Issued under the seal of The United States Copyright Office in accordance with title 17, United
States Code, attests that registration has been made for the work as follows:
Brownlee, Jonathan
PO Box 65, Perrysburg, OH 43551
Soliloquy
Registration number TXu 2-087-872
Effective Date of Registration: February 28, 2018
ISBN: 9780692083284

Printed in The United States of America
Columbia, SC

Dedication: *To Magnolia and Chaz*

Soliloquy

By Dr. Jonathan J. Brownlee

Soliloquy

Act I

I am a man (more or less),

And everything human is foreign to me.

Chapter 1

<u>*The Good, the Bad, and the Untenable*</u>

It is a beautifully curious thing to be an actor on stage. There is nothing in the world quite like it. As far back as I can remember, I'd prayed (well, not prayed exactly—more like hoped) for one solitary moment up on stage, in front of all the captivated people, underneath all of the vibrant lights. The thought of acting was my perpetual and reliable daydream. It was my most consistent and happy thought.

I love the theater more than I have ever loved anything in my entire life. I have always loved it, and I always will. The graceful movements, the potent words, the colorful costumes, the absorbed audience; they can all have a euphoric effect on a person. Plays are like magic shows without the nasty aftertaste of knowing you've been tricked. There is no trick in theater, just pure thrill and passion. Unlike most things in life, plays are uncontaminated, and they have a way of cutting through the bull and getting to the truth.

To a guy like me, acting is more than just those things, though. It's more than just lights, stuffy costumes, and a big wooden stage. Acting is much more than an exercise in getting rich and famous, getting on heroin (or some other brain-rotting opioid substance), getting shipped to a lavish celebrity rehab facility, and repeating the process, vigorously, until the inevitable death by "natural causes." Acting is, I truly believe, all about one's innermost self. It's about one's true psyche or whatever you want to call it. Some people might even call it the "Soul."

I don't know if I would go that far, but acting is the empowerment of a person's determination to be free. It's a chance to experience real life existentialism in its physical form. It's the freedom to experience all the different possibilities and perspectives of the human experience. It's the opportunity to be, *and not be,* who you are at the exact same time (if that makes any sense). Acting is the chance to tell the truth through fiction. It's a unique way to talk about reality without talking about actual material things. Ultimately, it is the right to explore all of man's possibilities, to be a shape-shifting God of the human experience.

A ridiculously bad writer (in a moment of literary luckiness) once wrote, "Actors suffer a transformation, they sink slowly deeper and deeper into the ocean of memory like weighted bodies, finding at every level a new assessment, a new evaluation in the human heart," and I completely agree with him. In my heart, that is what acting is really all about. Even though I wouldn't in my wildest dreams consider myself a *real* actor or anything, I know those words are true.

I've only been on a real stage once in my life, and it was much more than what I could have ever imagined. It was the moment when theater and my real life converged to become something new (and terrifying). The results of that convergence are still, at this very moment, being sorted out.

But, ever since I can remember, I wanted to be a real actor. A thespian. I wanted to be an actor for the feelings it involves: the emotions. In acting, all the feelings in the human spectrum are there for the taking. It's not every day that you can act out your deepest or darkest feelings and get away with it. Sometimes you even get praised for it. "You were splendid as Jack the Ripper. You brought him to life for me!" How odd is it to get praised for being a sick murderer? But with acting, the odd becomes the common, and the common can become the epic.

When I was little, I remember dreaming of no other job. But sometimes, when I was in school, when the teacher would ask me (in front of the rest of the class) what I wanted to be when I grew up, I would say I wanted to be an actor, or a writer, or a firefighter. Other kids would always laugh when I said I wanted to be an actor, so after a while, I just stopped saying it.

One of my earliest childhood memories is of me struggling to mimic my dad's hand motions as he debated with my mother in the kitchen. When he wasn't holding an old beat-up book or a crinkled-up, manically flipped-through newspaper, he used his hands when he talked more than anyone I've ever seen. I don't even remember if I could talk at that time, but I do remember how much I wanted to imitate him (not just his hand motions, but his *emotions*). Even as a tiny child, that's what I wanted. I wanted to feel what he was feeling, to convey what he meant. I wanted to be, just for a moment, him.

All of my life I wanted to be heard by those who long to listen, not those who let words fall flatly on deaf ears. I wanted to be heard by those who let words escape into their lives and pervade their beliefs and dreams. I wanted to be in front of those people who experience words as if they were objective things in themselves: physical, powerful, being-things, to be labored with and revered; not ignorantly spouted coercion bombs used for manipulation and hate-filled delusions. I wanted to act for the people who respect words to the highest degree, people who are clutched by them and held captive in them. I wanted to be heard by those people who participate in the incarnation of Word through actions; the people who love words, and art, and theater. People like me.

I know, I know. I know what you must be thinking. You're thinking that I'm one of those eccentric, emo, weirdo types. One of those over-the-top, annoyingly geeky geeks. You might be thinking that I'm an idealistic dreamer who doesn't *get* the real world. One of those feely freaks who lives vicariously through the characters he sees in plays, movies, and TV. And maybe you're right. Maybe I did read *Invisible Man,* and Harry, and Holden 10 or 20 times too many. Maybe I do have Surnames for my game consoles (I call my Xbox "Xavier." So what?). Maybe I do watch too much DBZ and know a few too many lines in all the Star Wars movies (including the prequels). Maybe I am "*one of those*" guys.

But even being all those things, I found a way to change my world forever. And I know I changed the world of others, too. I made it out of fantasyland and actually changed reality.

Breaking out of boxes is not an easy thing to do (or an easy choice to make). Breaking out of boxes normally takes a kind of craziness. A moment when your will makes its own decision and forces you to live with it. You are almost reborn in those moments. Who would have thought that a normal guy like me could change an entire community, an entire city? No one thought I could do anything, not even me. But I did.

My whole journey (basically, the journey of how I got from who I was to who I am right now) truly started when I decided ("*decided*" isn't really the exact word) to join a local acting troupe in my stuffy, quasi-conservative, assbackwards, creepy little city. I hated my city. It's really more of a town than a city, whatever the difference between the two actually is. (I'm sure my dad would know.) I think I still do hate it in a way. But I loved the fact that it, and the people in it, sparked my change.

I feel like the old me is a ghost. Except for my physical features, or lack thereof, it feels like I am a brand-new person. It feels like I was reborn through my actions, or through the events that precipitated my actions. I am not sure if my actions were due to free will, pre-determinism, animal instinct, quantum freakiness, bi-polar disorder, a psychotic break, or what, but whatever caused my actions pretty much erased the old me. The self I was before died after, let's call it: "The Incident." I feel like the new me boldly appeared and opened the old me up to a vast space of scary possibilities and even scarier consequences. But, I am getting too far ahead of myself.

Did "The Incident" change me for the better or worse? I am still not really sure. I haven't had enough time to decide. Not enough time has passed for me to think clearly about all that has happened in the last few months. I have just started to honestly recount all the actions or reactions behind "The Incident." I'm still trying to figure it all out. People have told me that writing it down might help me figure everything out, but I'm not so sure.

It could be that I've just slipped deep down into the dark depressing rabbit hole where good and bad are undistinguished. A hole where cause and effect dance together and the myth of being civilized is laid to rest. But one thing is for sure: I am different, my town is different, and I am glad.

Anyhow, maybe I don't really hate-hate my town. More or less, I feel sorry for the place. The town is defective on so many levels. There's so much robotic pointlessness to it. It's like all the people are responding to the same deterministic computer program, like they are all mentally coded exactly the same. All the people seem to want to *appear* perfect without really doing much of anything to actually *be* perfect (if that makes sense). In my town appearance is everything, and reality is taboo.

But the one good thing about the town, maybe the only good thing about it, the thing that I loved, was the fact that it had an amazing theater! I was more than a regular at the *Lyceum*. I practically lived at the place. I would bet that I was there more than most of the actors who regularly performed there.

From the time I was about ten or twelve, I practically lived to go watch plays. When my dad got tired of taking me, I would just go by myself. Watching plays was my only hobby. Those were the happiest days of my life.

Soliloquy

When I got older, I spent most of the money I earned from my extremely part-time job washing slimy dishes and bussing germ-infested tables at my uncle Mickie's restaurant to pay for tickets to any and every play or musical the *Lyceum* held. You name it, I saw it. From *Oedipus the King*, to *A Raisin in the Sun* (with an all-white cast for some reason), to *The Comedy of Errors*, to *Waiting for Godot* (in French), to *Uncle Vanya*, to *No Exit*, to *The Death of a Salesmen*, to *Wicked*, to *Cats* (with ill-fitting costumes), to everything you can ever think of. I saw it all, and mostly loved it all. The theater was a big deal in my town and an even bigger deal to me. You can say it was my *raison d'être*. It was my private, personal religion.

The *Lyceum* was the most beautiful structure in the whole boring town. It looked more like a modern art museum than a theater. When I was in it, it felt like I was standing on hallowed ground. It was an intense building that anchored, beautified, and validated the rest of the drab, kepple-filled downtown. It was bigger and better than our city hall (a city hall, by the way, that doubles as the courthouse, 911 call center, and the place where, as the billions of rumors had it, the judges let the prostitutes do their "community service," if you know what I mean. I mean, the prostitutes did sex stuff with the judges to get off the hook!). The *Lyceum* was nicer than all of the wanna-be-gothic churches that propagate the town and the surrounding area on every other street corner. It seemed like for every couple of homes in town there was one large church.

The theater was large, but not too large, about the size of one of the elementary schools. Everything about it was luxurious and grand. It was a fusion of classical grandiosity and modernist angular architecture: long, stiff, sharp, bulking, commanding, and mythical.

A row of cloud-white columns dominated the front steps, making the place feel like something designed for Washington DC (but in the future).

Soliloquy

The rest of the outside looked futuristic, like something Frank Gehry might have come up with in his saner period. Except for the columns and the vaulted roof, everything was razor-sharp. All the outside walls were bright white, and they took a tremendous amount of upkeep. (The quiet maintenance crew of paint-splattered Mexican immigrants would perpetually paint the perimeter walls. They were like a mumbling group of short Sisyphuses. I felt sorry for them.) It was a marvel of clever angles; Euclid himself would have admired the design.

The inside of the building looked like something out of Italy during the time of Michelangelo, like a cathedral built by Borromini (with the help of some intergalactic space aliens). The inside was filled with multicolored marble or granite that looked like chocolate, strawberry-vanilla, and caramel pudding swirled together and frozen underneath a fine layer of sleek glaze. The stone was like immobile clouds in a water-colored sunset, and there was a labyrinth-like tile pattern on the ever-buffered floor (reddish-pink, coffee brown, with grayish speckles) that I could never fully decipher. The floor was so beautiful and shiny that I felt bad for stepping on it.

In the main hall hung large chandeliers that looked like glowing, deep-sea creatures with shimmering chain appendages and golden exoskeletons. The sea-creature lights draped down on long spiraled spines of gold cable that looked like exposed gilded backbones.

There were large person-sized paintings and screen-prints depicting important scenes of classic plays: Greek tragedies, Shakespearean epics, modern comedies, and so on. The walls were filled with mammoth canvases that hovered like invisibly impelled giants. The paintings were beautiful, yet ominous and sad. Their frames were slathered with shiny gold-flaked paint that made them look like they belonged in an uppity New York art museum,

far away from my shitty town. There were two big bulletin boards crowded
with ads for upcoming plays and other events.

The *Lyceum* looked like the Louvre, not like a theater in a small town,
and that's what I loved about it. It took me away from immediate life. It took
me someplace much better, much greater.

In the main auditorium, where all of the major performances were held,
the deep crimson seats were almost too soft to sit in. It felt like you were
sitting on upholstered marshmallows. Sitting in the cushiony seats made me
drowsy, comfortable, and anxious, all at once. It was like sitting in the beautiful plush throne of a decadent tyrant: eerie, yet empowering. The seats
matched the color of the stage curtains perfectly; they always reminded me
of Superman's cape. I had a favorite seat that I would always sit in. I would
get to shows early just to make sure no one would sit there first. From my
seat I could see the whole stage perfectly, and when the lights hit the stage
just right, it was like looking at the stars with a massive telescope. It was
magic. It was the most beautiful place I had ever seen, and in it were beautiful things. As Henry James would say, it had an air of "luxury and of maturity" about it.

One weekend, at the start of the summer, before leaving a showing of
King Henry IV Part One, I saw an intensely bright red and yellow flyer tacked
to one of the massive bulletin boards in the theater lobby. It read:

Join the Troupe!
Miss Magdalene's Acting Troupe!
Are you between the ages of 16-21?
Do you want to learn the art of acting?
Call Miss Magdalene at: 843-3473

Soliloquy

For a long time, I just stared at the gaudy, luminescent flyer wondering: how could any chemist get paper so bright? It was so intense it looked radioactive. The way it glowed out from its spot on the bombarded bulletin board reminded me of the green slime I used to play with when I was little.

I had seen other flyers before, flyers about acting troupes and stuff, but I had never taken down the numbers or really considered giving it a try. But that day, for some reason, maybe because the people behind me at the bulletin board started to intensify in noise and number, I untacked the neon flyer, quickly folded it up, stuffed it into my pocket, and shuffled out of there.

I didn't take it down because I wanted to call or join. I didn't want to call or join because there was just one major problem with me joining acting classes: I fucking hated other people! I almost completely hated every single solitary person I had ever met in my whole entire life! —no exaggeration.

As far back as I can remember, I never liked other people; and I'm not at all joking or being sarcastic in any sort of way. But I, with every fiber and cell in my body, genuinely and utterly hated other people. It's kind of hard to explain. It's not really an active sort of hate of other people that I feel. I've never wanted to run out into the middle of a busy street dressed in a ninja costume, toting locked and loaded Glocks in each palm, with an automatic machinegun slung across my back like a Samurai sword, with a set of stainless steel katanas stuck in each sock, with two thigh sheaths full of ninja-throwing-stars, and a pink fanny-pack full of homemade explosives strapped around my waist in the hopes of killing a ton of random civilians that I've never met before, or anything like that. I'm not crazy. Guys who do stuff like that are banana-nuts-crazy. I'm really not. It's a different kind of hate.

It's just that I hate being *around* people, being near them, or having to hear them talk about random BS they haven't really thought all the way through. For some time, I've noticed that most people say a lot of nonsense they don't really mean, or generally don't really understand, for that matter. Their message, the underlying *thing* beneath what they are actually saying, it's rarely in the words they use. It's all in the *undertones*. The "from left field" lies, the mock candor and passion, the reliance on opinion alone—always opinion alone—it's all in the undertones, and I hate that.

For example, like people who talk about the Bible but haven't read it cover to cover, or even an entire chapter of it. Or, like people who talk about a popular book but have never read much more than the dust cover. Crap like that kills me.

I also hate hearing people talk about themselves because they usually exaggerate or flat out lie about things they have no business lying about ("left field lies"). I don't get it. I also hate hearing them talk about things other than themselves, for the same exact reason. I just hate when people talk in general because it's, more or less, always some type of rabid insecurity masquerading as valid information or truth!

I know I'm insecure and not that fun to be around, but that's one of the reasons I don't talk much. I think that one of the only truly good things about me is the fact that I know that there aren't that many good things about me. I am honest with myself. I'm not okay with my bad parts, but at least I know they're there. Why lie about them? Why spend all my time and effort trying to hide them from other terribly flawed people?

I don't hate the hypothetical thought of people. In my head, capital-H Humanity doesn't seem like such a bad idea. People from all walks of life coming together in peace and harmony to make the world a better, safer place—all joining hands—kumbaya—acoustic guitars—bare feet—hippy-dippy—live as one: that all sounds wonderful and great. But when I have to be near them in reality, in the real-deal world, that's the problem. All the happy hypotheticals go screaming out the window. I hate the physical experience of being around real people; it's as simple as that.

Most people tend to literally repulse me. I have a physical reaction, literally a physical reaction, when I have to deal with shitty people in one-on-one situations. Their behavior tends to give me serious migraine-level headaches and severe, almost crippling, stomach pains. I also get dizzy, uncontrollably dizzy. And if they are really bad people, really loud and overtly annoying, I get all hot and feverish, the whole world starts spinning, and in a few extreme cases, I would literally black out.

I've only blacked out a few times before, but it's happened. I had my first blackout in second grade, during recess. I remember it like it was yesterday. I struck out at kickball, if there is such a thing, and everyone started laughing at me and pointing their boogery fingers in my face. And Kim Beckman spit on me—right in the face. A hot gob of it got me right in the eye. I started feeling hot and woozy. Then, right then and there, I fainted. I fell face first onto the cold asphalt. The school nurse told my parents I had a mild heat stroke. But it wasn't a heat stroke. It was mid-September, and it couldn't have been more than 50 degrees out.

I know it seems over-the-top, but I can't help it. It's just in my physiological makeup. My doctor said it happens to lots of people who have psycho/social anxiety problems (But I think he was just trying to be supportive. I don't know anyone else who has fainted face first on a playground.). My doctor said it's a combination of panic attacks, emotional repression, fainting spells, and maybe mild psychosis. It's called "paroxysm tachycardia mania" or "monomania," or something like that.

For as long as I can remember, it has been that way: people making me uncomfortable and sick. It's not that I think I'm better than other people. I don't. I don't think I'm inherently *better* than anyone else. I'm just less delusional and less self-absorbed. I am not better, I'm just clearly aware that the world doesn't revolve around what I want or how I feel. "The World" couldn't give a shit less about how I feel or what I think about things I don't know very much about. It couldn't give a crap about whether I exist or not, let alone how I feel about other things that exist.

I am not saying that there are no good things about people, or that there are no good people. I'm sure there are, there has to be. All I am saying is that it's the unauthentically self-importance, the uber-unoriginal, the complete self-loathing crankiness, and the absolute petty shallowness of most people that I literally cannot stomach.

For a perfect example, there was this girl I knew, Delilah, Delilah Pastornail. Little Miss Pastornail was unnaturally beautiful. Unquestionably beautiful. I mean, completely drop-dead gorgeous. Maybe one of the most beautiful people I'd seen in real life. She stood about 5'3" with a slender shape. Her skin was shimmery and smooth. She was built like a Greek goddess, or one of the perfect human women the Greek gods always kidnapped. She was perfectly proportionate. She had this glossy, wheat-colored, perfect-looking hair that I bet took tedious time in the morning to prepare.

Every time I saw her, her hair was in a new, creative, fashion-showy style: from braided buns, to spiraling swoops, to curls, to prep-school pigtails, to askew-cocked ponytails, and so on, and so on, endlessly. Every day I was excited to see what she would do with it next. Not to mention, she never wore the same outfit twice. The sad sexiness of her assortment of how-did-her-mom-let-her-out-of-the-house-(or the principal let her into school)-with-those-shorts-that-are-so-short-that-her-pockets-literally-stick-out-of-the-bottom shorts made me want to puke and stare at the same time. The reliability of her omnipresent bra straps was depressing clockwork. And don't get me started on her chronic cleavage that bumped and rattled every time she took a step!

Her facial expression was always dripping with blatant sexuality. She looked like she was always on the verge of puckering for a kiss, and her voice sounded like that of a phone-sex operator. Everything about her was purposely sexual in one way or another.

But I swear, whenever little Miss Pastornail opened up her little mouth, it made me want to jump out of a window. I would have rather jumped onto thousands of dull, rusted, rabies-infected spikes rather than listen to her talk. Oh my god, she was totally terrible! Completely terrible in so many ways. I mean the stuff she talked about you wouldn't believe. Everything she said was patently superficial and utterly ignorant. Every word was mind-bendingly shallow. Her depraved little mind only functioned on three possible subjects: I called them the three B's: boys, booze, and girls she hates ("*bitchhhesss,*" as she called them). I mean she literally never ever talked about anything else. Only meaningless trash that could make your ears bleed from sheer boggled disgust.

When it came to boys, she talked about how ugly, or creepy, or hot, or sexy, or muscular, or scrawny they were. And she was not at all shy about going into medical detail regarding guy penis sizes, shapes, and nerve-fueled dysfunctions. She never talked about their personalities or anything of even minor importance.

You should've heard her talk. Better yet, you should've seen her act. She was always hanging all over some random douche-bag pretending she was madly in love with him. She always had some sad jock following her around. She had some new guy around almost daily. I was always aston-ished at how many jocks there were at our school to manipulate. If not daily, every other day, some poor bastard was getting his mind molested by her menacing charm. I never saw one that lasted a full week. Those poor little morons didn't have a clue that they were no more than free attention toys for her to chew up then spit out. They really fell for it, her entire act. They really thought she actually liked them. They thought they could be the one to make her settle down. They were wrong. But if I am being honest, I'm not sure if I could blame them. Her act was perfect. I doubt very many guys could have withstood her otherworldly looks and charm.

But still, she was pretty much always whoring herself out. There were countless stories about her weekend escapades. Her weekends have become urban legends in my town. It's like she did it for pure *sport*, or just to pass the time.

I often thought to myself: How could something so beautiful be so devoid and dead inside? How could beauty live on the outside of something so ugly and deformed inside? How could something so lifeless look so alive? The thought always made me sad.

Anyhow, when it came to alcohol, Delilah talked about how toasted, or wasted, or messed up, or belligerent, or shit-faced, or face-shitted, she and the "Tequila Twins" got (The "Tequila Twins" was the name for all her alcoholic, binge-drinking girlfriends. Even though there were way more than two girls in the group, they still called themselves "The Twins." I think they picked the name simply because it sounded cool, not for accuracy. To be accurate, they should have been called the Tequila-Sexaholic Sextuplets.). Delilah would always talk about how she threw up, or fell down, or passed out. She would always tell stories about how some hormone-hyper guy tried to spike her drink at some party, or how he tried to give her too many Xannies or Mollies, and how she almost died. All her stories were super crazy like that. For girls like her, that was <u>actually life</u>: blacking out in a foreign place. But that doesn't seem like fun or life to me. It is all sad and sick and heartbreaking.

She would always get this big arrogant grin on her face when she bragged about her moronic, worthless, Smirnoff-fueled adventures. She would say things like, "Girls! I got so super, super messed up last night—oh my God! You don't even know—so messed up. I don't even remember most of what happened last night. Amber doesn't either, she was too freakin' wasted. She is such a whore when she's wasted—oh my god. We were both black-out-drunk—I mean BLACK-OUT-DRUNK! Crazy, right? It was crazy! All I remember is that I had fun. So much fun! I hear there are pictures, but I don't even want to see 'um. I don't even want to know what all went on. So crazy, right?"

Crazy. For damn sure. In my view, she was crazy. Everything she said was a disgrace to herself and to the world in general. But there she'd be, saying very sad things, very loudly, for all of the world to hear. She thought stuff like that was sooo cute to brag about. When she said things like that, she would crack an enormous, genuine smirk, as if being in some kind of a stupor was the highlight of her "life."

When she talked about other girls, it was always far beyond cruel and unusual. I mean, it was evil in form and intent. "Teen Terrorism," I called it. I bet ADC even plugged his ears when she talked about other girls. I won't even repeat most of the stuff she said about them. The profanity of it would melt a sane person's brain cells.

She tore them down with an oddly talented, cold, professionalism. What type of person has a talent for evil? When she went after other girls, she was a mixture of Doctor Kevorkian and Anne Coulter. Let's just say she got a kick out of mutilating other girls' reputations, by any and every means unnecessary.

Soliloquy

I'm surprised that no girls ever killed themselves because of what Delilah said about them. Come to think of it, maybe a few of them did, who knows? The way she would glow when she whispered her nasty rumors, shredding her victims down to the bare bone, with a big group of her so-called friends surrounding her like a cult of dark disciples doing some sort of wicked ritual, I could tell she was a real sadist. It was truly frightening.

She couldn't talk about anything other than those three things: boys, booze, and "bitches." It was beyond sad. It's like she couldn't talk about real things, the things that really matter in life, even if she wanted to. Her mind was trapped in a self-obsessed coma, stuck on a spin-cycle of frantic vanity and meaninglessness. Whenever I heard her talk, without exception, she was stuck on those three stupid things.

I only talked directly to her once, thank god. It was at lunchtime, a long time ago. We used to go to the same school. She was in a lot of my classes, too. One day I was in the lunch line. She and her alleged friends were standing behind me being loud as hell, as usual. Then, all of a sudden, out of nowhere, this dumbass Frankensteinian Neanderthal from her group crashed right into the back of me. And I'm not saying he slightly bumped me. No! I mean he almost broke my spine he hit me so hard! I got whiplash!

So once I was done checking myself to make sure that none of my organs were damaged and that I wasn't paralyzed, I turned around to see what was going on. And guess what I see? I see little Delilah Pastornail and all of her wannabe friends laughing their asses off as if "Frank" almost breaking my back was somehow unbearably funny. So I said, "Is everything all right?"

Most of them couldn't hear me over their impossibly loud cackling. So I said it again, a little louder. Delilah looked at me with this nasty smirk on her face and said, "Yep. Everything's fine, thanks." Then she went right back to laughing like a dumbass.

Soliloquy

I wanted to say something to her, something mean. Something over her empty head like, "'*O sancta simplicitas!*' You have contrived to retain your ignorance in order to enjoy an almost inconceivable freedom, thoughtlessness, imprudence, heartiness, and gaiety in order to so-called enjoy your completely useless life! Your existence is not a life! It is a non-state of being— merely movement alone—conscious-less, emotionally inert, fugue— existential fear. Your being is worse than purgatory, death, or oblivion. It is a waste of potential, could-being, which is the worst of all conceivable states of being."

That would have been so far over her head she would have thought I was speaking a foreign language. She would've hated that. She would've probably scoffed, rolled her vacant eyes, and cat-walked away. Or she would've had one of her jocks punch my head off. Either way, I bet she wouldn't have had a clue what I meant. But I know she would have felt stupid.

In the end, I didn't say anything to her or her friends. It wouldn't have been worth it. I just turned around and stood there, trying to block out the pain and the sounds of their childish laughter.

And that's my point. That is exactly my point; most people make me sick like Delilah Pastornail makes me sick. Maybe not to the exact same extent, but they make me sick, nonetheless. There are hundreds of thousands, maybe even billions, of people that are just as terrible, just as phony, and just as empty as she is.

How could I speak to people like that on a meaningful level? How could I act—pour out my heart and soul—for people like that?—people who would laugh and grin and smirk at the truth.

I would feel like Rothko when he saw those shallow, vainglorious, aristocratic jerks shoving their faces full of overpriced food, not seeing the *real* food around them: the art. They consumed the trivial while ignoring the real. That's why I always assumed that my greatest dream would never become reality.

But I was wrong.

Chapter 2

To Be... Or Else!

When I got home from the play, it was around eight o'clock. I went to the kitchen and magnified the red and yellow flyer to the refrigerator for safekeeping. I stood there for a while just looking at it, admiring it.

I thought about putting the flyer in my room, but my room was always a complete sty. It might have gotten eaten by "The Clutter Monster." That's what my mom calls my room—the Clutter Monster— as if I were a five-year-old child. She still talks to me like I'm a little boy. She just never grew out of it, and I strongly doubt she ever will. But she was right about my room. It was a mess, where most things went to disappear.

Later that night, I was summarily summoned to dinner by my mother. It was one of our family-traditions-type-things to have dinner together at least three nights a week. My mom came up with the idea some years back. She probably got the idea from some daytime talk show or some news program. Or maybe Oprah told her to do it. I don't know, but it sucked. It was a huge waste of everyone's time. It accomplished nothing other than long blocks of uncomfortable silence, and it made all of us really good at creating innovative new ways not to make direct eye contact with one another. (I got really good at looking at food.)

It's not like we really even talked to each other when we were at the table. Our conversations consisted of weather reports (and our feelings about the weather reports), robotically reciting the events of our day, or random rants from my mother on politically incorrect topics. There were only three of us in the house: me, my mother, and my dad. No pets.

Soliloquy

I think the reason she came up with her tradition was because she was always by herself and she seemed really lonely. Her loneliness drains her like a disease. It clearly had affected her mental health. She doesn't work, as in, she doesn't have a real job or a career. I kinda feel sorry for her.

I've told her hundreds of times that she should get a pet dog or a little cat, but she always says, "You and your father are as filthy as animals! I don't need another animal to clean up after!"

You have to understand my mom: she's not really mean, or a bad person, but sometimes she comes off a little, well, rude and belligerent. I think that her wish to keep up appearances is what causes most of her emotional problems. For instance, I've never seen what she really looks like; I've only seen what she *appears* to look like. I mean, I know what she looks like, I could pick her out of a crowd, but she is always hidden behind a defense of heavy clothing and a mask of thick makeup. She's nearly always covered from neck to ankle, even in the yellow heat of summer. But she never gets sweaty, which is weird. She always wakes up early, at like 4:30 in the morning, to put her makeup on.

She wears lots of oddly shaded, very dark-colored makeup that doesn't really match her skin tone. I think she goes for quantity, not quality. There is always a sharp ring around her jaw and chin where her makeup mismatches her actual skin color. I don't know why she never has makeup that matches her face. I thought about asking her a few times, but I'm sure she'd get upset. She gets upset a lot, very easily. She's kind of an emotional time bomb.

She always wears bright, pastel lipstick that never comes off, no matter what she eats; although, I've rarely, rarely seen her physically eat (even though we have dinner together all the time. I rarely see her take actual bites of food; it just mysteriously evaporates from her plate while no one's looking). I can't remember ever seeing her without her makeup and lipstick. I

wouldn't say that her looks are important to her; I would say that it is important to her that people not know what she *really* looks like.

But she does have one physical feature that she can't hide with a mask
of dark makeup or a uniform of dark woolen clothes: her eyes. She has these
enormous moon-colored eyes that have their own personality. She likes to
say they change colors with her mood. They are like twin birds of prey
perched on her round face. They swivel and glare and judge. Her eyes are
always intense and poignant with a shy uncomfortable vulnerability that
makes you want to feel sorry for her no matter the situation. They are sad
eyes. When you look at her, it's like you can see all of her insecurities, yet
they somehow still seem stubborn and strong. They are bright and depressing at the same time. My dad always said he married her because of her
"wildly gravitational eyes."

She likes to refer to herself as a "Homestress," but there is no reason for
her to stay home. When I lived at home, I was never at home (and if I was
home, I was locked in my room—of my own volition). When I was younger,
it made a little more sense, even though I was always at daycare or some sort
of schooling or the library. It wasn't like I was home-schooled. Now, she
basically stays home for no reason.

My mom spent most of her days cleaning the already clean, watching
her soaps, meticulously reading the Bible—highlighting nearly everything
with different color highlighters—or reading some ridiculously cheesy ro-
mance novel that had a picture of some Fabio-looking character on the front
in the midst of rescuing some busty, white-clad, blonde-haired damsel in
distress. Or she was worrying the piss out of herself about petty things like
the carpet stains (that were only visible to her), or the validity of her vase
and figurine arrangements. ("Is this vase too tall to be next to *this* vase?")

Soliloquy

She doesn't have very many friends, but she does have a group of church-lady friends who used to come over and keep her company every once in a while. They had this quasi-Bible study, slash counseling session, slash gossip gathering where they would read scriptures aloud to one another, talk about their personal problems, and give simple solutions for the world's infinitely complex problems. ("All they need to do is clean the water. Is that so hard to do?")

Then they would cry and say "*Awww!*" to just about everything one of the others would say. Then they'd tell profoundly inappropriate stories about their husbands and children and just about anyone else they could think of. They would describe in intricate details just how hard it was to orchestrate and care for an unappreciative family. And they would brag about how amazing a feat it was for them to love the Lord with their leftover strength. Then, at the end of their get-togethers, they'd gossip about all the ladies from their church who didn't attend the quasi-Bible study.

Even though my mom is Bible-thumpingly religious, she loves gossip more than anyone I've ever met.

I said to her once, "Didn't God say only he can judge people?"

With an appalled frown she said, "No! Not at all. Who do you think thought up judges and the Supreme Court? If He didn't want people to judge other people, the court system would be all out of whack! No prisoners would be in jail!"

She always talked crap about other people, but she would do it in this magnificently unwitting, innocent way, as if she didn't even realize she was talking crap. Like when her and her church-lady friends talked about the other ladies from their church, my mom would say things like, "It is really sad that Marcy can't see that Jim doesn't love her anymore. Maybe if she prayed more and gave it over to the Lord—gave God the glory—maybe the situation would be better for her. But clearly, she doesn't pray enough, and that's why she's not in the loop. Praying keeps you in the loop, you know? That's why she can't read her own situation. That's why Jim is cursed with a wandering eye."

She said judgmental things like that all the time. When she said things like that it would make me sick, but I don't hate my mom like I hate most people. Yes, she can be annoying and completely unreasonable at times, and overemotional, and hypocritical, and, yes, even hysterical, but I don't hate her. She may have a lot of bad qualities, but I think she really wants to be a nice person, which should count for something. She just doesn't have the will or wherewithal to change. She's like a smoker who's been promising to quit smoking for forty or fifty years but hasn't. I feel sorry for people like that.

Most of the people who have lots of bad qualities tend to love their bad qualities. They act like their lack of interest in their mental and emotional defects somehow makes them immune to the fact that they are actually hideous people. They act like their defects, if not cared about enough, somehow can be transmuted into merits. It's like they have turned their perverted weaknesses into some sort of reverse strengths. They have this "I-don't-care-about-nothin'-and-you-can't-make-me" anti-strength. Somehow, they find strength in their lack of strength. But that's not my mom. She's different. My mom's bad qualities haunt her. They cause her real pain. I can tell. I think she wants to change, but she is too weak or too lonely to. It's heart breaking.
***

When my mom called me down to dinner, I paused my game and dragged myself to my assigned seat. We all had special "assigned" seats for our mandatory dinners. Three people, assigned seats, another one of my mom's bright ideas. When I got there, my father had not made it into the kitchen. He was always the last to arrive. My mom was scurrying around like a hamster on a Five Hour Energy drink, trying not to burn her "World's Famous Meatloaf," as she liked to call it.

"Dinner's ready!" she shouted in a weary voice.

"On my way!" my father shouted back.

***

My father is a very unusual, yet incredibly wise man. He is excruciatingly smart. Some people might call him a genius, although he would never call himself one. He is severely unique (in an intentional sort of way). He's an austere man who loves to talk, but doesn't love to communicate, if that makes any sense. He's kind of stuck-up, or so people think. He knows a lot about everything, but he never tries to talk to you on *your* level. He tends to talk over and beyond people. It's his level or no level.

He's always out on some obscure island of speculative, philosophical thought, completely alone, and it never appears that he wants anyone else to join him on his personal island. He seems most content with just his books and his thoughts. Every conversation that he has ends in one of two ways: either with him going on some inductively logical, obscurely referenced tangent, or with him turning up his nose and changing the subject altogether.

My dad lives to read. Reading is like his religion. We have books all around our house—probably over five thousand—and I bet he's read them all, two or three times even. He reads anything and everything that has to do with anything; novels, poetry, science, anthropology, zoology, sinology, genealogy, and all the other -ologies out there. Anything he can get his hands on, he is interested in.

He's read and has opinions on everyone: Henry James ("the greatest psychologist to ever live, including Sigmund"), James Baldwin ("Perhaps the most courageous and forthright writer ever to have lived on this earth"), Roth ("the vile, angry grump"), Emerson ("the philosopher poet"), Ellison

("Oh, the existential fire"), F. Scott ("the wordsmith"), Mr. Faulkner (he always refers to him as "Mr. Faulkner"), Morrison ("the poet of sadness and earth"), Tommy P. ("He tries too hard!"), Jack K. ("There was sincerity and energy there"), Hemingway ("the brut essence of The True") Ken ("crack-consciousness") Kesey, "Crazy" Pound, Bellow ("my good fellow"), Bukowski ("Only a mailman could deliver such withering beauty"), and Ginsburg ("simply a provocateur"). Basically, everything ever written in English he has read and has a thought about.[1]

But the one subject or thing he loves unconditionally is philosophy. Western, Eastern, it doesn't matter. He loves it all. His favorite book of all is *Beyond Good and Evil*. He's read it maybe a hundred times. I bet he has it memorized. He made me read it one time as a punishment. When I was younger, he used to punish me by making me read really difficult books to him aloud.

My dad was always either working or reading or trying to figure out how to do both at the same time. My mom would always say, "He lives in the world of books, not the world of bricks."

I guess he's an idealist or a dreamer. Maybe that's where I got it from.

"Hello, hello," my dad said. He rushed clumsily to the table. He was carrying a newspaper and his beat-up leather briefcase, one in each hand. "How is everyone this evening?"

---

[1] Although he loves literature, he *really hates* what he calls the "neo-postmodernist writers." He says that most of them are "writers of dark matter. Writers whose means of substance only exists in the relativistically grandiloquent minds of their melo-pretentious, robo-sycophantic, uncourageous, unenlightened followers; not in the realms of reality: causation-proper, bravery, and capital-f Fact-based reality." He loves to say that the current world of literature is dominated by "M.F.A.s, not Hemingways." He always says that "The aesthetic value of poetic expressions and witty turns-of-phrase can never rival the worth or splendor of pure, true, unselfconscious meaning." Meaning will always withstand novelty, he says.

Soliloquy

"Fine," I said. My mother was too busy with the meatloaf to hear him, or she was just ignoring him (which was one of the things she seemed to actually get pleasure from).

After a minute or two of my mom rushing around like a decapitated chicken, dinner was finally on the table. The whole room smelled like spicy Italian seasonings and ketchup.

"Well, I hope you enjoy," my mother said sounding like she had just run a meatloaf-carrying marathon.

"It smells delightful, dear."

For a while we all just sat there trying not to make awkward throat-clearing sounds. It was easy for my father because he had his newspaper completely covering his face; he was reading silently.

Then my father, still flipping through his newspaper at mechanical intervals, said, "So, how is Mickie's treating you, son?"

"All right, I guess."

"Just all right?" my mom said indignantly, rhythmically clanking her fork on her plate. "You should be happy just to have a job. You're lucky to even get a job these days, with the economy being as dreadful as it is. There are tons of people, well-qualified, proud American people, that have gotten their jobs taken away by those Mexicans, or Chinese, or the Indian people. It's a real shame. I don't have anything against those people, but they are taking jobs from proud American-born people. That's just a fact.

"You know Marcy's husband, Jason? — God bless 'um. The factory he worked at for the last eight years shipped his job and the whole factory, every single brick of it, over to China or India. Or someplace like that. Some sad place over there. Eight years, then poof! What a miserable mess, you know? Those people over there will work for nothing, dimes and pennies a day. They don't care one bit; as long as they can work and eat they are in bliss.

Soliloquy

Any food is heaven to them: dogs, pigs, cats; it's all the same to those people. What is Jason supposed to do now that he's laid off? You're lucky to have a job at all!"

"Now calm down, Mary Lou. Don't get yourself all upset," my dad said softly. His eyes were still shielded behind his newspaper.

"I'm not all upset. I'm not upset at all. I'm just telling the truth. Be thankful and *excited* for every gift God gives you. That's all I'm saying."

I thought to myself: She must be forgetting the part that says, "The Lord giveth, and the Lord taketh away!" But, I didn't say anything. I just forked through my ossifying meatloaf, wishing to her God that she would shut up.

I rarely ever argued with my mother because she cannot be reasoned with. She's almost completely illogical. Her mind functions on pure untreated emotion, that's it. It's useless to argue logically with someone who doesn't see any benefit or authority in logic. She goes on and on and on when she gets on some topic she feels passionately about, and nothing can stop her, especially not me or little old logic. She will just keep saying illogical stuff until I almost forget what we were talking about in the first place. Or she will just get all upset, as if by disagreeing with her you are intentionally trying to hurt her feelings.

"So, son, how was the play? Did you enjoy yourself? '*My honourable lords, health to you all! Sad tidings bring I to you out of France, of loss, of slaughter and discomfiture: Guienne, Champagne, … Orleans, Paris… are all quite lost.*' Oh, old William Shakespeare. He was a great, great artist, indeed. How was it?" my dad said, trying to change the subject.

"Oh, it was fine. It was better the first time I saw it. They had different actors this time. But it was fine."

I was bored with the cold, ketchupy meatloaf, and even more bored with the conversation, so I started staring at the flyer on the refrigerator.

Soliloquy

"...don't you think?" my mom said.

I had no idea what she'd said. I wasn't listening. I was completely absorbed in my daydream.

"Hello! Are you ignoring me?"

"Oh. Ummm, no. I was just daydreaming. Sorry, mom."

"What's that you're lookin' at?" she said, following my eyes to the red and yellow flyer.

"Oh, nothing. Just something I got from the *Lyceum*."

My father, looking up from his paper for the first time all dinner, said, "What, what?" We must have aroused his intellectual curiosity, because he carefully folded up his newspaper and began peering through his thick glasses with anxious confusion.

"The red thing on the refrigerator," mom said.

"Oh. Beautiful! What is it about?"

"It's just about some acting classes, I think. I just took it down because I liked the colors or something."

My mom chimed in, "Acting classes? Really? Well, you should look into joining. That would be good. When you were little, you used to always set up your stuffed animals and act out parts from Sesame Street. You were so, so cute back then. You would always talk about how you were going to act in school plays and be a famous play actor. But you would never try out. Why? I tried to get you to try out, but you would get so nervous, and you would start to cry from just talking about it. You would cry and cry and cry.

"Now, all you do is sit around and do those videogames, and go to that expensive theater, and who knows what else you do while you're locked away in that room up there. If I didn't know any better, I would think something was wrong with you; like you were one of those weird anti-socials, or one of those hackies or whatever. One of those hackies who tries to break into the CIA's computers, you know? But I know better than that. Your father and I didn't raise you improperly. Did we?—no. We raised you well.

"I bet the people that don't know you think you're some kind of mute because all you do is go to that library, read those weird comic books, and play those noisy games all day long.

"You should just think about joining those classes. I think that would be really good for you. Get out more, meet new people, have fun. Maybe meet some people you could be friends with. Friends are the fruit of life. Everyone needs a few friends. It's natural. It would be nice if you got some nice new friends to play with and talk to, you know? That would be good for you."

"Your mother has a valid point," my dad said, rubbing his hands together. "Acting would be a powerful pastime for you. It is a great mechanism for expressing one's emotions and angst, and a young man like you needs a sufficient avenue for psychological expression, introspection, and growth. True, videogames may be fun and marginally gratifying, but they do not grow you as a human being; as a psychosocial whole. However, art does. Acting is one of the greatest art forms to exist up until this point."

Though I was completely annoyed with them and the conversation, they did have some sort of point. All I did, other than go to plays, was hide out at the public library or in my room. I mean, hiding out from my mom and her church-lady friends was a part-time job in and of itself (and my real part-time job was extremely part-time), and I hated being alone with my mom. When I was alone with her, all she would do is tell me how much stuff I needed to fix about myself. So, when I wasn't at work, I would go to the library, practically all day, or I would go to plays. Then at night, I would come home and play videogames or read books until I fell asleep. It wasn't much of a life. Even I knew that.

Soliloquy

But I did like the library because most of the people at the library didn't tend to really bother me. Maybe because they minded their own business, for the most part, and kept quiet most of the time, and didn't bitch at me about stupid stuff. The people there were okay. However, there was one exception: the book checkout/computer sign-in guy. He always had this quizzical, constipated look on his face. He looked at people (me in particular) as if they were trying to stuff books down their pants or something. It was this goofy, gumshoe sort of look that you see in low-budget spy movies: the protruding, darting eyes, with the moist, nervous eyebrows. Another thing I didn't like about him was the fact that he smelled horribly! He smelled like old baloney and rotten goat cheese. I don't really know what the smell was, honestly, I've never smelled rotten goat cheese, but it was utterly disgusting! Even though I never got that close to him, I could still smell him from far away—up to maybe ten paces away; that's how bad he smelled. He bothered the crap out of me. But other than him, it was a pretty cool place to hide. It was my other hideout, my second home away from home.

But in all honesty, I was getting tired of going to the library every freaking day. I did want to do something productive, but the fact that I didn't like people much would make acting impossible, or at least horrible.

I was contemplating the cons and more cons in my head when my dad said, "Son! I propose a deal. If you try out for this acting troupe, I mean give it a wholehearted effort and attempt, I will help you get a new car. How does that sound? Sound fair?"

That bastard! I thought. He was trying to bribe me. He knew my biggest weakness, and he was trying to exploit it. He knew how much I needed a new car. I needed a new car badly, because I was driving a piece of crap, mustard-yellowish, rusted-up, fire-hazarded, 1979 Chevy Malibu! It looked like clown vomit on wheels. It was so tattered and hazardous it shouldn't have been street legal. I didn't want a new car to be cool or anything. I just wanted one because once every seven or eight times I went out to start it, it wouldn't start. Or even worse, every couple of weeks the mustard-stain would spontaneously overheat while I was driving down the road, causing dark grey smoke to block my vision, almost causing me to kill myself! The scene would be so embarrassing, I almost wanted to kill myself. I really wanted a new car. I really *needed* a new car. Not for style, but for safety. The thought of a new car made me feel relief.

"I don't know," I said. "You know how I feel about talking in front of lots of people and stuff. I get really nervous and sickish. You know how I am."

"Well, I guess he doesn't want a new car then, does he, Jamison?" my mom said in her snooty, taunting voice.

"Well, son. Just give it some thought, okay? Sleep on it a night or two before you make your final decision. No need to be rash. I think it would be an amazing idea for you to at least give it a try. Maybe you'll enjoy yourself, maybe you won't. You can't be sure unless you try. If you don't enjoy yourself, you can always quit. You will not be signing a legally binding contract with them. You don't like it, no harm done. No harm, no foul. But maybe the people in this group will be more like you than you think; maybe you all share common emotions, experiences, and ideologies. They at least like one of the same things you like: the theater. Otherwise, they wouldn't be in the group. And who knows? You may have other things in common, as well. You never know until you try."

"Okay. I'll think about it."

I was finished with my cold burgundy meatloaf. It had gotten coagulated and gross. The ketchup had hardened. My dad had drifted slowly back into his own world, reading his newspaper with one hand and eating with

Soliloquy

the other. And my mom was starting to quickly clank around, gathering up the dishes. So, after a minute or two of silence, I excused myself from the table, grabbed the flyer from the refrigerator, and headed to my room. I thought about cleaning up the place, because I wasn't tired, and I didn't feel like videogames, but I didn't clean a thing. I figured I'd try to read a little bit of James, I only had a few chapters left of *The American*, but I couldn't focus on that either. All I could do was sit on my bed and think about the discussion at dinner.

I really, really wanted a new car. And I really did kinda want to do more with theater, but on my own terms. Not in some random group of strangers. I damn sure didn't want to have a bunch of obnoxious jerks I didn't know watching and judging me.

But even though I had pride (or fear that mimicked pride), I wasn't dumb. I knew that sometimes, if not most of the time, in real life, people have to do crap they just really don't want to do. They have to do it to get to where they want to be. Then other times, they have to do it just because. I got that—I completely understood. And sometimes I didn't even mind that fact about life. But I just wasn't sure I wanted to put myself in that situation if I didn't *really* have to. Why complicate things if it wasn't absolutely necessary? But how else would I get a car? My dilemma made my head spin. I started hearing an unnatural ring in my right ear.

Lots of the money I had made from the restaurant went to repairing my piece-of-crap car, and I hated that. I didn't work much, but when I did, I didn't want my money going to fix a car that was on its deathbed. I had a little money in my savings, but that money was for a trip I was planning to take to New York, so I could finally visit Broadway. I would've walked to the library before I spent that money on a new car. There was no way I was going to be able to save up enough money to get a new car by myself, and still be able to do the other things I wanted to do. I needed help.

I sat on the edge of my bed for about an hour or so, chewing over both sides of the argument. But in the end, I decided that in the morning I would at least give Miss Magdalene a call to get more information about her acting troupe. I wanted to talk to the lady on the flyer before I gave my dad a final answer. Maybe there weren't that many people in the troupe or something. I wouldn't hate it that much if it had just a few people. I just wanted to see what she had to say—see if she seemed nice. That couldn't hurt anything.

***

When I woke up, I dicked around on the computer for a while, a long while. It was around the beginning of summer, so I normally woke up around 10:30 when I didn't have to work. While I was on the computer I remembered that I had planned to call Miss Magdalene to feel her out. I wasn't as sure as I was the night before that I wanted to call. I was having some serious second thoughts. But after an hour or two of aimlessly surfing the web, I remembered why I'd decided to call her: I was bored out of my mind and I had nothing to do! And I needed a new car. I had to call that lady, or I was going to die of pure boredom (or in a car explosion). I was going to go crazy if I didn't find something to do between plays.

I thought about using my cell phone, but I couldn't find it. (A cell phone isn't all that important to keep track of when no one ever calls or texts you.) I got the house phone and went to my cluttered dresser where the flyer was sitting in an origamical mass. My heart started beating fast from just looking at it. I didn't like talking to people I didn't know. It usually turned out badly. I barely liked talking to the people I did know, so talking to strangers was enough to raise my blood pressure or give me a minor panic attack.

Soliloquy

I found myself pacing around my messy room, trying to build up the courage to dial the number. I held the boxy phone in one hand and the flyer in the other (for about ten or twenty minutes) before I could get up the nerve to dial. I kept going over the opening lines of what I was going to say to her. I kept repeating them aloud to myself. I figured if I had what I was going to say completely prepared ahead of time, I could get through it.

When I finally did dial the number, the phone seemed to make one long "*Brrrrringggggggggggggggggggggggggg*" sound. When something did finally pick up, its voice scared me half to death. The thing that answered the phone had a steely, scary voice. The voice seemed to be clawing and cutting through the phone like an electric carving knife, and there was what sounded like small rodents screeching in the background. It only said, "Heeeello!" but it said it as if I owed it, the voice, a debt just for putting it in a position to speak.

"Heeeello!" the voice said again. It was impatient; the second hello was no more than a half second after the first.

I was already flustered. What little composure I had built up was being siphoned by the harshness and impatience of the voice. "Hello," I said quickly. "I am calling to speak to Miss Magdalene about the acting troupe. Um... I found a flyer—"

"—This is she," the voice said.

"Um, I'm calling because I found... um... this flyer at the *Lyceum* that said that you offer a, umm... acting classes. And I was... umm... just wondering what all that would entail... I guess."

"Oh. Well, yes. I am *always* offering acting classes." Her voice had slightly softened; it became human. I was finally able to tell that it was the voice of a woman. There were still rodent screeches in the background. "But the classes are only offered to people between 16 through 21 years of age."

"Yes, miss." Did I sound older? I thought.

"So what else would you like to know?" I could tell that she was start-ing to get impatient again.

"Oh… I'm just wondering… um… what days you conduct practice. Um… where are the practices are held? How much do the classes cost? Ummmm… how many people are in the troupe? And dum… are there any prerequisites for joining?"

"Well. That's a lot of questions," she said with a sarcastic laugh. It al-most reminded me of my mother's condescension. "Practices are conducted at my house, in my spacious garage, one or two nights a week, depending on people's work schedules. The cost of admittance varies due to a person's income or family income. I try to make it so that people of all economic cir-cumstances can join; acting is for everyone. But normally it's around 20 to 50 dollars a month—very inexpensive. The fees pay for costumes, food, travel and things of that nature. What are your other questions?"

"Um. I just wanted to know, how many other people are in the group?"

"There are around eight to ten people, maybe. It varies. Well, I do hope you consider joining us. We can always use some new talent in our group. What is your name, young man? It would be very nice to have a new mem-ber in our group."

We exchanged a little more information and a few more pleasantries. She'd somehow talked me into setting up a meeting with her before the next practice. "Just to get the feel of one another," she said.

After the talk, I felt a lot less negative about everything, but I was still very uneasy. I started thinking that joining might not be such a bad idea, but I was unsure if I was really capable of doing it, acting in front of other peo-ple. I felt almost happy that she would want me as a new student, a new part of her group, even though she didn't really know me.

Soliloquy

For a long time, I just sat on the edge of my messy bed, clutching the phone and the red and yellow flyer, smiling. Maybe joining wasn't such a bad idea, I thought. Maybe joining wouldn't be such a terrible thing.

<u>Act II</u>

"Am I an other? Strange am I to Me?

Yet from Me sprung?

A wrestler, by himself too oft self-wrung?

Hindering too oft my own self's potency,

Wounded and hampered by self-victory?"

F.W. Nietzsche

Chapter 3

Introductions to Fire and Futuristic Dreamscapes

During mandatory dinner, I sat there bored. I was silently dozing off. In order to break up the long silence, I told my mom and dad that I would give the acting troupe a genuine try: but if, and only if, the help-me-pay-for-a-new-car deal was still on the table. My dad was extremely excited.

"Well, that's amazing, son. Simply amazing!" my father exclaimed. He clapped his hands and smiled so big that his eyes were closed beneath his glasses. "I am very proud that you chose to venture out into the unknown and take a risk!" He seemed giddy about my announcement.

"Well, I hope he doesn't quit the group right away," my mother muttered under her breath.

They both were unaware I had already set up a time to meet Miss Magdalene at her house the next day. Miss Magdalene wanted us to meet in person before I made up my mind about joining. She said the meeting would be "an informal meet and greet."

"So, son," my father said, "when are you going to start with the troupe?"

"I'm not sure yet. I still have to call her and get more information. I have to call her to set up a meeting."

I was lying. But it was not a big lie. Don't get me wrong, I think lying is a bad thing. Most philosophers and religious groups would say deceit is "immoral," or "detrimental to social utility." And I would agree. But lying to my parents was not immoral or detrimental at all. Lying to my parents was necessary, even welcomed by them, it seemed. They didn't seem to mind. They just wanted me to say something. And they're not the only people who

didn't seem to mind lies; lots of other people fall into that same exact catego-
ry. It's as if lying has lost its negative association for most people.

I sometimes lied to my parents just because I knew it wouldn't make
that much of a difference to them one way or the other. They would believe
just about anything anyone said, especially my mom. You could tell her the
sky was raining jumbo hotdogs, and she would literally go outside and
check. (Her unbreakable belief in miracles might have something to do with
that.) The truth of the matter seemed to be of little significance or concern to
them. This fact always depressed me.

Both of my parents like hearing what they want to hear much more
than they like hearing the truth. Sometimes they even find ways to transform
the truth into what they want to hear. Every person I know is capable of a
sort of self-deceiving magic. I don't understand it; how can people want to
hear lies more than they want to hear the truth? The truth will exist and im-
pose itself whether we like it or not.

The facts are the facts. And the truth is the truth. So why do people love
their lies so much? They are passionate about their lies. They are more passionate about lies than anything else. They covet lies and bigoted beliefs.
What do their lies really do for them? Can their lies change their fate? Can
their lies keep them safe from the one thing no one is safe from? Can lies hide
them from their shame? What do they do? How crazy can people be?

I, myself, am an avid fan of truth. Even though I don't always tell it, I
always want it. No matter what truth it is, good or bad, useful or not, I want
it. Even though I'm not all that talented, or handsome, or funny, or rich, or
perfect, or anything like that, I am willing to accept the truth, which should
count for something.

I would die if I had to live my life pretending all day long, acting like
things aren't what they are. I wouldn't be able to keep everything straight. I

would rather live unhappily in the real world than insanely happy in an insane world. "You get what you get, and you don't throw a fit," as my mother used to say, and the world is all we get.

***

It was dazzlingly stunning the next day. Everything was unusually vivid with clear bright blues and pale yellows. The sun was beaming everywhere. It was warm, and there was a circumference of cloudless skies for miles and miles. It was late afternoon, and I was on my way to Miss Magdalene's house. It was one of those quintessentially beautiful days you see on postcards. All was perfect, except for my emotional state of being.

I started getting incredibly nervous about the visit. I was nervous for a ton of different reasons. First of all, I was driving the mustard-stain, and I was hoping with all hope that it wouldn't blowup in my face while I was jerking and staggering down the road. If I was going on a trip over a mile or two, explosion was a real possibility. But it's not like the praying helped; the car still sucked. I never knew when or if it was going to breakdown or detonate. It was nerve-racking.

Second of all, I was absolutely terrible with directions—I mean terrible! I swear, without a map, I couldn't direct my way out of a bathroom stall. Even with a map I might have had some trouble. It took me until I was seven or eight to learn my left from my right (even though I could read years before that). I can remember getting lost on my own street. But in my defense, all the houses on my street looked almost exactly the same. I lived in one of those additions where all the houses looked like they were made on the same factory assembly line. The place was called *Dream Garden Greens*. Everything there was the same color, the same shape, the same numbers of bedrooms and bathrooms, the same perfect outer appearance, and everyone had the same unexamined values. Everything was the same.

Soliloquy

I didn't want to get lost on the way to Miss Magdalene's house, so I was completely prepared. I had Google-earthed the directions several times before I'd left home. I almost went as far as to put one of those safety car kits in my trunk, but I thought that might be a bit much.

The third reason I was nervous, the worst reason of all, was I was going to meet a new person, or even worse, new people.

New people judged other people, new people pointed and whispered and made strange, mangled, animated faces at other people. New people snickered, cackled, and giggled like obnoxious little children at other people. New people were hateful, shallow, spiteful, and hollow. New people were hell. I hated new people, and if I got in the way of their moronic tsunamis of instant judgment, they tended to hate me, too. So most of the time, I just tried not to meet them or get in their way.

All in all, I was so nervous I was pretty much ready to piss my pants.

After about twenty minutes of driving, with very few mishaps, I found Miss Magdalene's street: Wichita Street. I was extremely proud of myself. I slowed my car to a clanking crawl to make sure I wouldn't miss the house, but after a few seconds it was very easy to distinguish her house from the others. Her house was completely different from every other house on the street, and her house number was plastered on her oversized mailbox with big, navy-blue whopping numbers: 4328.

Her house was, in a word: extreme. The other homes on her street were like mine; they were big, bland-colored boxes. But Miss Magdalene's house was unique. It was considerably bigger than all the other homes on the street. Structurally, it had clearly been added to, with no concern for visual harmony. The paint was a screaming sky blue. It reminded me of a cheap Popsicle wrapper.

Soliloquy

Her front yard was stuffed with sculptures, trinkets, and general front yard muddle. There were garden gnomes, and hobbits, and elves, and scary gargoyles, and big wooden bird houses, and bird baths, and a plastic children's play set, and all sorts of other miscellaneous junk. There were even flashing Christmas lights draped around the porch. It was a chaotic mess of sculptures and fixtures and mess. Taking it all in made me a little dizzy. As my car inched past, I couldn't help but think to myself: What in the hell have I gotten myself into?

I tried to gather my thoughts. I parked a short way down the street to compose my nerves. I sat there for a few minutes going over what I was going to say when she opened the door. I kept trying to figure out what makes a good impression if you don't know what the other person is looking for. And I kept imagining what Miss Magdalene would be like. Would she have glasses? Would she be short and elegant like the actresses of old? Would her teeth be misshapen or straight?

After I felt as comfortable as I was going to feel, which wasn't very comfortable at all, I stiffly staggered toward the door. The walkway (if you could call it a walkway; there was no place on it to walk) was filled with trinkets and tons of cutesy things to trip on. It was a virtual landmine. Maneuvering through the path was more like maneuvering through an obstacle course. When I finally reached the doorbell, I was nearly out of breath from all the stretching and crouching and hopping to get over and around all the clutter.

I rang the doorbell. It played some jingle that I had never heard before. Arriving almost instantly to greet me at the door was... well... not who I expected. I'd hoped that it would be a well-dressed actress-teacher-looking lady, but instead I was greeted by a very strange-looking man. The man was extremely frail, pasty, bug-eyed, and generally crazed-looking. However, he looked very familiar to me. Not like someone I knew personally, but more like someone I had seen on TV.

"Hello, hello, helloooo! You must be the new guyyyy!" he said in a high-pitched, sing-songy voice.

I was stunned by his voice, and I was even more stunned by his flamboyantly odd attire. This guy was adorned in the most ostentatious outfit I'd ever seen. He had on a crimson, crush-velvety dress shirt, with one too many buttons undone, and two small gold choker chains with oversized diamond encrusted crucifixes on them. He also had on skintight, silver high-water pants and blue suede shoes—literally—blue suede shoes with yellow-and-black striped socks. I couldn't believe my eyes. All my energy was spent on keeping me from running away in fear and/or busting out into laughter. I was hesitant as hell to step into the house because, well, frankly, the guy looked dangerous. My legs were stiff and wobbly at the same time; they were weak, but they wouldn't move.

I managed to eke out a few words. "Hi… is Miss… ummm… Magdalene a-va-bowl?" I was peeking my head inside to make sure someone else was actually there other than Mr. Creeper Cut-me-up. My neck was in the house, but my body was still planted semi-firmly on the flashing porch. I was afraid that it was some kind of set-up, some kind of kidnapping plot or something.

At that moment I remembered who the guy reminded me of: Jeffery Fucking Dahmer! You know, the "I like to eat people and make human hamburgers out of them like Hannibal Lecter," serial killing, Jeffery Dahmer? Yes, they were spitting images of one another. The wild blond hair, the over-the-top mustache, all of it matched up. When I realized the spooky similarities, I let out an accidental: "*Hah!*" This guy looked almost exactly like a notorious serial killer, and he was inviting me to come inside. He even had

those spooky, oversized, 1984 serial killer glasses on. He was a doppelganger! Were they in the middle of working on a play about serial killers or something? I thought. I was about to crap my pants until I saw a lady coming to
the door.

"Hello, hello," she said. "You're right on time. Come in and have a seat.
I see you've met my brother, Paul." She made a confusing flicking hand motion in the creeper's direction.

I could tell it was Miss Magdalene from her sharp voice. She looked
close to what I had hoped she'd look like, except her face was very different.
I'd figured her face would be the face of an elegant older actress struggling
to keep the beauty of her youth. But Miss Magdalene's face was not soft in
any way. It was tight and steely, just like her voice. She had the face and
permanent scowl of a career army officer.

It wasn't like she was frowning; her look seemed to be due to the fact
that her face was composed of all frown-like features. Her hair was jet black
and thick, and she had a bush of squiggly bangs that covered her forehead
down to her eyebrows. Her face looked as though she had seen too much of
life and knew better than to smile. She had a strong, symmetrical, depressing
appearance. Her cheek bones were spiky and taut as though she was re-
straining a profound emotion by gnashing her teeth together.

I was inching into the house with my Jell-Oy legs and a heart that was
beating so loudly that my eardrums started ringing. I wobbled up to her and
shook her hard hand. She had very strong hands, hands stronger than my
dad's. I was afraid of her, yet comforted by her at the same time. I didn't
want to stare, but I could not look away from her face.

She broke my trance by doing a Vanna White-like hand gesture toward
a loveseat across from an oversized, thronish sofa chair.

Soliloquy

Mr. Cut-me-up, so-called *Paul*, had seemingly vanished into warm air. "He probably vanished into some basement-dungeon where he worked on his sedated subjects that he had marinating in a vat of bar-b-cue sauce," I thought to myself. I was more nervous than I thought I'd be. My stomach was starting to bubble violently. I could hear my heart drumbeat.

I was so scared and nervous that I hadn't noticed just how much the inside of her house mirrored the outside. It was packed with clutter. It was like a circus merged with an awful antique shop. The carpet was orange-and-yellow shag with tons of some kind of animal hair all over it. There were baby toys scattered across the floor and old black-and-white pictures on every inch of one wall. The furniture was placed in an irrational arrangement (if you could call it an arrangement). All the black-and-white photos appeared to be of Miss Magdalene. I saw none of the creeper. They seemed to range from the time she was a baby all the way up to the present. I was inundated with Miss Magdalene's life story, her colorless history.

"Would you like anything to drink? We have lots of soda and juices. We tend to keep the juice for the kids. It's very nice out today, isn't it?" she said. Paul had rematerialized out of nowhere with three large cups of dark colored cranberry-apple juice.

"Here you are, mister," Paul said, handing me a cup. "So, please tell us a little bit about yourself?" he said. His face had a menacing, yet somehow genuine, grin. He set the tray on the messy coffee table next to Miss Magdalene. She was sitting completely erect in her oversized seat with her stocky legs crossed. Next to her chair I noticed yet another peculiar sight. Beside her trudged a huge, dog-sized, obese cat! The massive cat was a dingy pearl white, and it had to weigh at least 70 pounds! It moved like a fat man carrying another fat man. It just kept slowly circling the perimeter of Miss Magdalene's chair like Samson circling a grain grinder.

Soliloquy

"Yes, why don't you tell us just a little about yourself?" Miss Magdalene said.

"Well... ummm... there really isn't much to tell about myself, really. To be honest, I'm a pretty boring person. I do love watching plays and stuff. Ummm... I'm also an only child. I guess I'm kinda shy, I guess. I don't know really, there's not much to say about me. To be honest, I'm pretty boring."

A few super-uncomfortable seconds crawled by. Miss Magdalene and Paul looked me over with contemplative glares. I felt like a sad animal in a zoo. They looked as if they were contemplating buying me or something. I felt objectified.

Paul said, "There has to be more than thaaat. Tell us more!"

I was already starting to hate Paul. I had said all I wanted to say about myself, but for some reason, he wanted more. Why? I don't like being pushed, especially when I'd given them all the information I had.

"No, not really," I said. "I'm serious. I'm really boring. I'm a very boring person. I wish there was something else. But... ummm... so Miss Magdalene, how did you get started giving acting classes, if you don't mind me asking?" I had to do something to get the focus off of me. My whole body was starting to sweat.

She took a long moment of silence as she sipped the last of her drink. She slowly adjusted herself in her jumbo seat and put her glass back onto the coffee table, slowly. She cracked a small smile as if she had been waiting for me to ask her that question from the second I'd arrived. It was like she was preparing to go on stage, preparing to give her own personal soliloquy. My question set the stage for her, and she seemed very happy to take it.

"Well," she said, taking another dramatic pause. She clasped both hands over her lips like a person in prayer. "I'm not exactly sure how to answer that question." Her gaze was slightly above my head as if there was a vision of her past right above me; a portal that she could see through that would help her answer the question.

She stroked her chin for a few moments, looking into that invisible portal. "I guess it all started when I was a very little girl. Yes. My family lived at our church. My father was one of the pastors at our church. My mother was a Sunday school teacher for many, many years, and she was in charge of all the dramatic performances the church put on. You know, plays for Easter, Christmas, Thanksgiving, and all the other little productions churches like to put on.

"When I was really little, way back when, my mother would take me with her to all the play rehearsals and let me run around and dress up in the pretty little costumes. When I was about five or six years old she gave me a small part in my first play. A play called *Jesus and Small Places*. It was a play she'd written with...."

She paused for a moment and slowly pointed to one of the pictures on her wall. The picture was of her and (who I figured was) her mother. The pictured showed a dark-haired woman and an excited little girl. The woman in the picture had a stern, strong face, but she was smiling at the child, holding the child hoisted on one hip. The child was leaning toward the camera with her eyes and mouth wide open. The little Miss Magdalene had on a costume that looked to be from the 1800s. A young Miss Magdalene and her mother, happy. She seemed to be paused in silence in memory of that moment. She just stared at the fuzzy black-and-white picture, rubbing her hard chin.

"Yes. I guess it all started with my mother. After she introduced me to drama and literature and all the goodness of emotion, I was hooked! When I was in school, I played the lead in nearly every school play I participated in. I

Soliloquy

played Juliet. I played Stella. In college I majored in theater arts, psychology, and music. My ultimate dream was to be a Broadway star."

She was absorbed into her memories. Her dark brown eyes were firmly fixed in a far-off memory land; everything else seemed nonexistent. She was more or less talking to herself now. She no longer needed an audience for what she had to say. She did not acknowledge Paul or I as she talked, only her memories and occasionally one of the pictures on the wall.

"After I graduated from college, Paul and I moved to a broken-down little studio apartment near the Theater District in New York. We were chasing the dream! I received a few very small roles in a few very small productions, but I didn't make enough money on acting alone to make a living. I told myself, and Paul, that I would give myself five years to break into the business, to get my big start, and if I didn't, it would be time to find a real career, a realistic one that would pay the bills.

"There is only a small window of opportunity for a person to catch their dreams, and if you don't catch it when the time is right, you are likely to never catch it.

"After the five years were up, thousands of auditions that didn't pan out, no real acting job for me and no money, Paul and I moved back here to find real work. I started a baby-sitting business, a daycare, and the rest of the story is history. Now Paul and I run a daycare during the day called: Daily-Care. And we run acting classes at night in our free time. We are very passionate about what we do. I may not have made it big, but I could never give up acting completely. I guess it's just a part of me. It shaped me into the person I am today. I hope it will do the same for some of the kids I teach."

Paul was leaning over, elbows on knees, and his fists on his cheeks. He was smiling from ear to ear. He was slowly nodding. I could see that he had loved the scene Miss Magdalene recreated of their past. He was smiling but he had tears in his eyes. It was like she had spoken both of their life stories with perfect clarity. Miss Magdalene was just sitting there looking off into the space of her memories, as they seemed to slowly fade away.

"I love it every time you tell that story, Sissy!" Paul whimpered. "She always tells that story; it is one of her favorites to tell. It's my favorite of all her stories. But I could never pick a favorite because she has so many good ones. Sissy, you're a great storyteller, you know that?"

Miss Magdalene did not respond. She was still looking into the firmament, rubbing her chin.

Then there was silence, minutes and minutes of it. During the quiet I looked around the house at the pictures, trinkets, and the orbiting fat cat. After her story, Miss Magdalene's junk seemed more understandable. After hearing her story, I understood how sentimental she was about the past. Maybe she had so many trinkets and things because she felt she needed to hold on to her past, since her dream slipped away.

Paul sat up straight, took off his glasses, and wiped the few tears that were trickling lazily down his strange face. His smile of awe faded as he wiped, and for the first time his face was free of a smile.

He looked directly into my eyes. Then, like a fire siren on the most peaceful of nights, Paul burst out of nowhere, shouting: "So, fella! I've been thinking, why do you want to join our group, anyway? To be frank, you don't seem to talk much or be very enthusiastic about acting. Why do you want to act? You have to give us a reason to put you in our group, you know; we're not doing charity!

"We don't accept just anybody you know. We have standards for our group and we are serious. There has to be something that makes you want to be a part, or makes you stand apart from just any old Joe. We only have time to teach those who really want to learn. If people are not here for the right

Soliloquy

reasons, they should go elsewhere. Sissy and I are not running a charity group! We are actors, we are an acting troupe and you…."

Before he could go on, Miss Magdalene stopped his tirade by yelling, "Calm down, Paul!" Her voice was more jagged and powerful than ever before.

"I'm sorry," she said, "My little brother is a very emotional person, and he loves our group. He takes acting very seriously, sometimes too seriously." She turned to him and scowled. Paul did not turn his head. To avoid her look, he just kept looking directly at me.

I was sick of Paul! Literally sick to my stomach of his pushing and questioning. What was previously a small bubbling in the basement of my stomach had become a spewing volcano of blistering hate that traveled to my chest and turned into a deep heartburn. I felt like I was going to puke up a fury of fuck yous and get off my backs, but I didn't. For a moment I was bewildered and speechless, choked up by the heartburn. I was having a hard time swallowing.

Despite the choking, I got out, "Oh, no, I understand. I… um… I can see his concern. I'm very sorry if it seems that way, Mr. Paul. But I do really want to join the group. I want to join your group because, umm, words are important to me and drama is important to me, and I'd like to learn more about it. Stories and characters are important to me. I think I understand, to a certain extent, why writers write the things they do, some of them, anyway. I think I can feel what they are trying to do with the characters they create.

"If a story is true enough, I think I can sometimes physically feel the characters' pain and pleasure when I read a good book or see a good play—I don't just read or watch them—I feel like I'm right there inside them. I think that a good story can guide a person's life, right or wrong. A good story can tell a person how to act or how not to act; and a great story can tell a person

<u>why</u> to act a particular way and why not to. I think that great stories are *encounters*. A story can illuminate the power of love and its weaknesses in perfect synchronization. Good writing and great stories can set the world on fire, changing people for the rest of their lives. Just look throughout history. Good stories transcend time and place and personal experience. They are fundamental truths that will never be overturned as long as humankind is humankind. They reach the universal DNA, the guiding archetypes of life. I'm shy, I know, yes, but I do love stories more than I love most things. And I think this group could put me closer to what I love, I think. I hope."

I was completely shocked by myself (which rarely ever happens). I had never consciously thought those thought before, let alone spoken in that fashion. I don't tend to talk about my feelings to people, ever; especially not to strangers. I must've been inspired by Miss Magdalene's speech and desperate to calm Paul's onslaught.

People don't tend to get the truth when I'm telling it to them. I don't know if they ever do get the real truth no matter who's telling it to them. Maybe people do get what I am saying, but if they do, they do a damn good job of pretending they don't. I stopped opening my mind and letting the truth come out to the world a long time ago; when I realized the depth of childish, reverse-Darwinism, and the self-deceiving judgments people would heap on my head when I would be honest with them. When I saw the strange, contorted faces they would make when I told someone what I really thought about something, and not what they wanted me to think, I began to see their truth. The truth that, to them, the truth is the most frightening thing on the planet!

The truth frightens stupid people (and by stupid I don't mean those who are not formally educated). It can stop a stupid person in his tracks, mid-sentence. For a split second, you can see the fear in his eyes and the tension in his voice. It is as if he has heard the voice of a ghost shout something profound. When the truth hits a fearer of truth, a foe-losopher of truth, you can sometimes see a slight moment of panic rush through him, a moment of stinging discomfort, a moment of strong mental pain—but just for the shortest of moments—then they catch themselves. They remember that they can still hide from it.

Most of the people I have met shrink from the truth; and that is why I was so surprised at myself for telling Miss Magdalene and Paul, two odd-looking strangers with judgmental eyes, the truth about my view of acting.

"Well," Paul said, looking down his slim nose. "That all sounds good."

I didn't know what he meant by that: that all *sounds* good. Was he trying to be a prick, or had I convinced him? I was confused. His face gave no clues.

Miss Magdalene said, "So how do you plan to pay the monthly fee? Do you have a job or are your parents going to pay?"

"Could you stand up for a moment; stand up for me for just a moment, please," Paul uttered, sitting crossed-legged with his disturbing smile smeared on his face.

"Paaaaul!" Miss Magdalene said firmly, glaring again at the side of his head.

"What, sis? I'm not going to do anything mean to the boy. I just want to see something really quick. I'm not going to do anything mean."

I did not want to get up. I was ill from Paul's lack of tact, the poking and prodding. My physical sickliness, which I'd hoped I could contain until I got back home, had become overwhelming. I thought to myself: If I get out of this seat I can guarantee that I'm going to puke all over this fucking guy! My bowels were about to erupt!

"Come on, come on. I'm not going to do anything. Just for a sec, please."

"Oh. Okay." I muttered, clutching my stomach.

I started to stand up very slowly, so as not to burst. I felt a complete looseness in my throat, midsection, and gut—as if I could no longer control any of my bodily functions. A fiery bubbling was in control now. As I rose to my feet, I felt the hot volcano of vomit rush from my stomach to my chest, and rise to the tip of my throat and the back of my nostrils. I only held it down by swallowing as hard as I could two or three times and sucking through my nose. But the bubbling heat kept rising, flooding back up through my throat.

Paul said, "Okay. This is what I want you to do... are you okay?"

"Ohg—I'm-k—bathroom moment—pleggg?" I was looking at Miss Magdalene who had been quiet, with an unchanging look on her face. I addressed my question to her, hoping she would give me directions before Paul shouted me down with a smile. She broke her stare from Paul's profile. "Sure, you can. It is right down that hall there, first door on your left."

I didn't know if it would be better for me to run, walk, or jog to the bathroom. They all seemed like very bad ideas; if I ran, the vomit might erupt faster from my stomach jarring around; if I walked, I may not make it to the bathroom in time to have a place to puke. So I took the middle path: I jogged.

I was growing frighteningly dizzy. The hallway started to rock back and forth like a small ship on a treacherous sea. I had to put a hand on the wall to stabilize myself. I thought about yelling for help, but who would've helped me? They would think I was crazy or something. By the time I reached the bathroom door my temperature had increased by twofold and I felt hot stanching vomit running down the hand I had covering my mouth.

Soliloquy

I was trying to hold the puke in, but it was coming up too fast to stop. I couldn't hold it down anymore. A gusher of hot vomit was flowing quickly down my arm, drizzling down to my elbow, and dripping onto my damp blue jeans. By the time I lunged over the cold toilet bowl, I had already made quite a mess of things. The whole right side of my shirt was steeped with chunks of half-decomposed food and my pant leg was a mess.

I was half sprawled over Miss Magdalene's toilet, heaving violently and gagging, choking. I was on the floor lying like a damsel in distress, with both of my arms draped faintly around the toilet bowl. I felt absolutely ridiculous. I felt like I was dying! My entire body was overheated and weak and the heat and dizziness were growing by the second.

As I lay there puking my heart out, choking and coughing up puke chunks, with my head hunched firmly in a foreign toilet, I felt like my body had been set on fire—it was the oddest feeling I had ever felt in my life. I was sweating profusely, and my sweat was sticky. My shirt was sticking to my skin and I felt like it was suffocating me. I had already gotten vomit on it, so I decided to take it off—along with my soiled jeans. My arms were feeble and flimsy, so it took a ton of effort to get them off. I said to myself:

Cool down... you can do it... just try to get... don't pass out... just get this stuff off and you'll...okay... be fine... fucking calm down!... just be okay... don't freak out... just think... cold stuff... cold water... ice water... ice cream... i... snow....

But my thinking didn't help. Though I was down to my socks and my tidy-white underwear, my body's temperature continued to rise. I thought about taking an ice-cold shower before I stroked out from the heat, or the anger, or the nerves, or whatever had me on the verge of combustion; but I thought that Miss Magdalene would think I was a crazy pervert for using her shower without permission. And besides, I doubted I had enough energy to get up from my spot on the floor and get into the bathtub. But I had to do something because I was becoming delirious and I felt that I would rather die than feel the feeling I was feeling.

So after flushing the toilet a few times, I did the unthinkable (unless you were in my shoes); I mustered up enough energy to plunge my head into the frost cold toilet water! I didn't know what else to do to keep from passing out, or worse, dying! I held my head down in the chilled water as long as I could, seizing my eyes and mouth together as tightly as I could so as not to let the toilet water in. When I was done, when I could no longer hold my breath or withstand the thought of what I was doing, I dried my face with the clean side of my shirt, I scrubbed my mouth with it until it felt like the skin on my lips would come off. But for a minute or two I was cooled.

Although it sounds completely nasty (and believe you me, it was!), I have to admit, it was close to the best relief I ever felt. The water was so cold, and it was the only thing that could stop the heat from overtaking me. I needed that water to survive.

It's like hanging onto the edge of a cliff with one hand, and right as you begin to slip and fall to certain death your worst enemy offers you his hand to save you. Though you may not want to take his hand, you take it! That is what it was like—exactly what it was like. Some people might let their pride get the best of them and die, but everyone knows that pride is a commodity only for the needless. Everyone should know that for the weak and needy, pride is a mask and a two-faced frenemy. I took that filthy, polluted, toilet water with puke chunks floating in it, and until this day, I think it saved my life. I would have died without it.

Soliloquy

After cleaning my face with my shirt, I pushed aside the pink furry floor mats and slumped on my stomach on the linoleum floor. I rested my head on a pillow of my shirt and pants. I just wanted to cool down.

***

Knock-Knock!

Knock-Knock!

Knock-Knock!

Knock-Knock!

"Hello? This is Paul. Is everything all right in there? You've been in there for quite a while, 15 or 20 minutes or so. Are you okay?"

I had completely passed out on the bathroom floor!

"No. Um… I'm okay. I just got a little sick that's all. Maybe food poisoning. I just threw up a little bit. I must have had something bad for lunch or something. I'll be all right. I'll be right out. I'm almost done. Thank you. I'm okay, though. Thank you."

Before Paul's knocking, I had been having the most wildly vivid dream. It was more like life itself than a dream.

I dreamt that I was on a gleaming outdoor stage in brutal summer heat. The stage had a floor of sparkling silver with claret velvet curtains. In front of me was an infinite, stunning stretch of tree-covered land with large patches of sand in some places. The land was filled with a near naked group of aborigine-looking or native-looking people. There were millions of half-naked (some completely naked) tribal men, women, and children. The strange-looking, stout tribal people were frozen like mannequins; they were just staring at me as if I had landed on the stage from outer space.

In my dream, I was adorned in a thick, pitch-black, hooded monk robe, with a long silver rope wrapped several times around my waist. I was shouting something to them at the top of my lungs in an alien language—their language. I have no idea what I was saying, but it seemed to be dire. I was in a panic. I just kept shouting and shouting frantically and passionately to them, but they would not respond. They would not move. It felt like life or death! It seemed like the louder I shouted the more frozen, and distant they became. Some of them receded into the sand.

Then, after what seemed like hours of shouting, a group of them began to slowly move in my direction. As they moved closer, their speed increased until they were running at full speed, sprinting directly toward the steps of the silver stage. It was like a stampede. As they reached the steps, several of them brandished shiny, skinny gold and silver knives. The knives were blindingly bright. They seemed to be glowing from the sunlight. The men grabbed me swiftly and threw me to the floor—I was surprised—but I did not fight them.

As they held me down, one of them (the one I clearly remember thinking must have been the leader) pulled out a very, very long sword that was rich gold and brighter than all the other men's knives combined. His sword was like the sun. The man with the gold sword began to cruelly cut off my robe, while one of the others undid my long belt. As I lay there stark naked, the man with the golden sword held my silver belt over his head in the direction of the unbounded crowd. When he did this, a deafening noise erupted among the onlookers. They all began to cheer. They were applauding, screaming, raving, mad!

The other men hoisted me up harshly and took me down the silver stairs. They took me to where a big circle of the onlookers had gathered. They all looked at me with blank, alien eyes; they were now back to complete stillness and silence. It seemed to take the men and me forever to reach the middle of the somber circle. When we reached the center, there was two huge burnished black horses waiting. They were stallions. The man with the golden sword, the only man with seeing eyes, looked at me for a few eternal moments; then he cut my silver rope belt in half. He tied one half of the rope around my neck, and then he tied the rope to one of the horses. He put the other part of the rope around my feet, and then he tied it to the other horse. My hands were tied behind my back.

For a long time, everything was soundless and unmoving.

As the tribal men let me slowly down between the two horses, to be supported only by the ropes and my body weight, I began to choke. My breath began to evaporate, and I began to flail hysterically. The man with the golden sword moved behind the horses and gave both of them a swift slap on the butt—jolting them into dead sprints. They began running for their lives, maneuvering through the thick, motionless, crowd.

The rope around my neck drew tighter as the horses ran. I was dying— and there was nothing to do about it. The horse that my head was tethered to started to veer away from the other horse, pulling the rope tighter around my neck causing an unbearable pain. I thought that I would pass out from the pain, but the opposite occurred; I felt more aware, more sensitive. I felt more keenly. I felt like my head was going to pop off, and I was racked with fear and anticipation of that devastating moment. I could feel my skin beginning to chafe and cut, causing a hot gush of blood to flow from my neck to my chest. My head was being torn off, but I remained cogent and alert. The closer I came to the unchangeable event of death, painful death, the more crazily aware of my life I became. I knew it was inevitable, so fighting was useless—I was going to die and there was nothing I could do but die. So instead of trying to escape, I decided to accept it and take it all in. I was going to understand what it meant to die.

Eventually it happened. My head was snatched from my body by the speed and terror of the big black shining horses.

Soliloquy

But in my dream, at the moment when my head was wrenched abrupt-
ly from my neck, something very strange happened; I became *more*. Not
more human or more me, but more *one*!

At the exact moment, my head was separated from my body, for a split
second (that seemed like an eternity; we all know how deeply dreams alter
time), everything, I mean everything in the world, made perfect, simple,
united sense. For a moment I saw everything as it is and was, as one. From
the most microscopic of things to the largest and most complicated of inter-
connections—the world was mine to be understood—and I understood. All
knowingness was near, but only for an instant.

In that small window of utter understanding, I felt a power that can only be imagined in a language-free dream world (of which no one can speak),
a power that cannot be contained by time or space or matter or anti-matter.
The power was painfully wonderful, pleasingly overwhelming. Due to the
immensity of the power I felt, another ripping sensation—not bodily—but in
my understanding. My animating force was torn in half by transcendental
knowledge and flung into ultimate empathy. This tearing and flinging overwhelmed me again—which gave way to transcendental knowledge again
(and so on and so on for the eternity of that short but infinite loop.)

No moment in my life had ever been so vivid or so real! And in that
moment, that moment of power-empathy and infinite shortness, I longed to
thank that man with the golden sword for the gift of power, empathy, and
for the total experience.

My dream seemed to grow me as a person in an instant. I can't say why,
but I felt different.

And that's when Paul knocked… waking me from my dream or nightmare. When I awoke, there was no longer a stage, no man with the golden
sword, no tribe or sand. There was the linoleum floor, a shitty smelling litter-

box, my pukey-putrid clothes, and me. I was back in the real world, and I had no idea what to do. I was practically naked; I didn't know if I should put my gross, wet clothes back on, or ask Paul for some of his crazy clothes; both ideas nearly sent me back into a state of panic.

So I just lay there, face against the floor, trying to get back into the real world and wrap my head around the crazy situation I found myself in. Finally, I pulled myself from the floor; I was still dizzy, so I had to be very careful. I decided right then and there that I would try to wash the puke from my clothes. I took the strawberry hand soap from the sink and squirted it on the most pukey spots of my pants and shirt. I ran the clothes under the water and tried to scrub the vomit out. I heard something brush the door.

"Hello?" I said. A few seconds passed, no answer.

"Hello?"

"Oh, it's just me still. It's Paul." He said it in a sweet, concerned voice. "I'm just making sure you're okay. I'm just making sure you didn't get lost in there. I don't want to have to break down the door to give you First Aid or CPR, mister," he jokingly said.

"Oh. It's okay. I'm just cleaning up. I kinda puked a little bit, so I'm just cleaning it up."

I heard rapid footfalls heading away from the door. It sounded like running, and I heard Paul's fading voice saying, "Okay. Be right back!"

I tried to ring out as much water from my sopping wet clothes as I could, but with my lack of strength, it wasn't very much. So I put on my fruity-smelling, dripping wet clothes. I put my shoes back on, but I didn't want to chance leaning over and tying them. My clothes felt sticky and disgusting, but at least I wasn't hot anymore.

I walked out of the bathroom, slowly, and back down the hall toward the living room. As I walked down the hallway it still seemed to be spinning like it was when I first went to the bathroom, so I had to use the wall again as a crutch. When I got to the living room, Miss Magdalene was still calmly sitting cross-legged in her chair. Paul was hunched over her shoulder whispering something into her ear. When they saw me, they both froze. Paul's eyes showed huge and frightened through his tan-framed glasses. Miss Magdalene's face began to slowly form a frown of concentrated concern.

"Why are you all wet? Are you all right?" Miss Magdalene said.

Paul was still hunched over her staring. He was wide-eyed like a little child.

"I'm ok."

"You were in there for quite some time, and you are wet."

"I got a little sick while I was in the bathroom, I think it was something I ate for lunch. Yeah, maybe it was my lunch. It got on my clothes, so I tried to wash it off in the sink. Sorry I look so disheveled, but I'm okay now. Just a little dizzy is all. I'm fine, though."

Paul chimed in, "You look like hell. I hope you feel better than you look because you look like death is at your doorstep! Come and have a seat. You are wobbling around like an upside-down milk jug. Come sit down and I'll get you some cold water or some crackers to calm your stomach."

"Oh, there's no need. I think I'm going to head home and try to get some rest. What time is it?"

"It's around eight or so; maybe a little after."

Miss Magdalene's face was still frowning. "Are you sure you're in the proper condition to drive yourself home? If you're not, I can have Paul take you. It wouldn't be a problem."

"Oh, I'm sure I can make it home okay. My dizziness is clearing up as we speak. I'm fine." I was lying, of course. I was just as dizzy as I was when I passed out, but I had to get home ASAP. And Paul, the main person who

Soliloquy

induced my sick-spell, was the last person on the planet I wanted to take me home. He might have said something super crazy that would have made me want to jump out of the car! I couldn't chance it. I would take my chances alone with my dizziness. At least if I crashed by myself, I could crash of my own free will.

They both were quiet for a moment. They looked at me like a doctor looks at his patient who wants to be released before he's ready.

"Okay," Miss Magdalene said in a questioning voice. "If you're sure you're fine, I guess I have to believe you're fine. You sure you don't want Paul to take you? We can even get in touch with your parents if you'd like."

"I'm sure." I did not want my parents involved.

"Well, okay. Here, come take this card." She leaned over in her seat and pulled a card from a small glass card holder on the coffee table. She took a pen from her pocket and wrote something on the back of the card. I carefully walked to her chair. I had to make sure I walked as if I wasn't too dizzy to drive. It was difficult, and it took all of my strength and concentration. But I did it; I made it to her without falling, puking, or having to lean on to something.

"Here," She scrunched up her nose as I moved closer. I guess she could smell the mixed aroma of vomit, stress sweat, and strawberry hand soap. I took the card. It read:

<u>*Magdalene El Richardson*</u>

Professional Care Giver: Daily Care Sitters

Professional Acting Coach: Miss Magdalene's Acting Troupe

843-3473

"Always Remember You Are Braver Than You Believe!"

[Handwritten on the back side of the card]

Practice/Thursday at 7

Soliloquy

As I was reading the card Miss Magdalene said, "The next practice will be held next Thursday. If you feel better, and you still mean what you said earlier about acting, feel free to join us. We would love to have you as part of our group. Go home and get some rest, okay?" She was trying her best to be sweet.

"Write your number on the back of this card, so I can give you information if anything changes."

I did.

"Well, thank you very much for your hospitality. Sorry I got sick," I said, trying not to blow the smell of vomit breath in her face. I started slowly for the door. I looked back and saw Paul standing a few feet behind me. He was looking at me like a dog looks at his owner when he pees on the carpet.

"I hope you feel better."

"Thank you. I'm sure I will."

He reached for the handle and opened the door for me. As I staggered onto the porch, I realized I had my work cut out for me. It was going to be a serious task to make it safely to my car. Making it back to the sidewalk with all the crazy crap Miss Magdalene had scattered in her walkway would be a great challenge for me in my weakened condition.

"Bye, bye," Paul said in a babyish voice.

Through the haze of wooziness, I spotted a small path of clutterless grass that I could take without tripping.

Paul was standing on the porch with his hands on his hips, looking like an overly concerned mother.

I bobbled through the small slick of grass until I reached the clear sidewalk. I turned back to see if Paul was still peeping at me, and of course, he was. I gave him a halfhearted wave and headed for my car.

Soliloquy

When I reached my car, I was as happy as a rich pervert at a strip club. I had never in my life been so happy to see my piece-of-crap car— not even when I got it as a birthday gift. I rolled down all the windows and took a huge sigh of relief. I had made it out of the crazy house, and away from peeping Paul, but now I had to make it home through traffic and the onset of dawning darkness. A nice breeze was kicking up, and I thought that the fresh air might help my condition, and in a way, it did. Even though it was still warm outside, the cool breeze on my wet clothes made me cold. It was not the killer heat that I had felt in the bathroom, so I was happy.

For a moment I contemplated driving around the addition to make sure my motor skills were functioning well enough for me to make it home. But I decided I would chance it, and if anything went bad and I didn't think I could make it, I would just pull to the side of the road or into a gas station and take a rest until I felt strong enough to drive the rest of the way.

All I wanted to do was to make it home.

As I drove away, I began to feel better almost immediately; the further I got away from that house the better I felt. My bout of vertigo had passed, and I felt steady for the first time that whole day. My mind was exhausted of being exhausted, and my thoughts had returned to the strange dream I had in the bathroom. What did it all mean? Knowledge, power, sympathy, empathy, time, space, the man with the sword; what was it all about? I'd read Freud's *The Interpretation of Dreams,* but even that craziness could not help me interpret my Dada-esque experience. Did it mean that I wanted to die? I didn't think I wanted to die! Did it mean that I wanted more knowledge; did I want to be all knowing? What did it mean? I was baffled by it.

My concentration was broken by a leaping barrage of car horns. I was drawn back to earth by the noise, and I realized that I had been sitting at a stoplight for quite some time. Traffic was at a standstill. I heard the deep horns of a fire truck siren sounding in the distance. As I poked my head out the window to see what all the fuss was about, in the distance I saw huge puffs and pillars of smoke bellowing from a large apartment complex. It was a powerful sight. As the building burned, the smoke glowed gray, yellow, and tangerine. The smoke was flowing high into the purple darkness that had consumed the formerly clear blue sky.

The fire was awe-inspiring. It was frightening yet beautiful. I have never been so close to something so large and powerful. Although I was maybe a hundred yards away, I could feel it. The fire seemed to be a living being. It moved, pulsating and heaving like the chest of an exhausted man. It was gorgeous and devastating at the same time. People were losing their homes and belongings in a beautiful spectacle of horror, light, and combustion.

I wanted to be closer to the fire. I wanted to see it up close.

For years I could never understand why crazy bastards chased tornados. I used to think: God, those people are idiots for running around trying to find tornados, but when I saw that fire it became clear to me why people do it. They do not chase tornados because they are crazy, and they do not chase tornados simply because of the adrenaline rush (though perhaps some of them might); the reason that the sane, rational guys chase tornados was because they want to be near great power. No man on earth has the power of a fire or tornado.

Seeing Mother Nature at work is the closest man will ever come to seeing God. The closest man will ever come to *being* God is the atomic bomb. The bomb is man bring the sun to earth. Devastating.

Anyway, a ton of emergency vehicles rushed onto the scene beaming their flashing lights: extra fire trucks, a cavalry of cop cars, and a few slow-moving ambulances. Some of the cop cars were parked horizontally across the street, blocking my route home. Every exit was closed. Traffic was completely frozen.

So I put ole-shit-stain into park and turned on my flashers. I got out of my car and headed toward the smoke. As I made it up the sidewalk, I could see people running from the apartment complex. A large crowd had gathered around the entrance, and I could hear yelling and weeping coming from the growing congregation. I made it about twenty yards closer to the fire before I ran into a small blockade of cops.

"Hey! Where do you think you're going?" a pasty cop said. "You can't go this way."

For a second I froze. I needed to see the fire. I needed to get closer, but the cop's face said it all.

"Oh, but sir, I live in those apartments. I live with my grandma and my little sister, and I have to see if they're okay. I have to see if my family is okay!"

"Why are you wet and why are you coming from that way?" the fat cop shouted. The other cops had sympathetic faces, but his was not. He had a stern, rosy, suspicious face.

"I'm coming from my best friend's house. We were swimming and stuff. I just want to see my family, sir."

"You can't go up there. It's dangerous. What apartment do you live in, son?"

"I don't mean any harm, sir. I just need to see if my family's okay!" It was odd, even though I was lying again, I really started to feel as though I believed what I was saying. Emotionally, I felt like that crowd of weeping people was actually my family. As I created my lie, inside of me a true pain was created. Tears started to well up in my eyes, and I felt as if the cop was stopping me from seeing my actual family.

Soliloquy

"Let him go, Jack," a tall cop said. "He looks to be telling the truth."

The fat cop—Jack—looked sternly at me for a few moments. It was as though he knew I was lying.

"Okay. You can go. But I'll be sure to come up there soon and check on you and your family."

"Thank you, officer. Thank you." I ran as fast as I could run toward the crowd and away from the officers. I didn't even look back to see if Officer Jack was watching me. I just ran. I had a newfound energy. I was no longer tired, or sick, or dizzy. I was exhilarated. It could have been the excitement of reaching the powerful fire, or the adrenaline rush I got from lying to the cops, or both, I don't know. All I know is that I was running as fast as I'd ever run.

As I ran I was torn between looking at the crowd of distraught onlookers and looking at the overwhelming fire. The closer I got the more I could feel the power of it all.

Up close, the fire was more than I expected it to be. It was bigger and brighter. It moved of its own accord.

"What happened here? How did this start?" I asked an old man standing next to me in the crowd. The crowd was so packed that our shoulders were touching. The old man took off his dirty captain's hat and slowly scratched his gray chin. He did not look at me. He kept his eyes on the fire that was being battled by the arching waterfalls that were spewing from the fire hoses.

"I don't know. But I bet you I can guess," he said in a thick voice.

"What?"

"This is a small little place, but there's a lot that goes on behind the scenes. Things people don't know about."

Soliloquy

I thought to myself: What the hell is this old guy talking about? He didn't seem crazy or anything, but what the hell was he talking about?

"There are a lot of couples that live in the complex that have late-night get-togethers and what not, and they do God knows what. They're into some seedy business. I always knew, but nobody listened. People just don't want to listen anymore."

"Oh."

"The fire is coming from one of the buildings they tend to meet in. Co-incidence? Conspiracy? You tell me. My bet is that someone got that seediness they've been messin' around with in their heart and set this goddamned thing themselves over revenge or jealousy or some other vice that causes people to do crazy things like such." He still did not look at me; he kept his eyes on the fire.

"Passion and love are crazy things, young man, and sometimes it burns. Passion is an old force. It can create us and kill us—and tonight it seems to be killin'. I bet some of that bad passion is what started this here fire."

Somehow, I began to understand what the old man was saying. I stood next to him watching the fire. Despite the weeping and the horrified faces on some of the crowd, the spectacle reminded me of the 4th of Julys when I was a kid. Looking at the raw fire was like looking at some great fireworks show. I felt like a little kid again.

After ten or so minutes of looking at the fire, I remembered that I had to get back to my car before traffic started to move again. One lane of traffic was inching forward. I crossed the street, moving to the other side of the sidewalk to avoid the policemen. I made it back to my car without a hitch. My lane eventually began to move, and I slowly headed home.

On my way, I tried not to think about any of the day's events. It was just too much. It was too much to try to put into any sort of order or perspective. I just drove; listening to my car make struggling, clanking noises. The clanking got louder and louder, and the car started accelerating funny, but it made it home.

When I walked in, my mom was sitting on the couch with her Bible in her hand.

"Where have you been? I was starting to get worried about you. Why are you all wet?"

"Mom, it's been a very, very long day. I will tell you all about it tomorrow, before I go to work. I promise. But I'm just too tired to talk about it. I promise I will talk to you about it tomorrow, okay?" I was praying that she wouldn't press me for answers. I don't think I could have contained myself. Lucky for me she simply frowned and looked back into her Bible.

"Good night, mom," I said.

She didn't respond.

I dragged myself up the stairs. I took off all my nasty clothes and passed out on my bed. I was so tired I didn't even turn the light out. The day had been one of the craziest days of my life, but it was not quite over. I had another crazy, cracked-out dream.

I dreamt that I was Nero. I was sitting on the roof of my palace watching the city burn. But in the dream, I was not alone; Miss Magdalene was there, Paul was there, Officer Jack was there, and the old man in the captain's hat was there. They were all just sitting there watching the fire silently. But I was laughing. I just kept laughing, and laughing, and laughing. I laughed so much that my stomach started to cramp, and I could no longer breathe. But I just kept laughing, and laughing. But it was not happy laughter. It was laughter meant to keep me from crying. It was that kind of laughter. It was bizarre and frightening.

The dream was the bizarre icing on a very bizarre cake. The beginning.

Chapter 4

Bewitched, Bothered, and Bewildered

When I woke up the next day, it was after one o'clock in the afternoon. I had slept for over 13 hours. The sun was pouring bright pink rays of light through my room, and I sat up quickly, bemused and alarmed. I was surprised that I had slept so long. I was even more surprised that my mom had not come up stairs to shout me out of bed with one of her "How lazy can you be?" speeches. "Lazy" was one of her favorite words to use on me, which I've always thought to be ironic because she is a stay-at-home mom with one kid who is never at home. Maybe she thought I had left to go to work, but my car was still out in the driveway, so she must have known I was still home. I was confused and almost a little bit worried.

For a few moments I just lay in my bed thinking about how good my body felt compared to the crazy-ass day before when I had almost died of a heat stroke, or a panic attack, or whatever the hell had happened to me at Miss Magdalene's house. I was well rested physically, but the day before had completely drained me emotionally. All of the puking and the Paul and the cat piss stench had left me with a bad taste in my mouth. But at least I felt back to my normal temperature. At least I was in the relative comfort of my own home. At least I felt close to normal.

My stomach was frantic for food. I hadn't eaten for over 24 hours. And what I had eaten was resting in the deepest regions of Miss Magdalene's cold toilet, and on my sticky mildewed clothes. I had to get something to eat, fast.

As I tiptoed down the stairs, I realized the reason my mom had not come to wake me up: she was sitting in the living room entertaining a group of her church-lady friends. It was one of those quasi-Bible study thingies.

Soliloquy

They were sitting in a circle around the supremely polished coffee table (that my mother must have drowned in an entire can of Pledge), chatting feverishly and mauling arduously over their big, expensive, leather-bound, gold-embroidered Bibles. When they saw me, they froze like dumb deer in headlights.

A couple of the women seemed to resent me being there—their faces said it all—as if by simply coming down the stairs of my own house I had missed a sign that said: NO MALES ALLOWED! Had they forgotten that this was my house? I could tell that some of them were genuinely disturbed by my appearance because of the jolted glares on their faces.

One of the ladies looked at me as if I had seen her stepping out of the shower. She was considerably fat, or pregnant, with platinum blonde hair from the 1985, bangs teased to the point of suicide. Her eyes latched onto mine with a look of discomfort bordering on terror. My mom's face was slightly frowning, but that was not unusual for her. All of their peculiar looks stopped me in my tracks on the steps. They were all quiet, just looking at me, staring.

"Ladies," my mom said in an infomercial announcer's voice, "all of you know my son?" They answered with a sweet muttering barrage of yeses and head nods.

"Hello. I'm very sorry for interrupting your meeting. I'm sorry. I—"

"Are you just waking up?" my mom said, staring at me with crazy eyes that said what she really wanted to say, which looked like: "You can't be seriously interrupting our meeting dressed like that!" I had on checkered boxers and an old green Dawn of the Bridesmaids T-shirt. Her eyes could say much to a person with just one short look.

I tried to respond with my own look that said: "No. I've just been up in my room reading a little bit and cleaning stuff up," but I doubt that I looked anything other than confused or constipated. I tried to hurry into the kitchen. I bowed my head and ducked into the kitchen before she could continue her inaudible eye conversation with me.

I started making a cold baloney-and-ham sandwich to take back up to my room. I could hear them starting up a passionate conversation, but I couldn't make out what they were saying. I hurriedly tossed my sandwich together and quickly headed, head-down, back upstairs. I got about two swift steps up the stairs when I was stopped by a voice. An unknown voice. I turned to see who it was. She was not one of the regulars in the group; I had only seen her once before.

"Ladies," the anonymous woman said in a happy voice. "I think a male perspective could be very valuable on this particular subject, don't you? I know this is an all-ladies group, but proper perspective is everything," she softly chuckled. Regaining her poise, she continued, "Excuse me. Would you mind giving us a few moments of your time, please? We just need your opinion on a matter of current concern." She was a slender redheaded woman with old looking, round, bright-red-rimmed glasses. Her hair was cut very short, and she was dressed in a colorful bohemian outfit.

Oh, fuck! Not again! I thought to myself. I didn't want to deal with more craziness or complicated life equations. And although this lady seemed nice, well spoken, and well meaning, she seemed like a bearer of philosophical gibberish. I could sense it! I had had enough crazy for a while, and I didn't want anymore. But I was forced to join their conversation, regardless of whether I wanted to or not. I had walked into the lioness's den, and there was no way out. What could I have said to her to get out of the conversation? "Um, no thanks, little redhead lady. Thanks, but no thanks. I'd rather keep my opinions to myself, thank you very much. I've had my fill of crazy for the week—matter of fact—for the year, and I'd rather sit this crazy round out.

No hard feelings. But thanks for the offer!" That's what I wanted to say. But there was no way I could. If I said something like that, my mom would probably take a knife out of the kitchen and sacrifice me right there on the shiny coffee table. Or she would have an aneurism and die from pure shame and embarrassment. If I were to embarrass her in front of them, she would probably never forgive me. I had to be very careful with what I said, and I had to try to get back to my room as quickly and as harmlessly as possible.

"Sure. Yes. I don't know if my opinion will be valid or useful, or informative, or even make any sense, but I'll do my best." I said it with my stomach roaring loud enough for them to hear it. "Um, how can I help?"

All of the ladies were looking directly at me again, uncomfortably. There were about seven of them. Their Bibles lay open on their laps.

"Thank you," the redheaded woman said. "Well, young man, we were having a discussion on women in leading roles in the church, and society in general, actually. As in whether or not they should be pastors or priests and things of that nature. Don't be nervous. Just be as honest as possible. We won't hold anything against you." She laughed. She must have seen the anxious, starving look on my face. I was frightened and hungry. I was standing in front of strange women in my boxers! I wanted nothing more than to run to my room and jump in my bed, eat my sandwich, pull the covers over my head, and go back to sleep.

She said, "I just would appreciate your opinion; how do you, as a male, feel about women leading men, honestly? We are all friendly here. None of us are going to bite you if you say the wrong thing. There is no wrong answer to this question. I just want your candid opinion. There are lots of men who have a problem with it; women as well. Lots of people are against it; you can see it all throughout society. Everyone is aware of the glass ceiling. Woman in leadership; I'm not talking about in a family setting or in a classroom. Those fields are historical givens. I'm talking about in a big, important position like the leader of a Wall Street bank or a high government official or even the Pope. There are a few women in government, but they are few and far between. It's definitely not half and half. How do you feel about that? Our little group here is torn nearly right down the middle. I'd just like your opinion on the subject."

All the women's faces had changed throughout the redheaded woman's speech, except for my mother's. Instead of the strange look of contempt most of them once had on their faces, they were looking at me as a defendant looks at a judge who is about to render a verdict. All of their faces seemed to long for my decree. They all looked at me as if my answer was the absolute tie-breaking response. They looked as if my answer would settle their debate once and for all—as if I were the apostle Paul giving my current thoughts of my letter to the Corinthians or Pope John Paul the Somethingth giving a speech from a balcony.

I was shocked at the desperation of their looks. Why did they want my answer to validate them? Didn't their expensive Bibles hold a clear, cohesive answer? Couldn't they have asked someone else—someone more qualified? I wasn't a Biblical scholar. I was barely qualified to be considered anything.

I didn't know Hebrew or Latin or Greek or Aramaic! I don't even know Spanish, for God's sakes! I had only read the Bible (only the New Testament actually) once, and that was because my dad had forced me to do so as punishment.

I didn't want to answer any questions. Whatever I said was going to piss off at least half of them, so why should I say anything? It was rude for the lady to ask me to answer in the first place!

I looked closely at my mom to try to get some idea of what she wanted me to say; she was the church lady I wanted to offend the least, but her expression was totally blank. I was on my own, out on a conversational island, surrounded by bullshit and expectant church women.

"Well," I said, trying hard to compose my thoughts through the noise of my nerves. "Um, I've never really given it much thought. I don't give lots of things much thought, though, so that's not saying much. I know I should think about lots of things a lot more, but most of the time I don't. I have a bad habit of that. But, yeah, let me think. Oh, well, I guess I don't see anything wrong with women leading anything, really: men, other women, children, and businesses, governments, whatever.

"Um, I don't see why there would be an issue really, just off the top of my head. I don't know a ton of people, but women are some of the most capable people I know. Not saying men are not capable, some of them are, it's just I know as many or more capable women. Lots of them are much more capable than the guys I know, honestly. I've met some pretty crappy guys, though.

"If they are qualified—I mean, if they have the merits to lead something—I don't see why they shouldn't be able to lead it. But if they aren't qualified, and I'm not really sure what I mean here by qualified, but if they are qualified they should be able to lead whatever they are qualified to lead. That's just basic logic, I think. I don't know if that is really an opinion. But that's just what I think. And I haven't ever really thought about it, so I could be missing something concerning the logic of the other side of the argument. I could be completely wrong, too. It'd be better if I had more time to think. There could be an alternative argument that I am missing. But I really can't see what it could be.

"Don't get me wrong, I'm definitely not trying to go against the Bible or anything like that. I remember hearing something about women as pastors in it, but I'm not really all that sure what it says. If the Bible says that women shouldn't lead, I'm not trying to go against that. The Bible might know something I don't know. Of course, it knows things I don't know. It's the Bible. But I'm saying there might be a reason I don't know about that might be its reason for suggesting that. I remember reading something about it, but I can't recall the specific passage or anything.

"All I am saying is that there are a lot of men that are equally as incapable at leading as women. That's not what I meant to say. Sorry. What I meant to say is that there are a lot of unqualified men, and I'm assuming that there are a lot of unqualified women. I think that that is just a statistical probability. To me, there doesn't seem to be an inherent superiority built into a particular gender; and if there were one, I would guess it was on the female side—the superiority, that is. People are just different from other people. It's like a car air freshener and a candy bar, they cost the same, like a dollar, they are equal. They are just very different, structurally speaking.

"I heard on the news that there was some preacher that got caught selling cocaine out of a hotel room. He was the preacher at some mega-church! I don't know, but I would bet that there is some lady somewhere that maybe could have been a better pastor than the guy selling cocaine out of a hotel room.

"I also saw on the news another story about a pastor that killed his wife for no reason. Well, the reason was another lady in the congregation, actually. And he almost got away with it. I just think that guys like that are crazy."

My nervous, longwinded rant was thankfully interrupted when I noticed the look on the redheaded lady's face. She had an enormous smile. I looked around at the rest of the women, one by one; their faces were a grabbag of expressions, all different: from curious, to stunned, to intrigued, to pleased, to baffled, to mortified, to the stoic face of my mother, they all were looking at me intently.

"Well, young man. That is very interesting. You have some interesting ideas. You had some very thoughtful points, I would say. You did a good job for being put on the spot like you were."

"Yes, those were very thoughtful comments, son," my mother said. Her tone was mono and unrevealing, and her face was vacant.

"Well, thank you. I hadn't thought about it much. If I had more time to think about it, I might have come up with something better, or at least clearer or less fumbled. I was all over the place. I really hope I didn't offend anyone by my comments. A lot of the time I don't know what I'm talking about. I am truly sorry if I offended anyone, though."

One of the other women (the one with the intrigued look on her face) said: "Don't worry about that. You were just saying what you thought. No one can fault you for that."

The redheaded lady jumped in, saying, "Young man, you should give yourself much more credit than you do. I have a child around your age, and he tends to do the exact opposite; he gives his thoughts too much credit. What you said was very rationally based. Your oratory skills will perhaps improve with age and life experience. There's no need to be that nervous around a bunch of old hens. What you thought and what you said were good, it was very reasonable. Don't be so quick to dismiss your own insights, and never dismiss your ability to reason.

"Many people have degraded their thoughts so successfully that when they finally choose to speak confidently about a matter no one pays them any attention. They had degraded their intellect so thoroughly in the past, their words become mere attempts at meaning. Be confident in what you say, and others will be confident in you. But don't be falsely confident, be correctly confident. There is a big difference.

Soliloquy

"With correctness comes real confidence and an intellectual peace. The truth is more powerful and peaceful than most people can understand. But be sure not to grow arrogant or complacent when there is correctness on your side: correctness is a fickle old hen. You seem like a very smart young man, smarter than many young men your age. Don't waste your time being shy or self-deprecating, because that's all it is, a waste of time. Spend your time learning true correctness and self-confidence. In the face of self-correctness, all insecurities will be reduced to memories.

"I was once shy myself, but finding out the unity between confidence, correctness, and peace cleared me of my self-generated ailment. I'm sure your mother has told you before to be more confident in yourself. I know I tell my child these same words of advice all the time. I know it may be odd coming from an old lady you don't know, but I just thought I should remind you. Everyone needs a reminder every once in a while, right? Mary, you've told your boy these things before, haven't you? I know you have." She seemed to be fighting back a smirk.

"Of course, I have," my mom said with a forced, phony smile (I had seen that smile a billion times before). "My son is just shy, that's all. He has always been that way. Sometimes it's a good thing and sometimes it's not. But he's growing. He's just meek, that's all. But like the Bible says: 'The meek shall inherit the earth.' Remember that, son: God says the meek shall inherit the earth."

The redheaded woman laughed an introspective laugh and said, "Very true, Mary, very true. The meek shall inherit the earth indeed. But everything in life is balance; fine balance—the golden rule. Even Jesus was not meek all the time. Sometimes he was rude, and gruff, and sarcastic. Sometimes he was gentle. Sometimes he was angry. Sometimes he was somber, boastful, and dare I say, perhaps self-concerned. Jesus was balanced. He *was* balance. And he spoke with great confidence, ultimate confidence." As the redheaded lady spoke, the other women looked at her with shocked eyes and knotted mouths.

My mother looked directly into the redheaded lady's thick, round red-framed glasses and said, "That is very true; Jesus was completely balanced, but there was only one Jesus, to be sure. Only one All Knowing one. Only one Perfect one. Only one who could be sure when to be all those different things. And to be on the safe side, I would advise my son to lean toward meekness." There was a complete Western-shootout-level stillness in the room.

I broke the cold tension, saying, "Well, thank you all very much for your time. And thank you, for the advice, Miss. I'm going to head upstairs now; I don't want my sandwich to get cold." I tried to laugh, but a weird cough came out.

"No, thank you. And you are more than welcome, young man. I hope my and your mother's advice will help a little. You have a great mother. You had some very good comments. Maybe you can join this old group every once in a while, to give us old hags some new and fresh ideas. Some new things to think about." She was smiling widely with both rows of her perfectly white teeth showing.

"Maybe. Thank you. Thanks for your time. Have fun, ladies!" I shouted as I ran up the stairs.

When I got to my room my heart was speeding. I wondered what my mom *really* thought about what I'd said. She didn't seem angry with me, and that was a good thing. But maybe she did have something to say and was just waiting for the group to leave.

I didn't know which side of the issue she was on. I had never talked to her about anything of any importance, and that's the way I wanted to keep it. I figured that I shouldn't worry myself about it too much since she was capable of getting mad about anything, and I realized that I really couldn't be held responsible for my mother's actions or overreactions. I could only be responsible if what I said was honest or not. She would react how she wanted to react. So I pushed it to the back of my mind and began thinking of the redheaded woman's flurry of comments and commands.

What was she saying, anyway? I thought to myself. Was she just another crazy person trying to force me to think or act differently than I normally did? She spoke of correctness and confidence. "With correctness comes real confidence and the power of peace—the truth is more powerful and peaceful than most people can understand," she'd said. But what was all that? What did all that mean? What did she know about what people could understand? What made her an expert on confidence? The statement, "correctness breeds confidence," seemed completely untrue to me. It seemed to me that confidence would breed confidence—or stupidity would breed confidence. Look at some of the most incorrect people in history: the Hitlers of the world, the Francos, the Mussolinis, the Pol Pots, and on and on and on. Weren't they all stuffed full of confidence about completely insane ideas? They were completely wrong yet completely confident!

It seems like the more wrong you are the more confidence you obtain!

Just think about it. People from dozens and dozens of different, completely contradictory religions seem to be totally confident about their being correct. They are truly, fully, and utterly confident. They have something much, much more than humble faith propped up by "evidence." There are people from dozens of these contradictory religions that would die, or have died, to *prove* that they *know* what they believe is correct. And to try to force other people to believe what they believe. There have been people who believe enough to bet their one and only life on their beliefs. Now if that is not confidence, I don't know what is. To me, that is confidence, crazy fucking boatloads of confidence!

But due to the clashing nature of their thoughts, and what they call *evidence*, all but one of the groups has to be completely wrong about what they believe! But that does not take away from their confidence. What would the redheaded lady say about those people? —the completely confident and wrong!

She did say that real confidence comes from correct confidence. People who hold the correct beliefs, people who hold the real facts, they are the correctly confident. But what's the difference between real and fake confidence if they have exactly the same results? What would the redheaded lady call them? I guess she would call them the arrogant. I guess she would call them the falsely confident.

But in this world, in this great commotion of contradictory claims, in this mess of beliefs and thoughts and ideologies and dogmas, in this shit-fan of feverish faith, in this chaos and confusion, how was I to be confident about my thoughts and beliefs? How was anyone to be completely confident?

It's hard to be confident when for every single thought or theory you have there are a least a trillion others that deny and contradict it. It's hard to be correctly confident when all the greatest minds in the history of this world have always had other great minds saying the exact opposite at the same time! Correctly confident my ass! No one can know for sure about anything! Or can they?

Was she correctly confident? Did she know herself to be correct? She seemed like a regular middle-aged lady. She was not Siddhartha or Socrates or Aristotle or Gandhi or Democritus or Jesus. How could she be so sure about her correctness or her theory of correctness?

Soliloquy

However, she was a Christian. She was at a Bible study, for God's sake. Did that mean that she was sure about her religious correctness? Did she believe that she held the truth about the cosmos and the "after life"? Did she believe that everyone in the world who wasn't a Christian was damned to burn in eternal hell-fire for the rest of eternity? But that couldn't be the case; she couldn't be *completely* sure that her religion was correct. She seemed to be talking about something different than religion.

Faith is relative. Anyone can take it and do with it what they will— good or bad—right or wrong. Faith is no replacement for facts. Faith is the antithesis of fact unless your faith is in a fact! So for her to be sure was to be arrogant, unless she was talking about something else. Something deeper.

My flurry of thoughts about the redheaded lady's speech had me pissed off, confused, and on the heels of something I didn't understand. Who was she to tell me what to do? She didn't even know me. The redheaded lady was contradicting herself, yet she seemed so confident when she spoke that I was forced to take what she said seriously. I couldn't understand it. Couldn't she see the error in her statements? Were errors in her statement? Was I missing the critical point?

I lay there on my messy bed, running through her speech in my head, trying to understand confidence, and trying to understand her hidden or missing meaning.

At some point in my thinking, I realized that even though the lady had contradicted herself, there was something that seemed correct in her statement; something that I couldn't seem to shake off; something that refused to be pushed to the back of my mind. Even though, in my mind, she had lost all credibility by being a completely confident person of faith, there was a part of her statement that retained its importance. She had said, "Spend your time learning self-correctness; in the face of self-correctness, all insecurities will be reduced to memories." That statement remained. Was it true? Something about it rang true. I was someone who had never heard of this "self-correctness." I had read many, many books, yet I had never run across her idea of "self-correctness."

Although I knew nothing about it, I believed it, and I wanted it. I wanted to feel self-correctness…

I just laid there thinking, trying to find something in myself that I was unsure was there.

***

I was startled by a knock at my door. I jumped from my bed in a day-dreamy fog. I had fallen asleep again.

"Hello? I'll be right there," I said, scrambling around.

"It's me, open up."

"Just a minute, I'm coming." My room was in shambles, and I was still in my T-shirt and boxers, and it had to be around 4 p.m. My mom was going to freak out!

I quickly changed my shirt, kicked some stuff under the bed, and hurried to the door. I cracked the door as little as possible, peeking out with one eye. "Hey. How's it going?"

"You didn't hear me calling you from downstairs? I want you to come downstairs. I need to talk to you," my mom said.

"I'm sorry, I didn't hear you. I was on the computer. I had my earphones on. Okay, I'll be right down, just a minute."

When I got downstairs, my mother was sitting in the same spot she was in during the Bible study. I sat across from her wondering what the hell she wanted to talk about, all the while, in the back of my head, knowing exactly what she wanted to talk about. Before I could get out a preemptive apology, she said, "So what did you think about Rebecca?" She had an investigative look on her face.

"Is that the redheaded lady with the glasses, Rebecca?"

"Yes. Of course," she said impatiently.

From the look on her face and their previous conversation I could sense her contempt for the lady in the glasses. I could see in her eyes that she wanted me to dislike Rebecca because she disliked Rebecca.

"Oh, she seemed kind of out there, you know? She's different. Very opinionated, it seems. But I don't know. This is the first time I ever talked to her. Is she new to your church or something?"

My mother's inquiring look gradually lightened. She seemed content with my opinion.

"Yes, she is newish to my church. She hasn't been in town very long, actually. She came to this town with her son, after school let out. She's divorced. Newly divorced. She moved here because she has some family here in town, she says. I guess they moved to be closer to them, because of the divorce and all. Our church was the first church she visited, because she heard it was the best: the most spiritual and holy. We invited her into our Bible group to welcome her in her time of need. We thought it would be the right thing to do."

The lady didn't seem needy too me at all. But I think it made my mom feel better (or superior) to think so. "Well," I said, "what do you think about her?"

She sighed. "She's fine. I don't have a problem with her. But you're right; she is very, very opinionated. She likes to talk as if she knows more than other people. She's been that way since her first meeting. Maybe that's the way people are where she comes from, I don't know.

Soliloquy

"A lot of the other ladies in the group don't like her attitude very much. They think she talks too much, but I don't have a problem. I laugh at a lot of what she says. Not to her face, but I laugh. A lot of it is just extreme. It is way out there for my taste. But she's just trying to stir the pot, you know? Or that's my guess, anyhow. She's just trying to get people thinking." She spoke calmly, almost serenely. It made me think that maybe she liked this lady in an odd way; maybe she liked having a strong competitor.

"Well, she does seem kind of strange." It was silent for a time. I was wondering if that was all she wanted to talk about. She hadn't even mentioned my speech.

"So, is there anything else you wanted to talk about?" I said, rising from my seat to go.

"Oh, yes. I wanted to know how your meeting about the acting troupe went yesterday afternoon."

I was thrown off by her question. How did she know that I had gone to meet Miss Magdalene? I didn't recall telling her that I was going there. Did she follow me or something? I was confused and a little creeped out.

"Oh, it was fine. How did you know I went?"

"I am much smarter than you and your father give me credit for," she said, laughing like a villainous Disney character. "Last night, before you got home, a Miss Magdalene, yeah—I think that was her name—called here looking for you. She told me that you had left her house feeling sick, and she just wanted to make sure you made it home all right. Funny, you didn't tell me or your dad that you were going to meet her yesterday. I don't know why you thought you needed to hide something like that, something so petty.

"Her and I had a nice talk on the phone, a fairly long conversation, actually. She told me that you were welcomed to be in her troupe; you must not have made too bad an impression on her. She told me that you were invited to the next practice, and I told her, I *assured* her, that you would be there."

"What?" I shouted unconsciously. The word had flown out of my mouth well before I realized how loud I was. "Sorry," I said, "but what do you mean I would be more than happy to be at the next practice? I still don't know if I want to join or not. I'm not sure if that type of thing is for me." I couldn't believe that my mother would take it upon herself to "assure" Miss Magdalene that I would be at the next practice. Then again, I could believe it. It actually seemed more realistic for her to "assure" than not to "assure."

"Well, son, Miss Magdalene told me about the conditions you left in her bathroom—unpleasant to say the least. I think the least you could do is go to a practice and not waste her time. She seems like an extremely nice lady. Do you know how many young men your age are so bored they turn to drugs, sex, and devil's mayhem? Do you know how many? Do you want to turn up on drugs: all that crack, and smack, and wack-and-everything, and weeds, and methamphetamines, and Y2K that's out here killing everybody? Do you want some STD from some little floozy who's been with who knows how many people? Then you won't be able to have children! Do you want to become a pervert or some kind of pedophile chasing little boys and girls around the playground with pictures of fake lost dogs in your hands? Is that what you want? I see it on the news all the time! You want an old white van with no windows and a soiled mattress in the back? You want to spend all your time playing on the computer, and with those video games, or looking up pornography and lord knows what? Not in my house you won't! Not as long as you're under my God-given roof you won't!

"You need a hobby, a good, positive hobby. You need something pro-ductive to do. I'm not going to let you just sit around and turn into something evil on my watch. No-sir-re-Bob. That is not going to happen to any son of mine. I'm tired of it! The Lord says that an idle mind is the devil's playground, and by His name, He is right! I'm not going to have this idle sitting around all the time anymore.

It is done. I'm putting my foot down. Either you are going to join that group, and like it, or you're going to start working every day for 40-plus hours a week, not this two or three days a week. You are going to find a positive hobby or you're going to start paying room and board. Or I'm going to start making you go to church again. Remember church? And if you don't like either of those ideas, I'm going to take your car and your TV and your videogames away, and maybe even your darn computer. Or maybe you'd like to stay at your uncle's house for a few weeks. See how you like his rules. I will not let you wind up crazy and wicked from wasting all your time. No, sir! I'll not let that happen. There are too many kids in—"

I was done listening to her talk. At some point her words turned into the Charley Brown "womp, womp, womp, womp." I blocked her out as best I could. I had heard enough of her menopausal soapboxing. She was on her crazy horse and I knew that she wasn't going to get down anytime soon. I was not going to argue with her, it wasn't worth it. It was never worth it. So I just sat there pretending to listen.

After five or ten minutes more of her "moral" rambling, I realized that I couldn't take sitting there another minute. My blood was rushing, and I felt like I was going to have a heart attack. I said, "Mom: I don't mean to cut you off or anything, but I have to get ready for work. I have to work tonight, soon. But, yes, I totally understand what you are saying. I completely understand what you mean."

Soliloquy

"Okay, so we have an understanding? You're going to be a part of that group, or I'm taking all your toys away. We do have an understanding, don't we?" Her eyes were glaring like the moon.

"Well, if you are making me go, then I guess we do have an understanding. I don't seem to have a real choice in the matter. Will you and dad still help me with getting a new car? Will you guys help me pay to be in the troupe?"

"You'll have to talk to your dad about that. He's the one with all the money. I just pay the bills. But that's not the point. The point is you're going to join so you have something productive to do. Understand?"

"Yes. Okay."

And that was that. I was going to Thursday night's practice whether I liked it or not. I headed to my room, fully defeated. I plodded up the stairs before my mother could come up with more ridiculous clichés to hurl at me about "people my age" and "my lost generation." I was screwed, big time, no matter what. She was right because she was in charge. Power is a tool that the un-empathetic wield. She had the power, and she was wielding it like crazy. I could either be in prison (or basically house arrest) with my mother as the angry warden, or I could spend more creepy quality time with Creeper-in-Chief Paul and General Miss Magdalene at the cat-smelling, toy-littered, photo museum they called home. Those were my options; two very bad options. I was shafted and there was nothing I could do to change it. I didn't want to think about it, so I just got ready for work. It was done. *I* was done. I just tried not to think.

***

The rest of that week went by slowly. All I did was work at the restaurant, Xbox, self-satisfaction session, sleep, library, PlayStation, zzzz, work, library, zzzzz, more sessions, work, more Xbox, and finally, more zzzzz. I

Soliloquy

did all I could do to stay away from my mother. My mother seemed to be in a raving, righteous, ultra-Bible-thumping mood, even more than usual, and I was not in the mood to deal with it. I felt on edge, like my nerves had been cooked. I stayed out of the house and I stayed out of her way, except for mandatory dinners. At the dinners I ate faster than I'd ever eaten before. I ate like I was ten Sudanese children at an all-you-can-eat buffet. This did not make my mom or dad very happy (the looks they gave me were a clear indication of their surprise and concern), but neither of them verbally objected to my speed.

At Wednesday's mandatory dinner, the primary goal of my parents seemed to be: give me advice about what I should and shouldn't do to get the other people in the group to like me. It was nearly the same speech they gave me on my first day of kindergarten: the "JUST BE YOURSELF" speech.

"Son," my dad mumbled through his newspaper, "tomorrow, at rehearsal, just be yourself. That's all. Just be yourself, son. The setting of a rehearsal is very conducive to making friends. It is very different from the ambiance of a school or of a mall, and so forth. If you are friendly and mannerly, you should have no problem at all getting along with your fellow compeers. Talk to them about all the plays you've attended and read. That is where you are very strong, very strong. You have a vast knowledge base regarding literature and drama. If they are truly actors and actresses, it is very likely that they like the same things you like. I am sure it will all work out just fine, son."

"I really hope you at least try," my mom said. "I mean really, really try to make some friends—seriously. Whatever you do, don't make yourself look bad. Because if you make yourself look bad, you make us look bad—so please, for our sake, don't do that. Not that it's all about looking good, it's not, but it is important to make sure you show those folks that you have some proper home training. I don't want anyone thinking that we didn't raise you right—because we did! Your father is right: just be yourself. But don't try too hard to stand out or blend in. But blending in is always better than standing out. You know what they say, 'The nail that sticks up gets hammered down.' Just be who you are and if they don't like that, hey, that's their choice. Not everyone likes everyone else. Not all people have chemistry. Just go there, smile, practice, and try to have fun. And don't say anything out of line or philosophical. There are a few things that all people hate talking about with new people. Do you know what they are? They are money, and religion, and politics, and philosophy. So whatever you do, don't talk about those things. Talk about small stuff, like what they like and what they want to do when they're older. If you can do that, everything should be just fine. Okay?"

"Okay," I said, trying my very hardest not to sound completely exasperated. "So dad, when are we going to look for my new car?" I was trying to knock my mom off her kamikaze course with my nerves.

He lowered and folded his newspaper, straightening his frames on his nose, and smiled. "Well, son, don't get too far ahead of yourself. Horse first, cart second. Always remember that. You still have to make it through your first practice. Perhaps after four or five practices, we can have further, more serious discussions. Maybe then we can go look for a *newer* car."

"Okay, because we had a deal."

After dinner, my nervousness started to flare up again. As I got ready for bed, all I could think about was the meeting I'd had with Paul and Miss Magdalene. My physical faculties freaked out, completely. I was still trying to recover mentally from what had happened.

What was I going to do when I was on the spot in front of a ton of new people? Not just two. If I couldn't handle those two, how was I going to handle eight or ten or God knows how many more? The more I thought about it the more I realized how big of a disaster practice was going to be. I tried and tried to think of any possible way practice could not turn out to be a disaster, but nothing came to mind. All the scenarios that slogged across the landscape of my mind ended with me completely embarrassed, and my parents completely ashamed. For practice to be a success, something miraculous would have to happen.

***

Thursday arrived, and I was dreading every single second of it. It was clear to me that the rest of my summer was going to suck, one way or the other. I played videogames all day trying to keep my mind off of practice, but, of course, nothing could take my mind off of the dread. Paul, random new people, more Paul, the smell of obese cat shit and dander; it all was terrorizing my thoughts.

At one point, I thought maybe being stuck in the house for the rest of the summer without technology would be the better way to go. But I knew that if my mom and I stayed home all day together, either her or I, or both of us, would be dead, literally.

When five o'clock finally came around I began preparing for what I knew was going to be a night of absolute terror. I cold-showered, put on my nicest (or most acceptable by other people's standards) jeans and t-shirt, and went over the game plan I would employ: the "JUST BE ANYONE BUT YOURSELF" game plan. I would try to be what other people were most likely to accept, that was my game plan. I would try to smile a lot, but not too much. I would try to talk as little as humanly possible without coming off like a deaf mute. I would make some eye contact, but hold it for no more than a half a second. And I would leave as soon as practice was over without extra fraternizing, no exceptions. That was my game plan.

Soliloquy

On my way out the house, my mom gave me one last piece of advice: "Son, whatever you do," she said somberly. She was looking at me squarely in the eyes, as if I was going off to war, as if it might be the last time we would see each other again on planet earth, "Whatever you do, don't make a fool of yourself, okay? That's all I ask. Don't make a fool of yourself."

On the drive to practice I played my music as loud as I could. I really wanted to drown out my negative thoughts, the manic flappings of the butterflies that crashed frantically around my hungry stomach, and the distant train shrieks and inconsiderate whistles of an onrushing and uncontrollable panic! The music didn't really help much, though, because only one side of my car had working speakers, so the one-sided noise gave me a headache, which made me feel even worse.

I arrived for practice around fifteen minutes until 7. Several bright-colored cars filled Miss Magdalene's driveway and the surrounding street curbs. Once again, like the first time I had arrived at the sky-blue dungeon, I parked down the street to calm myself as much as possible. I was feeling incredibly anxious, and panicky, and feverish. I spent a few minutes trying a multitude of breathing techniques (that didn't work) and trying to find my happy place (which actually worked worse than the breathing techniques, because I panicked when I realized that I had no happy place). I eventually gathered enough confidence (for lack of a better word) to get out of my car, but once again, as I walked towards the house, my legs felt like liquid-filled garbage bags.

I approached the house with a mortified, yet (what I only hoped was a) composed attitude. Why be afraid? I thought to myself. Why be afraid when you're screwed no matter what? Just take it. I felt like a death row inmate walking down the sad white corridors of a prison to the execution chamber. It's not like he's going to pull off the great escape or something. It's not like he has any real options—he's dead and he knows it—all the guards know it—all the other inmates know it—and he knows it—dead! At some point he just admits defeat and gets ready for his dirt nap. He knows he is going to die; he has to somewhat come to terms with it, yet he still can't fathom the horror that awaits him when he reaches the end of the chemical-smelling corridor and enters that chamber. That's exactly how I felt as I maneuvered through the sidewalk covered with possible lawsuits (otherwise known as toys). I was entering the chamber.

As I moved I felt a massive piss coming on. But worse, I felt that the inner mechanism that stops a normal male from pissing himself indiscriminately was not functioning properly inside me. As I walked slowly, praying that pee wouldn't splash down my pants, I could hear loud, ebullient voices coming from the house. Many people were laughing with booming, wild excitement. It sounded like a house party. As I cautiously climbed the porch steps, I had fully accepted the fact that I was screwed (and I even accepted the possibility that I might wet myself in front of a gang of people I didn't know), and my realization of the un-dodgeable doom that awaited seemed to take a little of the pressure off. I was willing to accept whatever evils awaited me.

I rang the musical doorbell and expected the worst: Paul. The voices inside the house lowered as if a surprise party was in store. I heard heavy choppy footsteps approaching. To my surprise, when the door opened it wasn't Paul or Miss Magdalene; it was a girl who looked about seventeen years old. She was very petite, and she had curly jet-black hair. Her big bushy bangs swooped low over one of her eyes. It was hard to get a clear look at half of her face.

As she answered the door her expression seemed to be full of sad surprise, or more specifically, dissatisfied mystification. My looks or my strangeness or my basic existence must have startled her, because when she saw me she immediately called for Miss Magdalene in a wavering flustered voice as she retreated quickly back into the house. It was like she saw a ghost. She didn't even open the screen door, which was still locked. I thought she was rude. That's a pretty shitty start, I said under my breath.

"Oh, my," Miss Magdalene said as she approached the screen door squinting her heavily made-up eyes, "I'm glad you decided to show. I wasn't sure if you were going to come or not." She seemed genuinely happy to see me, which was totally confusing. Why would she be happy to see the guy who blew scorching spew-chunks all over her bathroom? She was smiling her militant smile, and for the first time I saw her top row of teeth.

"Yep, well, here I am." I was trying to match the believability of her smile with one of my own. I'm sure I failed.

"Come in. I'm excited for you to meet the rest of the troupe. Don't be nervous, now. You'll like the others. They're good people. No need to worry." She put her unnaturally warm hand on my back as she led me through the door.

As I followed Miss Magdalene into the photo-filled den, with each step my nervousness grew exponentially. My palms were wet and clammy. My heart was pounding 67 million miles per second. My ears were ringing a high-pitched continual "tingggggggggggggggggggggggggggggggggggg!" sound, and my chest shuddered wildly. I was freaking out again—I was freaking out again!

As I stepped into the brightly lit living room, my eyesight went blurry. It felt like walking out of a matinee movie into the bright mid-afternoon sun. I felt nearly blinded and everything seemed gauzy.

I heard someone near me say, "Hey there, little *buddy*!" Despite my visual impairment, I had no trouble whatsoever recognizing the voice. The voice was utterly distinct, and it was a voice burned deep into the black box of my memory, forever. I looked in the direction of the voice; I could still make out the wraithlike figure for the most part. Paul was standing against Miss Magdalene's chair: hands on hips, pelvis protruding.

"Hello, Mr. Paul."

"Welcome baaack, little friendee! Are you over the little sick spell you had the other day? You're looking much, much better, that's for sure." He came towards me and put his boney spider like hand on the small of my back.

"Yes, I am better. I feel much better, thanks. It was just something I ate, I think, thanks."

"Come, come," Miss Magdalene said, removing Paul's hand and leading me to the middle of the room. In a loud voice that filled the entire room, "Excuse me, ladies and gentlemen. Excuse me! I would like your attention for just a few moments. I am very happy to introduce the newest member of our troupe," she said.

I didn't really hear everything she said, because I was trying with all my might to concentrate on my breathing, so as not to pass out. Plus, the high *tinging* in my ear was reaching new octaves and tones that I had never heard before. I was not feeling as hot as I did when I had my bathroom meltdown, but I was getting lightheaded and the blurriness was steadily escalating as the rate of the "*tingggggggggggggggggggggg*!" increased. I kept blinking and rubbing my eyes, but that just made it worst. The icy sweat from my wet hands added a burning to an already-blurry situation. If I didn't get control of my heart rate, there was a very good chance I would faint, or die, or spontaneously combust. I began looking (or at least trying to look) around the room at all the strange, foggy, surreal faces that appeared to be staring ominously back at me.

Soliloquy

"He is an avid fan of theater. But he is very, very shy. So I want all of you guys to take it easy on him at first, okay?" They all laughed in harmonic unison, like a live studio audience. "I really believe that he will be a good addition to our troupe. Is there anything you would like to say?" she said, patting me on the back in a soft burping fashion.

"Um. I would just like to say nice meeting you all," I said, while still trying to focus on taking deep breaths. I must have looked like a fool in front of them, but at least I was still conscious. With all my breathing and blinking I must have looked like a woman on meth having contractions.

"I will give you all a few minutes to greet our new friend before practice officially starts. We will be starting in approximately five minutes. Enjoy the rest of your free time. You all can go back to talking now, if you wish. Thank you for your attention." Miss Magdalene seemed happy, completely in her element, and she knew it. The hardness in her voice had practically vanished. She was smiling. She was actually laughing. She seemed to be completely in her "happy place." It was clear that this acting troupe was what got her out of bed in the morning and what kept her up at night.

After her speech to the troupe, people began to come up to me. They formed a crude line behind the first solemn greeter. Through my visual haze I could make out about eight-or-so people. Even with my muddied vision I could recognize that the first person to greet me was the small girl with the swooping black bang that had come to the door, looked at me, then fled. The fright in her bang-shaded face seemed subdued. She seemed relieved and contrite as she stuck out her hand.

"Hi. My name is Hannah. Nice to meet you." She had a sweet voice.

"Nice to meet you, too," I said, groping for her hand. Her hand was soft and cold.

Soliloquy

The next person in line was an extremely fat bear-of-a-person with a forest of thick, rough facial hair. The hair on his head was wild in a sort of Einsteinian, hipster mess. He was sweating, and (from what I could see) he had an angry scowl on his large, domineering, wet face. He was a towering man-beast in the 6-foot-4, 6-foot-6 range. I had to tilt my head back to look for him. He looked big enough to be a starting NFL lineman or linebacker. What the hell was he doing at an acting troupe?

"Hello," he said in a booming, baritone voice. He was so loud that his voice caused my ears to begin ringing even louder than before. His wet bearded face dripped dimes of salty sweat onto mine. He gripped my hand incredibly tight with his hairy, perspiring hand.

"My name is David, but everybody around here calls me the D-train. It's nice to meet you." As he did his best to crush my hand, I noticed that his forehead had deep river-like wrinkles that trapped pools of his man-beast sweat.

"Thank you," I said quickly, trying to withdraw my hand from his bear trap. I was trying to conceal the pain in my voice.

I wanted to kick him in the nuts! I wanted to kick him in the nuts as hard as humanly possible. I wanted to kick him so hard that his nuts would come out of his hairy ears. It felt like he was compressing my hand in a trash compactor. I wanted to scream: Dude! What the hell is your problem? We're not about to arm wrestle, are we? If we are, no one informed me! Get the crap off of my hand! You crazy Cro-Magnon man! Were you raised by a pack of angry bears? Let go of me!

He finally let go of my hand after a few vicious shakes, like a dog with a toy in its mouth. Then he marched away, abusing the carpet and floorboards with massive stumps.

Soliloquy

A fast flurry of people came and went. They said their names, shook my hand, and hurried away before I could even get out a response. It was more like a mugging or a greet-bang than it was a chance to actually meet them. Everyone in the room came and went, except one person. After the line had dissipated, there was still a girl sitting on the couch reading a book, intently.

I stood there wondering if I should follow the crowd or wait for the girl with the book to greet me. I decided that it would be creepy for me to keep staring at her, blinking spastically, and saying nothing, so I decided to follow the others. As I started walking out I was stopped. "Just a second," she said in a soft, commanding voice. She spoke without looking up from the book. "I'm almost done with this page. Almost finished." Despite my blurry vision I could see that her eyes were completely fixed on the page. Her face had a scowl of intense interest.

As had she requested, or demanded, I stood there in the middle of the floor waiting for her to finish. I felt uncomfortable in the silence. I tried to look at some of the photos on the wall to give myself something to do, but it was hopeless. I kept looking back at the girl.

I just kept thinking: Who is this girl? Who is she to think she can make me wait for her to finish her page? Does she think I'm a little dog or something? Does she think I am *her* little dog? Will she ask me to sit or roll over? How rude and inconsiderate it is to tell someone you've never met to wait for you to finish reading your page! I started contemplating leaving and heading towards the others despite her demand, but I didn't want to be rude, too.

"There!" she said, still carefully looking at her book. She slowly placed a brown and gold bookmark in her spot. She stood up leisurely; still looking at her book, and slowly approached me.

Soliloquy

Her eyes finally met mine as she came near. Her eyes penetrated the fog of my sight like two beams of light. And for a moment I felt as though I was looking into the eyes of someone very familiar, someone I had known from something or somewhere I couldn't quite place.

She reached out her slim hand and said, "I'm sorry to make you wait, but I hate standing in lines with lots of people, and I hate when I have to stop reading in the middle of a page, you know? I'm impatient that way, and O.C.D, and I think I may be a little claustrophobic. I don't know." She smiled a coy smile as she shook my hand firmly.

"Oh, it's no problem," I said. "What book are you reading?"

"Oh, this? Oh, this is one of my favorite books, *Catcher in the Rye*. Have you ever read it?" She handed me the beaten-up book, still smiling.

"Have I read it? Of course, I've read it. Who hasn't read it? I've read it five or six times. I think J.D. Salinger is a very unique writer. He writes with an unflinching voice. He's not my favorite, I think he's a bit overrated, but he's very good. I like the book."

She looked me in the eyes, smiling excitedly. "Well, well, well. I am very impressed, mister. We have ourselves a young literary critic. So you are a Salinger fan? You'd be surprised how many people don't know Salinger or understand him. Or how many people don't know any great writers, for that matter. I've read all of his stuff, *Franny and Zooey*. I think he's great. This book is great, but his short stories may be even better, in my view. *The Laughing Man* is unbelievable! You like to read, I take it… from the six times thing? Who's your favorite author? What's your favorite book?"

"I guess, yeah. I guess I do like to read. I've read Salinger's short stories, too. *I've also read Franny and Zooey.*

"I don't know if I have a favorite author. I guess I never thought of it in those terms. It would be nearly impossible to pick one as my favorite, I think.

Soliloquy

I'd have to think. I love lots of books, but if I had to pick a book as my favorite, I would say it's between *The Metamorphosis* by Kafka and *Giovanni's Room* by Baldwin. I really like those two books. But I don't think I could pick one."

Her grayish brown eyes widened. "Oh, really? Kafka's *Metamorphosis* isn't bad. I've read it. But you want to talk about overrated; he might be more overrated than Salinger. But I've never heard of *Giovanni's Room* before."

"Most people haven't heard of the book or of James Baldwin. He's black. They never talked about him in school or anything. He doesn't get much respect. The book is kind of obscure, I guess, but it's a classic by most literary standards. It's amazing. I have a copy I can let you borrow if you ever want to read it sometime."

"Of course I want to read it. Why wouldn't I want to read it?" she said, placing her hand on my elbow. "If it's as good as you say it is, I will enjoy reading it. Maybe I can come get it from you or maybe you can bring it to practice next Thursday?"

"I think I can do that. That shouldn't be a problem. I think I will be here next Thursday."

For a few moments, while I was talking with this slim, big-eyed, smiley, peculiar girl, I was completely unconnected to my natural states of being: boredom and panic. I had forgotten my nervousness and my anxiety. I had forgotten my "tingggggggggggggging" eardrums and my fuzzy, dizzied eyes. I had forgotten D-Train's rain of sweat and his Hulk hand crush. I had forgotten Paul's creepy toddler voice. And I had forgotten the girl's rudeness for making me wait for her to finish her page. All I felt, all I knew, and all I remembered, was that I didn't mind talking to this girl. Another person who actually read of her own free will, I thought. How rare is she? How strange.

Soliloquy

"Oh, shit!" she said, grabbing my hand harshly. "Practice! Come on. It's already started. We're late!"

By the hand she led me, jogging quickly through the long kitchen into the large garage. As we went through the door, Miss Magdalene stopped speaking and looked at us with an annoyed glare.

"Excuse us," the girl said quietly. We walked behind the others who were already seated in their dark yellow-and-poop-green lawn chairs.

"As I was saying. Tonight, we are going to be working on new material. It's a new play that Paul and I have written. It's a completely original piece. It's called *The Poor Man's Prayer*. I have arranged for us to perform the play at my church in a little over a month's time, so we have a lot of practicing to do if we want to be prepared. All of you know how we strive for perfection here, so there will be little to no room for errors in the next few weeks, understood?

"Paul is coming around with scripts for all of you. I want you to take a few moments, fifteen or twenty minutes or so, to look over the script. I want you to look over it seriously. Look through it and see what parts you like, and start thinking about what parts you might want to try out for. Later, Paul and I will let you read for the parts you are interested in. There are only a limited number of parts in the play, so one or two of you may end up being understudies. So make sure you try out for a part you think you will be successful in, understand? Don't try out for a part you know you won't get. I'm not suggesting that any of you are not good enough for a particular part. That is not what I mean. I am saying that you need to try out for a part that fits you, a part that fits your emotional capabilities and your skill set. Okay, well—" she was interrupted by the door from the kitchen being flung open.

A loud voice said, "Hey, Mamma Maggie! Sorry I'm late!" The deep voice started laughing hysterically. Then everyone else in the troupe started laughing (except for me, Paul, the girl with the book, and "Mamma Maggie"). In the doorway stood a tall, overly muscular young man. He wore a very tight-fitting purple polo shirt that seemed to cut off the circulation in his arms, making his veins show through his skin like colored lines on a map. He was laughing and grinning as if he had just won some type of important award, and he looked around the room like a movie star looking at a group of screaming, admiring fans. Paul's face had an unrecognizable expression, and Miss Magdalene's face was tight, but without a frown. Everyone else in the garage was smiling and laughing as if God himself had entered the room and told a hilarious dirty joke. I was confused. I thought to myself: What's so funny? Why so much fuss? Who was this guy, anyway?

"John," Miss Magdalene said, in a piercing voice, "may I ask why you are late?"

"Oh, it's a super long, but super hilarious story. I'll tell you a little later. It's sooooooo long! God, I'm exhausted. You'll love it, though. You'll love the story. It's a classic!" He was still laughing. "But what's up? What are we talking about? What's going on?" He insistently walked over to the front row of chairs and patted one of the other boys on the back. The boy, smiling, quickly got up and gave this so-called "John" his seat. Miss Magdalene said nothing; her eyes simply followed John as he walked over and Manifest Destinied his seat.

After a few seconds of awkward silence, Miss Magdalene started up again, saying, "We are looking over a new script that I wrote. Shall I continue?"

"Of course, of course. You're the boss! That's awesome! A new script? Really? What's it about?" He leaned over to look at the script of one of the guys next to him.

Soliloquy

"Just read it, John!" Paul said in a screeching voice. Paul hip-switched over to him and handed him a script.

"As I was saying: take a few minutes to look over your scripts. Try and pick out the part you may want to try out for—that most suits you. You can try out for no more than two parts, so pick your parts wisely. We need to get started learning and rehearsing as soon as possible; the sooner the better. A little over a month is not enough time to prepare for a proper play. But that is what we are going to do."

When Miss Magdalene had finished speaking, everyone quickly opened up their scripts. The first page had the cast:

Cast

Old Man Gleaner: Old Man Gleaner

The Old Man's Wife: Ruth

The Old Man's Daughter: Paula

The Old Man's Son: Abe

The Landlord: Landlord

The Landlord's Wife: Tulane

The Neighbor 1: Bubba

Bubba's Wife: Dally

The Other Neighbor 2: Jude

The Other Neighbor's Wife: Nana

The play wasn't very long, so it didn't take me very long to read it over. I was done well before everyone else. The play was your run-of-the-mill moral parable. It was written at about an eighth-grade reading level, but it had a few interesting parts, to my surprise.

For about half an hour, the garage was completely mute. The room was filled with a sour, warm silence. The only sounds were of paper being flipped, the lone fan jittering rhythmically in the corner, the occasional murmuring lips (sounding out unfamiliar words), and the sporadic nervous cough (followed by a spurt of other involuntary copycat coughs).

Since I was done before everyone else, I spent my free time looking closely at my troupe-mates. I was wondering if I recognized any of them from my old school or from the library. My eyesight was back to near normal; it would be easier to recognize faces.

There were five girls and five boys (not including myself) sitting in the imperfect lines of chairs. All of the guys looked very different from one another. They ranged from tall, to short, to dark, to light, to freight train huge.

But most of the girls in the group looked nearly exactly the same. They were slightly different shapes and shades, but three of the five were wearing purple graphic spaghetti strap tank tops (a fourth had on a pinkish-purple spaghetti strap tank top), ungodly short blue jean shorts, and dirty white flip-flops. Four of them wore their hair in a half up, three-quarters disheveled hairstyle that made me wonder if they had all just gotten out of bed or if they all tried really hard to make it look like they had just gotten out of bed (one of the four showed her uniqueness by wearing a huge bang over half of her face, but the rest of her hairdo was the same as the others). They even all sat with similar postures; it was a half-slumped, cross-legged, foot-wagging displeasure. I wondered if they had planned to dress in nearly identical outfits beforehand. I wondered if they practiced their uniform look of irritation.

But the girl with the book was different. Her hair, clothes, and disposition were hers and hers alone. She wore dark blue jeans that looked like they were a hundred years old with yellow rain boots that had van Gogh-style daisies on them. Her hair was almost curly, and she sat up tall, with her back straight, and she had her feet crossed at her ankles underneath her seat. She was completely different from the other girls, it was clear.

Soliloquy

I looked at her for a long time.

Miss Magdalene broke the silence, saying, "Okay. I know many of you are not done reading the complete script, but I hope that you have had enough time to look it over and get some kind of a feel for the characters. If you don't fully understand the characters, that is fine. I don't really expect you to fully understand them at this point. Like always, being the director, producer, and writer—co-writer—I will be here to give you insight into the thoughts, emotions, and eccentricities of the characters. So don't be intimidated." Miss Magdalene had a haughty enthusiasm in her voice. She was like a general who loved giving orders for battle.

"If you don't mind, sis, I'd like to say a little thing or two," Paul said, stroking the thick, dingy, dust-tan cat. The huge cat was sprawled corpsishly between his thin arms. "All of these characters are very complex and distinct. The play is very modernist and romantic. The characters all have something self-evident about them, but they also have many things hidden in their characters as well... subconscious intentions, if you will. Something *mysterious,* you could say. So we are going to be very, very particular about how you *shooow* their personality and feelings. None of these parts are easy or simple, trust me. They are all very difficult and complicated. They need people performing at their highest level—or even higher—to bring this play to life."

"True, Paul," Miss Magdalene said.

A large, burly arm shot up into the air like an explosion. The arm came from the front row. "Miss Maggie, before we read for our parts, will we have some time to talk to you and Paul about the background of the characters? I really want to get more information about what exactly you want the character to express before I decide which part is best for me. You know?" It was John.

"We all know you're going to go for the lead part, John!" one of the guys next to him shouted. John grabbed him by the scrap of the neck, roughly. Mostly everyone laughed, again.

"You never know," John's voice boomed over the wave of laughs. "I might let one of you little slackers finally get my spot!" He let go of the guy's neck and slapped him on the back forcefully.

"Enough!" Miss Magdalene said. Her strident voice cut through the laughter like a flying knife. "I am going to give you all an opportunity to get in small groups and go over the parts together before you audition for them. I want you to have the opportunity to talk amongst yourselves and give each other some ideas of what you think the character should express. A great actor has great acting instinct. He inherently knows what the character is meant to express, even before he's given direction. A great actor must be a great *reader* and a great evaluator. Great actors always know the character as much as the writer knows the character. But yes, I will be around to each group to give some input and advice; if that is what you need. And so will Paul. So you may gather into groups of three or so and go over the script."

Everyone began shuffling their yellow and green chairs around tentatively—forming small clusters. I just sat there, feeling like the new kid on the street, wondering if anyone would pick me for the stickball game.

"You can join Hannah and me, if you'd like," said the girl with the book.

"Thank you… very much." I was happy not to have to beg.

"No problem. I don't want you to get stuck up there with *those guys*," she said, pointing to John, D Train, and three others. She looked disgusted as she stared in their direction.

Hannah said, "Yeah… that could've been really bad for you. If you would have gotten up there with those *dicks*, you may never have been the same again." Her half-visible face wore the identical look of disgust that the girl with the book had.

"Why do you say that? What's wrong with those guys? They seem pretty normal."

The girl with the book blurted, "They seem normal? 'What's wrong with them?' What's not wrong with them? They are freakin' horny psychos, basically!—excuse my Latin." The other two groups shot darting glares at our group. "That's what's wrong with them, they are misogynistic a-holes. They are... pissants. They are all cocky, discourteous, hyper-horny, immature little morons. All they do is talk about girls as if we were pieces of dog meat. 'I'd do her! I'd do her! Look at her tits!' That's all they ever talk about. I can't stand being around them for more than a few seconds at a time, honestly. They make me sick. John, D, B-*trash*, Car, and J.P, every single one of them makes me sick.

"I haven't been in the troupe for all *that* long, but they have acted like morons from the first day I got here. They all acted like I was a slave on the auction block, like one of them was necessarily going to *have* me just because I had joined the troupe.

"I remember the first time John talked to me. He said something so offensive to me it made my stomach hurt, literally... it still does. The second and third things out of his mouth were sexual, too. I couldn't freakin' believe people really actually talked like that. I really couldn't believe it. I don't know why anyone in their right mind would deal with that big, steroid-infested moron—or the rest of those guys, for that matter. The rest of the boys are just his little cronies, anyway. His minions of 'yes men.' They do whatever he says, and they laugh at everything he says... even if it's not at all funny. And, believe me; the stuff he says ain't funny! Not at all. They are just immature morons, basically."

Soliloquy

Hannah cut in, adding, "Yeah, I've been in this troupe a long, *long* time, and they have always been like that. They say mean, rude stuff to everybody who doesn't give them their way, if you know what I mean. That's just how they are. They're sex-crazed maniacs. I think that John's dirty tricks actually worked on Rachel, though. And maybe Sam, too. Maybe."

"Who's that?" I asked.

"The girl sitting right over there," Hannah cupped half of her mouth and pointed in the direction of the group with three girls.

"Yeah, I heard about that! She's such a little nasty," the girl with the book said. "Sam and Rachel both are nasties."

"What about the other girl over there?" I said.

"Oh," Hannah said grimly. "That's my little sister, Essy."

"Essy?"

"Yes... Essy. We don't get along very well. But yeah, she's my sister."

"They don't get along at all," the other girl laughed.

"Is that why she's not in this group?"

"Pretty much," the girl with the book said.

"Well, then thank you guys for saving me from that group."

There was a silence.

"So, little ladies and little gent, what's cooking over here? I don't see any reading being done. Just talking? Or do mine eyes deceive me, thus?" Paul had condensed out of air, yet again. He was hovering over our group with the morbid cat over his shoulder like a mother burping a fat baby.

"Oh, we were just discussing the complexity of the characters. We were just admiring your work, Sir Paul, that's all," the girl with the book said.

"It's not just *my* work; it's me and my sissy's work. But, thank you," Paul said, with a wave of unconcealed sarcasm. He slowly moved, cunningly, to the group with three girls, looking narrow-eyed, over his shoulder, back at us.

The girl with the book said softly, "Paul is freakin' hilarious. He's *sooo* gay. But he's right; we probably should get back to the script. Hannah, do you know what part you are thinking about trying out for?"

"No. Not really. I spent most of the time we were supposed to be looking over the script daydreaming. I was distracted."

"What about you? Do you know what part you want?" the girl with the book asked.

"Ummm, no, I don't know which part I would like to try. I think I might need some training before I can get a part, right? I have no training whatsoever. What about you? Um…" I realized that I didn't know her name. Had she given me her name? Had I just forgotten it? I didn't want to be rude, but the only thing left to do was ask. "I'm sorry. I'm drawing a blank right now. What's your name again?"

"I never told you my name," she laughed.

"Oh. Okay. Well what is your name, if you don't mind me asking?"

"My name is Mira."

"Mira? That's a unique name."

"I know it is. Everyone says that. It's Miriam, but it's Mira."

Hannah said, "Guys, we are back off track again. Focus, please! We need to look at parts, remember?"

"I'm sorry."

"It's no problem, but we need to pick before we are stuck with parts we hate."

"I'm going to be stuck with a part I hate no matter what," Mira said.

"Well, you still are going to have to pick one, unless you want to be Rachel's understudy or something. And I know you don't want that. Or do you? Do you want to be Rachel's understudy? Maybe you guys could talk about boys and braid each other's hair."

Mira paused, thoughtfully. Then she burst out laughing, slapping her knee with her script. "I couldn't be Rachel's understudy even if I wanted to. I can't study under someone dumber than me; that wouldn't work at all."

"Okay, so what part do you want?"

"I don't know. I guess… I guess I might read—"

"Oh my God, Mira! Just read for the old man's wife, and I'll just read for the old man's daughter, gosh! Was that so hard? You know that's how the parts are going to go anyway."

"Not if you get beat out by Rachel." Mira laughed.

"If that ever happens I'll quit. You know that. I'll quit!" Hannah said with panic in her voice.

"Why don't you try out for the old man's wife, and I'll try out for the old man's daughter? I don't want to be the old man's wife if John is going to be the lead. I wouldn't be able to handle it. I'm so over it."

"Well, you know you're going to have to anyway; you're the best girl here, and he's the best boy here, and that's just the way it goes. Magdalene's going to make you read for it no matter what you say, and you know that. So let's not play around. I will read for it, but you know I won't get it. Magdalene basically hates me, you know that."

"No she doesn't, you're so dramatic," Mira said.

"*Nah-uhn*! No I'm not!"

"Yeah, you kinda are. You should try to get that part if that's the one you really want. Go for it. How about this: how about you read for it and do a really great job, do your best, then I read for it and really suck it up so bad it makes her want to rip her eyes out and feed them to that stinkin' cat. Then that way Miss Magdalene will give you the part and hate me. Then I won't

have to work with John, and you will get the lead, and everyone will be happy. How does that sound?"

"You're so dumb and immature sometimes, Mira," Hannah said with
an exasperated scowl. "You know that won't work. Let's just move on!"

"Okay. Okay. I got another even better idea! How about this: how about
he beats John out for the lead part." Mira pointed at me and smiled. "How
about that? Yeah, you should try out for the lead. Are you up for that? That
could solve all our problems, for the time being. So what do you say? Will
you try out for the lead? Will you be our savior, Mr. Messiah?"

"Me?" I said. Her eyes were staring at me with intensity. "Me? Try out
for the lead? I can't do that. I'm sorry. I don't know how to act. I don't know
the first thing about acting. It's my first day and stuff. I don't know how to
act. I can't lead."

Hannah put her hand on my arm. "Chill out, dude. Don't get all freaked
out about it. She's just joking with you. That's how she gets her kicks. That's
what she does. She's a jokester. She's like a real-life clown. You'll get used to
it. If you haven't noticed, she kinda likes to be a bitch that gets under your
skin sometimes—a little too much, sometimes. She thinks everything's a
game and a joke, but acts like nothing's a joke, you know? She likes getting
people riled up. Just ignore her."

As Hannah spoke, Mira made crazy cross-eyed faces and grasped at air
with her hands in the shape of dinosaur claws.

"See!" Hannah said. "That's exactly what I'm talking about. She's a big
joke!

"This one time, when I first met her, we went to the mall together. And
guess what this crazy girl did? She stuffed her jacket under her shirt and
walked around moaning like she was having contractions and about to have
a baby! I must say, it was pretty convincing. She just kept groaning and pat-

ting her stomach and saying, 'Not right now, little baby, not right now, mommy needs you to wait until she's done shopping for new bras. Mommy needs you to wait! Mommy needs Vicky's Secrets.'

"Everybody looked at her and stared. They stared and stared. They thought she was totally crazy, or they thought that she was really about to give birth right there, smack-dab in the middle of the mall. I was so embarrassed. She kept grabbing onto my arm. I barely knew her at the time, hadn't known her for a full week, and she was acting like that. I thought she was a crazy person, bipolar or something. I thought about leaving her there. People thought she was really having a baby! Even a security guard came and asked us if she needed an ambulance or a glass of water. She is crazy like that. She likes to get people going like that."

"Oh, I do. I do," Mira said. She was smirking a prideful smirk, twirling her pointer finger around her ear. "And thanks for the Freudy psychoanalysis, Hannah."

"Why would you do something like that? Why would you make those people think you were having a baby?" I asked.

"That's just what I do. It's true, I like to shock people. I think most people need it, a shock. People need to be shocked more often than they are, especially around this town. Most people aren't living lives. Biological lives, maybe—technically, but mentally they are asleep. Most people are mentally sleepwalking. That must've sounded strange. What I mean is most people are actually more like zombies than active, lively, thoughtful human beings. They live by a set of inconsistent rules and superstitions that they don't even understand. They believe, but they don't really understand. They live by a set of contradictory rules that someone else created for them, and that keeps them from being thinking beings. Yeah. A poet I like said:

Soliloquy

'Zombies are real,

See the slaves so depraved.

Trudging through life with their vegetable brains.

Despising the mountains

From out on the plains.

See this way every- day; I'm enthralled in the shame.'

And that's how I feel. People are living like they're dead, but they are alive. Does that make sense? They don't *live* life. They just *have* life. It's like a fixture just sitting on a nightstand, something that has little use and no purpose. It is sitting there, but it's not being useful. It's not doing. It's not active. I think that life is the same. Lots of people's lives are just sitting there, not being used—taking up space. Not being mentally active. They are on the sidelines. They're there, but they have no function, you know?

"I see shocking people as giving them a chance to get their lives back, a chance to get out of the daily trudge of mindlessness, of thoughtlessness. I see shocking people as the opportunity for them to get the functioning part of their lives back, the moving part, the being part.

"My crazy actions are like a defibrillator for their dying, mundane lives. The goal is to shock them back into reality. It is a very grand goal that practically never works. I know. It is a bit idealistic. I know it sounds weird, but it makes sense to me.

"Anywho, I don't shock people by going up to them and screaming in their faces, or trying to start a fist fight with them; that's not shocking. That's not what I do. That would just be ignorant. My goal is much more subtle and thoughtful than that, or at least I hope it is. I like to take what people secretly fear, sometimes what they don't even know they fear, and calmly put it up to their faces for them to see, like a mirror, up close and personal. I like to take

Soliloquy

people's prejudices and inject it into their everyday lives. It gives them an opportunity to get over whatever it is they are bigoted about.

"Like the mall thing Hannah was talking about. The people at the mall hate when girls my age are pregnant or have babies. They hate that. They like to talk about girls like that in the comfort of their homes. 'Did you see that little girl all pregnant? Lord, what a shame. What a shame!' They like to talk about them behind their backs. They like to feel superior when they see TV shows about young pregnant girls. But when I was dragging around the mall, huffing and puffing, acting pregnant, did they say anything? Did they have anything negative to say to my face? No! They kept their mouths shut! They didn't say a single word. You know why? Because it is harder to be ridiculous when it's real. Don't get me wrong, people are still extremely ridiculous in person, but they are much more ridiculous in the comfort of their own homes.

"When they realize that you are a real person, when you look a lot like their daughters or granddaughters, it's harder to be a jackass. Some people still are ridiculous and can be a jackass to your face, but those people aren't normal people anyway, really. They are the ones that have no regard for other human life and no sense of reality. Those people are animals, or psychopathic, or moronic sociopaths! That's what they are. They can't be shocked, because they don't have hearts or brains to be shocked.

"But the people who are human, the humans who have lives that are just on vacation and not mutated into something inhuman, they can be shocked. And I hope that the shock sparks their ability to be reasonable, or empathetic, or sympathetic, or kind, or just not assholes for once in their lives. The ones that still have hope are the ones I look to shock. I want to shock them back into the world of the active living. I want to shock them back from vacation."

"Wow." I said. I was in shock. "You seem really, really, really passionate about what you said. Do you do it a lot? Go out and shock people? What do you want to be when you get older?"

"Please, please, please, please, please, please, please, *please!* Can we please get back on track! For God's freaking sakes, Mira. Can't you give him this long speech later, please? We're going to get in trouble," Hannah said.

"Now who needs to chill out?"

"I guess we all need to chill out and get back on track. Can we please make a decision?"

"I could have sworn we already made one! You said I was trying out for the wife and you were trying out for the daughter, and he's not trying out for anything, because this is his first day? I could have sworn that was the plan. Was it not?"

"Okay, then," Hannah said softly. "Let's get to work."

The girls started to read some of the lines to one another. The tension between the two was gone as soon as they opened their scripts. I just sat there quietly, trying not to interrupt.

They were both very good actresses, almost as good as some of the actresses from the *Lyceum*. They read the parts passionately and smoothly. But they had very different styles. Hannah read very precisely, annunciating every syllable of every word. She studied the script with intense analytic eyes (or eye, I only could see the one). She reminded me of someone cramming for a final exam or a doctor looking over a new patient chart.

Mira, on the other hand, was composed, cool, and graceful like an old jazz musician. She just *knew* that she had a gift, but she didn't seem to want to hide her gift or show it off. She didn't seem to care. Her acting was instinctual, rhythmic, and pure. Nothing about it was contrived. She wasn't trying to be good: she was just good. She just knew what she was doing, how she was doing it, and how effortlessly she was doing it. She barely looked at her script. It was as if she had memorized it the first time around, and when she did look at her script, it was only a passive, uninterested glance, and then she dove right back into effortlessness. She barely broke character for a moment, but when she did, it somehow only added to her gracefulness. I loved watching her act. It was like watching a pro baseball player take batting practice.

When Paul looped stealthily back around to our group, both of the girls raised their acting to a more intense level. And when Miss Magdalene came around a few seconds after Paul, it was like they were auditioning for a leading role on Broadway or for some major Hollywood film project.

For the first time I saw the cocky sarcasm fade from Mira's face. She looked serious. She looked natural. She looked vulnerable.

"So, young ladies," Miss Magdalene said. Her stubby, muscular arms were folded across her busty chest. "Which parts are you two thinking about trying out for? Any ideas?"

"I think I'm going to try for the daughter of the old man, Miss Magdalene," Hannah said.

"What about you, dear?"

"Oh, well, I've been looking over the parts of the daughter and of the wife, but I don't know which one yet. I'm still trying to decide. But I don't really know for sure," Mira's voice was soft and indifferent.

"Well, dear, you need to pick quickly, because in a few minutes we are going to let all of you start reading for parts. So it would be wise to choose one. Quickly."

"Okay. Yes, Miss Magdalene, got cha."

"And what about you, young man? Have you decided on a part?" Her black eyes searched my face. I was surprised by the question.

Soliloquy

"Oh, no, ma'am. I thought that since it was my first day I would just be observing and learning about things. I didn't think I would be participating. Truthfully, I don't really know anything about acting. I do know that it takes much skill, which is something I totally lack. I love watching it, but I don't know the first think about acting myself." She gave me a stern look, so before she could speak I said, "But if you want me to try out for a part, I will do my best, but I can't promise my best will be good or anything. But I'll try if you want me to."

"We'll see. We'll see. But keep looking over the script, okay?"

"Yes, ma'am. I will. Thank you."

We all silently began looking back into our scripts. I decided that if she was going to force me to participate in the audition where I was bound to fail, I would choose the male part with the fewest lines in the script. The landlord had the fewest lines, so I looked them over nervously.

After a while Miss Magdalene called us all back to attention by clapping her hands together. Her clap echoed off of the large, humid garage walls.

"All right. I hope that you all have used your time wisely. Some of you seemed distracted. Now Paul and I will be calling you all one by one to tentatively decide what parts you are good for. This isn't the final audition, but I do want to get a good idea of who will have what parts. Again, we don't have much time to perfect this thing. We will call all of you into the living room, so you can perform in privacy. Who would like to go first?"

The first hand shot up like an Apollo rocket. It was John.

"I would be honored to go first, Maggs. This script is amazing. I would be honored to go first!"

"Okay. John will go first. I suggest that the rest of you use your time wisely. That is, read over the script until it's your turn. It may be the difference between getting and not getting a part."

Soliloquy

Paul held the door as Miss Magdalene and John marched through; it was reminiscent of Darth Vader being followed by a storm trooper. As they left, I could feel a weight being lifted off of the room.

"Okay," Hannah said. "Do you guys want to keep going over the script?"

"No. I'm tired. I think I'm going to read more of my book, but you can keep going over it if you want to." Mira stretched her slim arms over her head and yawned.

"Okay, suit yourself Miss 'I-don't-give-a-shit-about-anything-but-myself.' That's fine. Read your book for the billionth time." Hannah was giving Mira the evil eye, but Mira did not respond. She didn't even seem to notice. She simply bowed her head and started reading her tattered book.

One by one, people came and left, came and left; some of them returned smiling, some laughing, some looking to be in physical pain.

Rachel reentered the garage with a beaming smile. She walked up to me and said, "Miss Magdalene requested you. You're next." She looked at me smugly, flipped her scruffy ponytail, then quickly walked away. She didn't speak to the two girls in my group. She didn't even acknowledge their exist-ence.

"Okay. Here I go, I guess." Both Hannah and Mira looked up and, with mumbles, wished me luck. As I walked through the kitchen, I was amazed that I was not nervous. I figured it was because I was trying out for a part with only a handful of lines. The landlord said almost nothing the whole time, so I figured if I just read the lines as normal as I could, I might not make that huge of a fool of myself. I couldn't act, but I could read.

In the living room, Miss Magdalene was seated with her legs crossed. She was emotionless, with both stubby arms slung over the jumbo armrest.

Paul was next to her in a child-size, shiny red chair. He was scribbling frantically with a number two pencil on a pad of yellow paper.

"Did you decide on a part?" Miss Magdalene said, barely moving her
mouth.

"Um, I figured that I should try out for the part of the landlord. It's not
many lines so—"

Paul's head snapped up from the paper. "It has the fewest lines in the
whole play!"

"Oh, I know. I just thought it might give me an opportunity to ease in, I
guess. Um, it might give me the opportunity to focus deeply on getting the
few lines right… so as not to be overwhelmed."

"Huh." Paul rolled his eyes in exasperation. His thick glasses made his
eyes appear twice their normal size. He looked like a spoiled overgrown
child.

"It's fine. I have no problem with that reasoning," Miss Magdalene said
to Paul. "I understand your logic. It's smart that you want to ease into it. It's
good not to be over-confident. That means you are aware of what you are
ready to take on. It is good that a young man lacks the typical hubris that
accompanies youth. However, you should never underestimate yourself."
Looking back to Paul, she said, "You know, not everyone is ready to be Dan-
iel Day Lewis on their first day, little brother."

Paul looked up at her with puppy dog eyes. "I know, sissy. I'm sorry, I
don't mean to be snappy. I am just stressed about this play, you know? I
want everything to go well. I'm sorry, little buddy. Everyone will tell you I
get snappy when I'm stressed. You just have to get used to it. It's nothing
personal. Please don't take it personally, okay?"

"Oh, it's fine. It's fine. I didn't think you were getting pissy or anything.
It's no problem. I know… stress… it's bad."

Soliloquy

"Well, okay. Shall we get to it?"

"Yes, sure… Um, how does this work, exactly? Do I, um, just start reading or… I, um, have no idea how this works."

Miss Magdalene's face grew impatient. "You will read one of the landlord's lines and Paul will read the concurrent line, continuously, like that. Just relax and read the part the way you think the landlord would say it in reality. Simply. Ready?"

"Yes. Okay. I'm ready."

Paul and I read about five one-sentence lines before Miss Magdalene stopped us by raising her hand in the air. The reading took no more than a minute.

"Thank you. That's enough," she said firmly.

"Okay. Sorry if I was bad."

"You did fine. If you already knew how to act, you wouldn't need to be here. That's what you are paying us for, to teach you how to perform. Don't worry, that was fine for your first time."

"Yes, ma'am. Thank you."

"You're welcome. You did fine. Don't you agree, Paul?"

"Oh. Yeah. Sure. You did fine, buddy."

"Don't worry. We'll teach you all you need to know. You know the cliché: 'Practice makes perfect.' This cliché is very true. You will grow better with practice. Everyone does. I've never seen someone who did not. We have several fine actors in this troupe, but none of them started off as good as they are now. Trust me. Who's in your group?"

"Oh, um, Mira and Hannah."

"Okay, when you go back in, please send me Hannah, would you?"

"Yes, ma'am."

"Thank you."

Soliloquy

As I walked through the thick, dandered air, I realized something: I realized that there was something very kind and forgiving about Miss Magdalene. I had failed to notice this before. Despite her stern, militant face and the jagged tone of her voice, she never disrespected me. Even though it was clear that she could have unleashed on me at any second, she never did. She never questioned my authenticity. She never made fun of me or hinted at my weakness. She never raised her voice at me (without pulling it back down to a normal level by the end of her sentence). She never rolled her eyes or yelled at me, even when her propensity for impatience drew her cheekbones tighter than a drum's skin.

Even when her voice grew stern, she still showed me sympathy and tolerance. She showed me genuine kindness, not the illusion of kindness. Showing kindness is easy when you're a naturally kind person; it's still a good thing to do, but it is easy. But when you are a person who was born without patience, a person with a fierce, sharp soul, yet you force yourself to be patient, even to the most annoying among us, that is better than kindness. That is real charity. And Miss Magdalene had it and gave it. The thought of Miss Magdalene's charity made me smile.

When I reentered the garage, I contracted every eye in the room.

"Hannah, she wants you next," I said.

"It's about time, gosh." Hannah sprung up from her seat like an angry frog. She was clenching her script tightly like a relay runner holding a baton. She hit Mira in the head with the paper and said, "Well, wish me luck, girl."

"Luck."

"So how'd it go?" Mira muttered, looking down at her book.

"It went as well as I could expect, I guess. I'm not an actor or anything, so I guess it could have been much better. But for me, I'd say it went well. I didn't pass out."

Soliloquy

"Pass out? Well at least you don't have to go last. It looks like I'm going to be the last one to go. I've been paying attention, everyone has already gone."

"It wouldn't have bothered me any. I'm just happy to get it all out of the way. Maybe they saved the best for last."

She laughed loudly. Her laughter drew the attention of the groups. "Are you hitting on me?" she said, reeling back in her plastic chair.

"Oh, no! Not at all. I'm sorry if you thought that—I'm not. I was just saying maybe they wanted to end on a high note. Hannah seemed to be saying you are good, so I just thought…. I wasn't trying to hit on you at all, though."

Her laughter had gone in a flash. It was as if a somber switch had been flipped. She looked at me with a serious look and said, "So what are you trying to say? I'm not good enough for you to hit on? Is that it? Are you too good to hit on me? Am I not cute enough or preppy enough for you—huh— is that it?"

I was dazed at how far off base she was. Was she joking? I was baffled at how she could get that conclusion from what I'd said, and I was nervous at how offended her face and eyes looked. How quickly her mood changed. It was so fast.

"No, no, no. I'm sorry, there must be some confusion. That's not what I meant at all—that's not at all what I meant. You know that, right?"

"No! I don't know anything! If I knew that, I wouldn't have said it. Are you patronizing me? Are you talking down to me now, too? Do you think I'm beneath you or something? How dare you!" She was getting louder and louder. Her voice was echoing throughout the room. People were starting to stare. I felt like the world was closing in on me. I felt like I was in a movie where everyone was crazy but me. I felt like I was in a real live episode of the *Twilight Zone*. I wanted to just run away. She was fucking crazy!

"Um… I'm sorry… I don't know if… I mean I didn't—" Before I could finish my frantic fumbling stumbles, I was interrupted by her budding facial expression. She appeared to be fighting back a smile.

She promptly busted into laughter, saying, "Hahahaha! Oh my god, I had you goin'. You thought I was for real. Hahaha! You were freakin' out, big time. Ha! You should see your face! You should have seen it. You were looking like you saw an alien. Or like your mom caught you with your hand in the cookie jar. Ha, ha. That was perfect! You looked like you saw a ghost. Did I freak you out or what?"

Her eyes quickly welled up with tears of joy and laughter and stomach pains. She was clutching the side of her stomach as if she had been punched in the ribs.

"You were just joking?"

"Of course I was just joking. But it's clear from that look on your face that you thought I was serious. I was joking, but you bought it; you completely bought it. I'm sorry. I didn't mean to upset you. I don't mean to laugh in your face. I'm not laughing at you, but your face, you looked so stunned. I must really actually be a good actress, because you completely believed me. I'm sorry, I'm really not crazy."

She was right. I was stunned. I didn't know if I should laugh with her or slap her in the face! I didn't know. I had never slapped or punched anyone before, but I really thought about slapping her right on the cheek—then maybe *she* would be stunned. Maybe then she would know what it feels like to be "shocked."

But I could see her point; it was kind of funny, in a way. If she would have done it to someone else, I think I would have laughed. But I didn't laugh because the trick was on me. I didn't laugh. Instead I visualized slapping her in her pretty, smiling, smug face. I was confused. I was confused, angry, and relieved.

Just then Hannah walked up swiftly and said, "Guys, guess what? I killed it! Miss Magdalene let me read for the wife *and* the daughter; and I'm telling you, I don't know what came over me, but I read better than I've ever read before. It was so amazing. You should have seen Miss Magdalene's face. She seemed so surprised. Pleasantly surprised. And Paul commented that I've been improving. You should have seen it. Oh, Mira, you're up next. But it was amazing."

"Well, congrats," Mira said. "Well, if you did as well as you think you did, there's no way I can top that. Understudy... here I come."

"Well, I'm not trying to compete with you," Hannah said. Her voice was angry and smug. "I'm just really excited about how well I did."

"Of course. This is not a competition. Competitions need competitors, and I am not a competitor. I'm simply a student, if anything. I only compete with the limits of my own creativity and the depths of my concentration. Plus, you're a better actress than me nine times out of ten. You care more, and that's what makes you better," Mira said, smiling. Her eyes were stranded in space and her thoughts seemed to be far away from her conversation. She was daydreaming. But what about?

For a few moments she sat very still, quietly. She was looking reverently off into the abyss of her imagination. In her trance she seemed *real*. She didn't seem like she was putting on a show, or pulling a prank, or being sarcastic, or being offensive. She seemed real.

Her spontaneous swinging from offensive to authentic, from roughness to polished, from sweet to tart, made no sense to me. I couldn't understand it. I couldn't understand her. Did she even understand herself?

Soliloquy

How could this one person seem to be one of the sanest and one of the most insane people I had ever met, all at once? How could this one little person encompass so much emotion, apathy, and flashy forwardness? How did this complex confusion of wit, spite, crassness, humor, rudeness, and charm condense itself into this strange, small girl?

Hannah and I just looked at her. I was trying to think what she was thinking. I wanted to see what she was looking at, or I wanted to look for what she was looking for.

Mira broke her trance, saying, "Well, I better get in there. I don't want to keep Paul and Miss Magdalene waiting." She got up slowly and handed me her book. "Keep care of this for me while I'm in there, okay?"

"Okay."

"Aren't you going to wish me luck, Hannah?" she said with a playful grin.

"Good luck, Mira."

She moved slowly to the door. Before she went into the house, she turned back to us and put up the peace sign.

I didn't know what to think about Mira.

"I don't mean to pry. I'm not trying to get into your business, but are you and Mira friends? I mean like friends outside of the troupe?"

"Yes. We are. I haven't known her long, but she's my best friend. Why do you ask?"

"Oh, I don't know. You guys just seem to have a feisty conversational style. It seems like you guys try to get under each other's skin all the time."

"I know. It's strange. People always say that we fight like sisters or like a married couple. But really, we are just joking, for the most part. That's just our language. It's our sense of humor. I don't really get mad at her. Well, not very often. That's just how we talk to each other. We don't have to try to be extra nice to each other. That's how I know we are real friends."

"Well, it's interesting. When you were in the living room with Miss Magdalene, she freaked out on me. I thought she had gone crazy."

Hannah laughed. "I bet. She might just be crazy. She's crazy like a fox. You know most geniuses are crazy, or at least borderline crazy."

"Yes. I know. Genius? You consider her a genius?"

"Oh my god, yes! She may not seem like it, but she is crazy smart, like NASA smart. She skipped three grades in elementary and middle school. And she could have skipped her freshman year of high school, but she didn't want to. She told me she didn't skip her freshman year of high school because she had too much fun making fun of all the shallow people and drawing funny pictures of her dumb teachers. She took the SAT when she was in eighth grade and she almost got a perfect score—in eighth grade!

"She is smart, but she acts crazy. She likes to drink alcohol and stuff, but she's crazy smart. Most people don't realize how smart she actually is; that's the way she wants it, I think. But, believe me. I know. If you listen to her like I do, sometimes you'll get a glimpse of just how brilliant she actually is. But it's rare.

"Some of the things she says are *deep*. Sometimes too deep, they make my head hurt. She loses me sometimes when she's being all deep and psychological. But, yeah, she is a genius. That's one of the things I like about her."

"Wow. I would have never guessed all that stuff. A near perfect score? Wow."

"Yeah, she doesn't tell people about it. I'm one of the only people who know all that stuff I just told you; that stuff about her skipping grades and the SAT and all that. Don't tell her I told you. She would be mad at me."

"Why would she be mad at you? Why would she be upset if I knew she was really smart? That seems odd."

With her forehead scrunched, Hannah said, "I don't know. That's just how she is. I don't know why. She would be embarrassed about it, maybe. I don't know. She doesn't want to seem cocky, at least not about being smart, I guess. She wants people to 'take her in the moment,' she says. She says that a lot. I'm not completely sure I know exactly what she means by it, but she says it a lot."

"'Take her in the moment?' I don't think I know what that means, either."

"I don't think anybody does, except maybe for her. But that's my point; she lives in her own little crazy-smart world. But despite her crazy-smarts, she does care about other people. Even though she likes to start trouble, and do pranks, and joke around all the time, in her own way she means well. I know she would give me the shirt off her back if I asked her to. She's that kind of person."

"Those are very nice things to say about a person. You seem to have lots of faith in her."

"She's my best friend. I do. Speaking of the devil," Hannah said in a jittery voice as Mira drifted back into the garage. "That was quick."

"Were you talking about me while I was gone? What were you saying?" Mira said. Her face had a banal grin, and her eyes were dashing side to side, between Hannah and me.

"I was," Hannah said in a playful voice. "But it was all good stuff. I promise."

"Good stuff? I have good stuff?"

"Look at you, always trying to be modest."

"You know what they say, 'Modesty is always the best policy.'"

Soliloquy

"That's not how the saying goes," Hannah said. "It's '*honesty* is always the best policy'."

"Why, thank you, my dear Hannah, for that palpably apparent factoid. But I was fully aware of the historicity of the aforementioned aphorism! I was making what is commonly referred to as a joke, thanks."

"Refer to this!" Hannah was sticking up her middle finger and sticking out her white-pink tongue as far as it would go. They both giggled and swiftly jumped subjects as if the mock dispute conversation had never occurred.

"So, how'd it go in there?"

"Well, like you said, it was quick. It was fine—uneventful, really." Mira seemed indifferent.

"Is that it? Is that all you're gonna say? Be serious, tell me what happened."

"Wow. Chill out, girl! Okay, what do you want to know? I went in. I asked Miss Magdalene if I could read for the daughter, she said yes, but only if I read for the mother, too. I said if I'm going to have to read the part of the mother I might as well not read the part of the daughter because I was tired, and I didn't want it to take that long. She said that that was fine.

"I read a few lines of the mother—quite terribly. I thought I read terribly. Paul asked me a question. I don't remember what exactly. It was something about what I thought about the emotional brevity of the part of the mother, or something like that. I told him that I thought she seemed like a shy, crotchety old lady. He frowned and wrote something down on his yellow sheet of paper. Then they told me I was done. I said okay, I'll see you in the garage. They said nothing back. That is almost exactly what happened. Now, please, tell me Mother Hannah, is there anything else you would like to know before I go night, night with my binky and blanky?"

Soliloquy

"No," Hannah said with contentment. She seemed genuinely happy that Mira had told her every single detail. "No, my little bear," Hannah smiled. "Now was that so hard, my child?"

"No, mommy dearest."

Just then, the door to the garage was thrust open, and Miss Magdalene jaunted in with Paul following behind her like a coattail or the train of a wedding dress.

They stood at the front of the room for a few moments without saying a word. They stood impatiently as everyone slowly ungrouped; they waited until everyone had put their chairs back to their original spots and gave them their undivided attention. The dragging of plastic chairs filled the large garage with headache noise. When everyone was back in their seats, quietly, Miss Magdalene cleared her throat and began pacing mechanically back and forth like a brooding watchdog.

"Well, I must say," she said in a hoarse voice. "I must say that I am pleasantly surprised with how well most of you did in your somewhat impromptu tryouts tonight. I know you didn't have much time to prepare… but with what time you did have, you all did a very good job.

"Paul and I spoke about all of your performances, privately, and Paul took very detailed notes about how you all performed. What you did right and what you did wrong. Like I said before, this is not the final tryout by any means, but it was very important, nonetheless. It was important because it showed us who understood the parts and the tone of the play instinctually… and who did not. Tonight's practice has gone by very quickly, but I think we got a few good things accomplished, don't you? Before next Thursday I want you all to go over your script very thoroughly. Next Thursday we will have the real… a final tryout for the parts. It will be rigorous, trust me."

Soliloquy

"Sissy, can I add something, please?" Paul said. He voice was soft and shy. "I want you all to remember that this is not a game. This is art—not a game. When you guys perform, it doesn't matter how long you have been acting. People won't care about that. You are not just representing yourself when you get on stage; you are representing this entire acting troupe, God, and every single person in this whole town. 'Miss Magdalene's acting troupe!' That's the name on the marquee. You see? So if I am hard on you, really hard on you, the next few weeks, that is why.

"You better not take it personally. I don't hate or dislike any one of you. It is purely business. I love you all very, very much. I suggest you all spend at least an hour or two a night working over this play. We want you all to bring your *A* game, nothing less. Because nothing less will be acceptable. I promise you that."

Paul was as serious as I have ever seen him. He always seemed a little too serious, but this seriousness was in a whole new ballpark of seriousness. His expression was a mixture of sadness, scorn, and desperation. His speech and demeanor seemed to suggest that his entire life was somehow intimately tied to the success of the play—his entire worth. His face suggested that his life was based on this play and that the play was based on his life. His mood said: This play is me; and if this play fails, all of me will fail right along with it!

Miss Magdalene looked at him with stern, weary compassion, as if she could also hear the franticness in his tone. "With that being said: go home, practice, read and reread the material. Be ready for next week. Be as ready for next practice as possible. We are letting out early today, but we will make up the time in the weeks to come, trust me. Well, then, are there any comments or questions?"

Soliloquy

No one spoke. The warm air which filled the garage seemed to have put everyone in a pre-sleep daze. Everyone sat still and quiet.

Miss Magdalene said, "Okay, then. We will see you all next week. Drive safely. Be safe."

"Be safe," Paul said with the same exact inflection as Miss Magdalene.

"Okay!" a commanding voice said. It was John. He stood up and faced everyone.

"I have an idea! I have a great idea. I think we all should go to Steak and Shake and study the parts over dinner. It's not that late. Like Miss Maggie and Paul said, we need to get ready for next week and the weeks to come. What do you guys think? It would be so much fun. It's not really late. I think we all should go. Okay? Let's go!"

A slow chorus of voices started murmuring in agreement with John's "great" suggestion. I just sat there; I kept thinking about how I should get home before anything bad happened. The night was less painful than I had ever expected it to be, and I wanted to keep it that way. I did not want to break down, freak out, throw up, or pass out. I was still in control of my mental faculties and my bodily functions, and I wished to keep it that way. Who knows what terrible thing could happen at a Steak and Shake without adult supervision (or with adult supervision, for that matter)? I was going to cash in my chips while I was still ahead. That would be the smart thing to do.

John walked to the door, and everyone other than me followed him out like a parade of happy, headless chickens.

"So, are you going to go?" Mira said softly.

"Um. No. I don't think... I don't think tonight... I think I'm going to go home. It's getting late and stuff, so I think I should be getting home, sooner than later. I'm a little tired."

"Let's go!" Hannah shouted. She grabbed Mira's arm, trying to pull her towards the crowd.

Mira shrugged her off indignantly. "Hold on a minute! I'll just meet you at your car."

Hannah looked surprised. "Okay. You better hurry up, or I'm going to leave you."

"Well, it's too bad you're not going," Mira said. Her face was kind. "I wanted to talk more about books with you. What's your phone number? I want to borrow that book before next Thursday. I will read it and tell you what I think at next practice."

"What book?" I was flustered. The warmth and stuffiness were getting to my head. Or was it something else? I'd never had a girl ask me for my number before. I was confused. Hell, I had never asked a girl for her number before, so I was unsure of why or how it worked.

"Your favorite book, silly. What's your deal? You must really be tired. You seem tired. Maybe you *should* go home and get some rest." She laughed.

"Yeah, I know."

"So, what is it?"

"What is what?"

"What is your phone number?! Oh my God!"

"Oh. I'm really sorry. I'm just kinda out of it right now. I'm really tired. It is um… it's ummm… 56… I think its 567… 4… no wait… its 576… 4 maybe…"

"Oh my God! You are weird," she said angrily, but her voice was still playful. She pulled a small piece of paper from her pocket, and she pulled a pen out of her tattered book. "Here!" She scribbled hurriedly on the paper, then harshly stuffed the paper into my hand. "Here! Here, this is my number. Call me and let me know when I can borrow the book, okay? I'll come pick it up or something if I have to."

"Okay? I will."

She turned and ran out the door. I just stood there stunned, hot, and confused—trying to catch my breath. My heart was pounding fast, yet everything else felt like it was in slow motion. It was an odd sensation; one I had never felt before. It was a sort of exhilarating weakness (if there is such a paradox of feelings). I just stood there letting the lagging moment and the heat wash over me.

"Is everything okay?" Paul said. He had stepped back into the room with the stealth of a ninja. "I noticed that you weren't out there with the rest of them. Aren't you going out with them to eat?"

The sensation of the moment was broken by Paul's invasive questioning, but I was not mad. It had to end sometime.

"Yes, sir. I'm fine." I slowly walked to my old piece-of-shit car without a word. The rest of the group was pulling off in their colorful, loud rides. They all seemed overly excited about Steak and Shake. They were acting as if it was a free trip to Disneyland or something. They were shouting loudly, blasting their irritating music as they went. Someone from one of the cars shouted something to me as they flew past at an unsafe speed. But I was too tired, or I just didn't care enough to hear what they'd said.

On the ride home, I didn't think about anything, I just drove. I just kept looking at the cloudless night sky. Even though the sun was completely gone, somehow there was still multicolored brightness in the dark sky.

When I walked in the door to my house, my mother was sitting stock still on the couch.

"Hello, where's dad?" I said.

Soliloquy

"He's in his office finishing up some work. Did you meet any new friends tonight?"

"We will see. Tonight wasn't as bad as I thought it would be—which is a very good thing. But I'm tired."

"That's good to hear. See, things aren't always all bad."

"Well, night, mom," I said as I moved up the staircase.

"Goodnight."

Act III

Centuries of souls' shower down like strips of white lightning strikes.
Sinking slowly into Passion's quickening embrace.
Spinning holds like a bittersweet French ballet.
Shouting: "Toto, we're not in Kansas anymore!"

Henceforth, the unwell world of once oneness and loveliness,
Evaporates warmly into the solid mist of the beloved.
Saturated by possession until our black bead becomes a pearl.
Jaded pains of loss and zeal fill the mind with thick emerald envies.

Covering and conjoining every unconscious aspect of life: coherent.
Consciousness thunders loudly into quick, harsh, hastening clasps.
Shouting: "Some place where there isn't any trouble!"
Twinkling clenches glisten like love in a French ballet.

Chapter 5

"The Queerest Creatures in the World!" Daisies.

The next two days were pretty much hell for me. Not because of my mom's customary nagging or unwitting bigotry, not because of my dad's aloofness or egocentricity, not because of my mind-numbing, low-paying job, and not because of mundane mandatory dinner. It was hell for me because I didn't know what to do about Mira and the book situation. You'd think it would be simple, but the whole situation was nerve racking, frustrating, and to be honest, frightening. I was riled up over something that seemed small, which was normal, but I was riled up more than normal, for some reason.

It wasn't that I was afraid to call her (although I had only talked on the phone to two girls in my whole life: one of whom was a family member, the other a school project group member). It was just—I just didn't want to call her. I didn't want to call her at all. I really didn't want to talk to her. But it's not like I didn't like talking to her at practice—not to say that I *did* like talking to her at practice—I was indifferent, I guess. I just didn't want to talk to her outside of practice. She just made me nervous, extremely nervous. Just thinking about her smug grin and her expertise in sarcasm, irony, and practical joking made my stomach freak! Sure, she was pretty or cute, in a way, I guess. But cute looks were not enough to make me want to talk to her; it may have even added to my hesitation, to be honest.

I don't know what it was about her, but I felt a burning in my stomach like popping hot grease when I thought about her. I literally felt sick. Not a sick like I was disgusted by her, it was a different kind of sick feeling. One I had never felt before. Her sporadicism conjoined with her untamed mockery

Soliloquy

made me completely uncomfortable and off balance. She made me unbalanced. I never knew what the hell to expect from her other than a smart-ass
comment. It was like being around a "tamed" circus lion. Although there is
no such thing as a tame wild animal. The statement is completely oxymoron-
ic. They are never *really* tame, are they?—just waiting. And people get all
upset when "tame animals" wake up one day and claw or eat someone's face
off. What the hell do they expect from a wild animal? There were no guaran-
tees with her. I didn't know who the hell she was from one second to the
next. I couldn't pin down what she was really about.

Worst of all, I knew if I invited her over to come get the book from my
house—off the porch, preferably, so as not to have to deal with her directly—
my mom would make a huge deal about it. I know my mom. She would
probably try to arrange a shotgun marriage like right then and there, on the
spot. She would want to arrange a marriage in order to make sure I was not
"a gay," no doubt. Or she would invite Mira to mundane mandatory dinner
and ask her tons of completely inappropriate, judgmentally religious, and
sexual-orientation type questions, or something crazy like that. My mom was
all about finding me someone, so I wouldn't "die decrepit and alone" and/or
"under suspicion of being a gay" as she liked to say. That's just a few of the
reasons I didn't want to call Mira, but deep down I knew there were other
reasons. Reasons I couldn't or didn't want to put my finger on.

But in the more-or-less rational part of my brain, I knew that I should
call her—*had* to call her. I was the one that told her I would let her borrow
the book in the first place! And it would be rude of me to go back on my
word. And plus, she didn't seem like the type of person you wanted to make
mad in any way. She seemed like she could be a major bitch if you didn't do
what you said you would do for her or if you did anything at all to get on
her bad side. She seemed like she could be a major bitch if you were on her

good side, too, but the percentage of getting your head ripped off seemed higher on her bad side. And since she was one of the only people I actually talked to at practice, despite the fact that, at times, she was kind of a dick to me, she and Hannah had been kind enough to let me in their group when no one else seemed to want to. The least I could do was let her come borrow a stupid little book. The logic was simple enough, but the thing was: I didn't want to! I couldn't bring myself to.

So that was my hell: my incontinence (in the Aristotelian sense of the word). I knew what to do, but I just couldn't bring myself to do it. I was weak.

The inward struggle between what I knew to do and what I wanted to do took up almost my entire Friday. Not video games, not the library, not semi-sleep, not thinking about how much I hated my car, not the other things guys my age tend to do when they have free time in their bedrooms with a lockable door and the Internet, could silence the annoying voice of my nagging conscience. My mind was fighting itself, leaving my body in a nervous-stricken purgatory of anxiety and boredom.

At one point, I actually got up enough strength to pull out the number she had thrust into my soggy hand at the end of practice. The paper smelled like her; it was a mixed smell of some kind of melon and vanilla. She smelled like a fancy dessert. It was odd. I hadn't noticed the smell at practice, but the paper reminded me of what I hadn't noticed before or of what I had forgotten. I liked the sweet sugary smell. The smell went perfectly with the way she looked, but clashed with the way she behaved. But even with her number in my hand and a few deep breaths of fresh air from my opened window in my chest, I still could not bring myself to call.

That night I tried to sleep, but I couldn't. I went to bed early. I lay there in a fretful delirium, stuck between concrete reality and the trippy dream world of anthropomorphized figures. I was not fully asleep but not quite awake. I kept thinking over and over about the dream I had had the night I got sick at Miss Magdalene's house. Something about that dream wouldn't allow me to put it out of my head. The dream was the only real "relief" I had from the book situation. I was not dreaming, but the dream kept vividly playing over and over in my head like a hallucination, like a distant flickering silent film.

Saturday morning, it was clear to me that I had to call her if I planned on sleeping at all in the foreseeable future. I would call her and tell her to meet me at the library. I would give her the book there. That way, she wouldn't have to meet my mom, she would have the book, and I'd get some much-needed sleep. Then it'd be over with, at least until the next practice anyway.

I knew I was going to have to psych myself up to actually make the call. So I turned on some Morrison, got out the number, got out the phone, and started pacing through my cluttered room like a hungry tiger cub. After about 10 minutes of pace-stumbling around, I was able to anxiously dial the number. It was like mentally swallowing something disgusting. I felt like there was a large pack of elephants inside of my chest jumping up and down on my heart. I thought I for sure was going to faint, so I sat on my bed next to my window hoping the air would keep me conscious.

Her phone rang:

"Please enjoy the music while your party is being reached: (*Music from Phantom of the Opera*)."

"Hello?" Mira said in an apprehensive voice.

"Hey, it's me. The new guy from practice. I got that book if you still want to borrow it." My voice was shaking from all the nerves, and the pacing had me a little out of breath. For a second she was quiet.

Soliloquy

"Oh! Oh, yah! Hey, how are you?"

"Oh, I'm fine. Ummm. Did you still want to borrow that book from me? That Baldwin book I told you about, *Giovanni's Room*."

"Yes, of course. Are you okay? You sound kinda sick or something."

"Oh no, I'm fine. I just got done cleaning up my room and working out and stuff. But I'm fine."

With a giggle, she said, "You work out? I didn't know that. Did you just start? Why are you cleaning your room? Are you expecting company? Do you plan to have a sleepover?"

"Yeah. I work out sometimes. It's off and on, I guess. But just to be healthy. And no. No. I just like to be clean, that's all. That's why I was cleaning. I'm not expecting any company for a sleepover."

Full out laughing, she said, "I was just joking with you. Are you starting to get my sense of humor yet? I hope so."

"Yeah. I guess so." I was completely over the small talk. My unusually loud pounding heartbeat was starting to give me knife stabbing chest pain and a high-pitched earache. I hadn't called her for small talk. I just wanted to figure out if she wanted the book or not, so I could give it to her and get it over with. But she couldn't seem to stay on topic. I was starting to get frustrated. "But about the book," I said.

"Oh. Sorry. Yeah, I still want the book. Duh! Want me to come pick it up sometime later today, or do you want to drop it off at my house?"

"Well, I was thinking that maybe we could just meet at the library... downtown or something. I could give it to you there if that's okay. I'm going there anyway."

"Um, well I can't drive right now. I was just thinking Hannah could bring me there, to your house, when she gets off work. But I guess I could

Soliloquy

see if she would take me to the library when she gets off. What time are you going? What time does it close?

"I do have my license and stuff, but I don't have my own car yet, and my mom has the car and she's at work. So I don't know how I would get there anytime soon. I don't know where the library downtown is. I kinda know downtown a little bit, but not really. But I don't *know* downtown. I've only been a few times but—"

"How can you love books but have never been to the library? That's one of the only respectable places in this town!"

"I told you," she said defensively, "I just moved here not too long ago. All the books I read, I own. Or my mom owns. Don't judge me, I'm—"

"Oh, I see. I was just joking." There was a silence. "Well, I guess I can just bring the book to you? Or we could wait until practice? I could bring it to practice or your house. Which works best? I suck with directions, but maybe I can make it to where you live. I'm not sure. Where do you live?"

"Are you sure you don't want me to just wait for Hannah to get off of work?"

"No. It's fine." But it wasn't fine. I hated trying to find people's houses. I should have kept my mouth shut, but I didn't. I still don't know why I offered to go to her house. I really don't know. "I will just try to find it. Where do you live?"

"I live on the northeast side of town, on Miller Street. It's like five or eight minutes away from Miss Magdalene's house. So it shouldn't really be that hard to find. If you can get to Magdalene's house, you can find my house."

She told me the directions. Her voice was impatient. They didn't seem too difficult to follow. She was right. If I could make it to Miss Magdalene's house, I would have little problem making it to hers. I told her that it would

Soliloquy

take me some time to make it there, due to the fact that I had to finish clean-ing my room (which was a lie) and get dressed (which also was a lie). She said, "Take your time," and then hung up.

After neurotically dicking around for a time, I put on my shoes and a clean shirt, told my mom I was going to the library, and then I boarded the shit-stain express heading straight for crazy town. I took out the directions and followed them. On the drive I tried to keep myself calm by thinking about how nice it would be not to have her meet my mom. All I had to do was drop the book off and leave. No introductions, no stress. I thought to myself: I won't get out of the car. Maybe I won't even stop the car. Maybe I would do a drive-by booking—just toss it and keep going!

Before I knew it, I was rounding the corner to Miller Street. A wave of nauseating nervousness washed over me like an ice-cold tidal wave. I drove slowly down the street looking for the house number. Before I got to the house number, I noticed a girl sitting Indian-style in the bright yellow sun-shine. She was in the middle of a yard of perfectly cut grass. She was happily picking flower petals next to a young tree that was surrounded by a multi-hued, color-coordinated flowerbed. She was the only person outside on the entire street. In front of her was a small mound of grass and uprooted flow-ers of all different colors. There were huge daisies on top of the pile. She was picking through the pile slowly, looking at them analytically, and sniffing them unusually, as if she was getting high off of them.

As I neared, the sound of my car caught her attention. Mira sprung up to her bare feet and sprinted smoothly over to my car. "Pull into the drive-way," she said. I obliged. She was smiling a sweet, tranquil smile. I was sur-prised by how happy and un-crazy she seemed. Her happy look made me happy and even more nervous than I was already.

Soliloquy

"What took you so long?" She stuck her smiling head in the driver's side window.

"I got here as fast as I could. Sorry if I kept you waiting. I told you I was bad with directions. I'm sorry if it took—"

"So where's this amazing book? Hahahahah! What's up with your crappy car? It looks like 1977 took a steaming dump and out came your car!" She laughed, covering her mouth with a hand that was still full of flowers.

"I know. It really sucks. I know. I hate it so much, but I might be getting a new one sometime soon. Oh, here, the book is right here. Here." I reached into the passenger seat and pulled the book out of the plastic Ziploc bag. "Here you go."

She looked it over closely, reading a few lines from the back cover. "Oh, thanks!" she said. Half of her body was in my car. She was hovering over me like a friendly nurse hovers over a sick patient. A lazy breeze was blowing, and I could smell her. The scent of the warm summer air mixed with her flowers and perfume perfectly. Even the wind itself smelled sweet. She was so close to me that her dark hair was brushing the side of my hot face. She lightly draped her slim arm around my neck, hugging me. "Thank you very much!" she said, and she kissed me firmly on the cheek. Her warm lips held against my cheek for what seemed like a lifetime.

I was shocked! Physically and emotionally shocked! It felt like her lips had set my entire body on fire. Everything was a burning, itchy, scorching inferno. I was in a kind of agony that I had never experienced before. It was horrifying, worse than any form of agony I could envision. I felt like a fiery rash was bubbling over my skin: measles, mumps, chickenpox, smallpox, bigpox, Ebola, black plague, leprosy, scurvy, everything! A prickly pain was engulfing my whole body, starting at my head and aching its way down to my groin. The sweet breeze, the heat, the perfume, the smell of flowers, and her warm lips on my face were too much to take. They were too much all at once. I couldn't wrap my mind around it all. I was overwhelmed with thoughts and unfamiliar, uncomfortable sensations.

She had caught me completely off-guard. I wanted to disappear into the breeze, to just melt into thin air. I wanted to do something. I wanted to die! The feeling was torture. At that moment, more than at any other moment before, I wished I was back home in my bedroom, or at the least far, far away from her and everything else. It was too much.

I had never been kissed by a girl before. I figured I would get around to kissing a girl at some point, but I never expected that the girl would be pretty. Despite my age, I didn't get around much. I wasn't like most of the people my age. It wasn't that I didn't like girls, I just didn't know how to get them like the jokes and jerks did, let alone touch them, or get them to take their pants off. I had no idea how that stuff worked. The pickup lines in movies seemed ridiculous and smack-worthy; I couldn't pull them off. I figured the "girls" thing would work itself out at some point in my life, but not with some strange girl I barely knew infecting me with lips like burning gasoline.

What had she done to me? Why would she do that? Why would she do that without my permission? Why would she do that at all? What did it mean? What could it mean? Did she like me? Did I like her? Did it mean anything at all? Or did she go around kissing guys she just met all the time for no reason? I felt weak, sick, confused, and frankly, a little pissed off. I felt like I was going to pass out again, for the second time in less than a couple of weeks.

I struggled to mutter up the words: "N...o prob...hum...lem." My tongue felt like a thick cinderblock covered with chunky peanut butter, and my mouth felt like a humid Egyptian tomb. I could hardly breathe. My throat quickly began to harden like warm cement under a blazing sun. My neck was clogged with dense, paste-thick, rock-hard anti-saliva that would not go down or come up. I couldn't clear my throat to save my life. It felt like I had swallowed a cup of steaming salty sand. I thought that I was slowly choking to death. I started to panic.

My thighs were tingling mercilessly. I felt terrible! It felt like my bottom half had fallen asleep, and then been torched. Like when your legs fall asleep and it hurts like hell to move them. That was it. It was that tingling-needle-stab feeling that increased in pain and intensity as you tried to move; like I had been tased repeatedly in my groin until only a numb, non-feeling feeling remained. I was sensitive all over, yet numb. It was uncomfortable, and everything hurt with an unredeemable unnecessary pain.

Worst of all, I could feel an erection creeping on slowly, agonizingly. An erection! A morning, "I really have to pee" erection. I wasn't feeling sexual, I was feeling horrible. Why? No! The more I tried to focus and hold it down, the harder it got, and the faster it grew. I could feel it inching up faster and faster against the weight of my pants. It was rising—pausing—rising—pausing. Cranking up, like a rusty old tire jack. Not now! Oh, please, no! Not now, I said to myself.

"So, what are you about to do now?" she said. She was still near my face, still halfway in the car, and her arm was still around my neck. Her soft breath was blowing directly into my ear, making everything worse.

I tried to talk again, but nothing came out. Not even air. The sand saliva had my throat steadfastly stopped. I had to tell myself to breathe while I was trying to clear my throat. She was still close to me, touching me. The heat in my head just kept building. I was getting lightheaded and dizzy. I could feel my consciousness starting to turn into steam. I said to myself:

Soliloquy

No, no, no… not now… Jes'us no! You have to calm down… have to calm your ass down (I think I'm… going t…o black out again)… FUCK!!!!!!!! CALM DOWN! You can do it, please… I can do it… just calm down. Just don't think about it and it will go away. Breathe… That's i…t… Breath… do it, breathe… Okay now… Just calm down now. Just don't think. Eyes, stay open! Just think of something that doesn't have to do with anything… Just think of something or anything or nothing or something. Um, here, yeah: baseball, pink stuff, no… um, bikes, training wheels, training… um, airplanes, ice cream, um okay, warm milk, rock milk, rock salt, Rocky Horror Picture Show, Rocky Mountains, Rocky Balboa, Montana, Idaho… Okay. Okay. I can breathe… I'm gonna be okay. I'm…

"Hello… helloo'o? Did you hear me? You're so weird. Have you been drinking or something? You're acting funny. I'm asking you a question. What are you doing after this? Where are you going when you leave here?" She moved my chin with two fingers, so she could look me in my eyes.

Despite my attempt at personal Jedi-mind-trickery and lackluster self-affirmation, I was not okay. But I had not passed out or puked or crapped, and that had to count for something. My junk was as hard as reinforced metal piping, but when I glanced down at it, it wasn't all that noticeable, so that was good.

Forcing the words up through my stone-hard throat, I croaked out: "*S..r…y.* Uuuhuuummmm! Hummm… hnum… *Sorry*, I was daydreaming. I'm kinda sleepy or something, I think. The working out maybe. I'm sorry. I don't know…ummm… I think I might go to the library or just go home and get some sleep. Take a nap. I don't know yet. I just wanted to get you the book. That was my only plan for today, really. I don't have to work today so."

She un-leaned her head from the car window, her eyes searching mine with a questioning squint. She folded her slender arms across her chest. I noticed her tank top was low cut. She was standing fully erect, gazing at me. She was not smiling or frowning. It was just a solemn, thoughtful gaze.

"Well," she finally said. "Can I go to the library with you? I don't have much else to do today either, to be honest. I'm done picking, and Hannah's working. Earlier you were making fun of me for never going to the library, weren't you? You should take me. I think that would be a gentlemanly thing to do. What'd you think?" Her ruby bottom lip poked out slightly, and her head was tilted like a coy child trying to get candy from the grocery store check-out line.

I did not, I repeat, I did not want to take her with me. Not even a little bit. But it was as clear to me as daylight that it was not truly a question she was posing; it was a command in the thin disguise of a question. Something I would come to find out was a specialty of hers.

"Are you sure you want to go?" I said. "It's really not that fun. I was just joking with you about never going before."

"Yes, I really want to go, but if you don't want to take me… then fine. I will just wait for Hannah. But—"

"No. It's fine. I will take you. No problem. It's fine." It wasn't fine. "Do you want to go right now?"

"Sure!" She was smiling from ear to ear, bouncing up and down. "Let me just go change really quick. Wanna come in and get something to drink?"

"Um, no. It's okay. I'm okay. I'll just wait out here. It's nice."

She smiled. "Oh. Are you afraid to come in my house? You think I'm gonna kidnap you or something?"

"Oh, no! Nothing like that. It's not that. I'm just comfortable. It's nice out. And… umm… maybe some other time, maybe."

She didn't respond. She just gave me a wary look and gracefully sprang away.

Soliloquy

While she was gone, I tried to gather my scattered crumbs of thought and come up with a plan. But before I could, she was back, fully changed, carrying a big blue metallic purse.

"Let's go!" She slammed the heavy car door.

"Do you have a jacket? It tends to get pretty cold in there, in the library, even in the summer."

"No. I don't. Do you have one? If I get cold, I'll just use yours."

"Oh. Okay."

During the drive there was lots of silence. It was a good type of silence. The noiselessness was not just in my car, but everywhere. The hush that suffocated the surrounding space was warm and fixed. It was more profound than awkward. The pervasiveness of a Day-Glo yellowness covered everything with a happy brightness. Everything was clear yellow, except for the sky. The sky was a van Goghish light blue. It was devoid of all clouds. Just open space remained, stretching. The ginger sun was high in the bright blue openness. Its light made everything seem slightly phosphorescent and frozen. Everything was silent. It was a day unlike any I had known.

To speak, to remove the quiet space that hung in the air, would have been like dropping a rock into a peaceful pond of perfect stillness. Talking would have disturbed the endless possibility that hung between us.

There was something strange about the feeling I was experiencing. There was something fresh about it, something brand new. It was like time had, not stopped, but changed. As if time had become calmer, ticking ever more slowly and hopefully with each second. Time had become nugatory—the way it must have been before people existed. Time was no longer self-conscious. For the first time, I could feel that the time was eternal—forever before and above me.

Soliloquy

We just rode in the warmth. We were silent, and the day was ours to seize or waste in any way we wanted. Even the shit-stain drove quieter than usual, it seemed, in respect for the uniqueness of unselfconscious time.

I looked at Mira slowly, through the corner of my eye, wondering what she could be thinking. I wondered what the *real* her could be like, the person behind all the antics and edgy jokes. She was just sitting there with her little hands clasped together, looking straight ahead. She appeared to be meditating or something.

Suddenly, as if responding to my glance, she said, still looking forward, "Have you ever thought about what it would be like to die? Like genuinely thought about it? To commit suicide, I mean? I know it's a morbidly inappropriate question, but you seem smart enough to have thought about it, so I just thought I'd ask. Maybe you'd have something intelligent to say, you know?"

I took my eyes off the road to look at her. I was surprised. The question was heavy, weird, and out of nowhere.

"Umm… I think everyone thinks about it at least some time or another. I guess. I think it's natural to contemplate what it would be like. If you could <u>actually</u> go all the way through with eliminating yourself, your consciousness. Is everything okay?" I was trying to sound as calm as possible.

"Of course. I'm okay. Geez. I'm not crazy. It's actually a good question. I'm just thinking didactically, that's all. How come every time someone thinks a deep thought people think they're crazy? Has thinking deep thoughts become the new crazy? I'm fine. It's just that the thought of death is fascinating to me, as it should be with everybody. Don't you think, though? It's fascinating.

"I could never kill myself—ever! I hate pain way too much. And I love myself way too much. I'm complete chicken-shit when it comes to pain. But the thought of not being here, not existing, not thinking, not feeling, not *being*, it always frightens and fascinates me.

"Lots of famous huffy and puffy people say that great writing has to deal with the subject of death. If not, it can't be considered great. I think most writers are completely full of dog shit, to be honest. But my point is, I do think they may be right about how important it is to have people think about death, you know? If you don't ever think about death, can you truly have ever thought about life? Great writing is about shedding creative light on simple universal truth, evolving a reader's awareness of multiple perspectives. Perspectives people tend to take for granted or never get to see. That's great writing to me, plain and simple. But people *do* need to contemplate death, they are right about that. It's the thought that can never be fully thunk, you know?"

"Yeah." I was in awe of her ideas. Her words seemed wise beyond her years. I wasn't sure where it was coming from or why she was sharing it with me. She was deeper and more open with her thoughts than anyone I had ever met; yet I still felt like I had no idea who she was or what she was trying to accomplish with me.

I said, "It is definitely hard to wrap the mind around the thought of dying, because the conscious mind is the opposite, the antithesis of death. The complete *anti-*, I think. Complete opposites can never fully understand one another because there is no common ground, no common reference, for them to stand on or compare. 'God cannot think the devil and the devil cannot think God,' or something like that."

She chuckled. "My mom would freak out if she heard you say that. Where'd you get that quote?"

"Oh, I made it up just now, I think. Or I might have read it someplace."

"Nice," she said. "Keep going."

Soliloquy

"Oh. Well, when I think about death, I think about the instinctual cap that impairs our thinking of it, of death, if that makes any sense at all. I mean, since it is our instinct to live, to survive, and for some humans even to thrive, our minds are not programmed to understand the opposite of its most basic, most primal goal, which is death, or non-life, or non-thinkingness. If that makes any sense. I don't know if that made any sense at all." She was silent, still facing forward. She had not twitched one inch during our "death" conversation except for an occasional smile and giggle. I was afraid that I had said too much or scared her somehow.

She turned toward me and said, "See. I knew it. I knew you were like me. I knew deep down you had something to say—something real to say. I could tell when I first met you. I knew it!" She smiled the biggest, most contented smile I had ever seen. Then she faced forward again. It was the smile of someone who had been vindicated of a crime. It was a real smile. Her smile made me smile.

"So you understood what I said? That's good. I didn't think I was very clear."

"Yes, I understood you. I understand you. I think we are two of a kind. Two peas in a crappy car."

"Oh. Well… ummm… thank you, I guess."

"You're welcome, 'I guess.' All that death talk has got me thinking about this girl that I went to school with, back at my old school. We weren't best friends or good friends or anything like that, but I knew her pretty well. We had a bunch of classes together: Advanced Spanish, AP Chem, and some other ones.

"She seemed perfectly normal to me. Just like everyone else, you know? Then one day, without any warning or any hinting to anyone at all: BAM! She up and killed herself. Why? Why would she do that? No one could understand it. How could she do that, you know? Her life wasn't that bad. Not that I knew of, anyway.

"She had lots of friends. I would have been a *real* friend to her if I had known she needed one. People always blame the bullies, but no one bullied her. She was one of the most popular kids in the school. Everyone liked her. There was no bully to blame.

"When I think of stuff like, that I just can't wrap my head around it. Why would she do it? It just doesn't make any sense to me. None at all. What about all the people who cared about her? What about her family? Did she know how bad that would hurt them? I'm sorry. I know this is super sad and Debby Downerish, but sometimes I get to thinking and my mind just takes off, and I can't stop it. But then sometimes I think maybe I shouldn't stop it. Maybe it will take me to where I need to go, you know? Maybe if I think enough, one day I will end up in a place where I can find *real* answers. Maybe I'll be able to really understand people, really understand myself. I don't know, I think I talk too much. People tell me that all the time. They say, 'Mira, you think too much. You always have something to say. You always have an opinion about everything.' They always tell me I should tone it down. How sad, but it makes me laugh."

"No," I said. "I completely see what you mean. You don't talk too much. I think people should talk more. Not more always, but you know what I mean? I mean talk more about stuff that really matters. Stuff like we're talking about right now. Like they say, 'The unexamined life is not worth living.'"

"Socrates!" she shouted.

"Yeah. How did you know?"

"Ummm… Cause I read. Duh!"

"Yes. I see. Oh shit! I missed my turn. We passed it."

Soliloquy

"The library?"

"Yeah. I was so focused on what we were talking about. I wasn't paying attention to my turn."

"Well, at least you were paying attention to something. By the way, that's the first time I ever heard you swear!"

"Yeah? Oh. It happens now and then."

We circled around the block of sunny downtown one-ways, back to the library parking lot entrance. As we pulled in, I realized that I had still not made a plan for what we were going to do. What the hell were we going to do? Walk around looking at each other, or look at random books, then leave? It seemed like a big waste to me. I said, "Here we are. So… what do you want to do?"

"I want you to get your jacket just in case I get cold. Then I want you to show me around this library you spoke so highly of. Was that not obvious? You're the one that said this is one of the 'cool places in town.' I've never been here, so be a baby doll and give me the grand tour, *compendia*?"

"Well. Okay. I'll give you a tour. I can do that."

"You don't do this very often, do you? I mean hang with girls one-on-one? I never asked: do you have a girlfriend?"

"Um, no. Not really. I mean, no, I don't go places with girls all that often. And no, I don't have a girlfriend. Not at the moment."

"Do you have a boyfriend?" she laughed hysterically, clutching her stomach.

"No! I don't! I don't like guys!"

"Chill. Cool out. I was just joking with you, mister."

"I'm chilled. I'm not mad. I got that that was a joke. I'm just saying: no! I don't have anything against that, but I just don't like guys in that way." I was kind of mad. I didn't think that it was a joke. And even if it was a joke, I didn't think it was funny. "Do *you* have a boyfriend or a girlfriend?" I asked.

She recomposed herself and smiled. "Of course I do. Of course. I have lots of boyfriends and a few girlfriends. You're my boyfriend. I have a boyfriend named Jack that went to my old school. I have a boyfriend named Marteese who went to the school I went to before that. I have tons of boys-that-are-my-friends. Boy-friends."

"Oh. I see. That's not exactly what I—"

"So where are we going?" Her voice reverberated loudly through the hallway. We had been wandering through the library on the habitual path that I always took.

"Oh. Um… it's up to you, really. What do you want to see?"

"I told you: everything!"

"Okay, then. I'll take you to the novel section first. It's over this way."

We walked down the shiny ivory-colored main corridor past the "CHECK-OUT," "SELF-CHECK-OUT," "REFERENCE DESK" and "HELP-DESK." There were many, many odd hipster-looking women behind each of the long wooden desks. All of them were wearing very fancy, angular reading glasses, scarves, and long dark skirts. All the women were moving around very quickly, yet there were very few customers getting helped. I was confused. Near the end of the long hallway we took a left into the "READERS" department, and then another left to the four tall rickety racks of books designated: "NOVELS AND MORE." The racks of books were so tall you needed a chair-size stepstool to reach the top shelf.

"So. Here we are," I said.

"Yep, so we are."

"This is the novel section. There's some study rooms back around that way."

"Are these all the novels they have?"

"Well, ah, other than the ones that people have checked out, I guess so."

"Good one, smart ass! You guess a lot."

"Yeah, I guess you're right."

"So, have you read many of these books?" She walked slowly down a row. She was sliding her pointer finger across the weathered spines of the books. She walked leisurely down the row, and her little curved hips swung back and forth with every overtly feline step she took. It was like she was trying to seduce the books.

"Ah-hum. Yeah." I gulped down a medium-size rock of pre-drool that was stuck in my throat. "I haven't read all of them, but I've read quite a few. I've read maybe three-fourths of them, probably more than that, to be honest. The section isn't that big, but they have some pretty good choices. A lot of the classics."

"The section is not huge, but there is probably something like 700 books here—probably more. You're telling me you've read nearly a thousand books? I read more than anyone I know, and I know I haven't read anywhere close to a thousand books! I don't even think I've read five hundred books!"

"Well, I don't know how many books I've read in my life. I don't think I've read over a few thousand, but I don't know. Maybe close. I started reading when I was super young, and I never played sports, or did school clubs, or drove a cool car or anything, so I've had a lot of time on my hands to do a lot of reading. When I run out of things to do, which is all the time, I read."

She glared at me with interest and disbelief. "Well, I'll be damned. Nearly a few thousand books? *If* that is true, that's incredible. That's an incredible feat. When did you start reading?"

"Um… I don't really remember, but my mom and dad tell me I was about two and a half years old. But that's when I wasn't really reading. I mean, like, I was reading children's books to myself around that age. Or at least that is what they tell me, I guess. They tell me I could read simple words when I was younger than that. But I don't know. I don't really remember. They might be exaggerating to make me feel good. Or they might say it to make themselves feel good. I don't know."

"Get the fuck out of here!" she shouted.

"Hay... Shhhh... you're going to get us kicked out of here," I whispered.

"Sorry, sorry." Deep wrinkles formed a maze on her forehead. "I just can't believe you started reading when you were that young. That's really crazy. Are you a genius? What's your IQ?"

"No, I'm not at all a genius. I don't know my IQ. My dad says that IQ test are for people who are deeply insecure. He always says stuff like, 'Son, did Gandhi go around talking about his IQ? Do you think he ever took an IQ test? What about Honore de Balzac? Did he? Did Dr. King, Jr. go around preaching emphatically about how people needed higher IQ scores, or did he sermonize about how people need higher moral IQs? What about Marie Curie? You think she cared about her IQ score? No! I suspect her greatness was enough. The aforementioned *geniuses* are all true geniuses regardless of IQ scores. The people who need IQ tests to tell them who or what they are clearly have no idea what real genius is.

"You know who did have a high IQ, son? Ted Kaczynski. Do you know who else, son? Joel Rifkin. Both of those men had high IQs. Meaningless! IQ is nothing without courage, vision, and virtue.' That's how my dad talks. My dad gets on his high horse about things like that sometimes. He thinks intellectual standardization is just another *ism*. But, so, no, I'm not a genius. My parents just put me on that 'Teach Your Baby How to Read' crap when I was still an infant. I guess it really works. Maybe I was just so bored when I was a kid I had to find something to do. So I picked reading instead of playing with the toys I had, I guess."

She had come closer to me. She looked me in the eyes. "Wow. Your dad sounds smart. And maybe a little bit crazy. I don't know who half those guys are he talked about. But that kinda sounds like something my mom would say or at least agree with. She loves to go against the grain... even while being a part of the grain. It sounds like you had a pretty lame childhood. But hey, everyone I know had a lame childhood, too. So don't feel too bad. You don't have any brothers or sisters?"

"Nope. Only child."

"Me, too," she said softly. She looked down at her shoes. "Well, that's another thing we have in common."

"Yeah, I guess you're right."

"Yeah. It would suck to hate your sibling like Hannah hates Essy."

"Yeah, I guess it would."

"Anyway. Moving on. I'm getting bored. Where to next?" She quickly walked into the main hallway.

"If you want, I can show you the computer room."

"Sounds good." We walked back towards the entrance, to the granite-looking staircase next to the elevators.

"Hey!" she shouted. "Let's play a game. You take the elevator... and I'll take the stairs, and we can race. What floor is it on?"

"There are only two floors in the building. I don't even know why they have an elevator in this place."

"For handicapped people and parents with strollers and stuff. Duh! Don't be insensitive."

"Yeah. I guess you're right."

Soliloquy

"Push the button!" she said, then she pushed the button before I had the chance.

We waited for what seemed like forever for the elevator doors to "*DING!*" I was getting nervous. She had seemed quasi-normal all day. There had been no inconsiderate pranks, no temper tantrums, no philosophical outburst (other than the suicide conversation, which wasn't a problem), no fake pregnancies to draw negative attention, no being a big bitch to me for no apparent reason. None of that had happened. But she seemed, due to my lack of ability to entertain her, to be getting in one of her rabble-rousing moods. She seemed, from her overexcitedness, like a little ADHD kid who needed to be entertained or else he would explode and throw a self-amusing fit. If she didn't find some sort of entertainment or game, she might start dicking around with people, acting like a crazy person, or worse.

DING!

"Okay!" She was fidgety with joy. "Get in. When the doors shut, I'll go. Okay? Ready?"

"Okay."

When the doors opened to the second floor, Mira was lying on the floor a few feet in front of the doors in a crucifixion pose. I was mortified! A few people were looking at her as they walked by.

I walked up and stood over her. "Are you okay?"

Her eyes were closed. I couldn't tell if she was breathing or not. I couldn't tell if it was a prank or if she had actually fainted or something. I looked around to see if any object was near her that might have fallen on her head or for signs of blood.

"Hello? Are you okay?" I put my hand softly on her forehead. "Hello!"

An old gray-Afro-haired lady stumblingly approached us, her heels clicking like an old broken refrigerator. "Is that young lady okay?" The old lady's voice was raspy and breathless. She smelled like week-old coffee grounds and stale dog food.

"Oh, yes, ma'am. I'm okay. I'm just taking a rest. I just ran up all those stairs like the Flash! Shhhhwooooo! That was serious business! I'm just catching my breath," Mira said. She was smiling, still lying like a "t" in front of the elevator. A couple trying to get on the elevator looked strangely at the three of us huddled in their path.

"Oh. Well, get up from there, child! This is no place for a young lady to rest herself! Find a chair, there are plenty. There are germs on this here floor. Feet pass this way all day long. You don't want to get sick and dirty."

"Yes, ma'am," I said, grabbing Mira's arm and slowly helping her to her feet. I'll find her a seat. Thank you very much for your concern."

"You do that, young man. Keep your companion off the filthy floor." The old lady's face had doubled in wrinkles and sagginess. She was scowling and muttering under her breath.

Mira said nothing, but her face said it all. She was smiling, staring off into space like a person who had figured out an extremely complicated riddle. It was an inward, self-gratified smile. Her boredom seemed to have subsided (for the moment) and she was in a sort of bemused bliss.

"Mira. Seriously?" I was trying to keep my cool. "Please. You freaked that lady out. Let's not freak anyone else out, okay?" I was still leading her by the arm slowly, because she was walking like a dazed mental patient. It felt like if I let her arm go she would stumble back to the ground or crash into a wall or have an epileptic seizure. So I just held on.

"'You got it, dude,'" she said in a childlike voice. She was giggling to herself.

"Are you okay? Sit here." She plopped down in the soft cushiony seat.

Soliloquy

"I'm fine," she said. "I'm not really that tired. I'm fine. I beat you, by the way, in the race."

"Yes. I guess you did. I figured you would." I sat down in the chair next to her.

"Why? Why would you figure I'd—"

Words, surfing on the smell of putrid dairy and burnt baloney interjected, "Is everything okay over here, miss?" The reeking words came from the nasty librarian guy that I didn't like; the one that always gave me suspicious looks, as if I was hiding books in my boxers. He was standing robotically in front of Mira with an unreadable expression on his floppy face. He did not acknowledge me at all.

"Yes?" Mira said. Her voice sounded confused, but she had a happy smile on her face. "I'm fine. How are you?" She put her hand up and waved it at him slowly.

"Oh, okay. I was just checking. I work here… at the library. A few people came up to the desk and said that you might be having some sort of medical troubles. So that's why I came over to check. You were on the floor in front of the elevators, they said?"

"Yes," Mira said politely. "Yes. I fell down, but now I'm fine. Thank you."

"Okay. Well, I was just checking. It's my job to follow up on things like that, you know?" He spoke with a creepy, over-posed, fourth-grade-picture-day smile. His smile literally frightened me. I could feel the hair on my arms stand up, and I could feel myself getting hot.

"I completely understand. It's your job."

"Yes. Can I ask you something? Do you come to the library often? I am really good with faces, and I don't think I remember you. I'd remember if I remembered you. Have you ever checked anything out here before?"

Soliloquy

"Oh, no. This is my first time." She giggled like a schoolgirl. "My amazing new boyfriend brought me to your wonderful library today for the first time." She reached over and grabbed my hand, gently interlacing her fingers between mine. I felt a chill, then a hot flash, and then I tasted a metallic shot of adrenaline at the back of my throat. *What is she doing?* I thought. My hand started to sweat as if it was being held over a hot stove. She was saying to the creep, "He raved about how great of a place this library is, so I begged him to bring me. I really wanted to see it for myself. So here we are... my boyfriend and I."

The smile had evaporated from his saggy, rodent-like face. But somehow, without the smile, the creepiness grew. For the first time he looked toward me. On the surface of his face was no expression, but underneath I could see the indication of a frown trying to bubble over.

"Oh," he said, turning back to Mira. "I see him here all the time. That's cool." He turned back to me and said, "So... that's cool. So how long have you two been going out? I've never seen you here with a girl before. You're usually all alone. Why didn't you bring her here before?" His tone was accusatory and forceful, and his eyes were filled with suspicious disbelief. His eyes were saying: There is no freakin' way a guy like you could ever get a girl like her! I opened my mouth to speak, but the metallic taste at the back of my throat forced me to swallow several times to keep from choking.

"Lots of questions you have," Mira said. "We haven't been going out for very long. But he's amazing. He was worth the wait. But you'll be seeing a lot more of us together; I can assure you of that." She lifted my hand and kissed it gently, passionately. She closed her eyes (like a person who is about to pray a reverent prayer), and she held her soft lips to my hand for a very long time. My heart fell to my balls, and I could not make myself understand what was going on. All I could do was sit there frozen in a combination of horror, (what I assume was) pure horniness, and a state of infinite consterna-tion. I had never felt anything like it. If there were one word to describe it, it would be: *physical*. It felt *deeply physical*. It felt as if she wasn't pretending and every cell in my body felt her sincerity. It felt as if I was <u>actually</u> her amazing new boyfriend, as if she was full of real passion for me! Everything felt. It was like a chain reaction of sensation.

"Are you ready to go, babe?" She slowly opened up her eyes and gazed into mine.

Trying to clear my throat, I forced out an, "Uhmum."

The creepy checkout guy had accomplished a fully formed frown now.

"Okay. Well, I hope to see you soon. Try not to let her fall on your way out." He was glaring at me with an acute death stare.

"Come on, babe. We're going to be late," Mira said. She grabbed my hand and pulled me from my seat. My legs felt anesthetized, and I was al-most too weak to stand. "Come on!"

I trailed behind her like a dehydrated, three-legged dog. In an excited trot we jogged (I more or less stumbled) hand in hand down the stairs, through the main hall, and out the main doors. When we reached the front steps, she let my hand go, dropping it like a kid who was bored with a new Christmas toy. She rested and looked up into the cloudless sky. She seemed to be looking directly into the orange sun.

I stood next to her wondering what the hell was going on. What was this crazy girl doing? What was she doing with me? What was she talking about "new boyfriend"? What the hell was she doing holding my hand without my permission? What the hell was she doing kissing my hand with so much passion and tenderness? Where were we running to—late to what? Why did we stop on the steps, like crazy people? What the hell was it all about?

"Wow," she said, breaking my frantic string of inward questions. "It is so beautiful out today, isn't it?"

"Yeah," I said.

She was manikin still, gazing up at the sun. She seemed like some extra-terrestrial being waiting for the Mothership to return and pick her up. "So?" I was unable to come up with a logical question. Everything about Mira seemed to exist far beyond the realm of logical questions.

"That guy was creepy, wasn't he?" She finally took her eyes off the sun and looked at me.

"Yes. Very creepy. His smile gave me the chills."

"I know, right?" She bounded down the stairs like a joyful child. I followed.

"So, am I taking you home now?"

"Um, no! You can't get rid of me that easily."

"Oh. I wasn't trying—"

"Let's go get some ice cream, then you can get rid of me."

"Okay. But I really wasn't trying—"

"Let's go!"

We rode along the sun-soaked streets until we found a dilapidated DQ. After ordering Blizzards (she picked them out, I paid), she ordered me to an old picnic table near the parking lot. We sat there for several hours as she said strange things, until the pinkish-orange light submerged itself into the plum-colored horizon. I can't remember actually watching a sunset before that day. After she had her fill of whatever she was hungry for, we re-boarded my old car and headed for her house.

"Can I smoke in your car?" She reached into her big metallicy purse and pulled out a silver Zippo lighter and a crumpled pack of cigarettes. She gave me the same look that she had given me when she'd asked me to take her to the library. I hated cigarettes. I hated smoke. And I hated the idea of someone smoking in my car (even though it was a piece of crap car). But for some reason, I said, "Um… sure… I guess so… Uh… I didn't know you smoked."

She clapped her pack of cigarettes against her hand and said, "Yeah. I normally don't, just every once and a while. No one knows I do. Not even Hannah. But just sometimes I get a really bad craving."

"Won't your parents smell the smoke on you?"

"Hell, no," she laughed. "I am rarely close enough to my mom for her to smell me. And if she does smell it, I'll just tell her that it was you that was smoking while I was in your car."

She put a cigarette in her mouth and carefully clicked open the shiny silver lighter. There was a wax-like symbol on the side of it. I couldn't tell what it was.

"What's on the side of that?"

"Oh, this? It's a daisy. I love them. They are my favorite flowers. Cool, huh?"

"Yeah."

"Do you have a favorite flower?"

"Umm… I've never really thought about it. I guess I'd have to think about it."

The gray fog of smoke was starting to fill the car. I coasted faster in the direction of her house. I wanted the smoke to draft out quicker. About a block from her house, she directed me to circle the block. She was not finished smoking. I did as she'd directed.

When she was finished, she flicked her butt out of the window, opened her giant purse, and pulled out a big, half empty bottle of light-green body spray. Then she commenced to drench every square inch of herself in it, face-

and-all. The body spray was the same scent that I got from the phone number she had thrust into my hand at practice. The smell was strong and sweet.

"Now if she smells anything, it'll be this."

"I bet." I pulled into her driveway.

"Well," she said with an awkward, exasperated sigh. "I had a lot of fun. Much more fun than I expected to, to be honest."

"Yeah. Well. I did too."

"Thanks for everything." She swung her foot out of the car door. "Maybe we can do this again sometime."

"Sure… whenever you want."

"Oh, shit! I almost forgot. Since you gave me something, I'll give you something." She reached into her purse and pulled out her silver Zippo lighter. "Here, you can keep this until I give you your book back." She carefully grabbed my hand and placed the lighter in it.

"Oh, it's okay. You can keep it. I trust you. Don't you need it?"

"No. I have another lighter somewhere—I'm sure. But this is my favorite one, so be careful not to cock it up. And I'll be careful not to mess up your book, okay?"

"Okay." I cautiously placed the lighter in my pocket.

"Okay. I'll see you at practice, or maybe before. We'll see. Okay. Drive safe."

"Okay."

She looked me in the eyes for what seemed like an inappropriate amount of time. But it wasn't like she was looking at me. It felt like she was trying to analyze something about me. I felt uncomfortable, yet again.

"Thanks!" She winked.

Soliloquy

"No pr—" before I could finish, she turned away and ran quickly to her door. For a while I sat there in the car, exhausted, too tired to move. After some self-pep talking, I got up the energy to go home.

I was a bit frazzled. My thoughts whizzed around my head like a shiny silver ball in an old pinball machine, but none of my thoughts ever reached the game-ending holes of understanding or closure. My thoughts bounced from the girl, to the ice cream, to the library, back to the girl, to her playing with flowers in the grass, to the creepy guy with the death stare, to her smell, to the hand kiss, to the other kiss, to my painful erection, and round and round again and again. By the time I had reached my driveway I had settled on one concrete thought: I was freaking exhausted, and I needed to sleep as soon as possible.

My mother was on the couch when I walked in.

"Hey, mom."

"Shhhh," she said, quickly putting her finger over her lips. Her eyebrows were frowned with angry concentration. She was staring at the television, intensely. "The news," she said, patting a spot next to her on the couch. "Come."

I sat on the far side of the couch hoping she wouldn't be able to smell leftover smoke on my shirt.

News Channel 18 sounded from the TV set:

> Judith: Hello, this is Judith Moore and Donald Masterson with your first news at 9. Today there was another fire on the city's west side; the second fire this week. For more on the fire, we throw it to Patrick DeLuse, live on the scene at the fire. Patrick?

> Patrick: Thank you, Judith. I am here, live on the scene, where for the last two hours, the fire department has battled a blazing fire at the Church of Love and Christ on the city's west side. As you

can see directly behind me, there are still pillars of smoke and fire flying up into the sky. Also, as you can see, the police department is on the scene. They are setting up a perimeter to keep onlookers back at a safe distance away from the fire, just to be safe. There… are… two… three… five squad cars on the scene making sure the civilians are back behind the barrier. A lot is going on here, Judith.

Judith: So, Patrick, are either the police chief or the fire chief on the scene?

Patrick: Oh, yes, Judith. The fire chief, Chief Gilbertson, is right here… [Chief Gilbertson slowly lumbered into the camera shot: sweaty, large, in an intricate uniform, mopping his brow with the cuff of his shirt sleeve]. Chief Gilbertson, is there anything you can tell us at this time about the fire?

Gilbertson: Well, ah, Pat. Um… I ken tell ya this much for damn sure. This here fire was outta control when we pulled up, and it's been a hot bitch ever since—excuse ma French. I ken tell ya that much. But, yes'er. I can't tell ya much else 'cause we still have an on goin' investamagation.

Patrick: So, Chief Gilbertson, are you suggesting that this may be a case of arson? Do you believe that this fire is related to the other fire that occurred earlier this week?

Gilbertson: Well, now… If I'm suggesten anythang, I'm suggesten that if there is an arsonist around here burnin' up all types of stuff like the devil in lyin' britches, we gonna catch um and put um away like we just came home from the grocery store, if you catch ma meanin'! But, wait-a-second-na, naw, it's too early to tell what done happened here tonight. Assumin's for asses and scientists. We still got a long way to go for we figure dat out.

Patrick: Well, thank you very much, Chief Gilbertson [Chief Gilbertson, sweating profusely, dragged himself out of the picture]. Well, Judith, as you can see from Chief Gilbertson's comments, this fire was *definitely* related to the other fire that occurred earlier. Our city has an arsonist on its hands. Back to you, Judith.

Judith: Thank you, Patrick. Let us know if you find out any more details.

Donald: Wow, Judith. What a sight. I'm glad that everyone's all right.

Judith: Indeed.

"This world is going to hell in a hand-basket," my mother mumbled.

"Yeah. You're probably right." I headed for the stairs. "I'm tired. Goodnight, mom."

"Goodnight. These are the end times. You need to start thinking about your relationship with the Lord. You need to know where you're going to be headed when it's all over."

"Okay, mom. I will." I don't know exactly why I said it, but I said it. I just wanted to sleep.

I don't remember making it to my bedroom. I think I was asleep by the time I hit the stairs. All I remember was the dream I had that night. I dreamed that D-train and Mira kidnapped me and took me to a secret location (although I've never been to Germany, in my dream, it seemed like Germany or Russia or someplace like that). They had me tied to a wooden chair, naked. They both were dressed in all black and were talking with some weird accents: it appeared to be a mixture of weird German and psycho-gibberish. Mira was standing behind D while he tried to punch my face completely off my skull. I can remember thinking: *What do they want? Why are they trying to kill me? Why is Mira not helping me?*

Soliloquy

Mira emerged from behind D-train and said, "Twhere ez eint! Twhere ez it!" Her face was almost completely different from the real Mira's face. It looked like her face after a long future of very hard times. The pretty had turned into worldliness, the smile had turned into a conniving sneer, and the cheer had turned into a craving for violence. It was her, all right, but not the real her.

"Where is what? I don't know what you're lo —"

D-train punched my mouth shut. "Shud dup!" he yelled, as he punched away at my shattered face. Even though I was dreaming, the pain was real.

"Viw talkd vor I vill nd viw!" She looked directly into my eyes. Her black eyes lacked all humanity and compassion.

"Okay! I will tell you what you want to know! Just please, please, please tell me what you are looking for. What are you looking for?"

PUNCH! PUNCH! PUNCH!… PUNCH! I could feel my face turning into baby food.

"V vont talkd…" D-train said, rubbing my blood from his knuckles with a crimson towel.

"Go! Vring me de fluid." As D-train ran off into the darkness, Mira stood a few feet in front of me, arms crossed, staring at me with a stare that said: *You are all the filth that is wrong in this world.* Her eyes did not blink. When D-train returned, he had a canister of something with duct tape around it. He handed it to Mira. She uncorked the red top and started dousing me with the canister's stinky contents. It smelled like sulfur or death.

"No! No! Please! No!" I begged, trying to squirm out on my chair, but to no avail. The more I squirmed, the tighter my bindings became. "Please! Just tell me what you're looking for. Please!"

"No! Too vlate!" She pulled out her Zippo lighter and flipped it open. The flame that burned was enormous. "No! Too vlate!"

Soliloquy

"No! Please! I will tell you anything! What do you want from me? What do you want from me?"

But she didn't care. She held the flame there for a time, staring into my eyes. Then, with the flip of her slim wrist, she tossed the lighter into my lap.

I sat there. On fire. Burning. In pain. Immolated. The pain was beyond pain. It became something much worse, much more. The pain circled me, consumed me, and then fused with me to become a new being entirely. I was no longer myself and pain was no longer itself, we were one. And Mira just stood there frozen, watching it all happen.

When I woke up the next morning, my bed was wet. I had urinated.

Chapter 6

"Hearts on Fire, Aroused, Enraptured"

Despite the fact that my nightmares (or night terrors) seemed to steadily increase, for a couple weeks or so, things were looking up in my life. At least that's what I thought. Work at the restaurant was fine, MMDs went by at light speed, and the three weeks of practice before we were slated to perform at Miss Magdalene's church were, amazingly, not *that* stressful. At least not for me.

Don't get me wrong, there was loads of stress floating around at practice, but it was mostly relegated to the people who were actually going to be performing in the play. Due to the fact that I was new, I was told that I would be an understudy (the only understudy; everyone else had actual parts).

My main job was to put things in place, chairs mostly, and stay out of the way of the people who actually mattered. My task was easy for me because staying out of people's way was one of the things I was naturally good at. My official title was "understudy," but I was more of a glorified stagehand, which was fine with me.

The first week of all-out practice set the terrible tone for the "drama" that was to ensue. There were fierce spats about people's voice inflections during their line deliveries, drag-out quarrels about the benefits and drawbacks of adlibbing (adlibbing: a subject that made Paul's serial killer glasses fog up), and vicious brawls about who said what about whom behind whose back to whom, and why? Pure drama. It was like concentrating the most dramatic people you could find into a medium-sized, hot garage—a very bad idea.

Soliloquy

But all of the vicious fighting and verbal jousting paled in comparison to the main event: John vs. Mira! John and Mira were like Ali vs. Liston, or like cops vs. robbers, or like crazy people vs. context. They hated each other! They hated each other in a way I had never seen two people hate each other before. Their hate for each other made my hate for other people look like kindness. It was an inimitable, pure, unwavering hate. It seemed like they were born to be enemies, like the elder Montagues and the Capulets. It appeared that their ultimate success depended on the amount of hate they had and sustained for the other, as if the mere existence of one threatened the wellbeing of the other. It was a primeval hate that went below and beyond a simple logical reason. They fought, and fought, then fought some more.

At the first real practice they had an enormous fight about a scene where the two would have to hug one another. That was it: hug! Not kiss or make-out, but hug!

"I'm sorry, Miss Magdalene. I mean absolutely no disrespect by this, but I will not hug him. I won't do it," Mira said.

"Really?" John yelled. "You are so sick, you know that? You are sick in the head, seriously! You really need some professional help! You act like someone actually wants to touch you! I don't! But that's what actors have to do sometimes! That's their freakin' job! No one cares about how cool you think you are! No one cares! You are the only one who cares!"

"Really, John? I'm—"

"Are you two done acting like children? Or should I wait until you are done with the tantrums? I can wait." Miss Magdalene said. Her voice was calm and exhausted.

"I'm sorry, Miss Magdalene, I was not trying to start trouble. I am just stating how I feel. I think it is my right to state how I feel. I was not being offensive."

"Well, dear, how it came out *was* offensive. If you have a problem being touched, you should have come to me privately, not stated your concerns here, in front of the whole group. Also, John has a point. This is acting. It is not a game of match making. It is not *reality*. We are not here trying to set you two up. We are trying to tell a story that has little to do with you or John or anyone else here, for that matter. The story is what's important; we are simply trying to bring it to life. Sometimes in acting we have to do things that we don't always like.

"One time, while I was acting in New York, I had to kiss two girls directly on the mouth. Do you think that was something I wanted to do?"

Mira was looking down at the floor. "Umm, no. Probably not."

"No. It wasn't. But I wanted to be an actress. I wanted to help tell the story. So I had to do my duty. I did what I had to do to be an actress and to bring the story, not my personal point of view, to life. Do you understand what I am trying to say?"

"Yes."

"But I will see what I can do. If I can find a way to write that part out of the script and still be faithful to the soul of the play, I will do so. Okay?"

"Okay," Mira said.

John was looking at her with a hateful smirk.

Practices were full of John vs. Mira smash-ups. As the first show neared, Miss Magdalene added days (per week) to the practice schedule to make sure we (or more specifically, they) were "uncommonly prepared" for the show. But in reality, the more practices we had, the worse the play became. The extra time the troupe was forced to spend together only added drama and stress to an already dramatic and stressful situation.

But outside of practice, I was developing something that resembled an actual social life. After practices, I would hang out with Mira (and sometimes

Mira and Hannah). After our trip to the library we started seeing a lot more of each other. We went to movies (always horror films), on walks, and ate lots and lots of overpriced ice cream.

All the hanging out was cool, I guess, but extremely confusing. I didn't understand what it all meant. What was the point? Why was this crazy girl picking me, of all people, to spend her "important" time with?

It was easy for me to figure out why I was spending my time with her. That answer was simple. I didn't have anything better to do. I didn't really have any other friends. And other than work, MMD, and practice, I had nothing else to do, absolutely no other obligations. She was the first person that seemed to find me interesting (in a good way), so why would I reject her requests to hang out? How could I say *no* when she asked me? I couldn't. I couldn't pass up the opportunity to actually have a friend that thought I was more than just some weird nerd.

But the question that kept swimming around my mind was: What was *her* point? What was she doing spending her time with me rather than other people who matched her "cool" level? She was smart, most people would call her pretty (or extremely pretty), and she was sort of funny (if you're the type of person who thinks pranks are funny). She had all the attributes that make people popular in this world. So why was she wasting those attributes with me? Was she trying out an experiment on me, or something? Was I her charity case or her Guinea pig? Was she playing a joke on me? What was her point?

I bet there were tons of people, guys particularly, similar to her cool level that she could have found to hang out with. But she picked me. She picked me. Honestly, deep down, I felt, in a way, rewarded, proud, and privileged that she picked me. Despite all my questions and paranoia, I thought it was a good thing. But the feeling of worth and confidence it gave me was overshadowed by the unlikelihood of it being real.

I wanted to just be happy with my luck, but I couldn't. It was *too* lucky, *too* unlikely. My level of luck is what made me paranoid. "If it's too good to be true," as they say. It was as if I'd found a briefcase full of money in a bad neighborhood. We all know how that movie ends. But despite my paranoia, I tried to be content with my luck.

People say that guys and girls can't just be friends with one another. They say it always turns sexual. But even though we were hanging out quite a bit, it seemed like that was exactly what we were: *just* friends. There was no sexual component to what was going on with us. Except for the occasional joke where she would act like she was really into me and call me her boyfriend. But she would only do that when other guys she wanted to avoid were around.

Our friendship was purely Platonic. In reality, it was somehow even less than just friends. There was this one-sidedness to our relationship. It was as if I wasn't really there. I mean, when she talked to me it was like she was talking aloud to herself, or sleep talking, or as if she was narrating an entry for her diary, and I was simply there to transcribe it for her. It's not that she was ignoring me or intentionally being rude. It was just that when she got into one of her deep topics, she was taken up into a transcendental-like state. She seemed completely caught up in what she was saying and its importance. She was opening up her heart and soul, but it didn't seem like she was opening it up for me. Mira just needed someone there with her to witness her open up, to witness her as a feeling being, to witness her as a conscious thing. She just needed someone or something to hear her out.

Although I was not really participating in her transcendental trances, I was happy to be there. I was happy that she picked me to be her witness. I

Soliloquy

was just happy to be with her, a person who felt so deeply. I felt the pride of a witness at a spontaneous Las Vegas wedding. I wished that I could help her or say something to make her understand that I understood (even though I didn't fully understand). I wished I could have given her good answers or some kind of helpful philosophical advice. But I couldn't. Most of the time I didn't know what to say. I didn't have any way to help. So I did what I could do. I sat beside her and listened to every single word she said. And that seemed to be good enough for her.

She said to me, "You know, if it wasn't for you and Hannah, I probably would quit M troupe. I really would. I'm serious. You guys are what keep me in it. Yeah, sure, Miss Magdalene is a really nice lady who knows a lot about theater, and the acting can be fun sometimes, but overall, I'm over it. It's just too much work and too much stress. I can't stand all the drama and the bickering and the fighting. I can't stand being around John and all his ogre friends. Really. It just is beginning to be too tiresome. You have no idea."

"So why don't you quit if you're so miserable?" I couldn't believe what I'd said. My words came out all wrong. It was such a stupid thing to say. I wished I could take it back because it made me sound like I wanted her to quit. But I didn't. I needed her in the troupe more than she needed me. Without her, I would've been eaten alive by John and company.

She looked at me strangely. "Well, like I said, you and Hannah, for starters. You guys are my friends, the best friends I've got in this place. And I couldn't just quit right before our opening. That would be completely messed up. If I did that I would let everyone down. I'm not that selfish.

"Rachel wouldn't have enough time to learn all my lines correctly, and everyone would have to be switched around to make it all work. Miss Magdalene would hate me, and Paul would probably try to disembowel me. I couldn't do that to the group. And my mom wouldn't let me quit right now. She's all about, if you start something, you better finish it. So if I tried to quit she would completely freak."

"Well, I completely understand. But this play will all be over soon. So maybe things will be better after it's all over... maybe. Maybe everyone will be less stressed."

"I doubt it." She dropped her head into her hands. "D-stain and John and the others will still be there to bother the shit out of me, no matter what."

"Yeah. You're probably right."

"I know I'm right."

"You don't think you can find a way to get along with him or ignore him?" I said.

"Who, John? I've tried! I've tried and tried and tried and tried. He is just repulsive to me. He is just not a nice person. You know, some people are just not good inside. Something has gone awry in them. There's something fucked up in his insides. He's just so full of himself, and inconsiderate, and arrogant, and nasty. How can I get along with someone like that? How?

"I have tried to ignore him, but that just makes him try harder to get under my skin. Ignoring him won't stop him. It makes him worse. It's not like I want to fight with him. I don't like to fight. I don't want to be miserable every time we have practice. But as long as he is the lead, I am going to have to put up with his egotistical shit."

I didn't know what to say. "I guess you have a point. I have noticed that he kinda has a stick up his ass sometimes."

"Yes. He does. See? And him having a stick up his ass makes me have a stick up my ass. It's like a vicious cycle. But yeah, maybe after this play it will go back to a tolerable level of annoyance like it was before we started rehearsing for this stupid play. But if it doesn't, I am going to be forced to quit. At that point, I don't care who gets pissed about it. I have to do what I have to do."

"Well, I hope it gets better," I said. "It would really suck if you quit. Hannah and I wouldn't have a third for our group circles."

She giggled and touched my hand. "If I ever do quit, are we still going to hang out?"

"If you want to. Sure."

"Of course I want to, silly. The question is do you want to?"

"Yes. Of course."

"Are you sure?"

"Of course. Yes."

"Do you promise?"

"Do I promise what?"

"Do you promise that we will hang out even if I quit?"

"I promise," I said. I was confused. "I promise we will still hang out."

"Okay. Good."

***

Hell Week:

<u>Tuesday</u>

The second-to-last practice before we were scheduled to perform at Miss Magdalene's church (*The Holy Missionary Church of Brotherhood, Love, and Jesus Christ*) brought me face-to-face with my greatest fear: the possibility that I might actually have to perform in the play! Like I said, my job as an understudy really didn't entail much actual understudying. No one, myself most of all, ever expected that I might have to perform on stage, so why really learn and practice lines? Why pay close attention? Why be involved? I didn't waste my time learning lines or thinking about character development. I didn't waste my time because I was too busy moving chairs and homemade set props around the big garage.

I was completely comfortable with my permanent position as what most in the troupe called "prop-bitch." I had happily settled into chair moving, invitation mailing, and say-no-evil-do-no-evil silence. It was easy. It was me. "Prop-bitch" was a near-stress-free job; things were smooth. I was semi-fraternizing with people, and I didn't want to execute myself when I was around them. Being tolerated at practice was the closest I had ever come to being socially accepted. My fear and hate for people was under control more than it had ever been. My panic attacks had all but vanished. I had a girl who was my friend and she was "cool." My life was going as efficiently as my life could go. But as they say, there is always calm before the storm, and the dark gray storm clouds were forming with frightening speed, and I didn't even notice it.

When I entered the muggy garage that Tuesday, I could immediately tell that something was awry and that I was part of the problem. The first thing I noticed was two sets of eyes fixed on me like bright police spotlights. Paul and Miss Magdalene stared at me unblinkingly, with injured, stagnant glares. At first, I thought that I might have been late, but looking at the half-empty seats (and my trusty Casio calculator watch) and the horror on Paul's pasty-pale face, I was alerted to the fact that something much worse was going on. Paul's face had the terror of a child coming face-to-face with the real live, closet-residing, fang-toothed boogie man. The look on his face was twisted in a sad, confused panic, and he looked like he was literally going to let out a sob at any moment.

Miss Magdalene's look was much less terrified but much more serious. She looked angry, exhausted, and in a hurry. She started towards me, her

Soliloquy

low-heeled shoes popping on the ground with firecracker sounds. I was startled.

"We need to talk," she said in a stinging voice.

"Okay?"

"Follow me."

Miss Magdalene led me out of the garage, through a few sets of hall-ways I had never been down before, to a room that I didn't know existed. It looked to be a makeshift knitting-sewing-junk-storage room. The room was cluttered with tons of colorful eye-assaulting fabrics, piles of tan cardboard boxes, and moldering, disjointed, discolored manikins. There were photos and old magazine pages everywhere, on every wall.

"Okay." She slammed the door behind me. Her face was slightly twist-ed with irritation. "What I brought you in here to talk about is this: there is a possibility that you might have to take John's role when we go on this Sun-day. A few minutes ago, we got a call from John's mother, and she said that John wasn't feeling well, very badly, and he couldn't make it to practice today."

"Well, it's only Tuesday, maybe he'll be okay by Thursday's or Satur-day's practice," I said worriedly. I had spoken automatically. Terror had not set in, but I could feel it approaching in distant regions of my body. I couldn't fully fathom her words, but I knew the clearer they became, the worse I would feel. I felt like a bear starting to come out of hibernation. My panic had been sleeping, dormant, and her words were poking at it with a stick. I could feel the panic tossing and jerking.

Miss Magdalene was silent for a long time. Her forehead coiled tightly like a rattlesnake. The whites of her eyes were slowly becoming red, as if my words were drops of salt, and her cheekbones protruded like the shoulder blades of an emaciated person. A worm-size vein grew on the right side of her forehead, and I literally could see it pulsing. It seemed that she had completely run out of patience, and the only thing that kept her from physically tearing my head off with her bare hands was her near-empty tank of will-power.

"Excuse me," she said sharply. Her voice was so harsh that it made me flinch. "May I please finish?"

"Yes. Sorry. I'm sorry."

"As I was saying: he can't make it to practice today, and his mother said that his condition seems to be getting worse by the minute. She said if he gets any sicker she will have to take him to the emergency room. This means that we have to act as if he is getting sicker, and we have to prepare for the worst. If he comes back by Thursday or Saturday, great! But we can't hang our hats on hopes. Hope it not a *plan B*. Hope is not how one prepares for an important event. We need to take concrete measures to prepare for whatever the case may be on Sunday.

"We don't know what's wrong with him, and we don't know when he'll be coming back. It is that simple. So we have to act as if he's not coming back. That is the only sensible thing to do. Do you understand? So. Okay. You are his understudy. I know you haven't gotten very much practice with everyone, but do you know your lines?"

Her words made me confused. John sick… sicker? Me, know *my* lines? What she said seemed like foreign humor to me. John being sick or getting sick seemed unnatural. He was a muscular, athletic, Schwarzeneggion beast. Beasts don't get sick!—do they? You never heard of an NFL football star coming down with a cold or mono! Who comes down with the flu-or-something during summer? It didn't make any sense. It seemed like a joke, but it wasn't a joke. I couldn't process it.

Soliloquy

The air in the room felt thin. I was losing my breath, and my body started to heat up rapidly like a hog being rotisseried over a campfire. The bear was waking. The stick had worked. What? I thought. *What is she saying? This really can't be, can it? This can't be real.*

"Know John's lines?" I said.

"Yes! The lead's lines. Old Man Gleaner's lines. Do you know them?"

"Yes, I do." Again, the words had seeped out of my mouth before I could understand their significance. Again, my instincts had failed miserably. Again, I had said something that I did not really mean, something I knew to be absolutely false. Again, I had lied when I most needed to tell the truth. I was lying, completely lying, but I didn't know why. It just kept happening. I didn't think of myself as a person who lied all the time, but there I was, lying again, over and over again. Of course I didn't know John's lines, or anyone else's for that matter. I didn't ever study the script. The only time I would look at it was when I was tired of moving things around and was trying to look like I was doing something. Why did I tell her I knew John's lines? I had to fix my mistake, but how? "Um, I mean, I know some of the lines. I haven't really had a chance to memorize them all, because I never really practiced them, or anything, at practice, you know? Do you think one of the other guys might know?"

"Know what? Know the lines that you were supposed to learn? No. I don't think so. I don't think that someone would have learned the lines that you were supposed to learn. I think that at this point we don't have time for magic! We don't have time to switch a million people around. If I give someone else John's part, someone else would have to learn that person's part, and someone else, that persons' part, and so on. Do you understand? That means that multiple people would be trying to perform parts that they are not prepared for, not just one. If I give the person with the second largest part John's part, who's going to perform the *second* largest part? No one? That would ruin the entire performance as well. If you don't know your lines—"

"I mean, I know them. I know the lines, for the most part. And what I don't have memorized I can definitely have memorized by Saturday. I just haven't had the chance to practice them aloud." I kept lying! It was like I couldn't stop myself.

"Okay, then. You will have time to practice today. You need to get yourself together and realize how much everyone is now relying on you—counting on you. You are smart, aren't you?" she said, trying her best to sound sincere.

"I don't know. I guess so."

"No! You *are* smart. You know that. I know you know that. I know that. You can do this. Trust me. It's not as bad as it seems right now. Trust me. I have faith in you and your abilities. A lot of people are really relying on you, starting right now. If you pull this off, you will be a hero. Think about that. A real live hero. Everyone in the troupe will be so proud of you, and they will all look up to you. I'm sure your parents would be proud of you, too. Look, you might not even have to go on. Who knows? We don't really know what exactly is going to happen. John might just have the 24-hour flu. It happens. It is possible.

"But if you do have to go on: do it! Make yourself proud. Okay? That's what it's really all about, making *yourself* proud. You need to show yourself that you can do something difficult, if you put your mind to it, believe in yourself, and work hard. That is really all it takes. If you work hard, and believe, you can do almost anything.

"I remember you told me that you've watched numerous plays, right? You told me you love watching plays, and you love art. I remember you said that. If you love acting and you've watched a lot of things, tons of plays, then you have what it takes. You know what it takes. You've witnessed what it takes over and over again. You've seen it firsthand.

"I'm not saying that it is as easy as it looks. It's not. But I'm saying you already have all the references you need. Now all you need to do is pull the goods out of yourself and believe. They are all in there. This just might be your moment. This, what seems like a negative, might just be your big moment to shine and prove something to yourself. Many people never get their moment to shine, or they completely miss their moment when it comes to them. But you don't have to. You don't have to be one of those people who miss out. You could take this chance and make this your big moment, your big break. If you pull this off, we might write a play about you someday." She tried, unsuccessfully, to form a smile.

"I will try," I said. Despite her passionate words of wisdom, my panic was fully upon me. Although I could hear her, the panic that rang in my ears would not allow her words to register. I could feel cold lines of sweat parachuting down my back. Rows of perspiration were welling up on my forehead. My stomach was doing very crazy, abnormal things. I wanted to puke. I wanted to sit down.

She said, "No! Don't try, don't try… do!" The harshness was creeping back into her voice. "There is no reason you should feel like you can't do this! What's the worst that can happen? Really? The worst thing that can happen is that a person who has never acted a day before in his life, with just a few days to prepare, isn't Al Pacino or Marlon Brando! Really? So what? The new guy isn't at Oscar caliber? Would that be a surprise to anyone? No. No one expects you to be perfect. Almost no one is perfect.

"Stranger things have happened than an unprepared person not being the greatest thing since sliced bread. Much stranger things have happened.

Soliloquy

At least you have an excuse, a good excuse at that. But your excuse is also your opportunity.

"What you should ask yourself, what you really should care about is: what's the *best* that can happen? *That's* the question, the only real question. The best thing that can happen is that John comes back, and you go back to doing whatever it is you were doing before this whole thing happened. *Or...* *or...* the other best thing that can happen, the best thing that can happen is that you can step up to the plate and make a breakthrough for yourself. The best thing that can really happen, for you, is that a guy with only a few days of actual practice *is* the next Al Pacino! He *is* Brando! He *is* a great actor, perhaps the greatest actor of his generation. The best thing that can happen is that the strange actually happens! The best thing that can happen is that you are the best thing since sliced bread. Do you understand? Do you see?

"If we need you, and you don't step on that stage and give it all you've got, who knows what you are? Who knows what kind of person that makes you? Who knows what you have the potential to do or not do? Who knows if you were or weren't the next Oscar-worthy actor to be born? No one knows what they are capable of until they *do*. Doing is being.

"Do you think that De Niro knew he was The Robert De Niro before he ever stepped on stage? Of course not. He became who he was after he *proved* it to himself and to others. You will not know who you are unless you put yourself in a position to find out who you are. Courage is only shown through courageous acts, not through theorizing or hoping. Not through talking about courage, but from doing the courageous thing. Charity is only shown through charitable acts, not through wishing that one day the chance to be charitable will just randomly appear.

"'Without trial there is no progress.' So, I know I am saying a lot, but I am basically saying this: I need you to prepare yourself for the play as if you

Soliloquy

were going to be the lead on Sunday. I need you to believe that you are ca-
pable of doing what I am asking you to do, because I know you're capable.
And then, I need you to do it—do it. I need you to do your best, nothing less.
Do you understand?"

"Yes, I understand." My head was tingling. Her words had pushed my
mind away from the panic and placed it in her stern, matter-of-fact reality. I
realized that I did not have the option of letting her down. I had to prepare. I
didn't much care if I let most of the others down, but letting Miss Magdalene
down would have been inhumane. Letting her down would have been like
letting down an innocent child or a fairy godmother. I understood that I had
to believe what she said, no matter what she said, because she believed what
she said. She was true. I could tell. She was true and good.

Her words, her fixed face, and the laser-sharp trust in her eyes made me
realize that there were some people that I had to put ahead of my own interest (or disinterest), purely because they believed in their vision of life much
more than I believed (or disbelieved) in my own. Her belief was worth more
than my fear and incredulity combined. I could see that she felt what she
said more than I had ever felt anything in my whole entire life. And what she
believed in was potential: me and my potential. Somehow, I felt that she
believed in human potential much more than I believe in my own existence
("I think, therefore I am" rarely ever did the trick for me). On her face I could
see a guarantee of her statements and beliefs. There's something about
someone telling the truth. She did not have hope, she had knowledge, wisdom. I saw that her beliefs were beliefs that were stronger than the ones
people were willing to die for; hers were so strong that she was willing to
live by them. What she said and what she felt went beyond opinion and pep
talking; her words were built out of the same material that reality itself was

built out of. I had to believe what she said. I had to believe that I could do it, even though I believed I couldn't.

As I stood there with my mind spinning between worry, disbelief, awe, and shaky resignation, there was a small, almost inaudible, tapping on the door. Paul leaned his small face in timidly, as if he expected a knife to be thrown in his direction.

"Sissy?" he whispered in a baby's voice. "Mostly everyone's here. Do you want me to just go ahead and start practice?" His head was still barely peeking in the doorway; all I could see was his beady eyes behind his bulky glasses, his forehead, and his scraggly hair.

"Hold on a minute. We're almost done. I'll be there shortly. Just go back, and act like everything is normal."

"K."

"So, where were we?"

"Oh, um, I was saying that I would do it. Prepare. Do my best."

"Well, that's good. That is all you can truly do." She took a few steps towards me and put her heavy hand on my shoulder and smiled. Her smile was not forced like usual; it was full, tired, and frightfully genuine. She said, "Son, trust yourself. Trust yourself. Trust yourself. We need you, and you need you. Okay? Trust." She gave me two hard pats on the back and led me back out into the hallway.

As we entered the garage, I started shaking. Everyone was in their normal seats. Miss Magdalene took hold of my elbow and led me to the front. No one was paying us any attention until Miss Magdalene cleared her throat at the decibels of a severe thunderclap.

"AAHHAAAHUMMMMMM! Excuse me. We need to get started. But first, I have some important information to relay." Everyone looked our way with sluggish confusion and predetermined boredom. "The news is: first,

Soliloquy

please try to restrain yourselves from overreacting, which is for some of you your natural tendency. The news is that John is sick, and we are unsure when he will be ready to perform." A loud burst of melodramatic sighs went up from the front row, from all of John's cronies. Then most of the others echoed with less powerful, less authentic, but nonetheless, demoralizing sighs and gasps.

As the sighs went up, Miss Magdalene's hard grasp tightened around my elbow. She did not look at me. She just stood there stone-faced, waiting for the sighing to die down.

After a few seconds she said, "Is everyone done? Are you done acting like children? Is it okay for us to get back to business now? Okay, thank you. Are you sure? And thank you for not overreacting like I asked you not to. I appreciate it. Can I continue talking, please?"

The sighing subsided into low puppy moans. Then the moans were replaced by rustling seats and loud whispers. Eyes slowly started to land on me. Everyone was frowning sadly, everyone except Mira. I could see she had a clear look on her face. I could tell that the rest of the news Miss Magdalene had to give them was not going to go over well. I started getting sweatier.

"To finish, if I may. Since John is out for an undisclosed amount of time, John's understudy," she side-nodded her head towards me, "will be taking over his part until he returns."

Almost simultaneously, the entire front row doubled over in their chairs as if they were all punched in the stomach by an invisible bully. A few front-rowers put their hands over their faces in absolute horror and defeat. There was a small roar of rushed words, someone yelled "FUCK!", and Paul literally started sobbing in the corner where he stood. He was holding the big cream-colored cat like a mother holding a baby that needs rocking. The room filled with frizzed commotion. It was like Miss Magdalene had yelled: "FIRE!" Everything was moving and talking and rustling and freaking out.

Miss Magdalene just stood there like a hundred-year-old tree, holding my arm, still. My chest felt crushed and air-deprived. I felt like I needed to sit down or take a poop or something. I felt sick all over. I could hear my mind saying: I would rather be dead than be here. I hate these people! They act like I'm the plague. Forget them, I won't do it! They don't want me, okay! I won't do it!

I tried to pull my arm way from Miss Magdalene (my legs were visibly shaking. I needed to sit down), but her grip didn't budge. So I leaned over and closed my eyes to keep from getting dizzy. It felt like the commotion in the room was literally crawling on my skin. I just closed my eyes and tried not to be there in my head.

As I bent there shaking, in a kind of standing fetal position, I felt a soft hand on the side of my back. It startled me, and I cringed as if I was being seared by a cattle iron.

The voice of the hand yelled, "Hey!" I did not recognize the voice, but I recognized the hand. "Excuse me! Are you guys serious right now? Huh? You can't be freakin' serious!" The other voices quieted down. "How dumb is it for you to act like this is the end of the world? John got sick; things happen! Any one of you could get sick tomorrow—it happens—people get sick! But to hoop and act crazy like ferals and put more pressure on him than he already has is absolutely insane.

"It's completely counterintuitive if what you want is for this play to succeed! Isn't that what you want? The play to go well? For the play to actually happen? Isn't that what we all want? We've all put our heart and sweat in this. If that's what you want, the play to go on, then stop being stupid and inconsiderate!

Soliloquy

"How would you feel if you were new and had the responsibility to take over a major part of a play at the last minute, huh? Do any of you remember when you first started? Do any of you have any empathy at all? Remember? It was enough pressure just to meet new people and try to fit in, let alone learning lines and trying to perform them. So why are you guys acting like it's his fault that John is sick? You don't even know him! You don't know what he's capable of. If it's anyone's fault that John is sick, it is John's fault for not taking good enough care of himself. That's not what I meant, but you know what I mean: anyone can get sick and it may not be anyone's fault. So don't take it out on the wrong person. Don't be rude. Why put more pressure on him than he already has? That's just stupid!"

The entire time Mira spoke I was hunched over with my eyes closed, trying not to fall out of consciousness. But when she finished, Miss Magdalene lifted me upright by the elbow. I opened my eyes and saw defeated, resentful faces.

"Thank you, Mira," Miss Magdalene said. "At least one of you understands the gravity of the situation."

"I do understand. I was new not very long ago, and I know how hard it is. And if any of you keep acting like that you will have to find two new leads, because I won't be part of a troupe that is cool with bringing people down and hurting people for no reason."

"Quitting won't be necessary, Mira, because if anyone else acts out in that fashion again I will shut down the entire production. There will not be a show. I refuse to put my name behind something so negative and unethical."

The entire room was completely silent.

Mira put her arm around my neck and said, "Are you okay? You can do this. I know you can." I did not respond. I was too focused on my breathing.

Soliloquy

Miss Magdalene said, "Okay. Are we all back on the same page?" No one answered. They all just looked at her blankly, like heavily sedated mental patients. "Well, if we want to pull this off, we have no more time to waste. There are only five days until we go on, and we need every single minute. D, you and some of the guys arrange the chairs, please." No one moved. "Everyone move—now! Let's go. It is practice—move! Nothing has changed. Get into your groups and start working on your dialogue rotations. Thank you."

Everyone started to move as slow as humanly possible. They all slogged to their spots like lazy living-dead.

Miss Magdalene pulled me to the side. "Okay. Remember what we talked about. Now is the time for you to pull yourself together. Pull yourself together, okay? Okay. Now is the time for you to show up and prove to yourself that you can do something big. Let's go. You'll be working with Mira and me today, mostly, so don't worry. Let's go. Pull yourself together."

I wished I could pull myself together, but honestly, I didn't know how; I didn't know where to start. I felt like three-day-old trash, and there was little to nothing I could do about it. The troupe had rejected me, John had put me in an awful position, and I had screwed myself by not actually studying the script. Things were bad all over. What knowledge or abilities did I have to pull myself together? If I was good at pulling myself together… I would have done it a long time ago. Clearly, I wasn't. I was a mess. The most I could do was fight to stay conscious and not faint from lack of oxygen to my brain.

Still gripping my arm firmly, Miss Magdalene led me to a seat. Mira followed.

She sat down and said, "Okay. Now, first things first: do you have the soliloquy memorized yet?"

"Um... nnnnn... no... not completely." Of course, I had none of it memorized.

"Okay. Well, that is the most important part. It sets the tone for the entire thing."

"Yeah," I said. This soliloquy was the play's big opening. Old Man Gleaner was supposed to step out on the stage and give a deep speech about God, and Mankind, and blah, blah, blah. Paul had written most of it, or so he said, and he said it was his "most poignant piece of literary writing to date." The soliloquy was a big deal. It was the play's first impression. It would set the tone for everything else that was to happen. It was not everything, but it was almost everything, and I had to memorize it as if they were my own words. The soliloquy had the most consecutive lines in the play. If I could get it down, memorized, the hardest part would be over. But that was a very big *if*.

"Okay. Now. What I want you to do is read the soliloquy to yourself a few times, okay? While he does that, Mira, I want you to read to yourself as well. Then I want you to give him an idea of what you think it should be like: inflection, movements, rhythm, et cetera. Show him how John does it. Then I want you to read it aloud to her. Got it? Are we clear?"

"Yes, ma'am," I said. I felt entirely terrible, but I was ready to try.

We did what Miss Magdalene demanded. Mira and I read silently (which took a long time since I actually had to take it seriously), then she read it to me dramatically, with hand motions and facial expressions, then I read it to her from the page.

"'There comes a time in every man's—"

"No, no, no," Mira said. "You need to be more emphatic. You need to genuinely feel what you are saying, as if it is truly coming from your own mind, your own spontaneous mind. 'There comes a time in every man's life when he will have to make the choice! He will have to choose between be-lieving in a world where man is the determiner, the chooser of his *own* pur-pose, his *own* destiny. Or he will have to choose to believe in an omnipresent, omnipotent, loving God.' You see? 'It *does not* matter the man's education, occupation, or portion in so-called society. *Every man* must choose. I am a mere farmer. Nothing more, nothing less.' Okay. Do you see how I empha-size some of the words so you can get my meaning?"

"Yeah, I get it. That was really good."

"Thanks. But, okay. You try."

I tried a couple of times to do what she did, and a couple of times I failed. Before I knew it, Miss Magdalene was saying that practice would be coming to an end in ten minutes. She called us all together to give us all one more pep talk. I was too tired to listen.

On my way out of the warm garage, I was surprised by the fact that I had made it through rehearsal without messing my pants or fainting or up-chucking. A ton of stuff was thrown at me all at once: finding out that Johnxander The Great was sick (and mortal), finding out that I might have to be the lead in a play that I had only read through once or twice, having to stand up in front of all those jerk-offs for the horrible announcement that I might have to be the lead (which they took as the ruin of the play), and then actually having to practice as the lead, thoroughly disappointing my only real friend. It was a lot for me to handle in a year, let alone a span of a couple of hours. Excitement, uncertainty, and "drama" were three things I had al-ways tried to keep out of my life. There were so many times I was for-sure I was going to black out, but miraculously, I had held it off. My consciousness had held its ground against a tempest of dreadful surprises and oxygen dep-rivation. I was, in a way, like Miss Magdalene had predicted: proud of my-self.

Soliloquy

As I opened my car door, I felt a hand on my shoulder. "Mira wants you to wait for a second," Hannah said.

"Oh. Okay." I waited in my hot car for a minute or two.

"Hey!" Mira said. She skipped to the car with a broad smile. "Hey, are you okay?"

"Yeah, I'm okay."

"Okay. Listen. I know you're nervous." She stuck her head in the car window. "So, look, tomorrow I want us to get together and go over our lines. Okay? All day, as long as you want, until you get your lines down perfectly. Okay? We will stay up all night if we have to, pull an all-nighter. I am going to do everything I can to help you. I'm here to help, okay?"

"Oh. Thanks. But, um, but I think I might actually have work tomorrow."

Her caring look quickly turned into a judgmental, motherly frown. "Well, I suggest you call off work tomorrow. You understand that you don't have much time, don't you? You understand that, right? We have just a few days to get you to be the best you can be. Other than sleeping and eating, I suggest that you put all your plans on hold until after the play is over. Am I making sense? You can work anytime, just call off. The play is on Sunday, and you are just now learning your lines. You need practice, and I am willing to help you. It would be wise for you to take me up on my offer if you don't want to be embarrassed on Sunday night."

I tried the best I could to configure my face into a look of understanding and thankfulness. "Yes. You're totally right. I don't know what I was talking about. You're right. I need to focus on the play. I don't know what I was saying. I am just kind of tired and out of it from all the information I've had to take in today. But, yeah, you're right. I need to focus on the play. I understand."

Soliloquy

"Okay. I will call you tomorrow morning. What time will you be up?"

"Uuuumm—"

"7… 8?"

"I'll say 8. Yeah, around 8… I guess."

She pulled her head out of the window. "Okay. I will call you about 8 tomorrow. Then we can start rehearsing. Okay?"

"Okay."

It was not okay. I didn't want to spend all day rehearsing *The Poor Man's Prayer*. I just wanted to sleep and be alone. As I drove away, I realized that what appeared to be the best few weeks of my life was really just the prelude to my nightmare scenario: me on stage, completely unprepared, in front of tons of phony people I didn't know. It was like the nightmare that people always talked about, of being naked in front of a class with everyone laughing at you and pointing at your dong; that was more or less about to happen to me—except for the nudity. Hopefully, I wouldn't be naked, but I was sure to be just as embarrassed. I didn't know what to do.

As I drove, catching every red stoplight, an aching fatigue set in. My muscles and my brain both started hurting deep down. Even my bones were in pain. I started to wonder if I had the strength to make it home before one of my episodes took hold. The wondering about an episode started to cause me more worries, which only added to my anxiety and the likelihood of another episode. I could feel ambiguously flavored vomit slowly inching up my throat. I pressed on the pathetic gas pedal and hoped like hell that I could push through for just a few more minutes, just until I made it home. After running a stoplight and rolling through two four-way stops, I rounded the corner to my street. It was the first bit of relief I had felt since the news.

When I got out of the car, I felt too weak to make it to the front door. Everything in me was exhausted. My legs felt like bags of jelly. The grass looked like a good enough spot to rest and regain my strength (if there was any strength left to regain), so I hunch-crawled to a spot of green next to the driveway. It was 80-plus degrees outside, but the grass felt cool and spongy. I realized that I couldn't remember ever actually playing in the grass as a kid or even lying down in it. I couldn't remember climbing a tree or wanting a tree house. I couldn't remember doing anything all that reckless, childish, or dangerous. I thought: I bet Mira would love to see me lying here like this. She would be proud of me.

I closed my eyes, but I could still see the dull orange sunlight through my eyelids. I wasn't thinking about the play or my pain or anything. My only thought was how nice the grass was. In my head I kept saying: You have to do this more often. It's nice.

I must have fallen asleep or blacked out, because I was startled by a shout: "What are you doing there? Get up, now!"

It was my mother. Her head was peeking out from behind the screen door. She was frowning the most disgusted frown she could muster.

"What are you doing in the grass?"

"I'm just res—"

"Come in the house if you want to rest. That's what your bed is for. Come on."

As I rolled to my stomach, hoping to downward-dog my way to my feet, a hot half-gallon of brown mystery stench detonated from somewhere deep in my insides, spewing all over the soft green grass. My mother shrieked like someone being murdered.

I wiped my mouth with my shirt and went in the house.

***

<u>Wednesday</u>

I don't remember the rest of Tuesday, honestly. Not even a little bit. All I remember is the phone ringing at 7:48 in the morning.

I was not asleep when the phone rang. I distinctly remember not being asleep. I was sitting on the edge of my bed, wearing the exact same clothes I had on the day before. My shirt even had a smelly, brown bib of vomit about the neck from the day before. It was incredibly weird, surreal. Had I blacked out for an entire night? My hands were in my lap, my shoes were on my feet; it was like I was just waiting, waiting for the phone to ring.

After three or four rings I picked it up.

"Hel-*hum-um*... Hello?"

"Hey! You ready to get this party going or what?"

"What?"

"I'm trying to get you pumped up. Are you ready to get together and practice?" Mira said.

"Umm, yeah. Sure. Where, um, where do you want to meet?"

"You wanna meet me at my house? We can practice here or at the library." Both of her options sounded terrible to me, so I went with the devil I knew.

"I guess I can pick you up, and we can go to the library. I think that would work. They have some rooms in the back for studying and stuff. Maybe we can use one of those rooms. I'm not sure if you need a reservation in advance or anything for them though, but—"

"Okay. That'll be fine. I'm all ready to go."

"Oh, okay. I just have something to do, and I'll be on my way."

"Okay. Sounds great." She hung up.

I debated whether or not I should take a shower before I left. I could clearly smell myself. It was not a good smell. After realizing I still felt like shit, the same as the day before, I decided that I should just wash the vomit bits off my neck and chest, brush my teeth, change my shirt, and get on with it.

When I got downstairs, the house was silent and empty. My mom was gone, maybe at a Bible study, I thought.

As I walked outside, large, low clouds were bloated with a gray sadness. The dark saggy clouds made a murky canopy over the entire viewable area. How quickly the weather can change, I thought. It was like there was a bulky wool blanket where the sky used to be. As soon as I looked up I was instantly sadder. It looked like rain was just waiting to pounce at the most inopportune time. I thought about going in and getting an umbrella but decided to not waste that energy.

The car made extra-loud rhythmic rattling noises. I thought: Well, Shit-stain, if you break, at least I'll have an excuse not to practice today. But the breakdown never came; it just kept clicking and clanking to its own frightening beat.

When I clanked up to Mira's house, she was waiting on the edge of her driveway. She was clutching her big blue purse, and she was wearing a plastic-looking raincoat that had multi-colored daisies all over it (she had the hood pulled over her head). On her feet were neon pink galoshes that matched a set of flowers on the coat. The raincoat was short, but I couldn't see any shorts or who-knows-what underneath. She looked to be wearing only a raincoat and pink rain boots.

"Hey," she said.

"Hey. You sure you don't want to stay here and rehearse? Rain looks to be coming."

"Uaa, yeah. The library will be fine."

Soliloquy

She frowned, got in, and slammed the door shut. We didn't speak much on the way to the library. She asked if she could change the radio station, but that was it. She seemed upset about something, but I didn't want her to go into some philosophical tirade, so I didn't ask her what she might be upset about. I just drove.

She said, "Do you have your script?" as we pulled into the library parking lot.

"Yeah… I think… I think it's in the back seat. "

She violently threw off her seatbelt and crawled over the middle console to get the script from behind my seat. Then she rolled it up tightly and stuffed it in her purse.

"Do you have yours with you?" I said, trying to keep the conversation going.

"No! Why would I? It's just a few days before the play. I have all my lines memorized. Why would I still need a script?" Her tone was soaked in snappiness.

"Of course. I wasn't thinking. You're right. I wasn't thinking."

"It's fine. Let's just get this over with."

At that moment I was wondering if this was the "PMS" problem I heard about on TV. Why was she upset? She seemed upset for absolutely no reason. I hadn't done anything to her. To address her rudeness might make her mad, but I figured: What the hell, she's already mad. It can't get much worse. "Is everything okay?" I said, trotting up the library steps behind her. She was speed walking. I had to jog to keep up. "Did I do something wrong?"

"No, not exactly. It's just… I just don't understand why you're always so standoffish about coming into my house and stuff. It's really weird if you ask me. It's like you're cool hanging out with me as long as it's out in public. I don't get that. Are you too frightened to come inside my house or something? I don't get it. And you never have me over to your house, either. What's with that?"

I had no clue what she was talking about, where it was coming from, or why it mattered so much.

"Oh, no! I would love to see your house. The outside of it is really nice. I bet it's nice in the inside, too. I just thought you were trying to be nice. You know, offering just to be nice. You know, like people ask, 'Would you like something to drink?' when you go in their house, to be nice, because that's the socially acceptable thing to say to guests and stuff. I thought that's why you were offering... to be nice. The next time I'll come in. I'll come in for-sure. I misread that one, that's all. I just thought you were being mannerly." I had no idea if what I said would solve her invented problem, but I hoped to God it would. If it didn't, I was screwed.

A word of wisdom: When in doubt, always blame yourself; other people love that. That's always the safest bet.

She finally stopped walking, spun around, looked at me and said, "If I offer something, it's never just to be nice. Never. My offers always have a point! Otherwise they would be pointless." By this time, we were in the main hall of the library. Her voice echoed loudly, causing a few worker ladies to stare.

"Okay. I'm sorry. I am. Like I said, I misunderstood. I won't misunderstand the next time you ask me. That was my fault. I know now."

"Okay." My response seemed to appease her, but not quite cheer her up.

"I'm going to ask one of the librarians about a key for a study room."

She grabbed my wrist. "No. I'll take care of it."

As she "took care of it," I stood there thinking about how awful a start my day was off to, and how awful the other day had been. It seemed like I

Soliloquy

couldn't do anything right, couldn't catch even the smallest of breaks. Every second there was a new stab of pressure and discomfort being shoved deep inside my gut. Mira, the person who had said she would do everything she could to help me, seemed to be doing everything she could to concoct a reason to be mad at me. I had wasted the night before doing god-knows-what instead of studying, and I couldn't remember what god-knows-what was. I was falling apart right before my own eyes, and there seemed to be absolutely nothing I could do about it. Every turn was the wrong turn. As I stood there pitying myself, Mira waved for me to follow her as a tiny hipster librarian led the way.

The private study room was cold and snowed under in an awkward yellow light. The room had a tarnished dry-erase board bolted to the wall, an old round wooden table (decorated by deviants with obscene carvings), three small hard plastic chairs, and a large window that was muddled with a CSI's wet dream: tons of big greasy fingerprints and other unidentified fluids.

Mira reached in her purse and pulled out my script. "Okay. Is it warm in here? It's warm in here, right?"

"Umm. I guess it's a little warm," I said. It was actually cold.

She set her purse down in the empty seat. Then she slowly started to untie the belt on her bright raincoat. I sat there watching, riveted, wondering what she had on underneath the coat. The suspense was like unwrapping an overly wrapped birthday present. She took her time unbuttoning each button. I could feel myself getting nervous. When she was done unbuttoning, she slipped the coat off her shoulders like a lingerie model slipping off a silk bathrobe.

She had on an old cutoff Marilyn Monroe t-shirt that draped off one shoulder like an orbiting moon drapes its planet. The length (or lack thereof) of her black shirt suggested that the cutting-off was done by her; the bottom half of Marilyn's face was missing. Mira's entire smooth stomach showed. Her stomach was flat, but not skinny.

She had on dark weathered blue jean shorts that were incredibly tiny, about four or five inches from waist to fringe. They were tight everywhere except for the waist. There was a space between her waist and the short's waistband that a belt could have taken care of. Her hips were perfect. Womanly. And her legs were firm, shiny, and silky.

I had never seen her like that before. I had looked at her so many times, but I had never truly *seen* her body in that light. It was like finding out that someone you had known your whole life had an amazing talent that you never knew about. She was the loveliest thing I had ever seen in my life. All I wanted to do was touch her. Not in an aggressive way, but in a way that would tell her I understood.

As she stood there in front of me, for the first time in my life I understood. I understood what sex could mean to a reverent person. I could comprehend the hazard and calamity that rests deep within primal passions. I understood the urge, the compulsion, the *need* to reproduce, to pro-CREATE, and to co-CREATE. I could feel a connection to the future of mankind. I understood the perverse yet powerful nature of instinct and rush of lust. I could understand the saying: Thinking with your other head (and why the saying was true and sometimes inescapable)! I understood that most poets didn't mean sex when they said love; Sex was wanting, love was understanding. I became a believer in Muses. I understood why people made terrible decisions with stupid people in dreadful places. I understood why guys could care less about little Miss Pastornail's past or personality. And why they would only want to be with her in the present, completely absorbed in a set of fleeting present moments, lost in the carnal *Now*! I fully understood a new part of life that I hadn't known existed—a part I hadn't cared existed—a part that I had underestimated. Looking at her standing there in those few seconds, instantiating the perfected human form, I felt my first true flash of enlightenment and manhood, and it felt like being burned alive from the inside out. It felt bad, and it felt good.

I was staring at her with no regard for tact or shame. I stared like a loyal dog stares at its owner. I wanted her to see me staring. For the first time ever I felt bold, in control—full of something. I felt a flood of audacity jolting through me like an electrical current. It was like her raincoat was a curtain, that when opened, revealed the brightness of maturity and courage. When she took off her raincoat, something opened in me. Her light unthawed a frozen part of me.

"Now, let's get started. Is everything okay?"

"Yes. It's just… it's just you look amazing," It was like someone was talking in my voice through me.

Her head jerked quickly to meet my eyes. Her look seemed surprised, then confused, then humored. "Well, okay? Well, um, thanks. I try not to get fat." She laughed and looked away.

For four hours we sat at the old table going through line after line after line. But mentally, I was elsewhere. My mind was long gone. I just kept thinking about what I should do with all my newfound understanding. I wondered if all my understanding was actually real. Was what I thought I knew actually what I knew? Or was my moment of enlightenment just a tsunami of hormones washing over me, making me feel like a hungry caveman? I wondered a billion things, but the most important thing I pondered was if I should pursue her? Should I try and see more of what was behind the curtain? Should I try, for lack of a better phrase, "to be with her?" I was afraid.

Soliloquy

After a brief lunch break at a diner down the street, we went back to the study room and went over our lines a few more times. At some point Mira said, "I think you got it, honestly. I think you've got your lines down. Wow!"

I was fairly sure she was full of it. "Oh. Cool. So, uhh, what now?"

"Now? Now you take me home. Then you go home and keep practicing until you fall asleep. Then you wake up tomorrow and study until it's time to go to practice. Then you show everyone what you're made of. Tomorrow you show them that they were wrong and stupid and that you are better and smarter than they thought you were. That's what you do."

The ride back to her house was silent again; we didn't even have the radio on for background noise. The rain had not come, but the droopy, sooty clouds still blocked out the sky. We both were deep in thought.

Confidence was still inside me, searching around. It felt like my normal, weak body had been replaced with a better prosthetic one, one that could stand up for itself or even fight if need be. The feeling was like a drug, and I liked it. My confidence-high convinced me that Mira *was* interested in me, as in, wanted to be more than just friends. *Otherwise, why would she be spending all this time with you?* I thought. I had nothing to lose. I really wanted to touch her with intent, with meaning. The entire ride I just kept hearing a voice say: "Ask her on a date. You have nothing to lose. Ask her on a date. You have nothing to lose. Ask her on a date!" It kept repeating over and over again. It was like a chant, an aggressive incantation. But in the back of my mind: I was still afraid.

I decided (or was compelled to decide) that the chant of confidence was right. The fear was wrong. What was there to lose? A friendship? I doubted it.

We pulled up to her house. "Mira. Can I ask you something?" I said.

"Sure. Of course. What's up?"

Soliloquy

"But I don't want you to take this the wrong way."

She laughed. "I won't. I never take things the wrong way."

"Okay. Well, if you say no to this question, it won't mess up our friendship. At least not on my end it won't. I mean, whatever you say it won't make—"

"Just spit it out already."

"Okay. I wanted to know… I want to know if you would go out on a date with me at some point?"

"What do you mean?" Her face was serious.

"I mean we hang out, but it's not like a real date, is it?"

"No, not exactly. It's just hanging out."

"Yeah. Well, okay. What I'm saying is that I would like to make it a date. An official date. Not just hanging out. If that's okay with you."

She paused for a second. "Oh… Oh." She paused again. "Well how about this: how about after the play is done and over with, we go on a real date? The whole shebang: dinner, movie, all that. But right now, it's not a good time for me because of the play and stuff. Right now we need each other as friends. But afterwards, sure, let's go on a date. I've gotten to know you, and what I know, I like. You are sweet and smart and you're fun to be around. Sure, let's go on a date."

"Okay," I said. The situation felt unfathomable. It was like watching yourself watch a movie (in slow motion) starring yourself. I couldn't believe it.

She slowly stepped out of the car. "I was starting to think you'd never ask. I was starting to think you were asexual or something," she said.

I forced out a phony laugh.

I felt different.

***

Soliloquy

Wednesday night I had gotten just a little bit of sleep, two or three hours maybe. I had been up most of the night studying like Mira suggested. As I studied, without physical distraction, I realized that Mira was right about something: I did have all the lines memorized. My delivery was another story, but my lines, I had no trouble remembering any of them. It really wasn't rocket science. My realization should have been a relief, but it wasn't. Knowing lines by heart and performing them on stage in front of strange faces are two totally different things.

However, when I woke up that morning I felt, not refreshed exactly, more like *alive*. I felt the way a person feels after surviving a few days stranded in a desert and they think they hear a helicopter in the distance. The feeling isn't hope, because the person knows that the sound of the helicopter might just be a wishful hallucination. The feeling is like realizing you are not dead and have a life that is in the balance, a life to lose. I wasn't sure if the feeling even had a name, but whatever the feeling was it was better than what I had been feeling. I was still alive. I had a chance.

After showering for the first time in days, I went downstairs to have breakfast. My mother was already at the table with black toast, cold poached eggs, and cold black coffee.

"How are you, son? You don't look well."

"I'm fine, mom. I've just had a lot going on lately. But I'm fine."

"Yes. You've been spending a lot of time going around with that mysterious friend of yours," she said, giving me a probing look.

"She's not a mystery, mom. We've just been working on the play a lot lately." It was weird, despite how the hugeness of Mira's agreeing to go on a date with me was, I hadn't thought about it since it happened. I hadn't thought about her until my mom mentioned her. It must have been because it seemed completely unreal to me. Did she really know what I meant by a real date? What had gotten into me—taken over me? Did she really agree to go on a real date with me? Or had I blacked out again? Was I hallucinating?

"Mom, it's Thursday, right?"

She frowned at me over her *"JESUS IS"* coffee mug. "Yes. Are you okay? Of course it is Thursday. What other day would it be? You don't know the day?"

"I do. I do. I've just been so busy and stuff. I'm just making sure."

I took a slice of burnt toast and started heading for my room.

"Where are you going?"

"I'm going to my room. I have some more studying to do for the play. We have our second-to-last rehearsal later today."

"But I thought you weren't going to be performing in the play. Why do *you* have to study? I thought you were just a mover." Her voice was angry.

"That's what I thought at first, too. But I might actually have to perform. It's a long story. It's a big mess. But I have to study."

"Really? Why am I just now hearing of this?"

"I just found out a day or so ago. It's really just a precaution, I hope. But I just have to study."

***

When I pulled up to practice that afternoon, I was immediately relieved. Parallel parked with its backside sticking out into the street was John's yellow and black racing stripped Nissan Z. He was back! I was saved! Yay! I shouted. But, of course, my excitement was premature.

I walked into the garage expecting to see John and his cronies jumping around, laughing like dickheads. But that was far from the case. What I saw was much more disturbing. John was sitting slumped in his seat like a catatonic senior in a nursing home. He was wearing baggy grey sweatpants, a

Soliloquy

large purple Snuggie, and a light blue doctor's mask over his face. He looked like hell. I wondered what he was doing there looking like Patient 0.

People were standing around him like he was an art exhibit. D-train and Brad (who went by B-rash) patting John on the shoulders, and softly cooed: "*Bro... bro... bro.*" No one else spoke; they just kept vigil at his side, cloaked in awe and empathy.

Miss Magdalene walked up to me. "Hello. How are you?"

"I'm fine. So John—"

"John's still sick, but he is not contagious. He wanted to come and just watch today."

"Oh. Oh, I see."

"So we are going to proceed as if you are still going to be performing the lead Sunday night. All right?"

Out of nowhere Paul said, "Yes. So, are you better prepared, mister?"

"Yes. I think so. I am."

Another voice said, "He is ready. I know he's ready." It was Mira.

Practice was supposed to be the first dress rehearsal; Paul (with cat in hand) handed out all of the costumes. Everyone wore their hand-made farm outfits; they were mostly bright colored overalls for the guys and ankle-length skirts and patterned blouses for the girls. My costume was two sizes too big.

We went through the play from start to finish without a hitch. I performed with no blackouts, no slipups, and no problems. It was weird. The whole time I could tell that the group was shocked with my performance, my progress. Hell, I was shocked myself. Studying with Mira had paid off; I knew my lines as well as anybody in the troupe knew theirs. I could see it on all of their faces, no one in the troupe expected me to do anything but fail. But when I didn't fail they all looked a little impressed, relieved, and jealous.

Soliloquy

By the end of practice, I could tell that I had won over a few of my detractors. Most importantly, I had won over Miss Magdalene. Her doubts about me were not spiteful or cruel like the others; her doubts were simply a form of realism. She was skeptical because her default attitude was skepticism. She wanted me to succeed, but she did not expect me to succeed, she was too wise to genuinely expect. But, as I gave my lines her face brightened, and I could tell that she was stunned and happy.

John never moved from his green lawn chair during the practice. He was half-slumped over like a sleeping child in a car seat. His eyes had the alcoholics' sparkle to them, and he was sucking air audibly into his light blue mask; his doctor's mask made him sound a little like Darth Vader. He just sat there drooping, bundled in his big purple Snuggie. I kind of felt sorry for him.

At the end of practice, Miss Magdalene gathered us together and gave us a pep talk. "I am proud to say, from what I've seen today, you all are ready for Sunday. That was one of the best dress rehearsals I've seen since I started directing. You guys were on your game.

"But we can still do better. It was good, but it was not perfect. So Saturday's practice will be similar to today's practice, but better, flawless. Okay? It will be our last dress rehearsal, so we will have to work out any kinks that are left. I want everyone to continue going over your lines, and continue visualizing yourself on stage. That is a key. I know there will be nerves for some of you, but the best remedy for nervousness is preparedness. So prepare, prepare, prepare. Keep up the good work."

"Sissy, may I please say something, too?"

"Of course, Paul."

"Well. Well, I just want to say, I know for some of you it will be your first time, or almost your first time on stage performing in front of a lot of

211

people, so don't be overconfident. Overconfident is the worst thing an actor can be. I know you guys know what I mean. You've seen it. The best thing to do is what Sissy said: keep practicing at home. Pride comes before the fall, y'all," he said peering through his serial killer spectacles. Miss Magdalene gave him a stern look of embarrassed dismay.

"So, leave your outfits with Paul before you go, and be back here on Saturday. Ready to go. Practice dismissed!"

Before heading to my car I'd told Mira I would call her later to see if she wanted to get together and practice. She smiled and said, "Duh," then she foot-raced Essy and Hannah across the lawn to their car.

I felt... better, better than I had felt in days. I had done it. I had done something to be proud of. I had surprised my doubters, and I had surprised myself. As I was leaving, Miss Magdalene gave me a powerful pat on the back and a smile. I knew what the smile meant. She didn't have to say it; the pat and the smile said enough.

As I started up my car, I heard a loud knocking on the window. I figured it was Mira or Hannah coming back to congratulate me on how well I'd done. I was wrong. I looked up to see what appeared to be a purple phantom in a flowy shroud. John's face was partially pressed up against my car window. His eyes were wide and bloodshot.

"Vay. Det me dalk do oo!" Between his mask and my window, I couldn't understand what he was saying. I nervously rolled down my window.

He lifted up his mask and stuck his head in my car. "Hey. I don't know you that well or anything, but hey, good job and everything today. Miss Maggy was real impressed with you today, wasn't she?

"But, to be honest, you shouldn't get your hopes up about Sunday. I know for a fucking fact I'm going to be back by Sunday. I'll be ready to go.

I'm taking all kinds of meds. So, good job and everything *today*, but don't get too happy with yourself. Cause I'll be back for my part real soon. Thanks for keeping my spot warm. I'll be back!" His eyes were bulging centimeters out of their sockets and translucent lime snot was running from his nose. As he backed away from the car, he gave me a misdemeanor-worthy stare-down, the type of stare-down you normally only see from mental patients, murderers, or sky-high drug addicts. His red eyes didn't blink; they just burned at me.

I was genuinely frightened. I thought: What is wrong with this guy? What was that about? What did I do to him? He couldn't have felt threatened by me, could he? My hands were shaking so badly that I could barely get my keys into the ignition. He had succeeded at removing what little joy I had gained.

"No, no, no!" I screamed, punching my steering wheel. "Why can't I be okay? Why can't I be okay?"

***

Friday

I was in a black fog all of Friday. What I did that day and where the time went were both missing in my memory. The day had disappeared. Maybe I had detached from reality altogether that day. I don't remember. I don't know.

All I know is that I wanted it all to be over.

Soliloquy

Act IV.

Perched on high, like a swallow or the Raven,

Shaded by shards of sunlit leaves

You sit.

Soundless,

Just the reminiscence of the human heartbeat.

Heartbeats of an ominous rhythm

Statuesque pigeons fly effortlessly below

While you hover,

Eyes tilted downward.

Brazen, you are calm, yet completely perplexed.

"Some type of Napoleon complex," said the pigeons.

Fuming like the witches' pot; a devilish brew you are.

Plotting your awful anthropic vision.

"The devil's doppelganger?" all the pigeons squawk.

Whistling, while the rest of the world watches.

As you paint terrific torment on their eyelids

In rainbow-colored swatches.

Higher than elevation high

Looking down on Heath with a hate in your eyes

Disguised by the pigeon's feathers, I sing to you.

But you are deaf, to all of my surprise.

You are in a pious trance,

Taking sips of Lucifer's hemlock (a drinking man)

As if it were the finest of aged wines, swigging.

Soliloquy

Swirling circles in air the pigeons mock you.

But your eyes are too clouded to care.

Your eyes a pitch-black, silk Charmeuse

Signaling a neutron star's despair—

Endings and beginnings, then gravity!

Nothing escapes the gravity of your eyes,

Yet everything escapes your grasp.

"Will you stay that way forever?" I scream!

My voice now hoarse from all the singing.

"Forever, like the fear of the devil," says your eyes.

The doppelganger we watch in the twilight of the evening.

Chapter 7

The Sort of Things One Does

<u>Saturday</u>

I woke up feeling dread: unadulterated, indeterminate dread. The final day of dress rehearsal, I should have felt relief, excitement, or even happiness. But no. As I wiped warm drool from my wet cheek, with my eyes still closed, my first conscious thought was… dread.

Anxiety had arrived even before I was fully awake. I could feel that it had been patiently waiting for me to take notice of it for some time. The dread kept me from opening my eyes, kept me from sitting up. It was a sort of phantom physical ache mixed with an emotional atrophy. I was unwilling and unable to get up, unwilling to open my eyes and start the dreadful day. I was disinclined to think about what the day might bring. I didn't want to deal with it or them: John, cat smell, Paul, cronies, phonies, or feelings. I knew if I were to actually wake up and think about the day, I would be overwhelmed by a flood of unbearable thoughts and ideas of all the nasty things that could, and likely would, occur.

What finally forced me to move was the intermittent, incredibly loud *beep!* of my phone. How long had it been beeping? It was driving me crazy. (Was the beeping the dread?) It would beep every 36 seconds (I counted the time as I lay on my bed in the fetal position).

When I finally got to my phone (after a lot of staggering and angry rummaging) the phone read ten missed calls. Nine calls from Mira and one from a number I didn't recognize. I had four voicemails, all from Mira.

V1: "Hey, what's up? What time do you want to get together today? Let me know soon. I have a few other things to do today, I have to get my hair trimmed, so I want to make sure I put aside enough time. Okay, call me back, bye!"

V2: "Hey, why haven't you called me back? Why aren't you answering your phone? Call me back, please. Okay? Bye."

V3: "Are you serious? Are you ignoring me or something? You're starting to make me worried. Are you okay? If you don't start calling me back, I'm going to call the police and tell them you're a missing person. So call me back! I don't want to have to start calling hospitals to see if you're there. Call me back!"

V4: "Wow... unbelievable... I can't believe you won't pick up. If I knew where you lived, I would be at your door right now, banging it down. You're lucky. Unbelievable. I hope you're happy. You've ruined my day. Goodbye.

I dialed her number as soon as the voicemail was over. The dread had taken form.

Phone: "Please enjoy the music while your party is being reached: (*Music from Aladdin*)."

"Hello!"

"Hey, I'm so, so—"

"I cannot freakin' believe you!" Mira screamed. I had never heard her like that before. Her voice was shaky and deep.

"I know. I know you must be upset but just please hear—"

"Hear you out? Why would I have the courtesy to hear you out? Did you hear me out? No! You didn't even have the decency to pick up your damn phone when I called you. Do you know how I felt? Do you know what was going through my mind? I can't believe you!"

"I am so sorry. I have no excuses. I am so, so, so, so, so sorry. But honestly, I was sick. Like super sick. I really don't know what happened to me. But I was practically on my death bed."

Soliloquy

"You were too sick to pick up your phone?"

"My phone was off. I didn't even know. It was off, I think."

"No it wasn't! It rang when I called. If it was off it wouldn't have rung."

"I meant the ringer was off. I didn't pick it up because I didn't hear it ring. It was on silent. I was sleeping the whole time. I'm telling you the truth. You know, you know I would have picked up if I would have known it was you. You know I would never ignore you purposely. You know that, right?"

"I thought I knew that. But I don't know anymore."

"I'm so sorry. Did you call my house phone?"

"Of course I called your house phone! No one picked up! That's why I called your cell phone!"

"Oh, I'm sorry. My parents must be gone. I'm telling you the truth. I wouldn't do that. I'm not like that. I would never ignore you. I would never do anything like that. You're my only friend. I would never willfully disrespect you. I was sick, I promise. Honestly, I was feeling really, really badly. I would never do anything to hurt you. Never!" I was in a panic. My words seemed to be coming out of some new place inside me. I was not thinking of what to say. I appeared to be channeling my truest feelings, my honest emotions. I had never spoken like that to anyone. I had never felt like that. It felt powerful and vulnerable to be that honest. My true emotions were in charge. I was speaking truths that I hadn't consciously thought of.

"Okay," she said, finally, in a normal voice.

"Okay? So you believe me?"

"I don't know. I'm just not mad anymore. Anyway."

"Okay. I am really sorry," I said. "If you want to we can meet and practice before today's practice."

"Are you serious? Today's practice *starts* in 15 minutes. That was *one* of the reasons I was calling you so much. Miss Magdalene had practice pushed

Soliloquy

up today. She told me to call and tell you. She wants everybody there early. Hannah's on her way to pick me up now."

"Oh shit! I'll, I'll, I'm on my way. I'll be there."

She said, "Well, you better be, or Miss Magdalene and Paul will be pissed. You know that. They will be pissed." She hung up.

I didn't even change out of my Ninja Turtle pajama pants. I just put on shoes, put on the least rank hoody I had, and shot out of the house like a bat out of a bat cave. I pushed the shit-stain to its limits, clipping curves and chancing four-way stops. The car clanked and banged like an angry iron-smith.

I reached the garage with literally no time to spare. I got a few disgust-ed looks as I walked in (most of them came from the front row). Everyone was already seated, dressed in their costumes. I tiptoed over Rachel, Sam, and Essy to get to my usual spot. They all gave me frowns that said, "*Ewe, you smell!*" Mira didn't even acknowledge my presence as I sat down next to her. She just stared straight ahead.

Looking up at the front row, I realized that John had kept his word. He was taking his spot back. Even though his face (and disposition) still ap-peared sickly, he was wearing his costume, and he was wearing his overly cocky smile. He was leaning back with his head on the green chair and his oversized arms crossed over his inflated chest.

"Well, ladies and young men," Miss Magdalene said. "Today is our fi-nal rehearsal before the big show. Are we all mentally prepared?" A chorus of halfhearted yeahhhhs went up. The day was hot; the garage was scorch-ing.

"I wanted you all to come in early today, because I added a new facet to today's practice. I wanted to do a few walkthroughs, as expected, but after that, I want to do some quick individual one-on-one meetings to make sure

Soliloquy

that everyone is on the same page and to make sure that everyone's logistical questions are answered before tomorrow."

"What's ladistical?" someone shouted.

"Just any questions you might have," Miss Magdalene said sharply. "So the one-on-ones are why practice is slightly elongated today. We need to cross every T and dot every I before Sunday's performance. I want there to be no surprises.

"During today's walkthrough John will perform the part of Old Man Gleaner. If he is healthy, he will perform it tomorrow as well. Sickness cannot disqualify a person from their original role. That would be unfair." Miss Magdalene did not look at me as she spoke. Her eyes were gazing at the nothingness in the back of the room.

"Yes. I'm back to 100 percent," John shouted.

From the corner of my eye I saw Paul smile.

"Okay. Let's move these chairs, take our positions, and begin."

"Let's run it from the top," Paul shouted with glee.

I looked over at Mira. She did not look back. Her face was empty and sad.

I took the lead in moving the chairs; everyone else slowly drifted to their positions at the front of the garage. John eagerly started reciting the opening soliloquy in a nasally voice, sniffing snot down through his nose after every third word.

"There comes a [sniff] time in every [sniff] man's life…"

With those words my time as lead was officially over; it was time for me to go back to being invisible. I realized that being invisible (again) might be a good thing for my life and mental stability. When I was invisible, I had been less stressed out, less confused, and less depressed. When I was invisible, Mira and I didn't fight, we had fun. Our relationship was semi-uncomplicated before. When I was invisible we didn't go over lines until our brains turned to mush. When I was invisible Mira and I took walks, ate ice cream, and she talked.

As I went over all the positives that being invisible again would bring, I still felt something funny inside, something unwilling to relax. It wasn't like a physical pain; it was more like an old, quiet ache in my chest. My heart was lashing around like the detached tail of a dead lizard. I searched my head for the cause of the ache. Why was my heart twitching? Could it be because Mira was mad at me? But Mira wasn't it. That was too obvious, and that twitch felt indefinite.

I searched around my mind until I confessed to myself that the ache's purpose was right there in front of me the entire time: I wanted to be the lead! Something inside of me wanted to be the lead, wanted to take on that challenge! A part of me had *liked* being the lead. Not all of me, but part of me, the part inside me that was sore.

I felt like I had something I wanted to say, even if what I had to say wasn't in my own words. It was strange, it was not jealousy. I just felt that I could do it better than John could, but I wasn't envious. I felt that the part was better suited for me; most of what the old man in the play wanted to say, I wanted to say.

The remainder of the practice I moved props and chairs and pondered my confusing realization. It was not like me to want to be the center of attention, but my heart kept yearning and aching.

"Okay," Miss Magdalene shouted. "Now we will be calling each individual into the one-on-ones. You will be picked at random, so be prepared. The first person up will be Essy."

Soliloquy

As Miss Magdalene and Paul left the room everyone shuffled their chairs back to their spots and clustered in their normal social groups. Mira, Hannah, and I, sat in a semi-circle, saying nothing at first.

"Are you okay?" Hannah asked Mira.

"I suppose I am. Why? Why do you ask?"

"I'm just asking because you seem kinda funny. You're not acting like your normal self."

"Oh, yes. I'm fine. I'm just over this play stuff. I'm ready to be done so I can start something new."

"Is it my fault?" I asked.

"Of course not," she said. "Why would it be?"

"I don't know. But I'm glad it's not my fault."

When all the one-on-ones wrapped up (my one-on-one was uneventful, it lasted less than a minute), Miss Magdalene gave one of her patented speeches. "Tomorrow is a big day for all of us," and "Be prepared," and "Take pride in your preparation," and on and on. When she was finally done, the garage door was let up, and everyone poured out into the balmy evenfall.

As I walked out, Mira grabbed my elbow from behind. "Wait. Just a second." She stood looking around for a few moments as people passed. She spoke when everyone else was out of earshot. "I'm sorry for being mean to you, okay? It's just that I'm stressed about the play tomorrow. I know it seems like I am angry, but I'm just really stressed out. I get nervous before I have to perform. I know I don't seem like the nervous type, I try to hide it, but I am. And when I get nervous I get really bitchy, and I took it out on you. I didn't mean to take it out on you... but I did. I'm sorry.

"You are a good guy, and I shouldn't treat you like that, even if I am stressed. When this is all over, after the play is finished, I promise I will make up for it. Okay? Our date, our real date, it will be amazing. I'll make up for it, okay?"

"Oh. Okay," I said.

***

Sunday: It's not over until…

I woke up without dread or delirium. I woke up with the realization that I had dodged a fiery bullet. John's arrogance had saved me from having to be the main character in a play after very little practice. Sitting on the edge of my bed I thought to myself: If it wasn't for John, I would be feeling a lot worse right now. I would be in complete panic mode!

The part of me that wanted to be the lead was dormant and I was happy that my stress was almost at an end.

Knock, Knock!

Knock, Knock!

Knock!

"Son, your mother and I would like it if you would join us for breakfast. We are having French *pain grille*, over-easy eggs, and sliced bananas. Son? Are you awake?"

"Yes, dad. I'll be there in a second."

At the table I noticed a peculiar, undistinguishable look on my mother's face.

"Hello, mom. Thank you for making breakfast. Smells good."

"It does, does it?" My mother had both of her arms stretched out, her hands in fists on the table. Her large, crazy gray eyes were attempting to lock onto mine. It was apparent that something was on her mind and that she was in a fighting mood.

"Yes. It smells great."

"Mary, could you please pass me the eggs?"

"First, I think we all need to have a family talk. I'm very concerned about some things. And since we are all here, I think we should discuss them as a family." Her eyes were fixed directly on me.

"What's this all about, Mary?"

"It's about something I found in our son's room. It's about our son's recent behavior."

I was totally confused and pre-annoyed. I could tell that she was very serious, but it really almost seemed like a joke. What behavior? Found what? "What?" I said. "What are you talking about? And why were you in my room?"

"First of all, I'm talking about this!" She turned over her right fist and opened it slowly. In it was the silver Zippo lighter that Mira had given me after our first library adventure together.

"Yesterday, when you were gone, I went in your room, because when I walked passed it I smelled a terrible smell coming from inside. The entire hallway smelled like a decomposing animal. So I went in there to make sure you didn't have food laying around on the floor or an actual dead animal in there. When I tried to walk around in your cluttered mess, I stepped on something hard in one of your pants pockets. I almost broke my foot! When I picked them up, to my surprise, this fell out: a lighter! Why do you have a lighter? Why on God's green earth do you need a lighter?"

"Wow," I said. I didn't even remember I had the thing. "Um, it's a friend of mine's. It's no big deal. She just gave it to me to hold, because I let her borrow a book. That's all."

She didn't blink. "Is that right? Is this *friend* you speak of the mystery girl I've heard so little about?"

"Yes... no... Yes. My friend is the same girl we've talked about before: Mira. It's hers."

Soliloquy

"So is this girl a smoker? Is she on drugs? Why does she need a lighter? I do not like the sounds of this girl. She seems like a bad seed, a bad influence. There is something strange going on."

"No! I don't think so. I... She likes daisies. Daisies are her favorite flowers. I am not around her 24 hours a day, but from what I know of her she doesn't do drugs or smoke or anything. People can have lighters for other reasons. Maybe she likes to light candles in her room with it or something. I don't know. But she told me to hold on to it, so I don't think she can be using it for drugs since I have it."

My mother's face turned into a morbid frown. "You better watch your tone."

"I'm sorry. All I am trying to say is just because I have a lighter doesn't mean I am smoking cigarettes or doing drugs. I promise you, I don't smoke. Did you find any cigarettes with the lighter? I hate smoke. And I really don't believe Mira smokes either, but I can't be sure. I've been around her, and I've never seen her smoke—" which was a lie.

My dad, waving his hand it the air like a strandee spotting a Cessna, said, "Excuse me, if I may. I agree, Mary. There is no sufficient evidence to propose that the boy is a smoker. Were there any items of tobacco or cannabis found with the lighter?"

My mother did not answer him. She just pushed back her seat, stood up, took the platter of eggs, and walked away.

"Excuse me, Mary? What is the matter?"

"These eggs are cold. They need reheating."

"Son." My father stretched his hand high in the air, and then he placed it on his wrinkled forehead. "I know you are aware of the drawbacks of nicotine, tar, and tobacco—"

"Dad, of co—"

Soliloquy

"There was a time when tobacco and other such crops were socially acceptable. Actually, they were more than just acceptable, they were encouraged. Some physicians would prescribe tobacco to patients for specific ailments. Can you believe it? Many great mathematicians and philosophers would give their lectures while puffing on a pipe or a hand-rolled cigarette. Smoking was fundamentally not understood in a chemical-causal sort of way. Some say it was. I disagree.

"The eccentric philosopher Hegel went a step further than simply smoking during his lectures. It is said that he would give his lectures with a patch of cannabis stuffed in the back of his cheek. This cannabis chew, some philosophers suggest, may be the reason why some of Hegel's ideas are so knotty, radical, and, perhaps, to some, convoluted. 'Self-consciousness is in and for itself in and through being in and for itself for another self-consciousness; that is, it is only as something acknowledged or recognized.' This is Hegel. Do you see what I mean, son?"

"Yes, that's very hard to understand."

"Are you trying to encourage him to smoke?" my mother said, sitting back at the table. Steam was rising off of the reheated eggs.

"Don't be hyperbolic, Mary. I was not finished making my point. I would never encourage the boy to harm himself in any unredeemable way. I was simply giving him a short history of things.

"However, as I was alluding to, my point: maybe this Mira person is simply an individual who enjoys pondering the proto-mythical eternality of fire. Fire was one of the first things to be deified or worshiped by humans: pyrolatry, it's called. It is, fire, like time, and like just a few other rudiments, a primary prerequisite for human existence, a precondition for self-cognizance and homin-psychological evolution. The universal birth: first fire, the big explosion—known to the hoi polloi as The Big Bang, then time, or, more specifically, both fire and time simultaneously, then pre-life, then life, then animal-man, then rational man, and then, perhaps, if we are fortunate, truly spiritual man. Fire and time are necessary, interrelated conditions.

"Contemplating fire's big beginnings is like contemplating the beginning of time and space, the enigmatic firmament of pre-time. They are thoughts of unthinkable awe! Sure, Hawkingites will tell you that thinking of pre-time is impossible and perhaps useless. They might say, 'Time is not separate from space, therefore, when space began expanding, so too did time, in concurrence and ultimate harmony. Thus, before the bang, the fact of time did not, for all intents and scientific purposes, exist as it does now.' Nevertheless, despite their robust, logically sound argument, I find it, the thought of pre-time, to be one of the most gratifying thoughts allowed to man, an ever-expanding gift of counter intuition. A crossing of synaptic wires if you will.

"Think of the first single moment in time, that first precise moment. It was over-rife with antagonistic activity. Think of before that moment: here is where our unsophisticated, ever-ambiguous language breaks down; our human ability to think in logical terms breaks down.

"Think of the first lightning strike to surge forth from earth's youthful atmosphere and set fire to the unmanned, chaste land. Visualize earth's *very first* fire! Was it large, raging? Was it small and sedate? Did it last for days or merely seconds?—before seconds were known as seconds or counted as such, when the earth was unified, undivided by the human mind.

"These thoughts and questions are pieces of contemplative gold that will always be, as will fire and time. Even when time is only a memory. These are thoughts that can and will never be understood on a visceral level, not the solemnity of fire nor the gestation and gamut of time. They are only so-called *understood* on a numinous, almost ante-religious, sub-rational, sub-visceral level. They are before words and beyond doubt. Although Parmenides' lover Zeno might be skeptical of my claim.

"Perhaps your young friend feels an unconscious, intra-spiritual regard for fire. Perhaps her lighter is a Jungian symbol, *Woman and Her Symbols*." My father seemed out of breath from all the hand movements and thinking he'd done. I followed almost nothing he had said. He seemed to be having a conversation with himself, honestly.

"I hardly believe that that girl thinks anything like you! No one really thinks like that," my mom said.

"Perhaps you are right. But sentencing this Mira person to moral reformatory school before you have even met her is just as presumptuous as my aforementioned assumptions. Balzac and Nietzsche insist that moralizing is personal wound exposure. Might they be correct, Mary?"

My mother stared at him coldly. "Here. Eggs." She slid the hot platter across the table at him.

"Thank you."

"What time does this play start tonight?" my mom asked.

"Oh. It starts at, I think, seven. And, um, but, we have to be there earlier, at four, so we can set up and maybe do another walkthrough. Are you guys going to come and watch? I don't think I'm going to have a part. The—"

"Of course we are!" my mother said. "Why would we miss it?! I have been waiting to go to an event for you since you were born. I want to see you interact with other people."

"Oh. I see."

"I may be a bit late, son. There are things at the office that need attending to—"

"On a Sunday?" my mother shouted.

"Yes, Mary. Sunday, today. However, despite my work obligations, I do plan to attend tonight, son. I am also excited to see what you are a part of, regardless of whether or not you will be formally participating. I am simply happy to see you taking in the arts as a participant rather than simply as a spectator. I am proud that you ventured out of your comfort zone."

"Okay. Well. Thanks, you guys."

"Thanks? For what?" my mother said. She was forking half of an egg into her mouth. "You don't need to thank us."

"Okay," I said. "Well, can we talk about me getting a new car now?"

My father clapped his hands together and laughed. "The play isn't over yet, son. It hasn't even begun."

***

Before heading to the church, we all met up at Miss Magdalene's house where she'd split us up into carpool groups. I was told to ride in the equipment van with Paul and John. Miss Magdalene was manning a 4X4 Durango truck (that I had never seen before) with Rachel primly in the passenger seat. The bed of the truck was filled with set props and junk. Mira and a couple others all rode in Hannah's car. And D-train, Carmi, Samantha, and J. P. crammed into D-train's undersized orange VW bug; they looked like a group of disgruntled clowns.

The equipment van was Paul's personal van. It was brownish white (from what appeared to be years of unwashed dirt), it had no rear or back side windows, and it was completely creepy. The van had two front seats, and the back was just an open, seatless space for "storage."

"Hey, buddy, I need you to sit in the back with the stuff, so you can make sure none of the stuff moves around and breaks. John, you can sit up front with me, okay? There're a couple things we need to go over on the way."

Soliloquy

Sitting in the back of a creeper-van wasn't as bad as it sounds (although it was extremely hot). Despite the fact that it was crowded with uniforms and fake farm supplies, I got some time to myself, and I didn't have to listen or talk to anyone. I couldn't really hear what Paul and John were saying over the Barbra Streisand CD that was blasting.

The ride there was bumpy and loud, but all I kept thinking about was how it was almost over. It, the drama, the stress, was almost over. And I kept thinking that maybe I would quit the troupe afterwards, and my life would go back to normal. Maybe I would get a really nice car and drive it around all day. Could I become a car guy? Maybe I would drive my new car to plays in other towns; that would take up a lot of time. Maybe I would work a lot more at my uncle's restaurant, maybe I'd get promoted. It was almost over, and I was ready for it to be over.

When I was done thinking about what I would do when it was all over, I started to wonder how the play would turn out. I hoped that I would get a chance to see Mira perform, but as a stagehand, it was unlikely. I could imagine how amazing she would be when she had a real live audience. I wondered how many people would show up to watch the play.

Every few minutes I would hear an explosion of laughter coming from the front of the van. Paul and John would yelp like hyenas for a few seconds, then go back to inaudible noise.

Eventually the Barbra was turned down low. "Hey, little buddy. We're here!" Paul sang.

Except for the forty-foot-tall white crucifix that protruded through the roof and towered over the building, Miss Magdalene's church was a beautiful place. The inside of the church was incredibly clean, and everything seemed to have a proper place and be in it. The wood and laminate-wood were dusted and polished to a holy shine. The pews were soft, and the whole place smelled like green pine car fresheners and cheap grape juice.

The sanctuary/stage was about four feet high, and it was covered in dark red carpet. It was not a stage exactly; it was just one huge elevation. In the center of the makeshift stage there was a large oak podium (with a crucifix craftily carved into the front). The podium had three microphones hooked to it, and there were wires curving from the bottom like ossuaries flowing from a river. There were several large chairs behind the podium, in what seemed to me a weird, nonsensical arrangement, and on the left side of the stage was what looked like a metal, foldable choir stand.

I felt awkward in Miss Magdalene's church. I had only been in one of my town's countless churches. I'd gone to church with my mom sometimes when I was very young, but other than that, the only time I went to church was for family funerals. I felt uneasy in church, judged, by who or what, I didn't know. But whatever it was that was judging me, I didn't like it.

When we arrived, the church was completely empty, except for the pastor and his wife. They were both very old, and they looked like paternal twins. They were both wearing the identical poop brown color.

"I'll show your group around, Sister Magdalene," the pastor said.

"That would be wonderful, Pastor Smithinson. Pastor Smithinson will be handling our lighting tonight. Pastor, while on your tour, could you perhaps show these young gentlemen the storage room, where we keep all the in-house props? That would be wonderful." Before the pastor could answer, she turned to us and said, "You guys follow Pastor Smithinson. There is a storage space that has a portable stage curtain. We need that. We also need the rolling chair carrier. We need to move the chairs off the stage onto the chair carrier. And we need to move the podium as well."

Soliloquy

Miss Magdalene turned to the girls who were standing next to us, all with their arms crossed and heads down. "Girls, I need you to get all of the materials from van and the truck. We—"

"*We* have to get all that stuff?" Rachel shouted.

Calmly, without looking in Rachel's direction, Miss Magdalene said, "Exactly. *We* need it all. What we don't need, the boys will take back outside."

"Well, off we go, boys, to see the Lord's house," Pastor Smithinson said with cheer.

After an unexpectedly lengthy tour, offices and bathrooms included, the setup process took us much, much longer than I anticipated. By the time everything was moved, arranged, re-moved, rearranged, and stored back into the truck, van, and storage closet, we had taken up most of our pre-play time. Everyone still had to have makeup applied (Paul was a virtuoso makeup artist.), hair styled, outfits adjusted, and on and on. By the time all this was nearly done, there was no time for a last-minute walk through. Miss Magdalene appeared to be holding back alarm.

Clumps of people were already starting to loiter inside the church.

Since I had no outfit to put on or cosmetics to apply, I just sat on the first row of pews waiting for someone to give me additional directions. No one did. For a while I thought that the troupe forgot about me. I thought I might get to watch the play from a pretty nice seat. Then, finally, I was summoned backstage by a frowning John. He popped his head out of the closed curtain and shouted, "Hey, we need you back here. Where have you been? There's some stuff you need to move!"

Paul instantly began ordering me around with palpable distain. He told me to move some of the stage props back to the places they had been moved from in the first place. I did as I was told. After a while (of me doing exactly what he told me to do) he got unwarrantedly frustrated with me and said, "Just move. Stop! Move! You're going *too* slow, too slow. What are you *doing*? Just stop and stand over there and try not to mess anything up, okay, bud?"

His rudeness didn't bother me like it normally did. I understood he was stressed. Behind the curtain the stress was conspicuous in the form of odd-smelling body heat. Everyone seemed incredibly tense, irritated, and frazzled. Everybody was mumbling under their breath and rushing around, bumping into one another, then mumbling even more. As I stood there watching everyone act like jonesing meth-heads, I caught sight of Mira. She was sitting in the back, on the floor by an outlet, curling her short, dark hair. She looked calm, almost peaceful. She must have felt my eye on her because she looked my direction, unplugged her curling iron, dusted off her dress, and waved me over. She smiled at me like we hadn't seen one another in years.

"I hope you have a great performance tonight. Break a leg, or whatever the right encouragement is," I said.

She laughed a little. Her eyes were lit up by her mass of mascara. "Thank you. Thanks." She slowly hugged me and gave me a long, soft kiss on the cheek.

"I'm so nervous," she said. "I wish I had something to drink."

"Oh, well, you don't look nervous. You look fine; you look perfect. I can go get you some water if you'd like. I saw a water fountain earlier."

"No, silly," she laughed. "I mean a *drink*, drink, like alcohol, something to take the edge off. But it's cool, I'm fine. I'm just whining. I'll be fine."

"Okay. I think you'll do awesome. You know your lines better than anyone. And you look really nice. You'll do fine—great."

Soliloquy

"Thanks. Yeah. Well, I just hope John remembers his lines; I hope *every-one* remembers their lines. But John still seems a bit off to me, like he's still sick. He better not get me sick. Well, anyway, I better get back to work. We're going to go over a few more things before the curtain goes up. It's almost time. We better hurry." She leaned in and kissed me again, and she grabbed my hand. "Thanks again. You're so sweet. You're the sweetest."

After a few minutes, Miss Magdalene called us all together for a final talk and the Lord's prayer.

"Well everyone, this is what you've all been working all this time for. All your very hard work comes down to this.

"Even before we go on stage, I must tell you all just how proud of you I am. You are like a family to me. You guys are like my children. And I am very proud of what you've accomplished in such a short period of time.

"I don't want any of you to go out there being nervous. There is no need to be nervous now. You can take comfort in your preparation. If you are prepared, you have nothing to worry about. And I believe that you all are fully prepared. We've done an ample amount of practice.

"If you make a mistake, all the people who are witness to it have also made mistakes, some much more costly than the one you may make on stage; you can take comfort in that as well.

"So, really, just go out there and have fun. Enjoy yourselves. Enjoy the crowd. Enjoy each other's performances. You deserve it."

Miss Magdalene took up both of the hands next to hers, Paul's and Rachel's, and bowed her head. Her dark hair covering her sharp cheeks. Everyone else followed suit, mimicking her sincerity.

"Let us pray," she said. "Our Father—"

After the prayer, I was told by Miss Magdalene that I would be standing backstage during the play, next to her and Paul.

Soliloquy

"You should be able to see pretty well from back here. You'll be in charge of opening and closing the curtain for us, okay? Paul or I will cue you when the time comes. Pull this down for open, this down for closed. Got it?"

"Okay."

After she gave me her instructions, she turned to the troupe. Everyone was huddled together in a fit of silence and nerves. She said, "It is show time." Then she walked through the curtain like a soldier onto a battlefield. She gave a short speech to the audience. Her voice was different; it was the voice of a caring speech therapist. Her words were soft yet loud, and every sentence was punctuated by a joke and a sprinkle of audience laughter. She reemerged through the curtain and walked up to me quickly and said in a whisper, "Okay, open it."

I pulled open the curtain. She looked to John and nodded. He was on first, alone. He took two big deep breaths, puffed out his chest, and slowly walked to center stage. After what seemed like a long time, I heard the words: "There comes a time in every man's life when he must choose!"

***

I watched the entire play from my spot by the curtain. The play was much better than I'd expected it to be. It was, in fact, a good play. No one messed up their lines, and Mira's performance was sublime, literally perfect. Even though I could only see the back of her head, I couldn't take my eyes off of her.

As soon as the play was completed, we all were brought on stage, my-self included, to take a bow for the audience. I stood next to Mira and P.J.; their hands were hot. It was the first time I'd really seen the crowd. The church was not full, but there were a lot of spectators there. As we bowed several times, most of the audience stood up and clapped. They appeared completely satisfied with the performance. I was happy to be there. I was happy to be part of the troupe.

I scanned the crowd for my mom and dad. They were both standing near the back of the church clapping and smiling like everyone else. Surprisingly, I was happy they came. When I met my dad's eyes, he began waving spastically. Following our curtain call there was a round of hugs among the group, and then a mingling session with the crowd. I fought my way to the back of the crowd to my parents.

"So, what did you guys think?" I said.

"Impressive, son. Very impressive."

"Was the girl, the lead girl… is that the girl you've been spending your free time with?" my mother said.

"Yes. She's the girl."

"Well—"

I quickly turned to my dad. "I really want to thank you guys for coming. I'm happy that you got to be here."

"Not a problem, son. I just wish you had a line or two. That is my only complaint, my reluctant complaint."

"Yeah. I know. Well, maybe next time. Well, I have to get back and start packing up the rest of the stuff. But really, thanks for coming. I'll see you at home." I hurried away.

As I ran I could hear my mother say, "Aren't you going to…?"

The crowd petered out slowly, and the troupe gathered all of the props and bag. Miss Magdalene called us all together once more before we headed out.

"Firstly, I just want to say: incredible job, incredible job. You guys exceeded my expectations by many miles. You went above and beyond. I want to say thank you all and congratulations.

Soliloquy

"Secondly, I have a question for you all: What is everyone doing this coming *Friday* night?" Everyone looked around confusedly, muttering to one another.

Then John said, "I don't know about them, but I'm free, Maggie. What's up?" After John spoke, the rest of the males chimed in saying that they too were free, and they too wanted to know what was up.

Miss Magdalene's face brightened. She looked to be holding back a grin as best she could; she appeared ready to blow with uncontrollable emotion at any second.

"Well, just a few minutes ago, I had the most important conversation in this troupe's history!" A few of the girls gasped. Miss Magdalene paused proudly, and then continued. "In the audience, during your great performance, there was a man. I mean an important man. He is the executive director of the *Lyceum*! His name is Mr. Saulmen. I have met him once or twice before, but…. Anyhow, he approached me and congratulated me on our performance. He mentioned that he thought we did an extraordinary job tonight, and so on and so forth.

"He *then* went on to tell me that everything was going well at the *Lyceum*: attendance has been up by twenty percent this year, et cetera. However, However, he has a performance opening that he is looking to fill! Something about a Russian opera company coming down with acute bronchitis at the last minute, and he said if the troupe was free this Friday evening and wouldn't mind filling in for the ill Russians, he would be very grateful and deeply indebted to us!"

Her smile broke through her composure like a full yellow moon through cloudy darkness. She was smiling a smile that can only be described as pure joy. Her eyes were starting to gloss with tears, and her teeth were showing. It was infectious.

Soliloquy

"Can you believe it?!" Paul screamed. He was clapping his hands together as fast as he could.

"So what do you all think?" she said happily. "Would you guys be willing to perform at the historic *Lyceum* on Friday night? I know it is short notice, and I know that some of you won't be able to answer until you've talked to your parents first or have dealt with your work schedules, but preliminarily speaking, by a show of hands, how many of you think you would be willing to perform Friday?" All hands shot up into the air.

Mira turned to me and said, "I've seen that place. It's freakin' beautiful!"

"Oh, I know. It's my favorite pl—"

"Well," Miss Magdalene said, "that is very reassuring. Performing in the historical *Lyceum* is almost as big as it gets. If it happens, it will be the chance of a lifetime!"

"I will be calling you all tomorrow to check and see if everyone is on board. And if we have enough people, we will practice—"

Paul cut in, "Please, please, please. I am sure that none of you want to be the person that keeps the troupe from performing at the L. Right? No one wants to be that person. Everyone raised their hand. We all want to perform. If need be, I will talk to your parents or employers and tell them just how important this opportunity is. It's huge! I will even take one of your shifts if I have to, or come to your house and help you clean up your room… if that's what it takes to get you there. This is, like my sissy said, 'the chance of a lifetime.' So please. Please don't be the person to mess this up for everyone."

Miss Magdalene's smile was gone. "I think what Paul means to say is that you should do your best to seize this amazing opportunity. It would be regrettable if you missed out.

Soliloquy

"Okay, well, let's head back to my place. We can put the props and costumes away, and then I want you all to head home and get some well-
deserved rest. I will be calling you all sometime tomorrow. Be sure to talk it
over with your parents tonight."

***

We had a serious impromptu practice on Tuesday, but Thursday's practice was little more than a giggling gloat-fest. Everyone was so happy and so
proud of themselves. There was laughing, joking, pranking, and general
childishness all around, pure mayhem. It was the least stressful and least
organized of the practices I had ever attended; but what was really odd was
the fact that Paul and Miss Magdalene didn't seem to mind all of the shenanigans.

Mira and Hannah were playing some weird form of tag I had never
seen before. The rules of the game seemed to be that if one of them was
tagged, she had to do the robot dance for an unspecified amount of time.
They were roboting and giggling all over the hot garage.

John seemed to be completely back to normal. He showed no signs of
sickness; the cronies had their undisputed leader back. He kept telling dirty
jokes and pining for attention, and everyone else was in a hurry to laugh at
whatever he said and give him all the attention he could swallow.

By the end of practice, we had somewhat accomplished a walkthrough.
Then Miss Magdalene told us the schedule for Friday.

"We are going to get there early and do a serious walkthrough. Today
was fun, but tomorrow will be serious. We need to be superb. There is no
telling how many people will be there tomorrow. And there is no telling who
will be there tomorrow. So—"

Soliloquy

As Miss Magdalene brought her pep talk to a close, Mira said, "I have something to say, if that's okay, Miss Magdalene." She stood up to address the troupe.

"Sure, go ahead."

"Okay, well, I just wanted to say thanks to everyone for working so hard on the play. The play was beyond. You've heard it already, but I too want to say: great job! And I want to show my appreciation for everyone's hard work and dedication. I want to invite you all over to my house tonight for a get together, pretty much just to bond and stuff. There'll probably be pizza and cookies and snacks and pop and games. Just a chance to have fun and bond before our big performance.

"I know I'm not besties with all of you, we all aren't all hunky-dory and buddy-buddy, and that's fine, but you're all still invited. If you don't come, I won't judge you. I really appreciate each and every one of you. I'm letting bygones be and all that. I just want to show my appreciation to everyone and show everyone that I'm not a bitch or anything. We've all had ups and downs and our emotional outbursts... but what we did together as a group, as a team... we all were amazing. So if you want to come and have some fun, you're invited."

For a second or two everyone was silent. Faces were twisted in confusion. I think that people were trying to determine if what she said was sarcasm or not. Most of the troupe couldn't tell what she was after, but I could. She was serious, genuine as she could be. She was speaking from an honest place; I had seen and heard things from that place before.

"That's a very mature offer," Miss Magdalene said.

"Cool!" D-train shouted. "Free pop and pizza? I'm there!" All the boys laughed. Then they all agreed. Then all of the girls nodded in agreement, Rachel included.

Mira gave everyone her phone number and told them to call her later for the address and specific time.

I was completely uncomfortable, upset even. I hated the idea. I hated the idea that she could up and have fun with people she'd talked so much shit about for so long. A few weeks before she was talking about how nasty Rachel and Samantha were, and how sick and misogynistic all of the guys were, but now, all of a sudden, she was letting bygones be bygones? Why? What had changed? Did she even believe all the stuff she had said about them before? The people were still the same. The play had changed no one's core. Not even a week before, she couldn't look directly at John. Now she was inviting him to a party? It didn't make any sense to me. I didn't like it. The idea of her "get together" made my stomach turn.

When Miss Magdalene let up the garage door, I tried to hurry to my car as fast as possible. I could feel myself getting hot and wobbly. I kept visualizing myself in bed, taking a long nap with the air-conditioning on high. I wanted to get away and be alone.

"Where the hell are you going?" Mira had caught up to me.

"Home."

"Why?"

"Why?" I said.

"Yes, why? You can't go home. I need you to help me set up for the party. We need to get all the snacks and stuff for the party. What's your deal?"

"Oh. You sure you want me to help you?"

"Duh, silly. That's why I'm asking you. Are you sure you're okay? What's wrong?"

I wasn't in the mood to go snack shopping, but I felt a little bit better due to the fact that she wanted to spend more time with me than the others.

She frowned. "So, are you going to help me or not?"

"Okay. Yeah. Sure."

"Good! I'm going to tell Hannah that I'm riding with you, okay? Be right back."

On the ride to Mira's house we stopped by the *Dickerton's Quick-Shop Mart* and picked up a few boxes of Zebra Cakes, six bags of different flavored Doritos, twenty ice teas, ten full-size bags of Chex Mix, a discounted cake that said, "Happy Birthday Lu-Lu" in green frosting, four frozen pizzas, and a bundle of paper plates and red plastic cups. Our cart was filled to the brim.

"How do you plan to pay for all this stuff?"

"My mom's credit card, duh. Do you think this is enough stuff for everyone? I hope so."

"Yeah. I think it's… yeah."

"Well, hopefully. I plan on still actually ordering more pizza later on, when everyone shows up."

"Wow. That's very generous."

"What?"

"That's very generous."

"Thanks. I try."

She seemed excited as we rode to her house.

"So you're finally going to come inside my house? That's a really big step for you, isn't it? You nervous?"

"No. I wouldn't say it that way." But she was right, I was nervous. I couldn't put a finger on exactly why I was nervous, but my heart was thrashing around like a suffocating fish. My hands were shaking on the steering wheel, but I was doing the best I could to act calm.

Unlocking the front door, she said, "Oh, I have your book. I'm done reading it."

"Oh. Cool. What'd you think about it?"

"You were right, it's an amazing book. It's really sad, but I loved it. I'm ashamed I hadn't read it before." She laughed. I tried to laugh too, but it came out like a mockery of her laugh. It was my nerves. I could feel myself acting strangely.

"Do you still have that lighter I gave you? The one that I gave you for the book."

Unwittingly, I slapped around my pants pockets like a smoker being asked for a cigarette. I settled on something hard in my right pocket: it was her silver lighter. "Yeah. I guess I do still have it. It's right here. Huh?" I didn't remember putting it in my pocket, but there it was.

"You keep it with you?" Her face was bright with a huge smile.

"Yeah. I guess, sometimes, it seems."

"Well, that's good; you should keep it with you. It's a good luck charm. It was my father's, and he gave it to me for good luck. After he gave it to me… he never had very much luck after that, so I guess he was right about it being lucky."

"Oh, wow. I didn't know that. If I would have known that, I wouldn't have taken it. It sounds super important and stuff. It's like sentimental to your family."

"No. It's fine. I make my own luck. I want you to keep it. That's why I gave it to you. I know it's sentimental, but now it's sentimental for you, for us now."

"Oh, that is… wow… I don't… I don't know what to say. Thank you." I was overwhelmed with gratitude. I didn't know how to express how much her kind gift really meant to me. I took her hand and kissed it. "Thank you."

She laughed loudly. "You're so silly. You're a real live chivalrous knight, aren't you? I should call you *Sir* from now on.

Soliloquy

"Let's go get the food before it melts in your car. I'll get your book when we're done."

Shortly after we had finished bringing all the food inside, the calls started coming. For two hours I was guided by her pointer finger and lipped words as to where things should go while she told the callers that the party was already starting and that they'd better hurry or else they'd "miss everything."

The first group of troupers to arrive consisted of D-train, B-rash, and Carmi. Hannah and Essy arrived next. Then a few others arrived in Rachel's car. And lastly, about forty-five minutes after everyone else, alone: John.

John brought with him a large nylon gym bag. It was bright blue with white handles and a tiger paw stamped on each side. The odd thing about it, other than the fact that Mira's home was not a gym, was the sound that the bag made. The bag sounded like it was stuffed with wind chimes. The clinking and clanking from the bag grabbed everyone's attention. Mira, as well as everyone else, peered at John's loud blue bag and his childish grin.

"What you got there?" Mira said.

"*Hahahaha*! Oh this? In this bag here? Oh, do you really want to know?"

"Um, yep, I sure do. That's why I asked."

"Okay, I'm going to tell you, but chill. Promise not to get mad? Okay?" He slowly set the bag down gently on the carpet.

"John, please. Just tell me what's in the damn bag. Don't draw it out. Just tell me." Everyone made a lazy semi-circle behind Mira to view the bag. John knelt down slowly, like a monk beginning a prayer. He unzipped the bag and began unloading glass bottles, one by one, stacking them in front of the bag in an incredibly straight line. There were gasps and hoots. I was not familiar with the particulars of alcohol, but the amount that John had unveiled seemed like a lot for a party of a hundred people, let alone a small one like ours. The glass bottles were filled with different color liquids: translucent, light browns, dark browns, brownish reds, and lime green.

"Where'd you get all that?" Mira said. Her voice did not divulge her feelings on John's blue bag of alcohol.

John smiled widely. "Oh. You know. I have friends in high places? I have a friend that gets it for me."

"I guess that serves as an answer," Mira said.

D-train shouted, "That's like 1,000 dollars' worth of alcohol! Holy *shit*, dude!"

John looked at Mira. "Are you mad?" he said.

For a long time, she did not speak. "No, I'm not mad. Why would I be mad? All I have to say is… if you drink that here, don't spill it, not a drop, don't drip it, don't go overboard, have at least one person that can drive you home or stay the night, don't get too drunk because no one wants to see a bunch of hungover people on stage stumbling around and getting sick tomorrow, and don't get sick anywhere but in the toilet. As a matter of fact, just don't get sick at all. Those are my rules. If you can't follow the rules, don't drink or get out. That simple."

"*Hahahahaha*! Cool! I hope someone brought the Coke… I mean, soda, not coke-coke! *Hahahahahaha*!" John laughed hysterically. He began carefully repacking his blue bag with bottles. "Where do you want this?"

"You can just put it on the kitchen table, I guess. I have some games we can play," Mira announced.

"Sure! Do you have Twister?" J.P. shouted.

"Actually, I do."

"I didn't know you had Twister," Hannah said.

Soliloquy

"Yes, Hannah, I have tons of games you don't know about. Yeah, J.P., I'll bring Twister out. I'll be right back. Can you help me with stuff, please?" she asked me.

I did not respond; I just followed her. I was in a state of confused contemplation. I was trying to process what all was going on. Was everyone going to drink? Why did John bring all that alcohol in the first place? What kind of person would give John a thousand dollars of alcohol? Why was Mira okay with him bringing it? My mind came up with question after question about the situation.

The more I thought about it, the angrier I got. I didn't want to be at a party with a bunch of drunken, stupid people. I was only there for Mira, no one else.

I followed Mira into the kitchen where we found John examining a bottle with scientific seriousness. He held it up close to his face, two fingers on the cap with a flat hand underneath. He really looked like an alcohol connoisseur.

Mira leaned close to my ear. "Please help him. I don't trust him in here with that stuff alone. John! He's going to help you—"

"Help me do what?"

"He's going to help you put all that stuff away. I actually don't want it on the table. Food is going to go on the table. You guys just put it on the counter over there, okay?"

John moved quickly to take his bag to the counter. He had already placed around half the bag's contents on the table.

As I went to lift one of the bottles, to carry it to the appointed counter, it slipped from my hand (the bottle was much heavier than I expected) and it crashed on the floor, making the sound of a baseball smashing through a window.

Soliloquy

246

John jerked his head around. I was just standing there; my shoes and pants were covered in liquid and flakes of hard glass.

Before I knew it, John grabbed me by the neck of my shirt; my face was no more than an inch away from his. He was so close that I could see the pores on his nose and the tiny red veins in his eyes. "What are you doing, retard? *What did you do?*"

"It was an accident," I mumbled. I was sure that what came out of my mouth was gibberish rather than actual words. His chest was heaving against mine. I thought I was going to piss my pants.

"Accident nothing, *you little homo piece of shit*! You did it on purpose! I saw you! You did it on purpose!" Small balls of spit were splashing directly into my eyeballs. He was breathing so fast he was almost hyperventilating.

"I'm sorry. But honestly, it was an accident." My voice was shaking like a scared dog in a thunderstorm and everything hurt when I spoke. I thought about pissing my pants again.

By this time people were standing in the doorway to the kitchen, watching the situation anxiously. A few people were smiling.

"What the hell's going on in here?" Mira said, running over to us.

"This stupid little bastard just tossed a thirty-five-dollar bottle of alcohol on the floor FOR NO REASON!" His mouth was opened so wide, for a moment I thought he was going to bite me. I could see his tonsils clearly. He looked me in the eyes with a level of disgust I had never seen before.

Mira grabbed the hand that held my shirt collar and tried to tug it away. She couldn't. "Let go of him! What is wrong with you, let go of him, asshole!" He finally let go, but he was still just inches from my face, scowling.

"You're going to take his side? He did it on purpose. I saw," John said.

Soliloquy

"Are you serious, John? It is one bottle, one! You have like twenty more. I'm not taking anyone's side, but I don't want you grabbing anyone like that. Not in my house! Use your words. Use your words. It's not worth fighting over, for God's sake! Are you okay?" Her face was covered with sympathy and fear.

"Yeah. I'm fine. I'm fine," I said.

She took me by the hand. "Come with me, come on." She turned to John and said, "I'll be back to clean all that up in a minute. And don't do anything; I'll move everything. That way if something breaks it'll be on me, okay? I'll be back."

She led me through a small hallway to what appeared to be a guest bedroom; the room was clearly unlived in. She sat me down on the bed like a person with sight leading the blind.

"Are you really okay? The bottoms of your pants are all wet. Look at you. What happened in there?" She was still holding my hand.

"Nothing, really. I just accidently dropped a bottle. I don't know. Then he flipped out. That's it, that's what happened. I don't think he likes me. I think he has something against me, but I don't know why. I've never done anything to him."

"Who cares if he likes you? Who cares? I like you and that's all that really matters." She smiled. "You can't worry about people like him. People like him have all kinds of twisted-up issues inside of them. No one will figure out why people are assholes or why people bully people or why people who were bullied grow up to be bullies themselves; albeit pathetic bullies that never got over their childhoods. You just can't worry about it. Just pity him. That's what I do."

"It's stupid. I'm not really worried or anything. It's just stupid."

"You're so right. It is stupid. He's stupid. But don't let him mess up your night, okay?"

"What do you mean?" I said. "I think I'm just going to go home. I don't want to start any more commotions or anything. I think I'm just going to go, just to be safe."

"You can't go. Don't go. It won't be as much fun without you. The best way to stop a bully is not to let him change you. Don't let him change your plans or mood. I'll protect you," she said with a giggle. She put her soft hair on my shoulder, nudging me gently.

"I'm not afraid. I just don't want to cause any more problems."

"Look, if anything else happens between you two… I'll kick him out, I'll make him leave. Okay? Is that a deal? If he does anything else he's gone. Just stay. I want you here."

I hesitated, contemplating what to do. "Okay. I'll stay if you really want me to."

"I do. Now let's get back out there." She stood up and pulled me up by the hand. "I'm going to give that John a talking to."

"I don't know if that's really necessary."

"Oh, it is. It really is."

John was standing in the exact same spot when we reached the kitchen. He appeared to be frozen in time, or like a robot that needed to be rebooted.

"John!" Mira shouted.

He turned toward us very slowly, his head bent down, eyes to the floor.

"Yes?" he said.

"We need to talk!"

"Yes." His face was a mixture of shame and grief. "I have something to say. I just want to say I'm really, really sorry, you know? I am. I'm sorry. I just lost it and that wasn't cool; that wasn't cool at all. I shouldn't have

Soliloquy

grabbed you like that; I shouldn't have called you a homo or whatever. It was just wrong. I am sorry for what I did. It's just alcohol. It's really not that big of a deal. I didn't even pay for it, I don't know why I wigged out so bad."

He seemed sincere, but I still felt like it was all an act. I felt he was putting on a show for Mira and the others who were listening near the doorway.

"I'm apologizing. Do you accept my apology?" He was looking at me with confused puppy dog eyes.

"Oh... um... yes. I accept it. Um... and I'm sorry. I should have been more careful. I'm clumsy and I know it; I should have been more careful."

"It's cool. We're co—"

"That was very mature of you, John," Mira said. "I didn't see that coming, to be honest. I was considering kicking you out of here a few minutes ago."

"No, no, no. You don't have to do that. I promise I've got my act together. I'll clean all this up and stuff and everything's fine. Where's your broom?"

"I'll get it for you. I have to get Twister, too. I almost forgot."

As Mira took off into her garage, I went out to the living room with the others. They were all standing around awkwardly, trying not to make eye contact with me.

I had no intention of playing Twister or any other games, so after Mira set up the game in the middle of the living room floor, I took her aside to ask a favor.

"Can I borrow a book?" I said.

"You don't want to play?"

"Um, not with wet pants. That would be weird. And I'm not very flexible. I'll just read until my pants dry."

"You want me to put them in the dryer for you?"

"Oh, no thanks, but thanks. I'll just let them air dry. It'll be fine. They're not too wet."

"Okay. What kind of book do you want?"

"A novel, please."

"Of course, a novel. But by whom? What kind? Long or short? Hurry, the game's about to start."

"Do you have anything by Bukowski or Eco, something medium-sized maybe?"

"Of course. They're up in my room. I'll be right back."

Within seconds, Mira was back with *The Mysterious Flame of Queen Loana*. Before I could thank her for the book, she was already twirling the color wheel for Twister and saying, "Who's ready to get their ass kicked?"

During Twister everyone was loud and annoying and extremely touchy-feely. There were piggy back rides and tag-you're-an-asshole and pushing games (a person would get on the ground behind an unexpected person and have another person push that person over the stooled person) and titty-twisters and nut-punching games that sent guys headlong to the floor holding their personal parts and groaning with a mixture of laughter and excruciating pain. I was confused, irritated, and mortified. The room was engulfed in a sort of joyful chaos, no one was speaking in normal voices; everyone was yelling to be noticed. It was like a Bacchus-sponsored bash where laughter multiplied on top of other laughter to become screams and cackles (and all of this before the drinks even started to flow).

The night quickly grew odder and odder, faster and darker—less controlled. Everything seemed to be spinning and turning upside down, getting very much out of hand. It seemed to go by in a torrent of shouts and glass clinks and jovial, profane outbursts.

Soliloquy

After Twister (and the first round of drinks) came Apples to Apples (with a side of Schnapps shots). The game quickly, within minutes, devolved into a shouting match. The shouting match deteriorated into a shirtless D-train getting B-rash into a rear-naked choke; B-rash nearly passed out. Then Essy jumped on D-train's back and did her best to choke *him* out, but his neck was too big for her to sufficiently get her arms around, so she got flustered, fell to the ground, and started crying hysterically.

Next came *Shot Pong* (on a small coffee table which made the game less like a real game and more like just a bunch of drunk people taking shots). After *Pong,* the group dispersed all over the house, simultaneously. Small, loud groups of clumped drunks formed small patches of racket all over the place. Some were on the couch mumbling to one another in very emotional voices, saying things like: "No, no, like, seriously. I've known you so long, man… practically my whole life, man. Seriously! I've known you for like ever, you know? It's like… It's like we're brothers, man. I love you, you know? Not gay or nothing, you know, but like really love, you know? You're like my fucking brother, seriously, man, seriously. I know it's crazy that we haven't hung out together in a while. I love you like a brother, man! Seriously!"

I could hear another group of people rummaging through the kitchen cabinets: I kept hearing wooden doors clap shut, then loud giggles, then shushing. I smelled severely burnt pizza and smoke.

I hadn't talked to Mira in hours, which upset me. She had more or less begged me to stay, but then she hadn't talked to me once since she'd gotten me the book. She was too busy playing hostess and waitress and taking shots to notice or acknowledge me. I felt kind of stupid for being so petty, but I couldn't help it. I wanted her to at least acknowledge me. I hadn't once moved from my seat, and despite all the chaos, I had gotten into the book she'd given me.

After a while, everything started to settle down more or less. It was like the quiet smoldering after a fire. Except for the occasional drunken grunt, the house was startlingly silent. The quiet hung in the air like eerie fog. A few people were starting to doze off on the couch. B-rash and Essy were cuddled up together on the floor, doing their best to make out.

I kept wondering where Mira might be. My mind kept repeating the fact that she had asked me to stay, but then she didn't talk to me at all. I could have read to myself at home. I didn't need to be surrounded by wasted drunks to read. My annoyance grew inside my chest, and I started to feel itchy. My stomach was starting to hurt; I realized I was very hungry. The pains in my stomach were like hunger pains but a hundred times worse. I decided to look for Mira and tell her I was going home. It was late, and I wasn't having any fun. My mom was probably wondering where I was. I needed to go.

I set my book, page-opened, on the arm of the once-comfortable chair. I tried not to make any noise; I didn't want to wake the sleeping drunkards. The first place I looked was in the kitchen. She had been in and out of the kitchen all night fixing drinks and rationing snacks, but the only person in the kitchen was Carmi, and he was lying on top of the table in the fetal position making gurgling sounds. (If he was lying on his back, he might have choked to death.)

I went back down the small hallway to the guest room I'd been in earlier, but it was empty. Outside the room, in the hallway, J.P. was face down like a building leaping suicide victim. I figured that maybe she was in her room. I headed carefully up the stairs, being cautious to avoid D-train's large, sprawled frame. He was passed out (or sleeping) with his huge body parts scattered over the majority of the five bottom steps. His head was drooping on his arm, and with his other arm he was hugging a vodka bottle like a clingy baby hugs her teddy bear. D-train looked like a paradox. He looked content and miserable all at the same time. I thought to myself: I know where *this* guy will be in five or ten years. He made a low growling sound as I stepped over him. I paused until the growling stopped, then tip-toed the rest of the way up.

At the top of the stairs there was a dark hallway with multiple rooms on both sides. I walked slowly, quietly, putting my ear near the doors to see if I could hear any voices inside. The first room was completely silent. I put my hand on the door handle as gently as I could; it was locked. The second room was what I assumed to be a bathroom. I could hear water running, coughing, and the loud, clanking ventilation fan.

Before I got to the third door I heard a faint, disquieting noise. It was a faint, mechanical, rhythmic sound. It had the beat of a rickety washing ma-chine, but much faster. The noise stopped me in my tracks, mid-step. I froze, trying to figure out what the noise was, trying to figure out if the sound was real, and why it worried me so much. It sounded like giant heartbeats.

Bump bump
Bump-bump-bump
Bump bump!

I heard a stifled voice that sounded like it was whining to someone about something urgent. There was a palpable strangeness: like the tense, immobile moments that hover in the air right before a fight breaks out. After a few seconds of frozen listening, I moved in closer, moving as slowly as humanly possible, holding my breath, trying not to make a sound, trying not to disturb the heartbeat.

The door was cracked just barely, and there was a small dull-yellow slice of light coming from inside the room. It was dark, but I could almost make out images; my eyes were slow to adjust. I could glimpse the spot where the noise was coming from. I was two inches from the door, my heart was pounding through my throat, I could hear the frantic heartbeat well now; I wasn't imagining it. The sound was real and dire. I didn't want to open the door anymore; I didn't want my eyes to adjust. I wanted to walk away, but I knew I wouldn't walk away. I knew that I was going to see in and see all. My curiosity was beyond my control (I realized then that the cat had no choice but to die, there was truly no other choice. Deep down, we all already know the horrifying truth. It's in us.).

I pushed the door slightly, slowly trying to make out the shady rustling images, trying not to make a sound. As the door squeaked open the noise grew louder, clearer. The pleading muffle sounded familiar to me, but odd, almost sick sounding.

I pushed the door open wider.

In the yellow wedge of light, I could see a bed. I could see two shadowy figures on the bed moving like frantic robbers. I could see they were both half naked (the small figure wearing less than the large figure, the large figure with his shirt around his neck. I could see who they were. I could hear the bed squawking like a mad tormented bird — the terrible heartbeat. I could see that is was John and Mira! I could see that it was John and Mira! I couldn't believe my eyes. I couldn't believe…

I was so confused by what I saw that I felt dizzy, disembodied. I spoke softly, to myself, to hear what I saw as a fact: "*John and Mira? Mira and John? Mira…but…?*"

Then suddenly my thought raced to the fact that he might be raping her. Maybe he was trying to kill her. The way he was slamming and thrashing at her seemed cruel, ruthless, and angry. My hands began pouring with sweat, and I got a lump in my throat that felt like a knife stab. I didn't move.

Soliloquy

Bump bump
Bump-bump-bump
Bump bump!

My heart jumped with a great discharge of pain. I wondered what I should do to help her. Should I find something heavy to bash him over the head with? But in that same second it became clear that it was not rape, he was not harming her. *It was mutual*! She…

Above the thudding heartbeat I finally could discern the pleading sounds, the voice, the whiny, thick words. Her voice was deep, drenched in something, some emotion I couldn't recognize. She sounded as if she had aged a hundred years since I had last heard her voice. Her voice was the voice of a jailer taunting a prisoner.

She was cheering him on in a deep, quiet chant, cajoling him, like a jockey pushing a hurt horse to the finish line. The more he flailed, the more she coaxed. Her legs flailed loosely. My eyes could see; I could make out her hands on his back. They were making small, passionate paws.

The truth of what I saw with my own eyes and the disbelief in my heart were playing a vicious game of tug-of-war with my mind. I couldn't believe the truth. I couldn't believe that reality could allow something like that to happen. It was like watching a family member be tortured… it felt like I was having open-heart surgery without anesthesia. It hurt so bad that the pain in my heart made me angry. Why would evolution let us hurt this badly? I couldn't breathe—I couldn't catch a breath. Dizziness came in cold white waves. I felt like even air had forsaken me. My heart was throbbing mush or jelly in my chest. It hurt so bad that the pain seemed alien, like a quick-acting virus taking over me, turning me into something entirely different. It seemed like an exponent of pain! Pain to the 100th! It felt like pain and sadness had a diseased baby and placed it in my chest and called it my heart. I was watching myself die in slow motion. I knew what it was to already be dead. Knowing was dying.

It's hard to explain. Words can't account for or make known the pain that I felt. But the pain was *more* and changing. I was instantly aware that I would never be the same again. It was as if the pain had fused with my DNA. I was instantaneously altered. I was angry and afraid and different. Afraid of what, I don't know. Maybe afraid of seeing behind the curtain, of seeing just how messed up reality could be, seeing just how unfair reality was, just how false, just how unjust.

I was witnessing Mira rip off her skin to reveal a hideous monster underneath. The whole world had changed in a few split seconds, and I was utterly unprepared. I could feel a part of me turn cold and malevolent; a huge hate snapped awake inside me like a child having its first nightmare, and the good part of me gave up and gave way. I felt bitter in my nervous system, in my cells, in my nuclei. I felt like I had been bitter for millions of years, jaded. It was like knowing just how powerless I was for the very first time. I could feel myself morphing inside. The little part of me that believed, that had faith and hope... it had died. Watching her do something horrible helped turned me into something horrible.

It all happened in a few seconds. (It doesn't take long to change or die.) I was changed. The old me was no more. I had hate and terrible truth in every part of me, every morsel. It was fuming inside me and it made my already-upset stomach more upset. My insides felt like I had swallowed a star.

I was full of two kinds of disgust: one kind for her, for letting this monster trick me into believing she was something she was not. And the other disgust I felt for myself, for me believing her, for not seeing what she was truly capable of. (I've always heard people say that you shouldn't underestimate people. They are right. But I learned that you should never overestimate them either.) I was disgusted for not seeing the putrid contradiction she really was. There was disgust for myself for believing in people, believing in this perverse, sick world that we live in. I was disgusted for believing in anything that occupies this world.

All these thoughts flashed through my head in a span of no more than 45 seconds. I kept peering through the cracked door. I eventually heard myself scream, not a normal scream, but a death curdle. The scream of someone being castrated or murdered. It was an animal shriek. I was not in control. The scream had come on its own, bursting from a place beyond my own voice.

John jump-flopped to his side and reached for his pants, which were bound around his ankles.

"What the *fuck*!" he yelled in a nervous voice. "Who's there?"

From the yellow slice of light, I could see Mira's face, her eyes mostly. They were as clear as day. They were full. They were full of fear, and confusion, and resentment. Her eyes didn't seem to even recognize me. They seemed to only recognize an object, a *thing* that was invading her privacy, her personal, sexual space.

"What are you doing, perv?" John yelled, still wrestling with his pants. "What the *hell* are you staring at?"

I finally broke free from my shock and sprinted, wobbly-legged, down the dark hallway. The bathroom door opened (and a female voice muttered syllables of nonsense). D-train's massive figure was blocking the opening to the staircase.

"What the hell's going on up here!" he boomed.

"Move!" I shouted, squeezing sideways past him. He moved just a crack, hesitantly, and I stumbled down the first few steps, and then fell head-first down the rest of the stairs. I hit my face on the rail. Blackness with flakes of perfectly round spots of white dots floated upwards in my dazed mind's eye. When the speckled sky of blackness faded, and I came to at the bottom of the stairwell, I was only moderately conscious. I felt submerged in invisible water. I could feel something like rug burn on my cheek; I could feel warm blood dripping down my face. Large dots of blood splattered from my nose, down my lips and chin. I tried to catch the dripping with the bottom of my shirt.

There was a cluster of people, half-sleeping, half-drunken spectators, in the living room looking at me with wordless curiosity, amazement, and revulsion. They all seemed submerged in the same heavy, invisible water that I was in.

I gathered myself as best I could and ran for the front door, but before I could reach it, I was stopped in my tracks by a pain in my stomach. I dropped to a knee, clutching my stomach with fear and puzzlement. I heard myself scream again, another inhuman scream. All of the onlookers gasped and backed away. I hunched over and heaved violently, hoping to get the pain out. Nothing came. I picked myself up again and ran out the front door.

I could hear John at the front door. He was shouting: "You little perv! What's wrong with you, you perv!"

I couldn't get Mira's eyes out of my head, the way she looked at me like I was a stranger, a nobody, like I was someone she'd never met before, like I was a frightening peeping Tom. Remembering her fear caused my heat to spasm. I couldn't get rid of the sight of her eyes.

I fumbled with the car's heavy door, got in as if I were being chased by hungry bears, and drove!

I drove and drove. And all I felt was pain.

Soliloquy

Chapter 8

"Everything Becomes Tragedy"

I woke up numb, completely void of all feelings. The pain had drained me (psychologically and physically). My left cheek felt dull and raw and clawed. My nose felt broken, well out of its normal position. Both of my eyes were swollen and puffy, my blinking was tight and awkward. My back felt dislocated in a few different spots; I was sure several disks had been slipped, but I was not worried or in pain; I was feeling emotionless.

I thought I should just stay in my bed and refuse to go to the play or get up at all. Maybe I should just lie here and die, I thought. I really couldn't imagine going to the play after what had happened. It was the day of the big, big play, and I was neither happy nor excited. They really didn't need me anyway, I thought. No one seemed to need me, not even my own pain receptors seemed to need me. My pain had left me before I could contemplate it or get annoyed by it. I was, simply, numb.

I wasn't depressed. I didn't care enough about anything to be depressed. What I had seen and understood had emptied me of all my illusions about everything, about people—about myself—about life—about reality. I was devoid of all sense and nonsense. Desire, hope, friendship, kinship, loyalty, all of that stuff was exposed in the same way: it was shit, one-sided wishful thinking. I didn't even know if I was capable of loyalty or friendship anymore. Was anyone really capable of those things? Was it all just a sick joke, a trick? Had those things, "virtues," ever been real? (I was too empty and bored to continue my train of thought.)

Mira was a deceiver, a contradictor. She had deceived me. She had me completely and utterly under a spell. I was a fool. I had actually thought she liked me. I'd truly thought I liked her too. I'd thought that there might be something there, inside her, that I could understand. I had believed that we were flowing in the same stream—in the same direction, operating under the same value-sets and belief systems. I had thought we were *alike*.

But lying in bed, detached, void, without any apprehensions or misapprehensions, I was fully aware that I had never known her. I was aware that you could be around someone for a lifetime and never know who they really were exactly—there would always be an ambiguity—a space—something missing—a secret.

I realized that this was because most people weren't even aware of who they were themselves, so how could someone else know them? If a person never became a *real* person, how could you know what kind of person they really were? I had never known what she was really about or what drove her. Attention? Boredom? Malice? Nihilism? Sadism? Insecurity? I had only known, if that's the right word, just the shadow she wanted to project, if that. Maybe I was projecting my hopes onto her? Maybe the time we spent was all an act for her, some sort of personal, social experiment. Maybe she was a dog and I was the chew toy. Maybe I had only known a character she had invented because she was lost, lonely, and in a new place. A character invented by a confused girl in order to… in order to what? What was her point in befriending me, then deceiving me, then abandoning me (with that look)? What did she gain by it all? What did she gain from badmouthing John every single time he was mentioned when, deep down, she was willing to stretch herself completely open for him and give away something she could never get back? What was her point?

None of my questions aroused any answers or genuine emotions. I lay there. I didn't even look at the clock. I may have even fallen back to sleep.

Soliloquy

After a time, I heard someone outside my door. The person did not say anything; they just shuffled about on the other side of the door. I heard soft foot slides and taps. The foot noise went on and on for a long while. Then came a knock.

"*Yes!*" I shouted. The deepness of my own voice frightened me.

"Son? Son, it is your father. Son, it's time for lunch. And, also, you need to start getting prepared for practice and the play."

"Practice?"

"Yes. The director called and told us to remind you that practice will be taking place at the *Lyceum* today before the play. Did you not hear the phone ring?"

"No. I didn't."

"Okay. Well, gather yourself together and head downstairs, as soon as possible. It's time." I could hear his footsteps recede.

I thought very long and hard about not getting up. I thought about barricading myself inside my room and never coming out. But what would I do about food?

All at once, I realized that I didn't have any real options. I couldn't really just *choose* to stay in bed and skip out, could I? I wasn't in charge. I didn't know who was in charge or what was in charge, but I realized, as clear as day, like in a frightening moment of enlightenment or epiphany, I wasn't in charge. *I was not free!*

It was crystal clear: I wasn't free to barricade myself inside my room. It wasn't really my room. It was my mom and dad's room, or maybe my room was a banker's room (did we have a mortgage?), or maybe the house was owned by some big Wall Street bank that was shared by thousands and thousands of little people and pension funds who owned part of the big Wall Street bank, but it wasn't my room. I didn't own it. Maybe my room was

Soliloquy

owned by thousands of people I didn't even know! I didn't own shares. I was in a room that wasn't my own. How could I be in charge?

I couldn't say, "No!" I'm not going to eat. I'm going on a forty-day fast, a hunger strike, for spiritual reasons, or "No!" I'm not going to go to a play where I'm not wanted or needed. I'm going to write my own play. I couldn't say *NO*! If I did, I would be punished by someone or something for not following the unwritten rules of society. I had never thought of the unwritten rules before—the invisible, heavy, thoughtless hand: the semi-universal cultural chains that bound me to things and people I didn't understand and never once gave thought to. It was frightening to think about (my first non-numb moment of the day… fear).

I thought to myself: What can I do? What do you do when you find out you're not really free? Lying there, I decided that in spite of the fact that I couldn't say "no" and that I wasn't in charge and that I was bound by indiscernible, maniacal forces, I could do something; there was still one thing. I could *say yes in my own way,* on my own terms, if I tried hard enough.

Yes: I would go downstairs as I was told, but I would not sit down at the table to eat. I would stand. And, yes, sure, I would go to practice and see John and that horrible girl, but I would not shower or put on clean underwear or clean clothes or brush my teeth. I would be dirty and foul and unkempt. I would be like a hermit in the woods, a dirty sage, a guru on a mountaintop, a metropolitan John the Baptist.

I would go where people told me to go, but I would not follow a direct, linear path; I would not walk in a straight line; I would curve where there were no curves, make my own curves, and zig, if I wanted to, for no apparent reason, maybe even do a whirl if I felt the need. And I would move as slowly as I felt the need to move, or as quickly, and I would not move things the way *they* would move things; I would put my own spin on it, my own personal touch. I would move things with the buoyancy and inattention of a carefree cavalier. I wouldn't care unless *I* wanted to care. I would be a permanent performance artist. I would not fake being happy or smile, and if I did happen to smile on my own accord, on my own newly minted semifreewill, it would be a new smile, a peculiar, unique type of smile that no one had ever seen before. It would be shameless and off-putting and daring, but it would be my own. I would not joke, but if it had to happen, it would be one single knock-knock joke, the same one over and over again, until people started finishing the joke's ending for me in exasperation; they would know my joke. *Yes!* That was it: I would do what I was told, but I would do what I was told in my own, personally chosen, anomalous, one-off, slipshod sort of way.

My realization gave me a warm rush. I could feel the dullness starting to lift. The pain was on its way back (which I took to be a good thing). I was excited to start my experiment, my life as an experiment. I kicked off my covers and jumped out of bed. I plunged into my smelly, unwashed jeans, and I rummaged around for the smelliest shirt I could find.

Downstairs, when I arrived at the table, I almost forgot to stand. (New habits are hard to create.) I reached over my chair for my plate of bright orange mac-and-cheese. My mother said, "What… what are you doing? My god, your face! What's wrong with the side of your face?! Your face—"

"Oh, um, nothing's wrong. Just a thing. I fell. Um… and I'm standing up to eat."

"What?!"

"Yes. I mean. I am going to eat standing up if you don't mind… if that's okay."

"Of course I mind! You don't live in a barn. And what is that smell?"

"I read… I read an article, an article in the Journal of Nutrition that said that if you eat standing up you will have much better digestion, okay? And… well… I don't know… lately I've been cons… constipated, okay! I've been totally constipated—"

"What?!"

"I've been constipated. My poop won't… See! Are you happy? Happy now? Are you happy that I said that out loud at the dinner table? All I wanted to do was stand. Is that a crime? Does that make me some kind of fu—"

"It's okay, son. It is fine," my father said calmly. He was stroking his jaw line with one hand and adjusting his glasses with the other. My mother's face was emotionless, as if all the life had left her body. She looked corpse-like. I was confused, I had no idea what I was saying or why I was saying it, but I felt excited and strong and afraid. I felt like I had breached a rip in the fabric of reality, as if I had seen behind the quantum curtain. I was bending and breaking rules before I could concern myself with the consequences.

"I may have read that someplace as well, son. That article. It sounds like a valid trial, don't you think, Mary?"

My mother stared at her plate solemnly. "I will not answer that. This is totally ridiculous, and I will not take part in it. I will not let these shenanigans ruin my day. I refuse." She adjusted her seat awkwardly, and then she began devouring her food by the forkful.

I was stunned by my audacity and by my victory. I didn't care about my mom's pouting. I stood behind my seat and ate my food in a triumphant daze, wondering if I was dreaming. I wondered if any rules were real.

For a while, no one spoke, not until my dad said, "Aren't you wondering why I am not at work, son?"

"Oh. Yeah. Why not?"

Soliloquy

"They, the company, is allowing me to—" He was cut off by the phone's dull ring. "I will get it," he said, scrambling from the table. My mother was still mechanically stuffing her face, barely chewing, swallowing with angry gulps.

"Son. It is your performance director, Miss Magdalene. She said practice is starting at this moment." He held the phone towards me.

"Oh. Okay. Um… tell her I'm on my way," I said. Then I headed towards the door, plate still in hand.

"Aren't you going to change your clothes? You look and smell terrible," my mother said.

"Maybe," I said, and then I walked out to my car.

***

On the ride to the *Lyceum* I felt a cold chill, and the numbness began to take hold again. The weather was changing, and I was caught unprepared. A harsh breeze was swirling heavily in the air, and the clouds hung down like old pale skin. The sun was out, but it seemed so far away. It was as far away as I had ever seen it.

About four or five blocks away from the theater I heard the distant sound of steak being fried, a low, fast hissing sound. The sizzling noise grew into a harsh crackling sound by the time I realized that my engine was starting to smoke. The smoke billowed from the rusted hood like a chimney excreting wood fumes. I quickly pulled over to the side of the road.

I had a gallon of water in my trunk for just such an occasion. But for once I had sympathy for my car; I was starting to understand the sort of toll outside forces could take on an object. I poured the water in carefully and let the car sit for a while. When I went to start it, the engine would not turn over. Not even a little bit. It was completely lifeless. I turned the key a few more times: nothing.

Soliloquy

Despite the cold wind, I decided to walk the rest of the way to the theater.

When I saw the *Lyceum,* I was amazed by how it made me feel. I felt... almost happy. I could feel my face smiling, my cheeks flexed, and my lips curled. My feet were moving faster and faster toward the beautiful building. I felt what I now think was euphoria. I ran, as fast as I could up the steps and through the doors.

I had missed the *Lyceum* (my only true friend). I had missed how it made me feel. I had missed its quiet consistency. It was a place that seemed outside of time, outside of my own world of emotions, outside of the daily mess and boredom, outside of the filthiness and uncertainty of all my relationships. What the *Lyceum* offered was beyond my life and the real world. It was beyond real. It was sacred.

Everything was still and factual in the *Lyceum.* The multicolored marble and huge paintings seemed to radiate gravity and sincerity. I could hear jumpy voices coming from inside the main theater.

As I pushed open the heavy doors, everyone stopped what they were doing. Everyone. They all looked at me with non-recognition and fear. Miss Magdalene waved me toward her. "Hurry. You're late," she said. I did not adjust my speed at all, but I did follow her wave.

Mira and John were rigidly standing in the middle of the large stage. I looked at Mira, but her eyes would not return my glance. She was looking off into space like a sick dog preparing to die. On stage Miss Magdalene gave me a slew of directions of where things needed to be moved. She told Paul to show me what she needed moved, and she commanded us to hurry.

There was a large space behind the thick red curtain, then a black curtain—a curtain I never knew existed. This black, taut curtain was a few feet from the back wall. Behind the taut curtain was a menagerie of ropes (dangling from various places), rolling staircases, old wooden ladders, a small stand-alone closet, different sized boxes with Sharpie inscriptions, costume racks stuffed with clothes, a roughshod of backpacks all over the ground, particle-board set pieces, and a huge cement wall. The setup was much more elaborate than the one at Miss Magdalene's church.

"Okay, buddy," Paul said. "Bags go there, house-sets there, roll those racks over to that side, and you need to move all the moveable things from the little closet back there, k?"

"Okay."

"You sure you got it, little buddy?"

"Yes. I got it, Paul."

"Good. I'll come back to check up on you a little later, to make sure you got it," he said, slapping me on the back with his yellow paper pad. He paused and looked over the top of his large glasses for what felt like a very long time; then he forced out a smile that was more grimace than anything else, then he flitted away.

Behind the curtain, I was glad to be alone. I had never enjoyed being by myself more than I did in that moment. I totally got what "nirvana" meant. Paul's departure was like heaven to me. I did not want to be alone with my thoughts or my feelings or anything like that; I just wanted to be completely alone.

I went about moving all the stuff without thinking. I was on autopilot. The voices of the cast were back, echoing loudly off the theater walls. The echoes didn't compromise my joyously alone moment, it reinforced it. The echoes made me feel like the words and the people who spoke them were worlds away, so far away that they could never reach me. But Paul's reappearance quickly brought me back to earth. His shadow startled me.

Soliloquy

"Buddy. It's time to come on back. Practice is about to wrap. Good job back here. You got a lot accomplished. Good job, buddy."

I was taken aback by the lack of sarcasm in his voice. "Oh. Thanks. I guess I did."

Everyone was gathered in a seated semi-circle around Miss Magdalene. She was standing like a statue of confidence. She looked like an army general reveling in a massive victory.

"There will be a two-hour recess before we meet back here for dress and make up, okay? I do not want you going very far off. My suggestion is that we all go to Burger Jack's and eat as a group. This way no one will show up late and compromise the performance. All in favor, raise your hands." Everyone looked around to see if raising their hands would conform to the will of the group. After one hand went up, the rest followed excitedly.

"It's almost three," Miss Magdalene said. "That should give us all time to go eat, relax, and be ready to—"

Before Miss Magdalene was done, Paul interrupted. "I need someone to help me move something backstage. John could—" he said.

"I don't mind," D-train shouted.

"No, it's fine. It'll only take one person to help me move it."

"I'll do it," John said. His voice was emotionless.

"Thanks, John." Paul said, looking down at his yellow notepad.

Miss Magdalene said, "Okay. Everyone else, follow me. To Burger Jack's we go."

"But what… but what about money, I need my purse to get—" Rachel said.

"Don't worry about it. It's on me, my treat to all of you guys for all your hard work to get us here, on this amazing stage. I am more than happy to pay."

Soliloquy

Mostly everyone cheered, jumped up from their spots, and ran towards the doors. They were a noisy, jovial horde. John went backstage with Paul, Mira trailed listlessly toward the back of the fast-moving mob, and Miss Magdalene and I pulled up the far rear. A few times on our way through the grand corridor, Miss Magdalene took a quick peek at me from the corner of her eye. She looked like she was going to say something, but no words ever came.

As we walked towards the restaurant, Miss Magdalene shouted: "Darn-it!" She grabbed my arm as if she was struck by lightning or the jab of a heart attack. I was startled and confused.

"What's wrong! What's wrong," I said in a panic. The rest of the group was now far ahead of us. It was just her and I, and I was not qualified to deal with any serious medical situation. I looked around for help, but no one was near.

She said, "Can you go back and get my purse? It's the pink one with a big silver buckle on it. You can't miss it. Trust me. You can't miss it. Hurry, please."

I was completely relieved and annoyed. "Yes. No problem. I'll go get it." I jogged back up the stairs and back through the main doors. It was eerily peaceful and silent. I stood there for a moment taking in the silence. I had never been in that place by myself before. I had always been there with lots of other people, lots of people I didn't know, but being alone in such a beautiful and magnificent place was different. It was supernatural. I just stood there for a while, almost forgetting what I was there for.

When my silent moment had moved past, I hurriedly headed backstage. I had placed all the scattered duffle bags and purses together along the concrete wall; I was trying to remember if I had seen a pink purse when I stumbled upon what can only be described as a life-altering, soul-kicking, reality-

Soliloquy

wrecking, mind-warp-of-a-surprise: pressed up against the side of the closet were John and Paul: the two were kissing, making out passionately (it was so intense, it was bordering on violent): John's pants and underwear were planted around his ankles: his penis was exposed: Paul was doing various things with his hands.

At first, I didn't move or even breathe. They were so into what they were doing that they didn't notice I was there, no more than twenty feet away. I looked away. I saw the pink purse, but it seemed like light years away. What was I to do? My head was pounding and spinning, and my stomach was in unbearable knots.

My only thought was: *Back away… slowly back away.*

As I tried to tiptoe backwards, softly, John must have heard me because he gasped and made frightened eye contact. The look on his face was literally indescribable. He screamed the most terrified and sad scream I had heard since my own scream just the night before.

"NOOOOOOOOOOOOOOOOOOOOOOOOOOOOOOOOOOOOO!!!!!!" he shouted. He sounded like his soul had fallen off a cliff. It was so loud; the echo was so unnaturally extreme. I was sure that people walking down the street must have heard him. I almost peed myself out of fear of his fear. "NOOOOOOOOOOOOOOOOO!!!!!!!!!!!!" he shrieked again. He reached for his pants, stumbled a bit, and then fell straight backwards, cracking his head with a thud on the wooden floor. His head made the sound of a bat hitting a baseball on its sweet spot, like a home run. The sound was sickening and jarringly similar.

Paul was grabbing at his belt and zipper area as if his pants and hands were on fire.

Soliloquy

I was instantaneously frightened, shocked, dizzy, and nauseous. Without thinking, I darted for the pink purse. I don't know why I went for the purse, but I did.

Paul shouted, "Whyyyyyyyyyyyyyy!!?? What the hell are you doing back here? Whyyyyyyyyyyyyyy? Why did you come back!!!!!?????"

I didn't answer him, but I kept looking at him as I reached the purse. John wasn't screaming or making any noises. He was motionless on his back. He looked like he was sleeping. His pants were still around his ankles. He was out cold. Paul dropped to his knees, his face over John's face, yelling, "Why!!!!! NO! Why!!!!!!!!!!!!!!!!!!"

I snatched the purse from the line of bags, and I ran. I ran faster than I knew I could run. I just ran as fast as I could back to Miss Magdalene.

I finally caught up with Miss Magdalene at the door of the restaurant. She instantly knew something was unusually wrong with me.

"What's wrong with you, boy? You look like you were getting chased by a ghost!"

"Oh. No. Purse. Here is."

"What? You're not even speaking English. Are you all right?"

"Oh. Yeah. Yep. Fine… I'm fine. Just… just… asthma."

"Are Paul and John on their way?"

"Um… maybe. Yeah. I don't know. I think they, yeah, I think so."

Inside Jack's the group was happy and playful. People were moving around like they were playing a game of silent musical chairs. Hands were flailing and clapping. The laughs were unbridled and mindless. My head was swirling.

I sat next to Miss Magdalene and ordered a banana and strawberry milkshake. My stomach was too upset for anything else. She kept looking at me out of the corner of her eye with distrusting confusion.

Soliloquy

"I thought you said Paul and John were on their way?" Miss Magdalene said.

"Yeah," I said, trying hard to sound calm and honest. "Yeah. That's what I thought."

"Ummm…" Her face was like cold stone, focused in irritated concentration.

Finally, after what seemed like hours, Paul walked up to the tables looking pale and mortified. He was fidgeting with his fingers and sweating profusely.

"Where's John?" Miss Magdalene immediately said.

"Sissy… can I… can we talk?"

With a voice like *de ja vu*, she said, "Where's John?" Her look didn't change. She just stared at him.

Paul's eyes quickly darted in my direction. He licked his lips a couple of times, started staring off into space, and said, "He got a phone call—his cell phone. I don't know, sis. He got a phone call, he started crying, and he ran off. I don't know what happened. I tried to stop him. I tried to follow him. I asked him what was wrong. I don't know. He just wouldn't stop crying. He just kept crying so hard that he couldn't talk. Then he ran off. I think it was a family emergency. It must have been some sort of family emergency because of how hard he was crying, but honestly, I don't know what happened at all. It wasn't my fault. I just don't really know what happened."

Miss Magdalene did not move or speak for almost a minute. She just stared at Paul's pale, dripping face.

"Okay, Paul," she said in a semi-soft voice. "Okay. I will find out. I'll find out what happened."

Paul glanced at me again. I looked away. He must have known that I hadn't told on him.

Soliloquy

Miss Magdalene reached for her pink purse, picked out her cell phone, and walked outside.

Paul walked to an empty table by the window and put his head down like a sleepy school child.

I drank some of my milkshake, but it did nothing but add to my stomach's excruciating pain.

When Miss Magdalene reentered her face was the same.

"He didn't answer," she said aloud, to no one in particular. She hurriedly walked up to me, grabbed me by the bicep, and said, "Come with me. Outside, now."

I was terrified. I hadn't ever seen Miss Magdalene's eyes look like that before. She looked like she wanted to hurt me. I figured her plan was to interrogate me about what I saw, what I knew. I didn't want to be questioned, and I damn sure didn't want to give any answers. My head was spinning; I just wanted to be done. I wanted to be home in my so-called room or at the library reading in silence. I wanted to be alone. I was tired of everything, and I didn't know what to say when she asked me what I saw.

"Well. Remember that talk we had? Remember?" she said.

"The talk aboooout?" my mind was scrambling.

"Our talk about if you had to go on stage," she said. Her voice was rushed but not angry. "Remember I told you that if you ever get your moment to shine, you should take it and use it. Not to shy away from it. Remember?"

"Yes, ma'am. I remember you said that."

"Remember I said you will never know who you are until you test yourself? Remember I said that?"

"Yes. I remember."

"Well, now just might be that time."

Soliloquy

"Oh. Now? Oh."

"No one can find John. I called. I called him several times, and I called his parents. No one knows. That means if he doesn't show up within the next... 45 to 50 minutes or so, you will have to go on and be the lead."

"Me?" The word dribbled out of my mouth like a heavy stone. I knew what she had been hinting at all along, but the mush of my trampled mind and the psychological vertigo of the previous 24 hours had made me very, very slow.

"Yes, you. There is no one else. We talked about this before. As I said, the troupe needs you. And you need to prove something to yourself. You can't hide in the shadows forever. Today is the day you step up. Am I clear?"

"Well... yes... yes, you're clear."

"I'm sorry to be so frank, but there isn't time to be tactful. We are almost out of time. I need you to step up for the troupe. And don't say 'you'll try.' Trying won't be enough at this point. At this point... success is the only option. Lots of people are coming to see us; lots of people. This is it."

"Okay," I said. I didn't know what else to say. There wasn't anything else to say.

"Well, I'm going to give you a few minutes to wrap your head around this. I know it's a lot, a lot to take in. Don't say anything to the others about this. I will break it to them in time. At the right time. Now is not the time to tell them. So, stay out here and gather yourself together. You can come inside when you're ready."

I sat down on the cold sidewalk. I crossed my achy legs and tried to wrap my head around the situation, but I couldn't. The only thing I could wrap my head around was the fact that I couldn't, due to my twisted tiredness, wrap my head around anything.

Soliloquy

My scratched-up face, my bruised ribs, my throbbing arm didn't bother me; they were the least of my worries. What bothered me was the fact that my exhaustion itself was a sort of terrible pain, a deep, unbearable achiness in every quirk of my body. I felt like gravity and air were instruments of torture. Existing, living, in and of itself, felt like the worst pain imaginable. My life was pain, and vice versa.

I sat on that sidewalk for a long time, just feeling it, a pain that was marrow deep. Feeling myself *as* pain.

I wondered if I had the strength to get up, let alone walk, or perform, or live. But in time it came to me again, my new-found ability: My *YES*! I could say yes to pain, couldn't I? Others had. Others had taken the pain out of pain. Some philosophers found that there was more to pain than meets the eye. Millions of martyrs had wrapped pain around themselves like a cloak of meaning. Billions of ravaged laborers had known pain better than they had known their own children. They all had found something in pain. They had understood it; they had *used* it. Could I?

I gathered myself and went back inside. I looked at Mira, but she didn't look back. Everyone was still floating in a loud happy mist. Their plates were stacked on the table like childish sculptures. Miss Magdalene was reaching into her purse. After the bill was paid to a hyper brunette waitress, the troupe exited the restaurant like a swarm of bees. Again, Miss Magdalene and I brought up the rear, but this time Paul lagged behind even us. I saw his face. He looked thunderstruck, sick, and scared. His walk was shaky. (If I had had the energy, I might have felt bad for him.) I thought about how he must feel. I wondered about what must've been going through his mind. I wondered if the pain he felt outweighed my own pain. I doubted it. Then I realized that everyone felt terror; everyone felt the crumbling of his or her own world. It was weird to me how one small group of people could be feeling such a wide range of emotions at the exact same time: joy, terror, betrayal, comfort, worry, nothing. We were all on the same sidewalk, but we were all in different places.

Back in the *Lyceum*, Miss Magdalene gathered us all on stage. I could tell by her tone that she was going to break the bad news. No one had asked about John (that I had heard). They were all so absorbed in their self-gratifying laughter that they were oblivious to the situation, except maybe Mira.

Her face was smothered in a false grin. I saw that her joy was fake. She was a marionette or a frightening doll. She smiled as if her jaw hurt. She laughed as if there was someone behind her with a knife making her laugh. I could see through her false smile to her sadness.

"Quiet down please," Miss Magdalene hissed. "I need you all to be very quiet right now."

Most of her speech was overshadowed by all of the hysteria and interruptions: "Jona... we need to... there is a poss... we all just need to cal... this isn't the end of the.... Hey! Watch your... this isn't... You all need to... d—" and it went on this way for quite a while.

I didn't mind the panic. I expected it, honestly. Why wouldn't they freak out that John had up and disappeared? Why wouldn't they be frightened that I was going to fuck everything up? Why wouldn't they? I was too drained to be offended. I understood.

After the majority of the hysteria, crying, and cursing was finished, Miss Magdalene ordered us to do a walkthrough without costumes. I guess she thought it would take our minds off the situation; it didn't. It was getting close to stage time.

The walkthrough could only be compared to a funeral. Dreary people in different stages of depression: grief, denial, bargaining, and anger. Most of them weeping with their twisted faces and walking around like zombies with extremely heavy monkeys on their backs. Everyone was distraught in their own special way. Some people would mumble their lines. Some would outright wail their lines. Paul looked terrified, Miss Magdalene looked like she had just found out she was pregnant, Mira looked like a comatose person with her eyes taped open. The whole scene was unreal.

We eventually set up some of the props, then we all took turns changing in the flimsy closet; all the girls went first. They needed extra time to put on their makeup and do their hair in farm girl braids, bonnets, and pigtails. I was the last person into the dressing room. As I took off my dirty pants (they literally smelled like a homeless person had donated them to me) and went to fold them, I heard a loud thump on the ground and something hard ping-ponging between my feet. It startled me. On the ground was the lighter Mira had given me, the Zippo lighter. I picked it up and looked at it closely. The lighter seemed to be always there, omnipresent. I couldn't shake it. I put the lighter in my sock for safekeeping, for luck, put on my grotesquely oversized costume, and went back out with the rest of the group.

Behind the heavy red curtain, I could hear soft voices and muffled footsteps. The audience was starting to trickle in. Their whispers were like scratches on a chalkboard of my weary mind. Miss Magdalene was never more than ten feet away from me. Every two or three minutes she would accost me with intense bursts of encouragement. "You've got this," and "You remember your lines, I know you do," and "Just do it how you did it in our walkthrough, you did fine." I would just shake my head in agreement, and then travel back to my terrified state.

The wait was purgatory. I stood in the same spot for what seemed like a lifetime.

I eventually heard the words: "Ten minutes to show time!"

Soliloquy

I felt like I needed to vomit, or sit down, or both. I looked at the faces of the others. They were all filled with nervousness.

The soliloquy was first. Just me and the words. I had them memorized. But I was first. Somehow that made things worse. I prayed that John would reappear and say, "What the hell are you doing in my costume, perv!" and take back his post. I was frantic and exhausted. I had zero left inside of me. I was not ready.

Miss Magdalene grabbed me by the shoulders. "Stop it. Don't overthink it. Just say the lines from your heart. Just say the lines. Okay? That's all. Think of it like you're just saying the Pledge of Allegiance. Think of it as if you are leading the audience in the Pledge of Allegiance. Okay?" The whole time she was leading me to my spot on the stage. The curtains were about to open. "Can you do that?" she said. "Can you think of it that way? Breathe."

"Okay. Yes. Okay," I said. I could not think. I could not breathe.

Miss Magdalene said, "If you forget your lines just look over to me, and I will help you." She went out of the curtain and gave a short, loud speech to the audience.

I couldn't believe that the curtain was about to open, and I would be the person who was supposed to speak. The world had changed, and I was standing there, behind the curtain I used to beg to open, shaking, hoping that it was all in my head and this was all some sort of big practical joke. I was visibly shaking. Then, Miss Magdalene came back. I could hear her softly count down from: "10 … 9… 8… 7…."

The curtain was pulled back; I was instantly blinded by the brightness of the light.

There I was. It was time. I had to speak. I had to say something! "Th… Ther… There comes a time… when… in every man's life when he must choose. Um… He must choose between submitting… submitting to himself

Soliloquy

and…" In that moment I froze. Something inside of me was out if its natural place. I had to do what I had to do. That was the only way. "He must choose between what he knows to be right… or submit to opinion, or convention, or falseness." My words were not from the script. I was saying things I wasn't supposed to say!

"The phoniest people among us are the quickest to throw the first stone, wield the bloodiest ax, and whisper the first baseless rumor. They scoff first. They backstab first. Annihilate first! We love to watch the good burn—the good have always been our sacrifice—the young, the weak, the innocent, the true. We love to watch 'the other' go up in fucking flames, so we can all say, 'See. I knew it! Nobuddy is perfect!' We love blaming our flawed nature for our evil, premeditated deeds. We love, 'I'm only human.' And I had bought into that belief. I believed that I was weak because everyone else was weak. Everyone else made excuses, why not me?"

Out of the corner of my eye I saw Miss Magdalene and Paul talking frantically. Paul started pulling the curtain closed. Unconsciously, when the curtain reached me, I took the silver lighter out of my sock and grabbed the curtain; I wrapped the curtain around my hand a few times. I placed the flaming lighter near the curtain. Paul stopped closing the curtain. "I… as I stand here in this moment… I have made my choice. I choose to submit to what I know is right. To facts. To the Truth. And the truth is… truth is, I can't stand this place… this town, you people, us! I can't stand you sick, vile people—criminals against hope—against possibilities! You make me sick. People are shit, you know it, but you don't care. As you sit there in your comfortable cushy seats, waiting smugly to be once again stuffed and gorged with entertainment, with fun, with pretention. I feel sick to my stomach. You are rotting away in a tiny, false prison of your own making. You are rotting in

the small, cramped prisons of your minds' waywardness, deceit, prejudice...
deliberate ignorance!"

I saw the faces in the crowd. Many people looked confused, some
looked humored, others looked upset.

"Let me assure you my words come from a lifetime of listening, waiting, and watching you and your evil ways. Smelling the putridness of this
sick and corrupt town. A lifetime of painful research.

"I have seen just how small your prisons are, and how knowingly you
strive to push all the generations to come after in an even smaller box then
the one you so ravenously inhabit. I have witnessed the lack of freedom you
preach as well as display, the robotic fearfulness of your actions, thoughts,
and your so-call 'passions.' Your passions are false, weak, disloyal, and fleeting. The inhumanness you all display is the norm."

Many in the audience started to boo. I screamed: "Shut your mouths or
I will burn this place down!" Most of the boos quickly subsided; I still had
the flame in my hand.

"It is inhuman because humans were not made for such small, stifling,
airless boxes, nor such dogged, filthy, disingenuous beliefs. Humans, us,
humans: we were not made to be less virtuous than dogs and nastier than
pigs and as cunning as snakes. But here we are. Here you are!

"There is a plague that has come upon this town, and that plague is the
ideology of falsehood! It is the ideology of lessness! It is the inhumanness of
current life which is, in itself, killing humankind altogether, killing the best
of human nature altogether! Where did all the good people go? Where are
they? What is the point? Look around you! There are so many cliques of
terrible people, wearing pitiful cracking masks. Look, they're right there,
sitting right next to you. Bogus faces: and what for? Why spend so much
time putting on your false faces? What are you hiding from, huh? The person

next to you who also has on a death mask? The person next to you who deep down hates your fucking guts? Is that who we're hiding from, but still trying to impress at the exact same time? Or are we hiding from the people who will never love us and never give us respect? What is the point?

"You fain religion—but for what? What does it change? You still are as bad as the day you were taught—the day you were taught that you were at the center of the universe and that your ideology could substitute for a thinking mind! You disbelieve in all unprovable beliefs besides your own unprovable belief—how silly!

"What can wake you out of your self-imposed slumber? Your coma of malcontent. Should I sacrifice myself for your crimes of sloth, greed, wrath, gluttony, lust, and envy, bigotry, and bullshit? For your crime of weak, bastardized, fruitless dogma. For your crimes of complacency, capriciousness, disconnectedness, prejudice, and worst of all, for your crime of extreme, obscene, unwarranted selfishness.

"I will pay for your crimes since you refuse to even recognize that you are committing one. I will light the way, regardless if you follow it or not. I will take the punishment because I am not you, and someone has to. Someone has to take responsibility. Someone has to be punished. Let it be me. Let me take the fall. I will take it for all of us.

"I would rather die than be like you. That is why I was forced to say these things. That is why I was forced to speak to you unrotten corpses. And that is why I must act now! I must do whatever I must do to change you.

"Virtue is dead. Futility and fertility is the norm. We've gone from Cro-Magnon, to Neanderthal, to human, to demon. This must have happened the moment consciousness and death found common ground: compulsory consumption.

Soliloquy

"I refuse. I refuse to be a part of it any longer. I refuse to be a part and play the game anymore. It's time to change! In the play of life, even the audience members are the actors!

"This fire is ours!"

Soliloquy

Act V.

I have heard all of Death's introspection
Such-sights-seen with no human eyes
Raped to death, Our depth of perception
Rationale: begs bound, gagged, and tied

I have seen how beliefs murder thinking
Saw confidence of serpents and stone
I have witnessed the poison of goodness
Raging naked their arrogance shown

I have suffered the death of the billions
Felt the jaws of hypocrite's pride
I have cried with the tears of the children
Received word that humanities died

I have witnessed the worship of Idols
Seen religions of personal gain
I was there and heard hatred's recital
Genocides in the name of a Name

I bared witness to the death of all men
So unwilling, but nevertheless
Gave my soul to do it again
Just to leave without any regrets

Chapter 9

"Strange Clauses of the Will"

I was apprehended very shortly after I fled the theater... allegedly. (This part is where my memory starts to fail me.) I was never really all that fast of a runner, so it figures. But I don't even remember running. I don't even remember exactly what all I said.

My first night in lock-up I had this strange dream that I had dreamt once before. The dream was about the Native American chief and the two wild horses.

When they told me what I had done, I didn't believe them at first. I denied it. But there were a lot of people there to confirm it was me and what I did. After a while I came to realize what I had done, although I still can't remember it. I was also told that no one got hurt in the fire. One of the guards told me that.

After being here for a few weeks or so, I finally had contact with my family, through letters. When I called collect no one answered; they didn't come to my bail hearing, and they didn't post my bail. I left messages, but they didn't answer. I'm sure that was my mom's decision. I couldn't really blame her for it. I had disgraced them both. It wasn't my intention, but it was a fact. I completely understood. I didn't expect them to save me. I had disgraced them in front of a few of their friends and some of my dad's co-workers. It was sad.

But finally, I got a letter from my dad. It didn't say much.

***

Soliloquy

Two days after my father's letter came, I got a letter from someone I never expected to hear from.

Dear Jonathan,

> *I am sorry for what I did with John. It was a mistake. I meant you no harm. It wasn't intentional. I am truly sorry. I never meant to hurt you. That was never my intention. I don't even know what else to say. What I did was stupid, I know that. I make myself sick. But it wasn't about you or to hurt you. I don't know what else to say. I'm so sad about everything that happened. Everything. All I know is that I meant you no harm, and I am really, truly sorry.*
> *Mira L.*

The funny or sad thing (depending on what side of the coin you're on) about her letter was that it showed me that she'd thought I set that fire because of her. She was wrong, completely wrong. You don't set a fire because of the spark; you set it because of a *reason*. She was just the spark, not the reason.

Yes, in a way she broke my heart. At first, I thought she destroyed the half of my heart that held affection and optimism. But then I realized that it was the half that housed weakness and false sentimentality. The world is set up to destroy romanticism, rationality, and assurance. It is meant to keep most people unbalanced. I now realize that what she did propelled me headlong in the direction of... the direction of something like real-life enlightenment or focus or monkhood or even greatness—when I wanted to take my sweet time or just stay in my place. The pain of propulsion (and alienation) is like the pain of heartbreak. It's like being stretched by two wild horses. Maybe they, pain and propulsion, are related, maybe like brother and sister. The pain of propulsion, of growth, is the pain of change and knowledge. But unlike heartbreak, propulsion entails purpose and destination. Action. Aim. Arrival. Purpose. While heartbreak entails self-pity, jealousy, greed, and shame. So in the end, what got destroyed by her strange act was my weakness and self-deception. My blinders were torn off, and of course it was painful. My naive non-action was forced to die and give way to something more.

There was just a sentence, a saying really, that kept repeating in my head the whole time I was on stage talking. It just kept repeating. I wasn't thinking about lighting a fire. I was thinking about the sentence. I still don't remember where I got the saying, but over and over I heard this: "To enable a sanctuary to be built, *a sanctuary must be destroyed*: that is the law." Over and over the words sped through my brain. So I guess I set the fire for myself, or to free myself from myself, or to free myself from my old self, or to make myself my own sanctuary, or to free myself from my overwhelming weakness. Sort of like self-castration for a sex addict, perhaps. I set the fire to give myself a future that could be free from what would have been. I set it to burn the cobwebs off my old, stale, scared life. I set it so I could never turn back to being what I was: a sad, frightened, little child—naive, wrong, blind. I set the fire so people would see its beauty and regret the beauty they took for granted every catatonic day of their catastrophic lives.

The fire was not for her, or about her, or about John, or about them. The fire was the beginning of a new future, the burning of a bridge, good or bad, for better or for worse. I was destroying my old sanctuary, and I was making myself *my* sanctuary. I married my decision that day, and the fire was the seal of my vows.

I take what I did as one of my first acts of freewill. I take what I did as an act that proves the existence of freewill itself; I don't give a shit what physicist or neuroscientists say; I know freewill is real. Before that fire, I only had the illusion of freewill. I'd never touched it or felt it burning through my veins. I never knew what it could do. I'd only thought I had control. I thought that going through the gate was what all the goats and sheep had to do or even wanted to do. Being free was being safe, being alike, being out of the way.

Some people might say it put me in a terrible position. They say, "You're in jail. You're going to be going to prison for a long, long time. You've ruined your bright future." And in a way, I agree. I should have found a better way to free myself. I agree. Putting people in danger was stupid and selfish. But I also say to them: My life was already a jail. My future was already a prison. Terrible was my state of being. You can't ruin what was already ruined. Living the way I was living was like dying every day (and I didn't even notice it—I couldn't feel it). Living not to make too much noise, not to make what lesser people considered mistakes, not to cause ripples in the big pond of life: that is no life at all!

People may take what I am saying the wrong way and think that I'm advocating anarchy, or that I'm sponsoring some sort of ethical-relativity, hedonistic, do-whatever-you-feel-like-doing-as-long-as-it-makes-you-feel-all-right hippy bullshit. No! If that is what you take away from my life then you are silly, phony, and dull. What these last months have taught me is that freedom is terrible and beautiful like a lion. What I am putting forth is true freedom: choice.

I've had so much time to think, and I've realized that a lack of freedom was my problem; a lack of freedom is *the* problem. People walk around for entire lifetimes thinking that they're making real choices, when in fact they are far, far away. These fools are the worst types of slave (I know because I was one of them). They are slaves to their weakness (even though they are unaware of their weakness). Every so-called decision they make is based on

Soliloquy

their weakness, or their fear of their weakness, or their fear of fear, or their fear of pain, and they completely lack the ability to choose otherwise.

The selfish man says, "I could give if I wanted to," but he never seems to want to. Does he have true choice, true freedom? He fears the pain he will be forced to endure when his possessions are gone. He is weak to pain; he genuflects before it and worships it as The Almighty. When the selfish man does give, it is only to spite those who point out his inability to give; this spite is not choice because it is predicated on his omnipotent weakness; so he still lacks the ability to choose. He, bound by his all-consuming weakness, still lacks true freewill.

Freedom is not the ability to choose, it's the ability to choose *otherwise*! Alcoholics still make choices, do they not? If not, what mental mechanism compels him or her to order a vodka? But to choose, to be fully capable of accomplishing otherwise, that is freedom. That is true choice. The Either-Or. The genuine Fork in one's Life. (I realized, after being in here for a while, and reflecting on my actions, that in certain moments in life, a person can choose to be "insane" or not to be insane. A person could choose to yield to sanity, or refuse it. A person could stop at a fork in the road, and instead of picking left or right, say: Fuck it, I will stand right here until it is my time to die! I realized that insanity was my right; freedom was more like having your skin ripped off than a beautiful vacation. Insanity was just as likely as sanity. I was free to choose.)

People love the freedom to be weak, to be misinformed; they love the freedom to be ignorant of what freedom really is. They love the freedom to stay in their little boxes and fester and stew in their stupidity.

Most people never think about this type of stuff. They are too busy pretending to choose to think. They are too busy to think, too busy to reflect, to introspect, too busy filling their lives with noise, gadgets, and drama, and things so they won't ever have to hear that little voice in the back of their minds. They make leaky rain buckets full of excuses about how they don't have the time. They use the ridiculous sentence: "You think too much." They are serfs to their excuses and diversions. They are slaves to their willingness to blame. But freedom is the ability to choose otherwise, to have all possibilities within reach. To choose takes will, force, and vision. I didn't have any of those things before. I didn't have the ability to choose *anything* until I started that fire, until I stepped on that stage. That fire proved that I could choose destruction if I wanted to. I could choose to be alien if I needed to. I could choose to reboot my life.

All my life I was a slave to doing what would ruffle the fewest feathers, what would cause the least amount of attention. But now, now I can truly do anything, everything once I get out of here. I can choose good or evil now that I am truly free. I can let reason, and only reason, guide my motivations, if that's what I *choose* to do. I can let irrationality run rampant, and I can follow it with delight. I have that choice. I can define my life with clarity and meaning, and I don't have to fit in or be afraid of that great abyss of reality or the maddening gift of truth.

When you are free, pain and comfort blend together like colors on a master's canvas; they become equals, two sides of the same coin. When you are free Truth matters, it's nearly all that matters. When you are free, heaven and hell are both equally accessible choices, and you get to choose the one you will follow. It is a beautifully terrible thing to be free!

What I did was a choice. A free choice. I am not happy with what I did; I would be more than happy to pay reparations for the rest of my life to see the *Lyceum* restored to its former glory. What I did, setting a fire, actually makes me sick. But I am happy with who I can become. I may not be much of a person yet, but now, I know what it means to be full of truth and to be free.

Made in the USA
Monee, IL
17 November 2020